Tryon Edwards

Our Country, Historic and Picturesque

A complete story of its development and progress from the first discovery by the

Northmen to the present time

Tryon Edwards

Our Country, Historic and Picturesque
A complete story of its development and progress from the first discovery by the Northmen to
the present time

ISBN/EAN: 9783337234942

Printed in Europe, USA, Canada, Australia, Japan

Cover: Foto ©Andreas Hilbeck / pixelio.de

More available books at **www.hansebooks.com**

DICKERSON'S ART HISTORY SERIES.

❖

OUR COUNTRY,

HISTORIC AND PICTURESQUE.

A COMPLETE STORY OF ITS DEVELOPMENT AND PROGRESS
FROM THE FIRST DISCOVERY BY THE NORTHMEN
TO THE PRESENT TIME.

EMBELLISHED BY
MANY HUNDRED FINE ENGRAVINGS,

Illustrative of War & Historic Incidents,

AND THE

GRANDEUR OF AMERICAN SCENERY.

ALSO

Life-like Portraits of Men who built the Nation, reproduced in
Colors from Oil Paintings now owned by the
Government at Washington.

BY TRYON EDWARDS, D. D.,

AUTHOR OF "LIGHT FOR THE DAY," "OUR FAMILY TREASURY," "DICTIONARY
OF THOUGHTS," ETC.

1891.

F. B. Dickerson Company,

DETROIT, MICH.

PREFACE.

OF all studies, that of History is one of the most interesting and important. It satisfies a natural and laudable curiosity as to what has taken place in the world, and makes some amends for the shortness of life by enabling us to live over, in thought, the days and scenes of the past, and to know, as by a second experience, the life and labors of those who have gone before us. So strong and universal is the desire to know about the times that are gone, as to their persons, events, and progressive changes, that it may almost be called an instinct of the soul. And, as Cicero says, "Not to know what has taken place in former times is to be always a child, for if no use is made of the labors of by-gone ages, the world must always remain in the infancy of knowledge."

This is eminently true of the history of our own country, the origin and growth of which have well-nigh the interest of personal experience. As we ponder its pages, we share the life and witness the progress of those who have passed away, while at the same time we are exempt from the dangers and self-denials to which they were subject, and through which they so patiently and faithfully struggled in carrying out the far-reaching plans of Providence, and laying broad and deep the foundations of our National Life.

To give a connected and clear History of the United States, from the days of the Northmen to the present time, is the object of this work. The aim has been to give an account of the origin and growth of *Our Country*, adapted especially to its families and youth; not, on the one hand, so full of minute details as to be tedious, nor, on the other, so brief as to be defective, but one that shall give, according to the best authorities, a full and proportionate narrative of the great events of our history, abounding as it does in the most stirring and instructive incidents. The work makes no claim to originality, for history is a matter of record, where one is, of course, dependent on the statements of previous annalists and writers, and where the chief merit is to so condense and arrange, as to be not only correct, but entertaining in matter, and attractive by illustration.

In such a work we may trace the first voyagers on their way over the ocean, the struggles and hardships of the early colonists, their various conflicts with the Indians, the gradual extension and growth of their settlements, the oppressions of the mother country which led to the war for independence, with its struggles and final triumph, the growing prosperity of the States, the war of 1812 and that with Mexico, and the fearful war of secession, leading to the overthrow of slavery, and to the renewed union of the States as *one great and prosperous Nation.* Years too, of peace, prosperity and progress, far more in number than those of struggle and conflict, may well fill us with thankfulness as we ponder the blessings they have brought, while the story of our statesmen, scholars, inventors, and explorers, and that of our progress in agriculture, commerce, education and religion are seen to be such as justly to place our country in the front rank of the great Nations of the World.

As the maps of a country make plain its geography, so engravings of its scenery, passing events and its distinguished characters, give vividness and interest to its written history, and aid the memory in retaining the knowledge imparted by it. The great number of such illustrations given in this volume cannot but aid in making the work both interesting and instructive to all.

Detroit, 1892.   T. E.

CONTENTS.

PERIOD I.
EARLY DISCOVERIES AND EXPLORATIONS.

CHAPTER I.
The Northmen or Vikings,   13

CHAPTER II.
Columbus and other Discoverers,   21

CHAPTER III.
The Progress of Colonization,   25

PERIOD II.
THE EARLY COLONIES AND ORIGINAL STATES.

CHAPTER I.

Virginia, .   32
Massachusetts,   40
Connecticut,   49
Rhode Island,   54
New Hampshire,   56
Maine, . .   59
Vermont, .   63

New York,   64
New Jersey,   74
Pennsylvania,   76
Delaware, . .   81
Maryland, .   83
North Carolina,   87
South Carolina,   89
Georgia,   92

PERIOD III.
LIFE IN THE COLONIES.

CHAPTER I.

The New England Colonies,   95
Virginia, . . .   106

The Other Colonies,   115

CHAPTER II.
French and Indian Wars,   127

PERIOD IV.
THE REVOLUTION.

CHAPTER I.
Causes of the Revolution,   137

CHAPTER II.
The War of the Revolution,   143

PERIOD V.

THE CONSTITUTIONAL PERIOD.

CHAPTER I.

The New States. .   164-207

CHAPTER II.

The Territories.   207-227

CHAPTER III.

Administrations before the Civil War:
Washington, 1789 to 1797. .   229
Adams, 1797 to 1801, .   234
Jefferson, 1801 to 1809.   237
Madison, 1809 to 1817,   241
Monroe, 1817 to 1825,   .   249
John Quincy Adams, 1825 to 1829,   251
Jackson, 1829 to 1837,   .   254
Van Buren, 1837 to 1841,   .   258
Harrison and Tyler, 1841 to 1845,   260
Polk, 1845 to 1849,   .   . 263
Taylor and Fillmore, 1849 to 1853.   267
Pierce, 1853 to 1857,   .   271
Buchanan, 1857 to 1861,   273

CHAPTER IV.

The Civil War and Emancipation:
The Causes of the War,   278
Lincoln's Administration,   .   280
Campaigns of 1861. .   .   284
Campaigns of 1862,   .   290

Campaigns of 1863, .   300
Campaigns of 1864,   .   313
The Final Campaign, 1865.   320
Review of Campaigns,   332

CHAPTER V.

Administrations after the Civil War—
Reconstruction and Peace :
Johnson, 1865 to 1869,   335
Grant, 1869 to 1877,   340
Hayes, 1877 to 1881,   .   348
Garfield and Arthur, 1881 to 1885,   351
Cleveland, 1885 to 1889,   .   359
Harrison, 1889 to 1893, .   362

CHAPTER VI.

Our Country's Growth and Improve-
ment :
Territory,   370
Population,   373
Government,   375
Education,   377
Religion,   .   385
Literature,   .   .   .   387
Inventions, Discoveries, Improve-
ments,   .   .   .   395

CHAPTER VII.

National and other Parks,   416

GREAT HISTORICAL PAPERS.

Franklin's Plan of Union, .   .   433
The Declaration of Independence, .   435
The Confederation of 1778,   .   438
Constitution of the United States,   440

Amendments to the Constitution, .   452
The Farewell Address of George
Washington, ...   457
Proclamation of Emancipation,   .   467

INHABITANTS BEFORE OUR HISTORICAL PERIOD,   469

LIST OF ILLUSTRATIONS.

	PAGE
First Sight of Land,	*Frontispiece*
Vessel of the Northmen,	15
The Dragon Ship,	16
Ruins of a Norse Building,	17
Old Tower at Newport,	18
The Dighton Rock,	19
Christopher Columbus,	20
Vessels of Columbus,	22
Balboa's Discovery of the Pacific,	23
The Eclipse of the Moon,	24
Gate at the Entrance of St. Augustine,	25
Street Scene in St. Augustine,	26
The Sun at Midnight in the Arctic Regions,	27
The Aurora Seen in Greenland,	29
The Natural Bridge, Virginia,	30

	PAGE
The James River near Richmond,	32
View on the Potomac,	33
Tower Rocks, Virginia,	34
Baptism of Pocahontas,	36
Introduction of Slavery,	37
View on the Rappahannock,	39
Plymouth Rock, Massachusetts,	43
Scene on the Hudson River,	44
Silver Cascade, Crawford's Notch,	46
Old South Church, Boston,	47
Turner's Falls, Massachusetts,	48
Attack on the Early Settlers,	50
Yale College, Connecticut,	52
Woodland Scene in Rhode Island,	55
Squam Lake, New Hampshire,	57
St. John's River,	58

	PAGE
Bar Harbor, Maine,	59
Off the Coast of Maine,	60
View in Acadia,	61
Scene in Maine.	62
Trout Stream in Vermont,	63
Sabbath-day Point, Lake George,	65
Sketch of Niagara Falls by Father Hennepin in 1698,	66
Niagara Falls, American Side,	67
The Falls of Niagara,	69
Opening of the Erie Canal,	70
Trenton Falls, New York,	71
First Passenger Railway, 1831,	72
Rapids of the St. Lawrence River,	72
Catskill Mountain Scene,	73
Arrest of Carteret,	74
Chateaugay Chasm, New York,	75
Penn's House, Philadelphia,	77
View on the Susquehanna River,	78
Penn's Treaty with the Indians,	79
Pennsylvania Forest Scenery,	80
Scene on the Delaware Bay,	82
Fight with the Maryland Pinnace,	84
The "Golden Lion" Firing on the Maryland Boats,	85
Cumberland Gap, Maryland,	86
A Vista in North Carolina,	87
View of a Cotton Chute,	89
Scene in South Carolina,	91
A Planter's House in Georgia,	92
Scene in a Georgia Meadow,	94
On the New England Coast,	96
Shore of Cape Ann,	97
Evening at Sea,	97
Church-Goers in the Early Colonies,	98
A Pioneer Home in Winter,	101

	PAGE
A Mountain Stream,	102
Indian Burial Ground,	105
View on the James River, Virginia,	107
A Virginia Summer Scene,	109
Group of Trees,	111
Summer on the Rappahannock,	112
Upper Au Sable Lake,	114
A River Scene,	116
A Cotton Field,	118
The Cascades,	119
The Alleghany Mountains,	121
A Coast Scene,	122
Roger's Slide, Lake George,	123
A Dutch Household,	124
Early Settlers Ascending the Hudson,	125
Quebec,	128
Washington's Attack on the French,	130
Wolfe's Cove,	132
Night Attack on Colonial Schooner,	133
Attack on the Fort at Presque Isle,	134
Meeting of Washington and Rochambeau,	136
Eventide,	138
Building in Boston Where the Tea Plot was Hatched,	140
Building in Philadelphia Where the First Congresses were held,	141
The Brook,	142
The Monument on Bunker Hill,	144
Statue of Jefferson,	145
The Prison Ship "Jersey,"	146
Washington Crossing the Delaware,	148
Attack on Chew's House,	150
Surrender of Burgoyne,	152
Washington Reproving Lee at Monmouth,	153

	PAGE
Arnold at New London,	155
Washington's Headquarters at New-burgh,	156
Exploit of Arnold,	157
Attack by the British on the Block House at Tom's River,	158
The House Where Cornwallis Surrendered,	160
Washington Surrendering his Commission,	162
Attack on the Rioters,	163
Mammoth Cave, Kentucky,	165
Look-out Mountain, Tennessee,	166
Red-mill Falls, near Elyria, Ohio,	167
A Mississippi River Boat,	168
Loading a Cotton Steamer,	169
View on the Mississippi,	172
A Nook, Fox Lake, Illinois,	173
Scene on the Mississippi River,	174
Cathedral Spires on the Merrimac,	175
Hot Springs, Arkansas,	176
Detroit River Scenes,	177
Scenes on the St. Mary River,	178
Government Canal and Locks, Sault Ste. Marie, Michigan,	179
Amelia Island, Florida,	181
Sam Houston,	183
A Nook on Spirit Lake, Iowa,	185
On the Brule River, Wisconsin,	187
Big Trees of California,	188
Yosemite Valley,	189
Three Brothers, Yosemite Valley,	190
Mirror Lake and Mount Watkins,	191
The Falls of St. Anthony,	192
Lake of the Woods,	193
Portland, Oregon, and Willamette River,	194

	PAGE
A Kansas Harvest Scene,	196
Basaltic Pinnacles, Colorado River,	199
The Cascades,	200
Near the Summit of the Rockies,	203
View in Grand Cañon,	204
Rocky Mountain Scene,	205
Flowers and Butterflies,	206
Mountain Scenery, Utah,	208
White Cliffs, Utah,	209
Colored Cliffs Near Kanab, Utah,	210
Marble Cañon of the Colorado,	211
Cliff Dwellings, Arizona,	212
Distant View of Moqui, with Sheep-pens in the Foreground,	213
Sitka, Alaska,	215
Scenes in the Inland Passage,	216
Washington (Two Views),	218
Washington in 1810—The Old Capitol,	219
The Capitol—East View,	221
The Bartholdi Fountain, Statues—General Scott and others,	222
The Naval, and Other Statues,	223
Statues—General Rawlins and others,	224
Washington Monument,	225
The White House From Pennsylvania avenue,	226
Mount Vernon from the Potomac River,	227
Washington's Reception at Trenton,	228
George Washington,	230
Franklin's Grave at Philadelphia,	231
View of Washington's House, Mt. Vernon,	232
Washington's Bedchamber,	233
John Adams,	234

	Page
Martha Washington's Bedchamber,	235
Washington's Grave, Mt. Vernon,	236
Thomas Jefferson,	237
Duel Between Burr and Hamilton,	239
The Officers of the Chesapeake Offering Their Swords,	240
James Madison,	241
Perry's Victory on Lake Erie,	243
The Burning of Washington,	245
Capture of the Cyane and Levant,	247
James Monroe,	249
A Scene in the Early Settlement of Ohio,	250
John Q. Adams,	252
Early Days on the Delaware and Hudson Canal Railroad,	253
Andrew Jackson,	254
A Negro Village,	255
Scene in Florida near Rock Ledge,	256
Scene on St. Clair River, Michigan,	257
Martin Van Buren,	258
William H. Harrison,	260
John Tyler,	261
Salt Lake City,	262
James K. Polk,	263
The City of Mexico,	264
The City of Vera Cruz,	265
A Woodland Scene,	266
Zachary Taylor,	268
Millard Fillmore,	269
Franklin's Expedition in the Polar Regions,	270
Franklin Pierce,	271
Mount Hood,	272
James Buchanan,	273
Harper's Ferry, Virginia,	274

	Page
A Skirmisher,	275
General Robert E. Lee's Old Home, Arlington,	276
Defense of Fort Sumter,	277
A Railroad Battery,	279
Early Home of Abraham Lincoln,	280
Abraham Lincoln,	281
Federal Iron-clad River Gun-boat,	282
The Swamp Angel,	283
On the Baltimore and Ohio Railroad,	285
Destruction of Fort Ocrakoke,	286
Battle of Bull Run,	287
Fort Pensacola,	288
Capture of New Orleans,	289
Bailey's Dam on the Red River,	291
U. S. Military Telegraph Wagon,	292
Fort Pillow,	293
The "Destroyer,"	294
Battle of Malvern Hill,	296
Antietam Bridge,	297
Sinking of the Alabama,	298
Fight Between the Monitor and Merrimac,	299
The "Nashville" Destroying the "Merchantman,"	301
Battle of Chancellorsville,	303
View From Gettysburg—West,	304
Pickett's Charge at Gettysburg,	305
Gettysburg From Little Round-Top — East,	306
Gun-boats Passing Before Vicksburg,	307
Longstreet's Arrival at Bragg's Headquarters,	308
Federal Lines at Chattanooga,	309
Moist Weather at the Front,	310
Attack on Charleston,	311

PAGE

Fairfax Court House, . 312
Explosion of Mine Before Petersburg, 314
General Sherman's Scouts. 315
Death of General Polk. 316
Savannah, ... 317
Opening of the Fight Between the
  Kearsarge and Alabama, 319
End of the Oyster War, . . 320
The Peace Commissioners, . 321
Raising the Flag over Fort Sumter, 322
Destruction of the Nashville. . 323
Sunset Over Atlanta. . 324
On Picket, . 325
Retreat of Lee's Army. 326
Surrender of General Lee, . 327
The House Where General Lee Sur-
  rendered, . . 328
The Capture of Booth, 329
Lincoln's Grave, ... 330
Review of the Union Troops at
  Washington, . . 331
The Lincoln Monument, 332
Residence of Andrew Johnson, 335
Andrew Johnson, . . . 336
Ruins of Richmond After the War, 337
Picking Up the Atlantic Cable, 339
Ulysses S. Grant, . 340
Birthplace of U. S. Grant, 341
The Joint High Commission, 342
Storming of the Corean Forts, 343
The Burning of Chicago, . . 344
" I Declare the Centennial Exhibition
  Open," 345
Attack by Modocs on the Peace Com-
  missioners, . 346
Custer's Last Fight, 347

PAGE

Rutherford B. Hayes, . 349
View on the Panama Railroad, 350
James A. Garfield, . 351
Put-in-Bay Harbor, Ohio, 352
Chester A. Arthur, . . 353
General View of the Brooklyn Bridge, 354
Arrival of the French Transport Isere, 355
Statue of Liberty, ... 356
The Farthest Point North, Reached
  by Lieutenant Lockwood, . 357
Caldwell, the Birthplace of Cleveland, 358
Grover Cleveland. 359
Decoration Day, . 360
Earthquake at Charleston, S. C., . 361
The Funeral Train of General Grant
  Passing West Point, 363
Benjamin Harrison, . 364
Hon. Thomas W. Palmer, 365
Kentucky Scene. . 367
A Harvest Scene in Michigan, 369
A Western Prairie, . . 371
Improving Leadville, 1877, . 372
Leadville in 1887, . . 374
Gulf Coast near Galveston, . 378
Wild Flowers, . . 381
The Bend, . 383
Along the Shore, 385
Ferns and Leaves, . . 387
Wild Flowers of the Pacific Coast, 391
Mountain Flowers, 395
Pennsylvania Scenery, 398
An Early Steamboat, . 407
A Modern Steamer, 408
A Scene in the Rockies, 410
The Hunter's Retreat, 413
Fort Scenes. Mackinac. 414

	PAGE			PAGE
Robinson's Folly, Mackinac Island,	416	Lime Tower near Hot Springs,		428
Plummer's Lookout,	417	The Yellowstone,	.	429
Sugar Loaf Rock,	418	The Grotto Geyser,	. . .	430
Arch Rock, .	. 419	Lower Falls, Yellowstone Park, .		431
Yosemite Valley, . .	420	Map, ...	. .	432
Grand Canon, Colorado River,	421	Signers of the Declaration of Inde-		
Steeple Rocks, Yellowstone,	422	pendence,		439
The Grotto, ...	423	The Golden Gate, .		468
Boiling Springs, Yellowstone Park,	424	Observatory Mound, .		470
Boiling Sulphur Springs, Yellowstone		Works at Marietta, Ohio,	.	473
Park, ...	425	Islands in the Detroit River, .		v
Great Falls of the Yellowstone River,	426	American Country Scenes,	.	vii
Old Faithful Geyser,	427	The First Icebergs,		xii

Our Country.

PERIOD I.

CHAPTER I.

THE NORTHMEN OR VIKINGS.

THE history of our country is full of interest, both to the old and young. Long before its discovery by Europeans, it was inhabited by the "Mound Builders," a prehistoric people whose monuments are now found in various parts of the land, and who, some suppose, were the remote ancestors of the modern Indians, while others think they were an entirely different people, conquered, and possibly in part exterminated, and in part merged in the tribes of the conquerors, and so disappearing as a people. Squier, Davis, and others take the former view; but the traditions of at least two large Indian tribes give the latter, saying that the modern Indians conquered and drove out a people before them; that that people conquered and drove out a race before themselves, and that the last mentioned people conquered and drove out those known as the "Mound Builders." Long before America was known to Europeans it was occupied by the Indians, whose numerous tribes were found in every part of the land, and the descendants of whom are still in the country, partly on reservations allotted by the government for their occupation, and partly in regions where they have long wandered or dwelt. Of the origin of the "Mound Builders," or of the Indians, comparatively little is known, but more full notices of them may be found at the end of this work.

Nearly four hundred years before Christ, the inhabitants of the Eastern world had believed that there were undiscovered lands far to the West. Plato, who said his information came through Solon, from an old Egyptian priest, had told the well-known story, or fable, of Atlantis, describing its climate and scenery, its mountains, rivers, animals and inhabitants, and speaking of the Island as almost a paradise. And about a hundred years later Aristotle had taught that the earth was a sphere, and that the waters on the west side of Europe washed the eastern shores of Asia. And Seneca the teacher of the Emperor Nero, who lived in the first century and died A. D. 65, as his words are translated by Archbishop Whately, said: "There shall come a time, in later ages, when the ocean shall relax its chains, and a vast continent shall appear, and a pilot shall find new worlds, and Thule (which was thought to be the end of the world) shall no more be the earth's boundary." This idea, kept alive through the middle ages, gave the impression which was widely spread, that by sailing westward, countries beyond the sea would some time be discovered.

It is said that as early as A. D. 800, Japanese junks, driven by severe storms, had landed on the western coast of our great continent, and Modoc, a Welch prince, is said to have reached the coast of Virginia as early as A. D. 1170, though no permanent settlement was the result. And tradition had long asserted that nearly five hundred years before the time of Columbus, the Northmen had landed and made settlements on our eastern coast. These Northmen or Vikings had nothing, as the term "Viking" might seem to imply, of a kingly or royal character. They were not *Vi-kings*, but *Vik-ings*, simply the dwellers on the *Viks* or bays of the Scandinavian coasts, from which they went forth as bold and persevering buccaneers of the sea, much like the Algerian corsairs of a later day, except that, unlike the Algerians, they were not merely pirates and conquerors, but were also colonists, founding settlements in the lands they subdued and robbed. They were of the same race as those who, as Saxons, had, at an early day, overrun and subdued England, and afterward, as Normans, had conquered France, and still later, crossing over from France, had again conquered England, and mingling with the English and Saxons, laid the foundation of the Anglo-Saxon people.

For a long time the Vikings were the terror of Europe, entering the ports and landing on what are now the British Isles, raiding up the rivers of France, and through the Mediterranean sea, reaching and plundering Africa, which they called "Saracen's land," and sending back the wealth of their booty to Norway, where, to this day, Greek and Arabic coins and chains of gold are found, as may be seen in the museums of Christiana and Copenhagen.

Of the history and movements of these Vikings, Mr. Keary, in his "Vikings in Western Christendom," has given full and most interesting accounts. As early as the year 789, as he quotes from the *English Chronicle*, "These Vikings sought the land of English folk," three ships bearing the first of these buccaneers, that, so far as is known, had not since the sixth century, made incursions on any Christian shore. These fierce freebooters had long and strongly built vessels, manned by from twenty to forty oarsmen on each side, and each having a mast thirty or forty feet high, set in a block of wood so large that, it is said, no block of equal size could now be found in Norway. These masts had no standing rigging, but with their square sails, were probably taken down when not in use, the dependence, in the absence of favoring wind, then being on the oars. In these powerful vessels they swept down from their old homes in the Scandinavian regions to the milder and richer South, and across the North sea to England, Scotland, and Ireland, conquering and robbing wherever they went, and making many settlements under leaders who took the name of Kings. The ninth century saw their rise to greatness, and it saw also their decline; but during this hundred years they were the terror not only of France and the continent, but of the British Islands and every part of the coast.

The model and structure of these vessels are now as well-known as if they were just built and launched from our ship-yards. They are depicted on the celebrated Bayeux tapestry, and cuts of them are still seen on the rocks of Norway, and their remains are now and then found in different parts of that country. One of them, represented in the cut, which is taken from an engraving in possession of Mr. R. B. Anderson, of Wisconsin, was dug up at Sandefjord, about half a mile from the sea. It had evidently

VESSEL OF THE NORTHMEN DUG UP AT SANDEFJORD, NORWAY.

been used as the burial place of its owner, and a full account of it has been given in a volume by Mr. N. Nicolayson, published at Christiana in 1882. It was about seventy-seven feet long, over sixteen feet wide at its greatest width, and between five and six feet in depth, drawing less than five feet of water. It was not like the "dug-outs" or bark canoes of the savage or half civilized tribes, but was "neatly built and well preserved, constructed on what a sailor would call beautiful lines, and eminently fitted for sea service." It was clinker built, that is each of its thick oaken boards overlapped the one below it, like shingles on a house-top, just as our best boats are built to-day, and all were bound together with strong iron rivets well made and clinched. The vessel had no decks, but seats were arranged for from forty to sixty rowers, and there were corresponding holes for the oars which were some twenty feet long. In the vessel was a tent-like chamber in which were found human bones, the bones of a dog, the bones and feathers of a peacock, some fish-hooks, and several bronze and lead ornaments for belts and harness, and about the vessel were the bones of several horses and dogs, which, it is supposed, had been sacrificed at the burial of the owner. Vessels much larger than this were called *Dragons*, and other sizes were known as *Serpents* and *Cranes*, each ship so built, or having some part or figure such as to represent the name it bore.

The Vikings who went forth in these vessels fought with stones, arrows and spears, and had grappling irons, with which to fasten to other vessels for boarding and close fighting. At a council in Norway some were clad in iron, some wore leather cloaks and had halberds over their shoulders and steel caps on their heads, and their leaders wore rich and costly garments. One of their leaders, or kings, as they were called, who, landed in Ireland to carry away cattle and other booty, is mentioned as having an iron helmet on his head, a red shield inlaid with gold, a sword the handle of which was of ivory, a short spear, and a red silk cloak over his coat, on which was embroidered with yellow silk, the figure of a lion.

Ireland suffered more from the Vikings than England itself, for it was in the fullness of their strength and when their eagerness for plunder was still unsatisfied that they came down on the Irish coasts. Ireland, at that time, was rich in monasteries, abbeys, and convents, which offered most tempting inducements as well as opportunities for their attacks, for in the fifth and sixth centuries that country abounded in religious establishments in which was gathered a large part of the wealth of the people. The jeweled mass-books, the richly adorned vestments of the priests, and the gold and silver sacrificial vessels, both invited and rewarded those daring robbers of the sea. Up to the year 807 their attacks had been mostly confined to the outlaying islands Iona and Man and to the Northumbrian coast, but in that year they came down upon the mainland, and by the year 825 had plundered most of the churches and religious establishments of the country.

By the middle of the century they had established three Norse or Viking settlements in Dublin, Waterford, and Limerick, under rulers whom they called kings. Great as were the losses and sufferings from their conquests some advantages resulted from their occupation of the country. They taught the people great improvements in ship, or rather boat-building; the first native coinage was introduced by the Norse king of Dublin, and the Irish were practically instructed in the uses and benefits of navigation, for both commerce and war. The capital of ancient times had been in the middle kingdom, but the Norsemen brought it down to the coast, and when they broke

up the monasteries, and scattered the monks and clerks who were the scholars of the times, the latter went forth in great numbers to the continent, to be instructors there, and in place of the religious houses from which they had been expelled, trading stations grew up, especially along the coasts, starting the germs of a new civilization and prosperity.

THE DRAGON SHIP.

The attack of the Northmen on England was later than on Ireland, and though for a time successful, they were in the end defeated and checked by King Alfred and his west Saxons in the great battle of Edington, and compelled to conform to the terms of the treaty of Wedmore, and from this time on their power in the country was broken, and their success as freebooters of the land as well as of the sea, steadily declined. It was toward the end of this century that they found their way to the New World.

In coming to America the Northmen were not intending or thinking of discoveries. They did not go forth like Columbus in the faith that a new world was to be found in the West. They were, rather, accidental discoverers, making "what might almost be called coasting voyages from Norway to Scotland, from Scotland to Iceland, and at last to North America, each passage extending but a few hundred miles," and, so, unexpectedly to themselves, reaching the new world.

After they had colonized in Iceland, and made it their home, Eric the Red, having, on account of a quarrel, been declared an outlaw, went to sea and discovered Greenland, which he thus named, that people, by the name, might be attracted to it. Taking a colony with him, he there took up his abode, about the year 986. With Eric was a friend, whose son, Bjazzi Herjulfson, was absent when they left Iceland, and who in endeavoring to follow them to Greenland, landed at three different places, and at last at Greenland, where he found his father and remained with him. His fellow adventurers determined to make further explorations, and to the number of thirty-five, led by Lief Ericson, sailed south and west, touching at several places, and at last discovered land which they called Vinland. Lief was followed by his brother Thorwald with thirty men, and Thorwald was followed by a larger expedition of sixty men and five women, who took with them cattle and provisions, and formed a settlement on the eastern part of what is now New England. Some have supposed the place was in the northern part of Maine, or even further north. But according to the writings of the Sagas, the region was not only one of forests and meadows, but of so mild a climate that cattle did not need to be housed for the winter, and grapes abounded, and corn grew abundantly — a description that could not apply to Labrador, or even to the northern part of Maine.

For a long time the accounts of the landing and settlement of the Northmen on the Atlantic coast were regarded with doubt and even disbelief. But they rest on writings and traditions as authentic as most of the statements which we have in the earliest annals of European history. They are mentioned in manuscripts of good authority still in existence in Iceland, in the Saga of Eric the Red written in Greenland,

RUINS OF A NORSE BUILDING IN GREENLAND.

and in that of Karlesnefni written in Iceland. These have been translated into different languages, and may be seen in Beamish's translation published in London in 1841, which has been reprinted by the Prince Society of Boston, and also, in part, in the Massachusetts *Quarterly Review* for March, 1849. And in later Norse manuscripts of undoubted authority, there are references to "Vinland the Good" as a region in America well known.

Where it was that the Northmen so settled has long been supposed to be utterly unknown. But from recent and careful investigation, Professor Eben N. Horsford, of Cambridge, Massachusetts, claims not only to have confirmed the statements of the Sagas, but to have found that the land on which these colonies settled was in Massachusetts; that after landing at Cape Cod and other places they finally fixed their main settlement at the mouth of what is now known as Stony Brook, on the Charles river, some nine miles from Cambridge, at or near where the town of Waltham now stands. Here, as he tells us, are found the remains of the buildings they erected, the fort, docks, wharves, walls, dams, canals, and basins, and also excavations ten and twelve

2

feet deep, extending hundreds of feet in length on both sides of Stony Brook, and for much of the distance carefully graded and paved with stone. The old tower at Newport, Rhode Island, and the well known Dighton Rock, were at one time conjectured

OLD TOWER AT NEWPORT.

to have been the work of the Northmen, though the former is of much later date, and is said to have been a windmill, copied from one at Chesterton, England; and the inscriptions on the Dighton Rock are supposed to have been made by the Indians.

Norumbega, the name given to the region spoken of, was the ancient form of Norvega, or Norway, and of this, Vinland was supposed to be a part, the whole extending from what is now Rhode Island to the St. Lawrence river. It was first seen by Bjazzi Herjulfson in A. D. 985. The "landfall" of Lief Ericson, on Cape Cod, was in A. D. 1000, in which year he discovered the region supposed to be about Charles river, explored by Thorwald, his brother in A. D. 1003, and colonized by Thorfin Karlsnefni in A. D. 1007. The first bishop or minister of the settlers, Eric Gnupson, arrived in A. D. 1121; and the various industries of the settlers are said to have been carried on for three hundred and fifty years, till, finally, the last Norse ship went back to Iceland in A. D. 1347. The region was afterward occupied by the Breton French in the 15th, 16th and 17th centuries.

THE DIGHTON ROCK.

Coming down to later times, it is an interesting fact that a Norwegian colony was founded in Bergen, New Jersey, in 1624; that the Swedes settled in Delaware in 1638; and that the first Swedish church was built at Wilmington, Delaware, in 1698; though both these colonies lost, to a certain extent, their identity, first by the infusion of the Dutch element and later by the English. Immigration from Norway to this country began on a larger scale in 1821, when religious persecution led large numbers, like the Pilgrims and Puritans of old, to seek new homes in some of our Western States. In 1824, the first emigration society was formed in Norway, and on the fourth of July, 1825, a party of fifty-two persons started for America, and after a voyage of fourteen weeks landed in New York, safely and all well. Since that time large numbers have followed to this country, where not a few of them have become distinguished in literature, and prominent as editors and in political life.

CHRISTOPHER COLUMBUS.

[Said by the present Duke of Varagua to be the most representative of the known portraits.]

CHAPTER II.

COLUMBUS AND OTHER DISCOVERERS.

THE inland rivers of Greece and Rome, and so the Mediterranean sea had long been navigated, but it was not till toward the end of the fifteenth century, and the beginning of the sixteenth, that the discovery of the mariner's compass and other inventions had prepared the way for long voyages out of sight of land, and that the great discoveries of that period were made. Then, in the hope of finding a short way to the East Indies and all their supposed riches, various expeditions were fitted out in Europe. The Portuguese landed in Brazil. Balboa reached the isthmus of Darien. (*See cut on page* 23.) Vasco de Gama went to India by the way of the Cape of Good Hope. And, at later dates, Davis, and Baffin, and Hudson, at the North, and Magellan and others, at the South, as also the French, through the St. Lawrence and the great lakes, were seeking the same desired end — a short way to the East.

It is, however, with Columbus, that the deeply interesting history of America begins. He was born at or near Genoa, about the year 1436, was the son of humble parents. His father, Dominico Colombo (as the name is written in Italian), was a wool-comber. He was the oldest of four children, having two brothers, Bartholomew and Giacomo or James, and one sister, of whom nothing is known except she married a person of obscure life. He attended school for a while at Pavia, where he became deeply interested in geography and astronomy, and, going early to sea, made several voyages on the Mediterranean. Settling at Lisbon, in A. D. 1470, he there married the daughter of Palestrello, a distinguished Italian cavalier lately deceased, who had been one of the most distinguished navigators under Prince Henry. The newly married couple resided with the mother of the bride. The latter, perceiving the interest which Columbus took in all matters concerning the sea, related to him all she knew of the voyages and expeditions of her late husband, and brought him all his papers, charts, journals, and memoranda. In this way he became acquainted with the routes of the Portuguese, their plans and conceptions, and occasionally sailed in the expeditions to the coast of Guinea. When on shore, he supported his family by making maps and charts, the construction of which, in those days, required a degree of knowledge sufficient to entitle the possessor to some distinction, as geography was just emerging from the darkness which had enveloped it for ages. The maps and journals of Palestrello and others impressed upon his mind the idea of land to the westward, which he then supposed to be the prolongation of the eastern shores of Asia, but which he afterward found to be a new and vast continent.

About the year A. D. 1482 or '83, he suggested his plans for discovery to King John, of Portugal, and afterward to the authorities at Genoa, Venice and other places, but, in each case, in vain. It was not till seven more years of effort and disappointment had passed, that, encouraged and aided by Ferdinand and Isabella of Spain, he was able to sail from Palos at day-break August 3, A. D. 1492, with three small vessels, and a hundred and

twenty men.   For a long time Ferdinand was opposed to the views and plans of
Columbus, but Isabella became so deeply interested in his projects that she pledged her
jewels for the undertaking.   The needful funds, however, were advanced by the royal
treasurer, and all needful arrangements were made for the undertaking.   Leaving Palos and
directing his course westward, in October he discovered the Bahama and other West India
islands, returning to Spain in A. D. 1493.   Sailing again, in the same year, with seventeen
vessels and fifteen hundred men, he discovered Jamaica and the Caribbee islands, and
returned to Spain in A. D. 1496.   In his third expedition, in A. D. 1498, he discovered
Trinidad, and landed on the coast of South America, thus, for the first time, seeing the
main land of the continent.   In his fourth and last voyage, which was made in A. D. 1502,
with four vessels and a hundred and fifty men, he hoped to have found a passage uniting

THE NINA.   THE SANTA MARIA.   THE PINTO
                        VESSELS OF COLUMBUS.

the Atlantic and Pacific oceans, but his crew became mutinous, and after many difficulties
and disasters, he returned to Spain in November A. D. 1504, having added but little to
his previous discoveries.   Isabella was now dead, and Ferdinand proved basely ungrateful
to the great discoverer; and so the noblest navigator the world has ever known,
misrepresented and opposed by those who were envious and jealous of his greatness, and
neglected by the King, at last died in poverty, at Valladolid, May 20, A. D. 1506.

Pages might be filled with anecdotes of Columbus and of his ships and voyages and
of his reception by the natives.   At first they received him with kindness, which was
continued during most of the year, which, on his fourth voyage, he spent in Jamaica while
waiting for supplies for which he had sent.   But the Spaniards being harsh and unjust
to the natives, they finally refused to bring in the provisions on which the lives of the
voyagers depended.   Columbus, however, led them to change their course by appealing

to their fears and superstition. Knowing an eclipse was soon to occur, he threatened the destruction of the moon if they did not comply with his wishes. And the eclipse taking place as he had foretold, they were so terrified that they hastened to do his will, and supply the wants of his people. (*See cut on page 24.*)

But though to Columbus belongs the undivided honor of leading the way to the Western world, to John and Sebastian Cabot belongs the credit of first landing on the coast of what is now the United States. Fourteen months before Columbus, on his third voyage, came in sight of the main land, and nearly two years before Americus Vespucius sailed west of the Canary Islands, the Cabots, father and son, under patents from Henry VII, reached the main land, June 24, A. D. 1497, and thus gave a continent to England. In a

BALBOA'S DISCOVERY OF THE PACIFIC, SEPTEMBER 25, 1513.

second voyage, after the death of his father, Sebastian Cabot reached Newfoundland, where he reported that the natives were clad in the skins of animals, and the fish swarmed in such vast shoals as to impede the progress of his vessels, while the deer were larger than those of England, and the bears were seen to plunge into the water to catch fish with their claws. Continuing his voyage in a southern direction, he explored the coast as far as Virginia, and possibly to Florida. In 1513, Ponce de Leon landed in Florida. In 1520, some Spanish vessels from St. Domingo were driven, in a storm, on the coast of North Carolina. In 1511, Cortez and his followers conquered Mexico, including what is now Texas, New Mexico and California, which thus became a province of Spain. In 1539-42, De Soto discovered and explored the Mississippi river. In 1584-5, Sir Walter Raleigh sent two expeditions to the coast of North Carolina, and attempted a settlement on Roanoke Island. In 1565 a Spanish settlement was made at St. Augustine, Florida. In 1607, Jamestown, in Virginia, was settled. New York, then known as New Netherlands, was settled in 1613, and Plymouth, Mass., in 1620. The country on the great lakes, and on the Mississippi was explored by La Salle in 1682. Settlements were made by the French in Arkansas, in 1685, and at Mobile and Vincennes in 1702. Some of these settlements were utter failures. Some of the more important and successful ones may now be considered.

THE ECLIPSE OF THE MOON.

CHAPTER III.

THE PROGRESS OF COLONIZATION.

SAINT AUGUSTINE, now the oldest city in the United States, and which still retains its ancient appearance (*See cut page 26*), was first settled, as said above, in 1565, by Menendez de Aviles, a Spanish navigator, who, with fifteen hundred followers, arrived off the coast on the 18th of August, and gave the new settlement the name it still bears. The Spaniards built a large moat or ditch around their settlement and at the entrance they built a massive gate of masonry, which has proven a providential opening to

GATE AT THE ENTRANCE OF ST. AUGUSTINE, FROM A PHOTOGRAPH TAKEN IN 1890.

the new world, and from which the colonizing work has expanded into a nation the progress and prosperity of which have become the wonder of mankind. The early settlers had hard struggles to maintain themselves against the Indians and against French and English adventurers. Twice the settlement was captured and pillaged; in 1586 by Sir Francis Drake and in 1665 by John Davis, a pirate, but still it grew slowly, and in 1763 was ceded, with other Spanish provinces, to Great Britain, and so at last became part of the United States.

The first attempt to colonize this country from England was made by Sir Walter Raleigh in 1584. Under a charter from Queen Elizabeth he sent out an exploring

STREET SCENE IN ST. AUGUSTINE FROM A RECENT PHOTOGRAPH.

expedition to what is now North Carolina, which after some six weeks, went back to England. The commanders of the expedition were delighted with the region, which, in the quiet beauty of summer, seemed to them almost a paradise; and on their return to England they gave such favorable reports as to the country and all they had seen, that

Elizabeth, who was called the "Virgin Queen," gave it the name of Virginia, a title which was then applied to most of the coast territory extending from Maine to Georgia.

Encouraged by these favorable reports, Raleigh, the next year, sent out a second expedition, consisting of seven vessels and a hundred and eight men, commanded at first by Sir Richard Granville, but soon coming under the charge of Ralph Lane. As there were no women in the colony the Indians imagined the colonists were not born of women, and therefore were immortal beings. The mathematical instruments, the burning-glass, the guns, the clocks, and the use of letters by which messages were sent on bits of paper and without vocal speech, all seemed to them to be the work of gods rather than of men, and for a time the Englishmen were reverenced as of divine origin and the special favorites of Heaven. But seeing the power of fire-arms the natives soon got the impression that sickness and death among themselves were caused by invisible bullets; and fearing that the strangers might intend to kill them, and so take their places, they soon began planning to get them away. Knowing that the colonists were desirous of finding a short way across the continent to India or China, they told Lane that the sea was but a little way to the West, and he, believing their story, set out, with most of his men, to find it. But being of course disappointed, and falling short of provisions, they came back just in time to save those they had left from being destroyed by the Indians. Their wants were supplied in part by Sir Francis Drake, who was on his return from the West Indies. He brought

THE SUN AT MIDNIGHT IN THE ARCTIC REGIONS—AS SEEN BY RECENT EXPLORERS.

them provisions, and left them a ship, but the latter being soon afterwards lost in a storm, the colonists became discouraged and went back to England.

Lane and his associates, while in the country, carefully examined its productions, especially those which they thought might be sources of profitable commerce. Maize, or the Indian corn, attracted his attention, both for its productiveness and its value for food; and the potato, though it was known before, had attracted but little attention till brought into use in England by these returned colonists. Lane also observed the culture of tobacco, and was the first to introduce it into England. He himself used it, and believed in its healthful influence. He learned from the Indians to smoke it; and his example was soon followed in England, some of the first tobacco-pipes being made of the shell of the walnut for the bowl, and a straw for the stem of the pipe. It is said that when Sir Walter Raleigh's servant first saw him with the smoke coming out of his mouth, he thought he was on fire, and poured a pitcher of water over his head to put out the flames.

Not discouraged by his previous failures, Raleigh determined to send out another colony which should be agricultural, consisting of emigrants with their wives and children, who should make their homes in the new world, and so establish settlements that should be permanent. John White was appointed governor, and with him were eleven assistants for the administration of affairs. They arrived on the coast of North Carolina in the summer of 1587, and hastened to the Isle of Roanoke, hoping to find the few men who had been left there by Granville; but they found only the ruins of the fort, and the scattered bones of the miserable men who had been murdered by the Indians. Soon after the landing and settlement of White's colony, his granddaughter, the first English child, was born on the continent and named "Virginia Dare." White, himself, going back to England for supplies, was detained by the war with Spain, and when at last he returned, the colony, composed of eighty-nine men and seventeen women, had entirely disappeared, though some twenty years afterward it was said that seven of them were still living among the Indians. So ended the efforts of Raleigh to establish settlements in America. Five times he had sent to search for his lost colonists, but each time in vain. Their fate was never fully known.

OTHER VOYAGES TO AMERICA.

The favorable reports of the early adventurers, and the still cherished hope of finding a short passage to India, led to still further efforts at discovery. In 1602, Bartholomew Gosnold, who had already sailed to Virginia by the round about route by the Canaries and the West Indies, endeavored to reach America by the direct route, and had well nigh secured to New England the first permanent English colony. Steering his small bark directly across the Atlantic, in seven weeks he reached the coast of Massachusetts, and landed, with four men, at Cape Cod, the first spot in New England ever trod by Englishmen. Reaching the westernmost part of the Elizabeth Islands, they built on it a store house and fort, intending to lay the foundations of what should be the first New England colony. But fear of the Indians, want of provisions, and disagreements as to expected profits, brought their plans to an end, and the whole party soon went back to England, after an absence of some four months.

So favorable, however, were their reports of the land they had visited, that another expedition consisting of two small vessels, with forty-three men, was fitted out at Bristol, and under the command of Martin Pring, sailed for America in April, 1603. The vessels were well provided with trinkets and merchandise for traffic with the natives, and the voyage was every way successful, reaching the coasts of Maine and Massachusetts, and returning safely to England in about six months. Other enterprises for discovery and traffic soon followed. Bartholomew Gilbert sought in vain for the remains of the colonies of Raleigh. An expedition commanded by George Weymouth, seeking a northwest passage, explored Labrador, and discovered the Penobscot river. And these and other voyages so spread information and wakened enterprise, as to lead to the later and permanent settlements which built up the United States. The daring and skill of these

THE AURORA SEEN IN GREENLAND.

early adventurers were wonderful. The ocean was untried, and its winds and currents unknown. The vessels were mostly of less than a hundred tons burden. Frobisher's vessel was only twenty-five tons; and two of those of Columbus were without a deck. Hudson, by the mutiny of his sailors, was turned adrift in an open boat, in the bay now bearing his name, and there left to perish by the waves or the savages. The vessels of several of the early navigators went down at sea with all on board. And such was the state of the art of navigation that the dangers of the sea were practically a hundredfold greater than they are at the present day.

THE NATURAL BRIDGE, VIRGINIA.

PERIOD II.

CHAPTER I.

Not counting Vermont, which did not come into the Union till 1791, the original thirteen colonies whose delegates signed the Declaration of Independence were Virginia, Massachusetts, Connecticut, Rhode Island, New Hampshire, Maine, New York, New Jersey, Pennsylvania, Maryland, North and South Carolina, and Georgia.

THE OLD THIRTEEN.

The curtain rises on a hundred years,—
A pageant of the olden time appears.
Let the historic muse her aid supply,
To note and name each form that passes by;

Here come the "old original Thirteen."
Sir Walter ushers in the Virgin Queen;
Catholic Mary follows her, whose land
Smiles on soft Chesapeake from either strand;
Then Georgia, with the sisters Caroline,—
One the palmetto wears, and one the pine;
Next, she who ascertained the rights of men,
Not by the sword, but by the word of Penn,—
The friendly language hers, of "thee" and "thou,"
Then, she whose mother was a thrifty vrouw,—
Mother herself of princely children now;
And, sitting at her feet, the sisters twain,—
Two smaller links in the Atlantic chain,—
They, through those long, dark winters, drear and dire,
Watched with our Fabius round the bivouac fire,—
One the free mountain maid, in white and green,
One guards the Charter Oak with lofty mien;
And, lo! in the plain beauty once she wore,
The Pilgrim mother from the Bay State shore;
And last, not least, is Little Rhody seen,
With face turned heavenward, steadfast and serene,—
She on her anchor, Hope, leans, and will ever lean.

— *Charles T. Brooks.*

31

VIRGINIA.

In the early voyages of Columbus, and of other early navigators, the great aim, as we have seen, was to discover a new and short passage to India, with all its imagined wealth. The passion for gathering gold, and the desire for the luxuries of the tropical regions were the leading motives to enterprise. The popular idea seemed to be that untold wealth could be gathered almost without effort in the new world. "I tell thee," says one of the actors in Marston's play of "Eastward, Ho!" which was written in 1605, "gold is more plentiful there than copper is with us; and for as much red copper as I can bring, I'll have thrice the weight in gold. Why, man, all the dripping-pans are of

THE JAMES RIVER AND COUNTRY NEAR RICHMOND.

pure gold, and all the chains with which they chain up their streets are of massive gold. All the prisoners they take are fettered in gold; and as for rubies and diamonds, they go forth in holidays and gather them by the sea-shore, to hang on their children's coats and stick in their children's caps, as commonly as our children wear saffron-gilt brooches and groats with holes in them. It is a pleasant country, withal, as ever the sun shined on, temperate and full of all sorts of excellent viands. Then, for your means of advancement, there it is simple, and not preposterously mixed. You may be an alderman there, and never be a slave. Besides, there we shall have no more law than conscience, and not too much of either,—shall serve God enough, and eat and drink enough, and enough is as good as a feast." Such was too much the theory that at first led great numbers to go forth as colonists, though afterward, as less influenced by such wild anticipations, came the higher aim of founding states, and planting permanent colonies, with all the elements of civilization and religion.

In 1606, under a patent from James I., the "London Company" was formed to send out a colony to America. And on the 19th of December of that year, a little squadron of three small vessels, with a hundred and five men, set sail for Virginia. The making up of the company was not auspicious. John Smith, one of their leading men, speaks of them as "poor gentlemen, tradesmen, serving-men, and libertines." Of the hundred and five of their number only twelve were laborers; and though they were going to a wilderness where there was not a dwelling of any kind, there were only four carpenters, and none of the men had families. After a tedious voyage of nearly five months, they at last reached the peninsula of Jamestown, which, in May, 1607, they selected as the site of their colony. By the middle of summer, when Newport, their leader, sailed for England, their provisions were exhausted, the Indians had become unfriendly, and the intense heat of the climate brought on disease, so that one half the members of the colony died before September, and the colony would have been entirely broken up but for Captain John Smith, so noted in the early history of the country, and perhaps the strongest and most representative man of all the colonists of Virginia. In spite

VIEW ON THE POTOMAC.

TOWER ROCKS, VIRGINIA.

of discouragements and almost insurmountable obstacles, Smith kept the colony together for two years, drilling the soldiers, compelling labor, repairing the fort, conciliating the Indians, whom he outwitted, and procuring from them the corn and provisions which kept the colonists from starving.

The story of Smith being taken prisoner by Powhatan, the head chief of some thirty tribes, and that when condemned to death he was saved by Pocahontas, the daughter of that chief, is probably a fiction, for it is not mentioned in his first account of his explorations, which was published in 1608, and did not appear in print till about 1616 or 1617, in the time of Queen Anne. But whether the story has or has not any foundation, Smith undoubtedly so influenced the tribes as to keep them for a long time in friendly relations to the colonists. He explored the Bay of Chesapeake to the Susquehanna; probably entered the port of Baltimore, and ascended the Potomac up to the falls at Georgetown. He was not only the leading man in the colony, but was made its governor; but when new colonists arrived who opposed his administration, and after he had been injured by an explosion of gunpowder, he gave up the government and returned to England, where he died in London in 1631. He gave to New England the name it now bears.

Smith, at his departure, had left some four hundred and ninety persons in the colony, but through indolence, vice, famine, disagreements among themselves, and hostility on the part of the natives, in less than a year only sixty remained; and these would have perished but for the timely aid which was brought by Gates and Somers, with part of the fleet, followed by Lord Delaware, who came over as governor and captain-general, bringing fresh emigrants and also supplies for the settlers. He reorganized the colony, which, with the additions he brought, consisted of some two hundred men. He held office, however, but a short time, and was succeeded by Sir Thomas Dale, who for five years was the ruling spirit of the colony, though aided for a time by Gates. Dale ruled with severity, but in most respects wisely, restraining the idle and worthless, and keeping on friendly terms with the Indians. The borders of the colony were extended and much was done for the permanent prosperity of the settlement.

Pocahontas was converted to the Christian faith, and in the quaint little structure at Jamestown, builded from the rough timbers of the forest, whose font was hollowed from the trunk of a tree, Pocahontas renounced the heathenism of her people, and in her broken English, uttered the responses in accordance with the rites of the Church of England. She was baptized under the name of Rebecca, and shortly after, April, 1613, was married to John Rolfe.

Six vessels coming from England, with three hundred fresh emigrants, under the leadership of Thomas Gates, gave fresh life and prosperity to the colony. The land, which hitherto had been held in common, was now assigned, in portions, to individuals, as private property. A new charter, given in 1612, enlarged the powers of the company, and the Indians submitted to the English, acknowledging themselves tributary to the king, an event which was brought about by the marriage of Pocahontas to John Rolfe, a union commemorated with approbation by the historians of Virginia, and to which many of her distinguished men trace their descent. When Dale went back to England, in 1616, Pocahontas and her husband went with him. She was received there with great attention and treated at court as a princess, but died in England the same year, at the age of twenty-one years. Rolfe, her husband, was the first one to cultivate tobacco largely in Virginia, and it soon became a valuable export to England, and was of great help in making the colony successful.

The allotment of land to individuals greatly encouraged industry among the people, and tobacco soon became not only the staple product but the ordinary currency of the colony. In 1618, many new emigrants came over from England, and the "Great Charter" was granted, under which the people of the colony had a voice in making their own laws, which was the beginning of free government in America, control of affairs being put in the hands of a governor, "a council of estate," and "a general assembly," thus establishing the threefold form of government which was afterward generally adopted in the colonies.

In 1619, Sir George Yeardley was made governor, and under him the new charter was put in operation, so that more than a year before the Pilgrims in the Mayflower left the harbor of Southampton, the first elective assembly of the New World was organized at Jamestown, July 30, 1619, and made, in Virginia, laws for the government

of the people. This assembly took steps for the establishment of a college; ordered that
the Church of England should be the established church of Virginia; passed laws for the
strict observance of the Sabbath; for instruction of the Indians, and for other interests of
the colony.

BAPTISM OF POCAHONTAS.

A bad element was introduced into the colony in 1619, when a hundred convicts
arrived, having been sent over from English prisons, by order of the king, to be sold as
servants. The same year was also marked by the arrival of the first African slaves,
twenty of whom were brought to Jamestown by a Dutch trading vessel, thus laying the
foundation of the slave system in the land.

At this time there were in the colony only some six hundred men, women and children, but in the course of the year some twelve hundred and sixty persons, mostly of an excellent class, were added to their number. That the colony might be more firmly established, in 1619 ninety respectable young women were sent over to be married to the settlers, the cost of a wife being from a hundred to a hundred and fifty pounds of tobacco. Within three years some thirty-five hundred persons had found their way to Virginia. In 1621, the colony was granted a written constitution,

INTRODUCTION OF SLAVERY.

under which representation in the government and a trial by jury became acknowledged as rights of the people.

The colonists at various times had had trouble with the Indians, but in possession, as they were, of fire-arms, they felt confident of always being able to protect themselves; and while Powhatan lived, the thirty tribes of which he was the head chief, numbering some twenty-four hundred warriors, remained peaceful and friendly. But afterward, becoming jealous of the growing power of the English, and fearing their complete ascendency, the Indians, while still pretending friendship, treacherously resolved on the destruction of the colony. Early in the spring of 1622, at mid-day, they suddenly fell upon the unsuspecting settlers, and murdered, with savage barbarity, three hundred and forty-six persons. Jamestown, and some of the settlements, through information given by a friendly Indian, were prepared for the attack, and so the greater part of the colony was saved. From this time on, for several years, there was almost continual warfare with the Indians, which ended at last in their complete subjugation, so that they dwindled away and were not afterward seriously troublesome.

In 1624, the colony underwent an important change in its government. The London Company was dissolved by the king, and Virginia was made a royal province, and so continued for a hundred and fifty years, down to the time of the revolution, except during the protectorate of Cromwell. But though ruled by royal governors, the people still elected their own legislatures, which they regarded as the safeguard of their liberties. The slaves which, as mentioned, had been brought in by the Dutch in 1620, and sold to the planters, were found to be most profitably employed on the tobacco plantations, and as a consequence others were brought in, and so slavery was rapidly extended through the colony. Several times the legislature endeavored to put an end to the traffic, but England would not consent, as it was a source of revenue to the king and the English government. The value of slave labor, however, was found so great that the colonists gradually gave up their opposition to the system, and so it was fastened on the country. At a later date, Virginia, and so several other Southern States, seeing the evils of the system, strongly opposed its continuance, and Jefferson, speaking of its existence and influence, said, " I tremble for my country when I reflect that God is just, and that His justice cannot sleep forever." But the British authorities did everything in their power to encourage and sustain it, saying it was "the pillar and support of the British plantation trade in America," and that they "could not allow the colonies to check or discourage, in any degree, a traffic so beneficial to the nation." And so slavery continued, until, as the result of secession, freedom came to the millions who had been held in slavery, and the entire country was free.

During the time of Cromwell and the commonwealth in England, the Virginians remained loyal to the royal cause, and at one time sent and invited Charles II. to come from France and become their king. He accepted their invitation, and was about to embark for the colony, when, after the death of Cromwell and the downfall of the commonwealth, he was recalled to the throne of England. And on his accession as a reward for her loyalty, he allowed the colony to quarter the arms of England, Ireland, and Scotland with those of Virginia, as an independent member of the "Old Dominion," a name which, to this day, is often given to Virginia.

In 1660, England passed what was known as the " Navigation Acts," the purpose of which was to control all the trade of the colonies, so that the Virginians, as well as others, were not allowed to sell or buy any of their products or goods except to and from England, and everything was ordered to be carried in English vessels. These laws bore heavily on Virginia, and were among the causes of the Revolution.

The progress of Virginia in population and wealth continued till the end of the colonial period, 1776, at which time its population was 575,000. The people were hospitable, the better class living mostly on plantations. Crime was rare, and theft almost unknown. The established religion of the colony was Episcopacy; but religious freedom grew rapidly, so that at the Revolution two-thirds of the people were dissenters from the Episcopal church. Before the Revolution, education was neglected, and even in 1671, the governor, Sir William Berkeley, said he "thanked God that there were no free schools and no printing presses in Virginia, and no prospect of any for a hundred years to come," adding "God keep us from both!" But in 1688 some free schools were opened, and in 1692, the college of William and Mary was established. The professions of law and medicine for a long time were almost unknown; and of the clergy, Bishop Meade, in his history of Virginia, says, "there was not only defective preaching, but most evil living among them." The planters, who were proud of their descent, were the influential and governing class, and from them, in the later days of the Revolution, came a set of leaders who have done the greatest services to the country and the greatest honor to the American name. A generation that could furnish such men as Washington,

VIEW ON THE JAMES RIVER.

Marshall, Patrick Henry, Jefferson, Madison, and many others like them, is one that is worthy of note, not only in the history of the United States, but in that of the English race and of the world. The firm and noble stand taken not only by such men, but by the great mass of the people of Virginia for their political rights, was of the greatest benefit as an example and stimulus to the other colonies, and greatly prepared the way for our independence as a nation.

Virginia has an area of 38,352 square miles. Its geology, climate, soil and productions differ in different parts of the State. It is rich in minerals, which are various and of great value, especially its coal and iron. The western coal region, cut through by large rivers, is one of the most valuable in the world. Mineral springs abound. Among the curiosities of the State are the Natural Bridge in Rockbridge county; the Blowing Cave, that sends out a blast of cold air in summer, and draws in the air in winter; the Natural Tunnel, 70 feet high; the Hawk's Nest, a pillar 1,000 feet high; and several ebbing and flowing springs, as well as some of valuable medical properties. The Potomac is one of its chief rivers, and cuts through the Blue ridge at Harper's Ferry, which is so noted from its connection with the John Brown raid, and with many of the important military movements of the country. The State has eight colleges, including the State University, besides several important literary and theological institutions of a high order, and numerous state institutions of benevolence, besides those sustained by private benevolent associations. Its public school system was organized in 1870, and in 1875 its receipts for school purposes were over $1,000,000. The population of the State in 1800 was 886,200, of whom 345,796 were slaves; in 1880, 1,512,565, and in 1890, 1,648,911.

THE NEW ENGLAND AND OTHER COLONIES.

New England was so named by Captain John Smith of Virginia, who, after his first return from Virginia to England, sailed to the American coast in 1614, for purposes of trade and discovery. He examined the coast from the Penobscot river to Cape Cod, and made a map of the region, which was first printed in London in 1616. All this northern part of the United States had been granted by King James, in 1606, to the Plymouth Company, which had tried, but unsuccessfully, to found a colony in Maine, and it was dissolved in 1620, when a new company was formed, called the "Council for New England," to which was granted all the territory from Nova Scotia to Pennsylvania, and extending from the Atlantic ocean to the Pacific. While this Council was considering its plans, a colony was founded in Massachusetts by the *Pilgrims*, at Plymouth, and a little later a settlement was made by the *Puritans* in the region of Massachusetts Bay, both settlements forming what afterward became Massachusetts.

MASSACHUSETTS.

The Pilgrims of New England are sometimes improperly confounded with the Puritans, who came over to New England at a little later date. The Pilgrims came out from the Puritans of England, going beyond them in opposition to the views and ceremonies of the Church of England. The doctrines of the Reformation began at an early date to have influence in England, but it was not till the time of Henry VIII, that they greatly divided the people. Then, and in the following reigns, strong opposition arose against the teachings and ceremonies of the established English church, those who dissented from the church while yet remaining in it and seeking its purity, being called Puritans, while those who separated themselves entirely from the establishment were called Separatists, and afterward were known as the Pilgrims, or the Pilgrim Fathers. The Puritans acknowledged the Church of England, but remained in it desiring, laboring, and hoping for its reform and greater purity. The Pilgrims went far beyond this, and denounced it as a corrupt and idolatrous institution, false to christianity and to the truth.

Being opposed and persecuted for their views in various ways in England, the Pilgrims, many of them, fled to Holland, under the lead of their pastor, John Robinson,

Remaining there some thirteen years, they finally resolved to emigrate to America, there to establish a colony where they might be free to carry out their views of religion and worship. Providing two ships, the Speedwell, of sixty, and the Mayflower, of a hundred and eighty tons, a part of their number embarked from Leyden. Twice they started, and twice put back, and at last the Mayflower sailed alone, with a hundred and two colonists, for the New World, September 6, 1620. They intended to go to the Hudson river, but after a stormy and trying passage, they landed, at last, at Plymouth, on the 21st of December. The leaders were not, with some exceptions, men of high social position or of great wealth, but they were men of thought and conscience and high character, and they bore with them the seeds of a great nation, and of a great system of government. As they had no authority from the king or the company as to the future of their enterprise, they decided, before landing, to make a mutual agreement with each other as to their government, and they drew up the following voluntary and solemn compact providing for their organization into a "civil body politic" for securing "just and equal laws," to which they promised "all due submission and obedience." It was signed by all the men of the company, forty-two in number, and is as follows:

THE COMPACT.

In the name of God, Amen: We, whose names are underwritten, the loyal subjects of our dread sovereign, King James, by the grace of God, of Great Britain, France, and Ireland, king, defender of the faith, &c., having undertaken for the glory of God, and advancement of the Christian faith, and honor of our king and country, a voyage to plant the first colony in the northern parts of Virginia, do, by these presents, solemnly and mutually, in the presence of God and of one another, covenant and combine ourselves together into a civil body politic, for our better ordering and preservation and furtherance of the ends aforesaid, and by virtue hereof, to enact, constitute, and frame such just and equal laws, ordinances, acts, constitutions and offices, from time to time, as shall be thought most meet and convenient for the general good of the colony; unto which we promise all due submission and obedience.

In witness whereof we have hereunder subscribed our names, at Cape Cod, the eleventh of November, in the year of the reign of our sovereign lord, King James, of England, France, and Ireland, the eighteenth, and of Scotland the fifty-fourth, Anno Domini, 1620.

Under this compact, James Carver was unanimously chosen their governor for the first year.

As they landed they found the region almost entirely unoccupied, for most of the Indians had a few years before been swept off by a desolating pestilence. The voyage had been severe; their provisions were limited; as they disembarked, the water was so shallow they had to wade ashore, and in the freezing weather severe colds were taken which brought on disease and suffering, so that forty-four of their number died before the winter was over, and at the end of the year more than one-half of them were dead. At one time only seven of their number were well enough to care for the sick. Fearing the Indians, some of whom had attacked the first exploring party, they levelled the graves of the dead, planting Indian corn over them to conceal the weakness of the colony from the natives. The rock on which they landed has been carefully preserved to this day; and their landing and the lofty character of their plans have been deservedly and widely celebrated both in prose and poetry, but nowhere in more soul-stirring lines than in those by Mrs. Hemans, which have been read and admired in every land where the story of the "Pilgrim Fathers" has been told.

THE LANDING OF THE PILGRIMS.

The breaking waves dashed high
    On a stern and rock-bound coast,
And the woods against a stormy sky
    Their giant branches tossed;
And the heavy night hung dark
    The hills and waters o'er,
When a band of exiles moored their bark
    On the wild New England shore.

Not as the conqueror comes,
    They, the true-hearted, came;
Not with the roll of stirring drums,
    And the trumpet that sings of fame;
Not as the flying come,
    In silence and in fear;—
They shook the depths of the desert gloom
    With their hymns of lofty cheer.

Amidst the storm they sang—
    And the stars heard, and the sea;
And the sounding aisles of the dim woods rang
    To the anthems of the free!
The ocean-eagle soared
    From his nest by the white wave's foam;
And the rocking pines of the forest roared,—
    This was their welcome home!

There were men with hoary hair
    Amidst that pilgrim band;—
Why had they come to wither there,
    Away from childhood's land?
There was woman's fearless eye,
    Lit by her deep love's truth;
There was manhood's brow serenely high,
    And the fiery heart of youth.

What sought they thus afar?
    Bright jewels of the mine?
The wealth of seas, the spoils of war?
    They sought a faith's pure shrine.
Ay! call it holy ground,
    The soil where first they trod;
They have left unstained what there they found,—
    Freedom to worship God.

As spring advanced the sickness and mortality decreased. But the hardships of privation and want had still to be encountered. At one time their provisions were so spent that they knew not at night where to find food for the morning, and at another, they were reduced to a single pint of corn, which being parched and distributed, gave to each individual only five kernels. But through all their self-denials and sufferings their trust in the goodness and guidance of divine providence remained unshaken. They threw out trading posts, hunted, farmed, fished, worked, and patiently stayed on, and so laid the solid foundations of the future State. The details of their life and progress may seem trivial in themselves, but they rise to grandeur when judged by the after results.

They were set down at the time, with minute care, by men like Bradford, who seemed to have an instinctive assurance that the future would long to know of their struggles for existence, and that he and his friends were laying one of the corner stones of a great and prosperous nation. The colony grew slowly, but it did its intended work, and opened the way for the great emigration and growth that were afterward to build up the powerful commonwealths of New England.

The system of common property here, as in Virginia, had worked badly and caused much discontent. But after 1623 it was agreed that parcels of land should be allotted,

PLYMOUTH ROCK, MASSACHUSETTS.

so that the members of every family could plant and cultivate for themselves, an arrangement that gave great satisfaction and led to universal industry, so that very soon enough was raised for quite a commerce with the Indians, who gladly bartered their beaver and other skins for the corn of the colonists and for the manufactured articles which these furs purchased from England.

One day, in the spring of 1621, Samoset, an Indian who had learned a little English from the Penobscot fishermen, came into the settlement, saying in English, "Welcome,

SCENE ON THE HUDSON RIVER NEAR WEST POINT.

Englishmen!" He brought with him Squanto, another Indian, who had been in England, who taught the colonists the Indian way of cultivating corn, and also acted as interpreter between them and the other Indians. Massasoit, the sachem of a neighboring tribe, came also to visit the colony, and formed with them a treaty of friendship—the oldest act of diplomacy recorded in the history of New England—a treaty which was faithfully kept as long as he lived.

The influence of the English over the Indians rapidly increased, many of the chiefs submitting themselves and their tribes to King James. One of them, Canonicus, the sachem of the Narragansetts, was for a time unfriendly, and sent to the governor a bundle of arrows wrapped in the skin of a rattle-snake, as a token of his hostility, but when Bradford returned the skin stuffed with powder and bullets, his courage failed, and he also made peace with the colony. Later than this a plot was formed by some of the Indians to destroy the English, but Massasoit revealed the plan to his allies, and Miles Standish, who had been appointed commander of the colony, seized the plotters suddenly, and put them to death with their own weapons, and so ended the danger.

Though the colonists exercised self-government, and were at peace with the natives, the progress of population was very slow. The lands were not fertile, the climate was severe and unfavorable, and at the end of ten years the colony numbered only about three hundred souls. Robinson had died at Leyden, and the remainder of the Pilgrims had come over from Holland to the colony, which afterwards acquired rights at Cape Ann and Kennebec, and also made a settlement on the Connecticut river. By a charter from William III., in 1629, the colony was united to the colony of Massachusetts, of which its territory thus became a part.

To enjoy religious liberty had been the great object of the first comers of the Plymouth colony. Their form of government was most simple. For more than eighteen years the legislature was made up of the whole body of the male inhabitants; the governor was chosen by vote, and had several assistant councilors; and the State was a strict democracy. But in 1639, as the population increased and the territory was extended, the system became representative, and each town sent its committee or delegates to the general court.

As guides and pioneers, the Pilgrims set the example of popular government, and moulded the civil and religious character of our country, laying broad and deep the foundations of republican freedom and national independence and prosperity. They were a thoughtful, intelligent, thrifty, God-fearing people; for their age, were liberal Christians, and never chargeable with the religious persecutions for which the Puritans of the Massachusetts colony have been blamed.

Not long after the Pilgrims came to Plymouth, other English people had visited the coasts of New England for exploration, fishing and traffic with the natives. At an early day Martin Pring had discovered New Hampshire; John Smith had visited the coast of Maine, and John Mason had established settlements at Portsmouth and Dover. And in 1622 thirty-five vessels were fishing on the coasts of New England, and settlements had been begun which afterward became the colonies of New Hampshire and Maine.

The Puritans in England had now greatly increased in numbers, and afterward, in the time of Cromwell, they controlled the government. Now, however, they were opposed and persecuted, and seeing the growing success of the Plymouth colony, a number of their leading and wealthy members formed a company to send out other

SILVER CASCADE, CRAWFORD'S NOTCH, WHITE MOUNTAINS.

settlers to New England. This company calling themselves the "Company of Massachusetts Bay," made purchase, in 1628, of extensive lands on the Bay, extending westward, as was supposed, to the Pacific ocean; and having in 1629 received a charter from King Charles, they sent out a party of Puritans, under John Endicott, which settled in Salem, and there laid the foundation of the colony of Massachusetts Bay. Others followed, the same summer, and settled at Charlestown.

In 1630 the charter and powers of government were transferred from the company in England to the colony, thus giving the colonists the right of governing themselves, the result of which was that a large number of Puritans, of influence and wealth, resolved to leave England for the colony. In the summer of the year, a fleet of thirteen vessels brought out fifteen hundred Puritan settlers, and with them horses, cattle, goats, and all things necessary for planting, fishing, ship-building, &c. With them came John

OLD SOUTH CHURCH, BOSTON.

Winthrop, as governor of the colony. He was greatly respected and esteemed by the people, and was frequently re-elected as governor. After being sixty-one days at sea, the Arbella landed her passengers; Boston was made the capital of the colony, and a church was organized with John Wilson as pastor. The colony, as usual, had many hardships and discouragements, and a hundred or more of their number, disheartened and fearing famine and death, went back to England. Before December some two hundred of their number had died, but the survivors persevering, brighter days came on, and between 1630 and 1640, some twenty thousand persons had come over to the colony. The people were thrifty and persevering, cultivating the ground, caring for their flocks and herds, fishing and hunting for food, and exporting cured fish, lumber, and furs of various kinds, which brought them, in return from England, articles of comfort and luxury. The laws were made by a legislature elected by vote of the citizens who were church members, till 1686, when the charter was taken away by James II., and the legislature abolished; but in 1692, a new and favorable charter was granted by King William, and Massachusetts continued to be a royal province down to the time of Independence in 1776.

From the days of the revolution Massachusetts has had a steady and healthful growth. The State has an area of 7,800 square miles. The country is hilly, and much of the soil is sterile, so that less than one-half of the acreage of the State is improved in farming, but in the low grounds, and especially in the river valleys, it is fertile. The great prosperity of the State, however, is not from agriculture, but from its great manufacturing and commercial interests, in which it is relatively in advance of any of the

States. The fisheries of the State have also been one of its leading industries. It has numerous rivers and streams giving waterfalls of great power for manufacturing purposes, as at Lawrence Lowell, and Turner's Falls.

In the State are some seven thousand schools of various grades, a university, and seven colleges, theological, medical, law, scientific, and industrial schools, and numerous hospitals and charitable institutions, and the railroad connections, thousands of miles in extent, give abundant channels for travel and transportation of every kind.

In the early days of Massachusetts the colonists suffered greatly from the hostility of the Indians. In 1675, King Philip's war broke out, lasting more than a year, and causing great loss of life and property. No less than twelve or thirteen towns were

TURNER'S FALLS, MASSACHUSETTS.

destroyed by the Indians, and over six hundred houses were burned. In one conflict twenty of the colonists were killed. It was during this war that an attack was made upon Hadley, on a morning when the people were all in church. Suddenly the Indians rushed in and surrounded the meeting-house, and though the people rushed to arms for resistance, all was alarm and confusion. Suddenly, in the midst of the people, appeared a man of venerable appearance, but dressed differently from the people, who took the command, and arranged and ordered the men in the best military manner. Led by him they repelled and routed the enemy, and saved the town. Then the stranger immediately disappeared, and the inhabitants, not being able to account for the phenomenon in any other way, believed that he must have been specially sent by God for their deliverance, and for some time afterward seemed persuaded that they had been saved by an angel taking the form of man. Nor did they know who their deliverer was till some twenty years afterward, when it became known that it was Goffe, one of the two regicide judges who had been secreted there.

Massachusetts, in its colonial days, was deeply involved in the struggles between England and France for control in the New World, which did not cease till the union of Canada to England, and of the vast region then known as Louisiana to Spain. From the earliest days the people of the New England colonies were a highly intelligent and thinking people, and their leaders were men of thorough education and just and broad views of legislation and civil and social rights. In 1650, in the Massachusetts Bay colony one in every two hundred of the people was a graduate of an English university, and many of them had been as prominent and distinguished in England as they afterward were in the New World. In the controversies that led to the revolution, and in the war itself, as in all the steps that led to our independence and to the formation of the new republic, Massachusetts took a leading part, and most of the ablest leaders in the great work were from Massachusetts and Virginia. In 1790, the population of the State was 378,787; in 1880, 1,783,085, and in 1890, 2,233,407.

CONNECTICUT.

The valley of the Connecticut river had early become an object of desire and competition to the settlers of Massachusetts Bay and Plymouth, as it had also to the Dutch. Its territory had first been granted to the Earl of Warwick, and then to Lord Brook and Lord Say and Sele and their assigns. A trading-house had early been established at Windsor by the Plymouth people, and another by the Dutch at Hartford, and small settlements had been made in one or two other places, but the great body of the future possessors of the rich Connecticut valley came from Massachusetts.

In 1635, John Winthrop, the younger, came out from England as governor of Connecticut, under the patent of Lord Brook and Lord Say and Sele, and took formal possession of the country, tore down the Dutch arms where ever they had been placed, and built a fort at Saybrook. In the spring of the next year, Thomas Hooker, "the light of the western churches," led to Hartford a colony of some hundred souls, gathered from the most valuable citizens of the Massachusetts settlement. Going on foot through the wilderness, with no guide but the compass, and no resting place at night but the ground, they drove before them their herds of cattle, and reaching the Connecticut river, founded the settlements of Hartford, Windsor, and Wethersfield, forming the "Connecticut colony."

For a time there was trouble between the English and the Dutch, as both claimed Connecticut, but the former at last gained full possession, and in 1644 the Saybrook settlement was united with the Connecticut colony. The settlements thus united were exposed to many perils, especially from the Indians. The colonists numbered, in all, only some two hundred persons, while the Pequots, who were hostile, had some seven hundred warriors, who soon began raiding and burning on the outlying farms, and murdering the inhabitants. Men going to their work were killed and scalped and horribly mangled. At Wethersfield a man was taken by them and roasted alive, and ten persons were massacred, and two girls carried away.

4

Roused by these atrocities, war was declared by the colony, and Captain John
Mason, with seventy-seven men and reinforcements of friendly Indians from the
Narragansett and Nyantic tribes, attacked and burned their intrenched fort, or walled
village, which was filled with their wigwams, and contained seven hundred of their

NIGHT ATTACK ON EARLY SETTLERS.

warriors. This stronghold, which the Indians seemed to think impregnable, was set on
fire on the end at which a strong wind was blowing, and the flames at once swept fiercely
through its whole length. It had but two openings, both of which were occupied by
Mason's men. The Indians, in attempting to escape from the flames, were at once shot
down as they rushed forth. And, the English throwing firebrands among the wigwams,

also, the whole village was soon in a blaze, and most of the savages suffered the same horrible death they were fond of inflicting on their captives. Only five of the six or seven hundred Pequots within the inclosure escaped with their lives, while only two of the colonists were killed and sixteen wounded in the conflict. The remnants of the savages were pursued into their hiding places; every wigwam was burned, every settlement broken up, and every cornfield laid waste, so that the Pequots, as a body, practically disappeared, and the warlike tribe which had gloried in its power, and had carried on its fierce warfare against the colonists, was wiped out of existence. Such terrible vengeance had never been known to the Indians, and the name of Englishmen now became a terror to the savages, so that for thirty-eight years the colonists were undisturbed and at peace, thus having time to perfect their constitution on principles which have stood the test of more than two centuries, and have made Connecticut what it is to-day. They toiled at their farms, organized society, opened schools, levied taxes, built churches, and established a purely democratic government, with the first written constitution known, not only in America, but the first ever known in the world, a constitution that gave them unqualified powers to govern themselves — to elect their own officers, make their own laws, administer justice, inflict punishments, and confer pardons, without appeals to England; in a word, to exercise every power as an independent colony, which it was in everything but in name. The first governor was John Haynes, who had already held the same office in Massachusetts. The second was Edward Hopkins, and these two were elected alternately to the governorship for many years.

During the Pequot war another Puritan settlement sprang up at New Haven, in 1638, under the lead of John Davenport, as its minister, and Theophilus Eaton, a wealthy London merchant, who afterward was annually elected governor (for twenty years) till his death. The colonists, coming from Massachusetts, settled on the sound, west of the Connecticut river, where they lived for a year under no rule but an agreement to obey the scriptures, after which they met in a barn and formed a church, which was itself the State — church membership and citizenship being identical. Two months later they formed a civil government — an independent religious democracy, much like that of Connecticut, but more strict, in that it confined citizenship to church members. Both the settlements steadily increased, laws were codified, and the boundaries between them and the Dutch were settled. In 1657 John Winthrop was chosen governor of Connecticut. The New Haven and Connecticut colonies remained separate governments till 1665, when, by Charles II., they were united in one, as " Connecticut."

The charter, under which they were united, gave the colonists unlimited power to order their own government, to make their own laws, choose their own officers, to administer justice without appeal to England, to grant pardons, in a word, to exercise every power in legislation and action. It made Connecticut independent in everything but in name; and where Charles and Clarendon were, as they supposed, making a close corporation, they had, in fact, authorized an established democracy. The charter which the younger Winthrop had obtained, extended the limits of Connecticut from the Narragansett river to the Pacific ocean, not only giving peace and prosperity to the colony for more than a hundred years, but preparing the way for the claim to those western lands, the sale of which afterward gave to the State its large school fund for the education of its children and youth.

The charter which, in 1662, had been granted by Charles was the most liberal ever given to any American colony. This charter, however, was annulled by James II., who was opposed to its free government. But the charter itself was not lost, for when Andros, who was sent out as royal governor, went to Hartford to demand it from the Assembly, the lights of the room where they met were suddenly blown out, and the charter was spirited away and hidden in the famous old "Charter Oak," from which, at the end of Andros' tyrannical rule, in 1689, it was brought forth, and, under King William the colony again enjoyed all its former privileges, their government under that old charter continuing the same for a hundred and eighty years, till long after Connecticut became a State.

In character, the people were intelligent, thrifty, industrious, liberty-loving, and earnest advocates of education. They were moral and religious. Every town and

YALE COLLEGE, CONNECTICUT.

village had a scholar for its minister. So honest were the people that bolts and locks were unknown. The frugality of private life made public expenditures comparatively small. Farming interests in the colony were prospered. The amusements of the people were rational as well as joyous; and for a century the history of the colony, with few and short exceptions, was a picture of general comfort and happiness.

An excellent system of common schools was early established (in 1644), and the State, in later years, had a large school fund to aid it. Yale college was founded in 1700, and received its charter in 1701. It was commenced by ten ministers of the colony, each laying down a few books — in all about forty,— each saying as they did so, " I give these books for the founding of a college in this colony," and from this humble beginning has arisen the great university, which in 1890 had 147 professors and teachers, and 1,645 students in its various departments, and which in the same year received in donations to its funds over a million and a half dollars. The college buildings, a part of which are shown in the cut, occupy one of the large squares of the city and front on another, on which stand several churches and public buildings and the design is to have the present and future structures in time form an enclosed quadrangle. In the State are also Trinity college, the Wesleyan university, several schools of law, medicine, and theology, and numerous seminaries, academies, and private schools of a high order.

The soil and climate of Connecticut are less favorable to agriculture than those of many of the newer States, but as a State it stands high in manufactures of various kinds, and its commerce is carried on with every part of the world.

The early settlers of the colony had all the religious earnestness of their age; but the spirit of persecution was never known in Connecticut. Their laws were strict, extending to the customs and moralities of social and private life, though what is known as the "Blue Laws," which many associate with Connecticut, never had an existence. What are so called were malignantly written by Samuel Peters, a renegade tory who was banished from the colony, and of whom Trumbull, the historian, says, "he was known as the greatest liar in the colony." One of Peters' stories was, that the Connecticut river in passing through the narrow gorge at Bellows Falls was so compressed that an iron crowbar would float on its surface like a chip or a dry leaf. And much of his "Blue Laws," is about as credible as this story.

The colony was active and energetic in the early wars with the Indians and French, and was among the most zealous of the colonies in the war of the Revolution, and in the war of the Secession the State did her full share, both in men and money for the support of the government. In every part of her history she has furnished to the country men who have been eminent in literature as well as men distinguished in our State and National councils, as also in the various professions and the callings of business life, and from her borders large numbers have gone forth to be pioneers and leaders in the rising and flourishing States of the West.

When the celebrated "Dark Day" occurred, May 19, 1780, covering, with its deep shadow, the country from Maine to New Jersey, the darkness was most intense in Connecticut and Rhode Island, spreading there the gloom almost of midnight. The legislature of Connecticut was in session at the time in Hartford, and the alarm at the strange phenomenon was so great that the impression spread that the end of the world and the day of judgment were coming. The house of representatives adjourned, and it was proposed also to Davenport, the presiding officer of the council, also to adjourn that body. "No," was his prompt and Spartan-like reply, "if the day of judgment is not approaching, there is no cause for adjournment; and if it is, I choose to be found doing my duty"; and he ordered the candles to be brought in.

As another interesting incident connected with the early history of Connecticut, after the accession of Charles II., three of the regicide judges, who had passed the sentence of death on Charles I., fled for safety to this country, and two of them, Goffe and Whalley, came to New Haven. They were followed and searched for by officers of the king from England, who, if they had been successful in their search, would have taken them back to certain and cruel death. Reverend John Davenport was, at that time, the minister of the church at New Haven, and though the officers were in the place, yet with the fearless independence of one of the old Puritans, he at once preached a sermon from Isaiah XVI., 3, 4: "Take counsel; execute judgment; make thy shadow as the night in the midst of noon-day; hide the outcasts; betray not him that wandereth; let thine outcasts be with thee; be thou a covert to them from the face of the spoiler," &c. It is hardly needful to say the people were of the same mind and spirit as their pastor, and that the regicides were concealed by them, and for a long time were hidden at "West Rock," in a cave still known as the Judges' Cave, where they were visited and cared for, and all their wants were secretly supplied, until, when the officers, foiled at every step of their search, went back to England, the wanderers, under assumed names, came forth from the place of their refuge, and quietly lived in New Haven until the end of their days.

The population of Connecticut at the breaking out of the Revolution was 200,000; in 1880, 622,700; in 1890, 745,861.

RHODE ISLAND.

The settlement of Rhode Island was begun by Roger Williams, who was banished from Massachusetts in 1635 for opposing the views of that colony on the subject of religion and government, both which were closely united in the plans of the colonists for their commonwealth. He was driven out, not, as is often said, merely because he believed in freedom of conscience as to religious matters, but because he insisted that the magistrates should have rule only in civil affairs, and that the people, in all other things, should be responsible only to God. These views were then regarded as politically disorganizing and dangerous, as they were opposed to the fundamental laws of the colony. Being banished, Williams passed a long and dreary winter among the Narragansett Indians, and finally, with five companions, established a little settlement at a place called Seekonk, at the head of Narragansett Bay, to which he gave the name of Providence, in recognition as he said, of "God's merciful providence to him in his distress." His doctrine, as already said, was, that the magistrates should have authority only in civil matters, and that there should be perfect freedom to all as to religious opinions, for which he claimed that men were responsible only to God; and it was not for holding these opinions, but because in carrying them out in practice he opposed the established government of the colony, that he was banished from its borders. Two years later another conflict of opinion in Massachusetts brought fresh exiles to Rhode Island, and Anne Hutchinson and her friends, buying land from the Indians, made a settlement at Portsmouth, as afterward, in 1639, some of their number went further south and founded Newport.

In 1643, Williams went to England, and came back the next year with a charter, which united these several settlements into one colony, and soon after the people met and framed a constitution, allowing to all perfect religious liberty. In 1663, a royal charter was obtained from Charles II., naming the colony "Rhode Island and Providence Plantations." This charter, which was the only constitution of the colony for one hundred and eighty years, was most liberal in all its provisions, and under it a popular elective government was established in 1664, with Arnold as governor, and Williams as one of the assistants. By 1672, the Quakers had come in in great numbers so as soon to

WOODLAND SCENE IN RHODE ISLAND.

gain a controlling influence and to make one of their own number the governor. In the Indian war with Philip, Rhode Island suffered not a little, and was the scene of many massacres and much hard fighting, and, like other colonies, was not free from troubles both abroad and at home. But the colony grew steadily, though slowly; its government became settled, and trade prospered to the end of colonial times.

Rhode Island is the smallest of all the States, having an area of only 1,306 square

miles. The country is hilly, and the surface of the soil rough and stony, devoted chiefly
to pasturage and orchards. The climate is mild, and on the islands, and where bordering
on the ocean, is for a large part of the year invigorating and delightful. Newport is
noted as one of the most fashionable summer resorts in the whole country, and abounds
in attractive scenery and elegant mansions. More than one-half of the population of the
State is said to be employed in manufactories. Providence has extensive manufactures
of machinery, steam engines, jewelry of various kinds, and cotton and woolen goods, and
for print cloths is the leading market in the United States. Large quantities of
merchandise of various kinds is landed and shipped at its docks for the Boston trade.
Brown University, which was founded in 1764, has become one of the leading colleges of
the country. The public schools, which are excellent, are supported by State, town,
district and other taxes, and the normal and private schools of the State are of a high
order. A newspaper was established at Newport as early as 1732. At the opening of
the Revolution the population of the State was 50,000; in 1880, it was 276,581, and in
1890, 345,343.

NEW HAMPSHIRE.

New Hampshire was different from the other New England colonies, in the one
respect that it was not all the time a separate colony, but at different times formed part
of Massachusetts. In 1622, Ferdinand Gorges and John Mason obtained a grant of land
"bounded by the Merrimac and Kennebec rivers, and the ocean and the river of
Canada," that is the St. Lawrence; and the next year small settlements were made by
them at Portsmouth and Dover; and when, in 1629, Gorges and Mason dissolved
partnership, Mason obtained a new grant for the territory between the Merrimac and
the Piscataqua rivers, naming it New Hampshire.

In the next few years the region was divided among several proprietors, which led
to disputes and lawsuits, and the settlers, suffering greatly from the Indians, were led to
put themselves under the protection of Massachusetts, which they did in 1641, and so
continued for thirty-nine years, till 1680, when New Hampshire was made a royal
province. During the two years of the despotic rule of Andros, 1686-88, New
Hampshire, like the other colonies, lost her independence; but in 1690, when Andros
was overthrown, New Hampshire again put itself under the protection of Massachusetts,
and so remained united to and a part of it till 1741, when it was finally separated and
made a royal colony.

Before this, New Hampshire, like all the early colonies, had suffered under
difficulties and troubles with several of the royal governors, but now had time for quiet
and progress. She furnished men and money for the attack on Louisburg, and took an
active part in the French war, as also in the conflicts with the Indians. No colony sent
better troops to the field, and her "Rangers," trained to a knowledge of savage warfare,
gained a continental reputation. The colony was greatly prosperous till the British
policy of taxation began, when the excitement caused by the Stamp Act spread through
the people, and led New Hampshire into the movements which united the colonies and
prepared the way for the overthrow of the English power in America.

The State of New Hampshire has an area of 9,280 square miles. Its population,
except the foreigners coming in, by immigration, chiefly to the manufacturing towns, is

SQUAM LAKE, NEW HAMPSHIRE.

almost entirely descended from the original settlers who came from England, Scotland, and the early New England colonies. It is a State of mountains and lakes, and has been called "the Switzerland of America." The White Mountain range is mainly in the central part of the State, its highest summit, Mount Washington, being 6,285 feet high. The celebrated "Notch" in this range is two miles long, and in the narrowest part only twenty-two feet wide, affording a passageway to the road and to a mountain stream.

ST. JOHNS RIVER, FRONTIERS OF NEW BRUNSWICK AND MAINE.

The soil, except in valleys and by the streams, is better fitted for pasturage than for culture. Numerous waterfalls give motive power to the many cotton, woolen, and iron factories, paper mills, &c., which are valuable industries to the State. Its foreign commerce is very small, Portsmouth being its only port of entry. Like all the New England colonies, New Hampshire suffered much from Indian wars and depredations during the colonial period. And in later days it has furnished a multitude of emigrants to the newer and more fertile western States. The State has an excellent system of free schools, a college, several noted academies, literary institutes, scientific and engineering schools, a medical school, and a school or college of agriculture and the mechanic arts. Railroads connect every part of the State with other parts of the Union. Population in 1880, 346,991; in 1890, 375,827.

MAINE.

Maine was not one of the thirteen colonies which, as such, engaged in the war of the Revolution, for at that time it was not a separate colony, but was a part of Massachusetts. As early, some think, as 990, the coast was discovered by the Northmen, and was visited by them occasionally until the middle of the fourteenth century, though they founded no settlement upon it. From 1350 to 1498, which was the time of Cabot's second expedition, there is no evidence that the coast was seen by Europeans. In 1524, it was visited by the French, under Verrazano; in 1525, by the Spaniards, under Gomez, and in 1527, by the English, under Rut; but none of these made any settlement within its borders.

The first attempt to settle on the territory was made by the French, under Du Mont, in 1604; but his plans were unsuccessful. In 1605, part of the coast was explored by Weymouth; and in 1607, by an expedition sent out by Popham and Gorges, which made a settlement at the mouth of the Kennebec river, which, however, came to an end in the

BAR HARBOR, MAINE.

following year. In 1613, the French Jesuits established a mission on Mount Desert island, but were soon driven off by the English. In 1616, Richard Vines, an agent of Gorges, was at Saco; and a company under Captain John Smith ranged the coast as far as Cape Cod; and Smith made a map of the region, to which he gave the name of "New England." In 1620, James I. gave part of the territory to the Plymouth Company, and part to the Virginia Company; and, in 1623, Gorges and Mason, under a grant from the Plymouth colony, planted a colony at the mouth of the Piscataqua river, which was the first permanent settlement in Maine.

After 1630, settlements were made at five different places, most of which by 1675 had been broken up and destroyed by the Indians, who for years were in constant conflict with the settlers. After several changes, the part of the country which had been held by Gorges, and afterward by the Duke of York, was surrendered to Massachusetts in 1686, and title to it was confirmed by charter in 1691; and by the treaty of 1783, at the close of the Revolutionary War, Massachusetts obtained full control and exercised jurisdiction over the territory, which was then called "the district" or "province of Maine," till 1820, when it was admitted to the Union as an independent State. At the time of the Revolution, Maine, of course, was not one of the thirteen colonies which, as such, engaged in the war, but her people were fully interested and active in all the measures that led on to our independence.

OFF THE COAST OF MAINE.

The surface of the State is diversified, much of it being flat on the sea coast, while back from the coast it is hilly or mountainous, the great Apalachian chain, of which the White Mountains are a part, crossing the State in a southwest direction. The region abounds in lakes, both large and small, which, with the various rivers cover some 3,200 square miles or nearly one-tenth of the surface of the State. The State is well supplied with minerals, though the metallic ores have not been much worked. Marble, slate, and limestone are abundant, and granite of the finest quality is both abundant and profitably worked. The great forests in the central and northern parts of the State have in the past furnished immense quantities of lumber, but are fast diminishing under the

VIEW IN ACADIA.

lumberman's axe. One of the chief industries of the State is that of shipbuilding; the fisheries employ several hundreds of vessels, and are highly profitable, as are also the manufacturing interests of the people.

A part of what is now Nova Scotia, was originally part of Maine, and was known as Acadia. It was settled by the French in 1603, and prospered as a colony, but in 1654 the French were subdued by forces sent out by Cromwell. The region was afterward ceded to the French, in 1667; but in 1713 was restored to the English. But when in the war between the English and French, the inhabitants refused on the one hand to aid the former, or to bear arms against the latter, the whole colony was cruelly broken up by the English, and its inhabitants, some thousands in number, were forcibly carried away from

SCENE IN MAINE.

their homes, and scattered to every part of
the country. The sad event, with its barbarous treatment, furnished to Longfellow the
subject of his *Evangeline*, one of the most interesting
and admired of all his publications.

The State has fourteen ports of entry, to and from
which an active commerce is carried on with every part
of the world. It has a good system of common schools,
and also many free high schools, two normal schools,
three colleges, a theological seminary, a college of
agriculture and mechanic arts, and several flourishing
seminaries of a high order. The islands and coasts of
Maine are more and more becoming favorite resorts for
summer rest and recreation, places like Bar Harbor
and Mount Desert being crowded with visitors for the
season. The population of Maine in 1880
was 648,926, and in 1890, 660,261.

VERMONT.

Vermont, the "Green Mountain State," never was a formal colony, and does not appear on any of the early maps of New England. It was not settled till 1724, when people from Massachusetts, supposing it to be within the bounds of that colony, built Fort Dummer, where Brattleboro now stands. In the French war of 1745, soldiers marched from this fort, and also from the New Hampshire colony, against the French, who occupied points along Lake Champlain. The rich and fertile lands through which they passed attracted the

attention of these soldiers, most of whom were farmers, and after the French war of 1755–58, emigrants began to come in in large numbers. Much of the territory on which they settled was claimed by New Hampshire, also part of it by New York, under former grants from Charles II.

TROUT STREAM IN VERMONT.

In 1776, the people petitioned Congress to be admitted to the Union, but through the influence of New York, their request was denied. In the following year, the settlers declared themselves an independent and sovereign State, under the name of Vermont, and so continued until 1791, when their rights were recognized by Congress, and they were admitted to the Union. New York was paid $30,000 for relinquishing her territorial claims, Vermont paying that amount to end the controversy, and New Hampshire relinquishing her claims altogether.

The leaders and soldiers of Vermont were faithful to the country through the war of the Revolution. A month before the battle of Bunker Hill, Ethan Allen, with his troops, had thundered at the gates of Fort Ticonderoga, and demanded its surrender, as tradition says, " in the name of Almighty God and the Continental Congress"; and it was chiefly the militia forces of Vermont that gained the victory of Plattsburg, in 1812. The State also contributed largely to the Union forces in the war of the Secession. The resolute spirit of the leaders as well as of the troops of Vermont, is well illustrated in Halleck's lines as to Stark, the noted general of Bennington. Speaking of the battle in which Stark led on the troops in the days of the Revolution, the poet says:

> When on that field the band of Hessians fought,
> Briefly he spoke, before the fight began;
> "Soldiers! those German gentlemen are bought
> For four pounds eight and seven pence per man,
> By England's king,—a bargain, as 'tis thought.
> Are we worth more? Let's prove it, now we can;
> For we must beat them, boys, ere set of sun,
> Or Mary Stark's a widow!" It was done!

The area of Vermont is 10,212 square miles. Its surface is rather hilly than mountainous, though in the Green Mountain range are eminences 2,000 to 5,000 feet high, but bearing vegetation and cultivated to their summits. Slate, iron ore, and soap stone are found, and also rich quarries of valuable marble. The soil is a rich loam; the country is well wooded, and the hills well adapted for pasturage; and the State has fine scenery, a healthful climate, and several beautiful waterfalls. It has a university, three colleges, several professional institutions, three normal schools, numerous excellent academies, and a good system of common schools. In the State, also, there are numerous manufactories in active and profitable operation. The population of the State in the past has increased but slowly, and in the last ten years has slightly decreased, owing to the constant emigration to the western States. In 1880 it was 332,286, and in 1890, 332,205.

NEW YORK.

New York was the only one of the American colonies that was settled by the Dutch, who came from Holland. The first white man who is known to have been within the present boundaries of the State, was Samuel Champlain, the French navigator, who sailed down the lake, which was named after him, in July, 1609, thus antedating by two months, Hudson's discovery from the sea. In September of the same year, Henry Hudson, an Englishman, then in the service of the Dutch government, landed on Manhattan island, now New York, and discovered the river now bearing his name. Soon

SABBATH-DAY POINT, LAKE GEORGE.

afterward, in 1615, the merchants of Holland organized the New Netherland Company, and sent out ships for traffic with the Indians, and two trading-posts were established, one on the island, and one up the river, near where Albany now stands.

In 1621, the Dutch West India Company obtained a patent for the territory of the New Netherlands, which, they claimed, stretched from the Connecticut river to Delaware. In 1623, they sent out a number of families, and founded New Amsterdam, now New York, on Manhattan island, which they bought from the Indians for sixty guilders —

about twenty-five dollars. In 1624, they established Fort Orange, now Albany. In 1626, they sent out Peter Minuets as the first governor, who proved himself an able administrator and wise governor. He was followed by Wouter Von Twiller, then by Sir William Keift, and then by Peter Stuyvesant, these four governors ruling the New Netherlands till 1664; At this date, the Dutch settlements, which had been growing slowly but steadily, had a

SKETCH OF NIAGARA FALLS DRAWN BY FATHER HENNEPIN IN 1698.

population of about ten thousand persons. The Dutch also had settlements on the Connecticut and Delaware rivers, and thus had troubles both with the English and the Swedes, as they also had with the Indians, but these difficulties were overcome by the energy of Stuyvesant.

The English, however, claimed the whole region of the New Netherlands as belonging to them, founding their claim on the discovery by the Cabots; and armed vessels were sent out from England to demand the territory for the Duke of York, to whom it had been granted by Charles II. At this demand, the city was surrendered to the English, September 8, 1664, and the whole province, as well as Manhattan island, took the name of New York. The city of New York, at this time, had a population of only about fifteen hundred, most of them speaking the Dutch language. Under the English, everything proceeded quietly, with little apparent change, except the new English officers and names. The Dutch customs still prevailed, and, except tax difficulties on Long Island, there was peace and comfort everywhere. This, however, was broken up by the second war between England and Holland, in which, in 1673, a Dutch fleet attacked New York, and the city was compelled to surrender; but in the next year, by the treaty of Westminster, the province was ceded to England, and so remained under British rule till the time of our Independence, when the Dutch power finally disappeared from America.

NIAGARA FALLS, AMERICAN SIDE.

At this time, Edmund Andros became governor, and ruled the province for eight years. In 1683, the people were granted the right of representation, but this was soon taken away, and printing presses and the holding of the Assembly were forbidden. Before the Revolution, New York was repeatedly engaged in warfare with the Indians, and in the wars between the English and the French in the contest for supremacy in the country, and the State took an active and energetic part in the war of the Revolution, as will be seen in the subsequent notice of that struggle. From the time of King William, 1689, to the Revolution, New York continued to be a royal province, ruled by the king's governors, the colony being allowed a legislature, though it had no charter of liberties like the colonies of New England.

The early settlers, as we have seen, were Dutch. They were honest, thrifty, and whole-souled, and through almost the whole colonial period, kept on friendly terms with the Indians. Afterward, large numbers of Scotch, Germans, and English, all from the old country, as well as settlers from New England, came in, and added greatly to the enterprise and prosperity of the city and province. The spirit of independence was strong among the people. Able newspapers in the city kept their readers informed as to their rights, and as to the unjust and oppressive measures of the British government. The New York Assembly was the first of the colonial Assemblies to propose, in 1764, the appointment in all the colonies of "committees of correspondence" as to the oppressive measures of the mother country. And as early as 1770, when the soldiers provoked the "Sons of Liberty," by cutting down their liberty-pole, a riot followed, in which several citizens were wounded and one was killed, so that the first blood shed in the beginning of the revolutionary struggles was in New York, more than a month before the noted "Boston massacre," which aroused such intense excitement, not only in New England, but throughout the entire country.

After the Revolution the State grew rapidly in population and prosperity. Its area is 47,000 square miles. The climate is mild on the coast and in the southern portion, but colder in the northern parts. The soil, particularly in the central and western parts, which are limestone regions, is very fertile, producing the finest of wheat and maize and all kinds of fruit in abundance. It has noble rivers, and is traversed by railroads in every direction. Among its natural curiosities, or wonders, are the falls of Niagara, about which Brainard has written the following lines, which are unsurpassed, if not unequalled in sublimity, by anything ever written about them, and of which one of our great newspapers says, "They could have been written only by a first-class poet, and under the inspiration of a full view of the falls themselves, pouring forth their immensity of waters with their superhuman power." And yet, the author was never out of his native State, Connecticut.

The thoughts are strange that crowd upon my brain
While I look upward to thee. It would seem
As if God poured thee from his hollow hand,
And hung His bow upon thine awful front,
And spake in that loud voice, which seemed to him
Who dwelt in Patmos for his Saviour's sake,
The sound of many waters, and had bade
Thy flood to chronicle the ages back
And notch His centuries in the eternal rocks!

"Deep calleth unto deep!" And what are we,
Who hear the question of that voice sublime?
O, what are all the notes that ever rang
From War's vain trumpet by thy thundering side?
Yea, what is all the riot man can make
In his short life to thine unceasing roar?
And yet, bold babbler, what art thou to Him
Who drowned a world, and heaped the waters far
Above its loftiest mountains? *A light wave
That breaks and whispers of its Maker's might!*

THE FALLS OF NIAGARA.

OPENING OF THE ERIE CANAL, 1825.

And as
lesser falls, there are
those of the Genesee
and Mohawk rivers, those
of the Genesee having
three cascades, of 96, 25, and 84
feet, in two and a half miles; those
of the Mohawk, at Trenton, a fall
of 200 feet, in five cascades; those
of the Taghanae, 230 feet, in five cascades; those of the Cauterskill, 175 and 85 feet, in
a gorge of the Catskill mountains.

The State, too, has noble rivers, and many beautiful lakes within its borders, beside
the larger lakes on or connected with its northern boundary. Soon after the close of the

war, in 1816, steps were taken by the legislature toward building the Erie canal, of which it is commonly said that it was suggested by Gouverneur Morris, in 1800, and that it was carried on and completed through the energy and foresight of De Witt Clinton, although, at first, he was ridiculed for persisting in digging what was called "De Witt Clinton's Ditch," and what so many believed was a costly and useless thing. The canal was begun in July, 1817, and was finished in October, 1825, thus opening the way for the stream of commerce from the great West, which has made the city of New York the metropolis of the continent. Although the canal passed through a region of great fertility, much of the country at that time was a wilderness. It gave a tremendous impetus to the settlement and prosperity of the State. Villages and towns sprang up as if by magic along its banks, and some of them now are important cities.

It is a fact that the first idea of such an improvement was suggested by Washington, who is known to have said that it was all important to the prosperity of the country to have water communication established between the great lakes and the waters of the seaboard; and Hamilton, also, is known to have advanced the same idea, though to Morris and Clinton is to be given the credit of carrying out the grand idea in the Erie canal.

TRENTON FALLS, NEW YORK

In and about the many cities of the State are many monuments and structures well worthy of notice. One of these is the splendid Bartholdi monument, a gift from France to the United States. Including its base and pedestal, it is 306 feet high above low water mark, the pedestal alone costing $300,000. It stands on Bedloe's island, in the harbor of New York, and by its brilliant light, which shines forth from the statue at the top, it becomes the most splendid lighthouse in the world.

Another remarkable, or even wonderful, structure is the great suspension bridge connecting the city of New York with Brooklyn. Its cost, including the land approaches, was about $9,000,000. Its length, including its approaches, is about a mile and a tenth; its height above low water mark is 135 feet, while the huge stone towers that sustain the wire cables supporting the bridge are 278 feet above high water.

One of the first passenger railways in the United States was that between Albany and Schenectady, chartered in 1826, but not in operation till 1831. A cut of its first engine and cars will give an idea of the immense and wonderful improvement in the facilities for railroad travel known at the present day, when in the State there are some

FIRST PASSENGER RAILWAY, 1831.

hundred and fifty different railroads, in all over seven thousand miles in extent, and opening avenues for travel and traffic not only through the State, but to every part of the Union.

The climate of New York is more varied than that of any other State, as in rich agricultural products it surpasses any other. The State has various and valuable minerals, and several important mineral and medicinal springs. It abounds in churches of various denominations; has an admirable system of public schools, and school property of over $30,000,000; has seventeen colleges or universities, several classical schools, important libraries, various and well sustained charitable institutions, and in all parts of the State private schools and academies of a high order. The feeling and action as to all the steps that led to our national independence, as well as the part taken in the war of secession, were such as were becoming the foremost State of the Union.

On the invitation of Massachusetts, the first congress for consultation was held in New York in 1765; it consisted of twenty-eight delegates from nine of the thirteen colonies, so that in New York were passed some of the earliest resolutions denying the right of taxation without representation, and demanding the repeal of the Stamp Act; and in New York, through the steps taken by that congress, the union of the English colonies in America was organized. The population of the State in 1880 was 5,082,891, and in 1890, 5,981,934.

RAPIDS OF THE ST. LAWRENCE RIVER.

CATSKILL MOUNTAIN SCENE — THE IRON DUKE.

NEW JERSEY.

The territory of New Jersey was originally part of New Netherlands, and when that became the Province of New York, New Jersey was included with it. But in 1664, the Duke of York granted a part of the province to Lord Berkeley and Sir George Carteret, and the part so granted was made a separate province by the name of New Jersey. The

ARREST OF CARTERET

next year, Philip Carteret, as governor, came over with a body of emigrants, and a liberal charter was granted, giving equal rights and liberty to all religious denominations.

The first settlement was made at Elizabeth, which was made the seat of government, in 1665, and soon there were settlements at other places; but as the population increased, troubles arose between the executive and the Assembly as to legislation, and also as to the payment of quit-rents, and in 1673 Berkeley sold out his share of the province to a company of English Friends or Quakers, and the province was

divided, the Quaker purchase forming West Jersey, and the part held by Carteret making East Jersey. The proprietary rights of New Jersey and New York for a time were unsettled, Andros and Carteret quarrelling as to jurisdiction in East Jersey, the former at one time sent a file of soldiers to Elizabethport, who took Carteret out of bed and carried him as a prisoner to New York. But at last, in 1680, commissioners, who were appointed, decided against the Duke of York, in consequence of which he abandoned his claims and gave a deed to George Carteret, the grandson of James; and two years after this, William Penn and his nine associates, in 1682, bought up East Jersey, and the two Jerseys being united, Robert Barclay was made governor. Difficulties arising between the people and the proprietors, the latter gave up their claims to the colony, and in 1702 the two Jerseys were united into one royal province by the name of New Jersey, and it was

CHATEAUGAY CHASM, NEAR CHATEAUGAY VILLAGE, NEW YORK.

placed under the governor of New York, though still having its own Assembly, and in this condition it remained till 1738, when, on petition of the people, a separate governor was appointed by the king, after which it was ruled by governors appointed from England down to the time of Independence.

The soil of New Jersey was fertile. The province was free from trouble from the Indians, and being shut in by the great colonies of New York and Pennsylvania, was little affected by the French war. The Quakers and Scotch, who, with many from New England, formed the main elements of the population were chiefly engaged in farming. They were frugal, industrious, moral, and always intelligent and decided in their love of liberty, and the province grew rapidly and was greatly prospered. As in all the other colonies, the people were opposed to taxation by England, and so excited against the Stamp Act that the stamp collector never ventured to attempt its enforcement. New Jersey sent delegates to the congress invited by Massachusetts, and so acted with the other colonies in that assembly. Some of the important battles of the Revolution were fought in New Jersey — at Trenton, Princeton, and Monmouth, — and her position in the center of the confederacy made her soil the principal theatre of the war.

After the time of Independence the State grew rapidly in population and prosperity. Its area of 8,320 square miles is of varied soil, the northern part being hilly and mountainous, the central part a rolling country, and the eastern portion a sandy plain declining to the sea, and affording some of the favorite summer resorts of the country. The State abounds in factories of various kinds, and its nearness to New York makes it a place of residence for multitudes whose business is in that city. Railroads traverse every part of the State. Some $3,000,000 are annually expended for its common schools, the buildings for which are valued at over $7,000,000. For higher education the State has five colleges, five collegiate schools for women, three scientific and agricultural schools, beside four theological seminaries, and large numbers of private schools and seminaries of a high order. At the Revolution the population of the State was variously estimated at 100,000 to 150,000; in 1880 it was 1,131,116, and in 1890, 1,441,017.

PENNSYLVANIA.

The region of Pennsylvania was first visited by Henry Hudson, in 1609, and then, in 1610, by Lord De la War, after whom the river and bay of Delaware are named. The Dutch, in 1623, took possession of the whole territory between the Delaware and Hudson rivers, and held it till 1664, when New Netherlands was conquered by the English; it was recovered by the Dutch in 1672, and again reverted to the British rule in 1674. The first European settlement was near what is now Gloucester, New Jersey, and the Swedes, who followed, settled on the west bank of the Delaware, in 1638. But in 1681 a large part of all this territory was granted by charter to William Penn, who founded the colony which has grown to be the great State of Pennsylvania.

In the mother country, Penn was the most distinguished of all the men who founded States in America. Though he was the son and heir of a leading, wealthy and worldly admiral of the British navy, yet he became a member, and then the zealous leader of the despised and persecuted sect of the Friends or Quakers, and as he grew up, gradually grew also in power and influence till he became the favorite and adviser of King James, then on the throne of England. "In his character," says another, "was a curious mingling of dissimilar qualities. He was, at the same time, a saint and a courtier, a religious fanatic and a shrewd man of affairs and of the world; but in American history he appears as the wise founder of a State, the prudent and just magistrate, and the liberal-minded law-giver and ruler."

His attention was first drawn to the work of colonization by the misfortunes of the settlements in New Jersey, in which the Quakers had become interested, and in which he himself took part, that he might be of help and service to them. And as he had from his father a large claim against the government, which was not likely to be otherwise paid, in 1681 he took in payment the large unoccupied region between New Jersey and

PENN'S HOUSE, SECOND STREET, BELOW CHESTNUT, PHILADELPHIA.

Maryland, containing some forty-three thousand square miles of territory, to which was given the name of "Pennsylvania." He published an address, explaining his scheme, and saying that the government of his new colony was to be just and righteous, and in accordance with Quaker principles, and guaranteeing perfect liberty of conscience and the right of trial by jury, not only to white men, but to Indians, and offering land, even to servants, at very low rates, subject only to small quit-rents to be paid to himself as proprietor.

With these prospects and promises in view, not only Quakers from England, but emigrants from various parts of Europe, especially from Germany, came over, three shiploads arriving the first year, and settling on the banks of the Delaware. The next year, 1862, Penn himself, with a company of a hundred persons, landed at Newcastle, having obtained from the Duke of York a grant of what is now the State of Delaware, a region then called " The Territories." The key of the fort at Newcastle was formally given him, and with this he locked himself into the fort, and then let himself out, as a

VIEW ON THE SUSQUEHANNA RIVER, PENNSYLVANIA.

sign that the government was his; and to show that the land also was his, with its forests and rivers, a piece of turf, the branch of a tree, and a cup of water from the river were also given to him. He was cordially received by the settlers who were already in Pennsylvania and Delaware, and on November 30 made his famous treaty with the Indians under the large elm tree near what is now Kensington, winning their confidence and paying them for their lands, so that as long as the Quaker control of the colony continued, which was about seventy years, friendship and peace continued between the settlers and the natives.

About the end of the year, Penn founded Philadelphia as the capital of his colony, and after reigning two years, wisely arranging the government, and giving the people a most liberal charter, he went back to England in 1684. Everything was now prosperous in the colony. In a single year some seven thousand settlers arrived, and before the end of the century the colonists numbered more than twenty thousand, and Philadelphia had grown to be the largest town in all the colonies.

PENN'S TREATY WITH THE INDIANS.

Penn remained in England about fifteen years, during which time dissensions arose in the colony. In 1691, Delaware withdrew from Pennsylvania, and in 1703 was made a separate province. Quarrels arose among those left in authority, and the people

PENNSYLVANIA FOREST SCENERY.

neglected or refused payment of the quit-rents due on their properties. To settle the various troubles, Penn, in 1699, came back to the colony, intending to remain there, but in 1701, he again went back to England, where he died in 1718, leaving the colony to his sons as proprietors, and by them it was governed, through deputy governors, down to the time of the Revolution, when it was bought by the commonwealth for $580,000. The boundary line between Pennsylvania and Maryland was long a matter of dispute and trouble, but was finally settled, in 1767, by the famous Mason and Dixon line. A thriving trade was carried on with England, the West Indies, and the southern provinces, employing at the time of the Revolution some five hundred vessels and over seven thousand seamen. Newspapers were early established in the colony, one of them by Franklin. Taxation by England, and the Stamp Act, were universally and strongly opposed; and when the Stamp Act Congress met in New York, in 1765, Pennsylvania was represented by her delegates, and her history becomes part of that of the United States.

Since the Revolution, Pennsylvania has been steadily growing in population and prosperity. Its area is about 43,000 square miles. Its climate and soil are various. In the mountainous parts are the vast coal fields and iron deposits that have enriched the State, and adjacent to the coal measures other minerals are found, and in the bituminous districts the great deposits of petroleum. While one of the best agricultural States, Pennsylvania is also largely engaged in mining and manufacturing, some of the largest carpet manufactories in the world being in Philadelphia. The State has over six thousand miles of railroads, connecting it with every part of the Union; some thirty colleges, including its great university, fifteen theological seminaries, several normal schools, and also schools of medicine; a thorough system of common schools, supported by an annual expenditure of over six million dollars, numerous private schools and seminaries of a high order, and a large number of hospitals, charitable institutions, and public libraries. The population of the State in 1880 was 4,282,871, and in 1890, 5,248,574.

DELAWARE.

What is now Delaware, was so called from Lord De La War, an early governor of Virginia, who, in 1610 sailed up and landed on the shores of the Bay, though Henry Hudson had been there a year before. In 1630, the Dutch planted a small colony near Cape Henlopen, but three years later the Indians had driven them out, and the settlement disappeared. In 1637 a colony of Swedes and Finlanders bought land and built a fort on Christiana creek, naming the region New Sweden; and a little later they erected another fort and a trading-house a few miles below Philadelphia. The Dutch of New Netherlands, however, claimed the territory as a part of their own, but when New York came under English government, in 1664, the Delaware settlements were claimed by the Duke of York, as they also were by Lord Baltimore for Maryland. But William Penn, in 1682, purchased the Duke's right and made a compromise with Lord Baltimore, and so added the Delaware settlements to Pennsylvania; and for twenty years they were governed as a part of that State, under the name of "the territories." In 1703, Delaware established a separate legislature, and became a distinct province, though it still remained under the governor of Pennsylvania up to the time of the Revolution when the State became independent.

Next to Rhode Island, Delaware is the smallest of the United States, having only 2,120 square miles. Texas alone would make 130 Delawares. There are no mountains

6

SCENE ON THE DELAWARE BAY.

in the State, and, except in the northern parts, the surface is generally level and sandy. The soil is for the most part fertile, and the climate equable and healthful. The shores are the resort of vast numbers of wild geese and ducks. The peach and apple crops and the production of small fruits are large industries of the State, though other various agricultural productions are in fair proportion. The people are mostly farmers, but there are numerous and profitable manufactories in the State, especially in the larger towns. Wilmington is largely engaged in car and shipbuilding, and has extensive machine shops of various kinds. The State has a normal university, a college at Newark, a female college at Wilmington, and numerous free and private schools, and charitable institutions. The oldest church in Delaware was that founded by the Swedish Lutherans, the ministers of which were sent from Sweden until 1786, when the custom of sending them was no longer continued, as their speech was not generally understood by the mass of the people. Delaware, from her position, was from the first, almost entirely exempt from Indian forays and wars. Her men were active in service during the French wars; and in the Revolution her soldiers were foremost in good service, as some of the best and bravest of Washington's troops. The population of the State in 1880 was 146,608, and in 1890, 167,871.

MARYLAND.

As persecution led to the settlement of New England by the Pilgrims and Puritans, and to the settlement of Pennsylvania by the Quakers, so it led to the colonization of Maryland by the Roman Catholics. George Calvert, who afterward became Lord Baltimore, had, in 1627, commenced a colony in New Foundland, but the climate there was so cold and severe that he went, in 1629, to Virginia, but as the Catholics were not allowed there, he returned to England, and obtained from Charles I. a grant of a part of Virginia lying north of the Potomac, for which he was to pay the king two Indian arrows a year, and one-fifth of all the gold and silver he might find.

The province was named Maryland, in honor of the queen, and by its charter was freed forever from English taxation, and was guaranteed entire freedom in civil and religious matters. But before the patent was finally adjusted and signed, Sir George Calvert died, and the territory was granted to his son, the second Lord Baltimore. The first settlers, consisting of twenty gentlemen and three hundred laboring men, were sent out under Leonard Calvert, Lord Baltimore's brother, in 1633, and reached Maryland in the following year. They came in two vessels, the Ark and the Dove, bringing Roman Catholic priests with them, and finally settled on St. Mary's river, not far from the Potomac. Here they bought land from the Indians, and the foundations of the colony were peacefully and happily laid, and in six months it had advanced more than Virginia had done in as many years, having a system of representative government, and all the liberties which were enjoyed in England itself.

The colony was for a time greatly prospered. But after a while the Puritans coming in, in numbers, so as to have a majority in the government, divided the opinions of the people, and led to acts of the legislature giving, in 1649, full toleration as to religious opinion. There were, for a time, troubles with the Indians, who were jealous of the growth and prosperity of the colony. And there were also difficulties with Clayborne, one of the Virginia council, who, having a royal trading license, would not submit to Lord Baltimore's rule, and kept the colony in trouble for ten years. In one of the conflicts arising from these difficulties, a vessel sent out by Clayborne was attacked by armed pinnaces from Maryland, and a sharp fight took place, resulting in death on both sides, and in the vessel of Clayborne being captured and taken to St. Marys. At another time, the Golden Lion, an armed merchant vessel, fired upon the Maryland boats, which were obliged to retreat to the more shallow parts of the river for safety, (see pages 84, 85).

The subject of religious freedom and toleration also led to difficulty, for after a time a class of Protestants came in, who, gaining control, passed a law disfranchising the Roman Catholics, a measure which led to civil conflicts, in which the Catholics were defeated. In 1658, the proprietary government was restored, and peace and the old liberties were again enjoyed till in 1689, when the Catholics were for a time opposed and oppressed, as were the Quakers, also, for a while, for refusing to do military duty. In 1691, King William made Maryland a royal province, and it so continued till 1716, when,

FIGHT WITH THE MARYLAND PINNACE.

under the fifth Lord Baltimore, the proprietary government was renewed, and continued till the Revolution. In the meantime, the colony was rapidly growing, settlers coming in from Europe and from the other colonies. Tobacco was largely cultivated, chiefly by slave labor; trade was extended at home and abroad, and Baltimore became an important commercial city. The people were intelligent, and like those of all the colonies, decided in their love of freedom and self-government. They took an active part in the French wars, and were among the first to resist the aggressions of the British government which led to the Revolution; and when organized as a State in 1776, they took a most efficient and honorable part in the Revolutionary war. In 1783, Congress met at the capital, Annapolis, and there it was that Washington resigned his commission as commander-in-chief of the forces of the Union. The State has an area of 11,124 square miles. The country rises gradually from the coast to the highest points of the Alleghany mountains, with great varieties of formation, including deposits of coal, iron, copper, marl, etc. The climate is temperate, and the soil in most parts fertile. Peaches and market garden vegetables and fruits grow in great perfection, and other agricultural products of various kinds give profitable employment

THE "GOLDEN LION" FIRING ON THE MARYLAND BOATS.

to the people. The State abounds in manufacturing establishments, and the annual value of canned oysters, vegetables, fish, and fruits is estimated at over $10,000,000. The foreign commerce is confined almost entirely to Baltimore. The expenditures for public schools are some $2,000,000 a year. In the State there are nine colleges, including the Johns Hopkins University, endowed by Mr. Hopkins with $3,500,000; the United States naval academy at Annapolis, a large number of schools and academies of a high order, and institutions for the blind, the deaf and dumb, the insane, for juvenile delinquents, &c. The population of the State at the Revolution was about 220,000; in 1880, 934,243, and in 1890, 1,040,431.

CUMBERLAND GAP, MARYLAND.

NORTH CAROLINA.

The region of Carolina was first explored by a party sent out by Sir Walter Raleigh, in 1584, in which year a settlement was made on Roanoke island. But trouble with the Indians caused the colonists to return to England and no further attempt was made to colonize the region for nearly eighty years. At that time the first permanent settlement was made by a considerable number of emigrants from Virginia, who left that colony to escape the oppressions of the Episcopal, which was there the established church. They settled, in 1653, in the region north of Albemarle sound, where they found a rich soil and fine climate, and where they were free and independent both in civil and religious matters.

A VISTA IN NORTH CAROLINA.

But in 1663, the king granted to Lord Clarendon and his associates the region extending from Virginia to Florida, giving them almost absolute authority, and the country then received the name of Carolina. A liberal government was given to the little colony on the sound, which was called Albemarle colony, and in 1665 a company from Barbadoes settled near the mouth of Cape Fear river, taking the name of the Clarendon colony, both these settlements being within what is now North Carolina. In 1670, an English company, under William Sayle, settled on the Ashley river, and took the name of the Carteret colony. This was the first settlement in what is now South Carolina, and was at old Charleston.

The proprietors of Carolina engaged the celebrated John Locke to draw up a plan of government for the colony, a plan which, though called the "Grand Model," proved to be an utter failure; and in 1677, the people of the northern settlements took the government into their own hands, so that things for a time went on well; but a new governor being sent out, who for six years plundered and oppressed the people, they banished him, and chose an Assembly from among themselves. After this, they had better governors sent out; and North Carolina had some excellent colonists, a company of French Protestants settling, in 1707, on the river Trent; and, in 1710, some German Lutherans, who fled from persecution in their own land, coming as colonists. In 1711, the Indians attacked the colony and murdered a hundred and thirty of the settlers, but they were soon conquered, eight hundred of them being captured, and the rest driven northward into New York.

In 1729, the king of England bought the whole province, and divided the northern settlement from the southern, calling the former North Carolina, and the latter South Carolina. Each remained a royal province, with a government and legislation of its own, but with royal governors, down to the time of the Revolution. In the beginning of the eighteenth century great numbers of emigrants came into North Carolina from Scotland, Germany, France and the North of Ireland, and about the middle of the same century many more came from Pennsylvania and the northern colonies. The interior of the country was explored and settled, and proved to be far more fertile than the coast. The people were mostly engaged in agriculture, and were trained by their mode of life to be both self-reliant and independent.

In August, 1776, the colony ratified the Declaration of Independence, and in the following December held a convention and framed a constitution for the State, which remained the organic law till 1835. After the Revolution, the State enjoyed much prosperity, but its history is marked by no specially eventful period till the breaking out of the rebellion, followed, as it was, by the four years of war, in which the State suffered many disasters and was the field of important conflicts, as will be mentioned in the accounts of the War of Secession.

The soil, as well as the climate is varied in different parts of the State. The low lands are hot and humid, but in the interior and higher grounds the air is singularly dry, pure, and bracing. The mineral products embrace not only coal and iron of superior qualities, but also the precious metals. Gold has been found in twenty-three counties, and silver, copper, lead, zinc, and other metals are known to exist, though not extensively mined. Other forms of mineral wealth in the State are abundant and valuable. The agricultural products are rice, cotton, tobacco, wheat and Indian corn, etc. There are large forests of the long-leaved pine, supplying immense quantities of resin, turpentine, tar, and pitch. The fisheries of the State are also important. The State has ten colleges, numerous academies and seminaries of respectable rank, a system of common schools, and numerous newspapers and periodicals. The population in 1776 was about 260,000; in 1880, 1,399,750, and in 1890, 1,617,340.

SOUTH CAROLINA.

South Carolina, as we have seen, was not set off by itself till 1729, its territory up to that time being a part of the Carolina province, though a settlement had been made within its borders, at old Charleston, in 1670. The region soon attracted a large number of very desirable settlers, among whom were the Dutch from New York, a large company of Huguenots from France, and many people from England and Scotland, both cavaliers and Puritans. In 1671, African slaves were first brought from Barbadoes, and so negro

VIEW OF A COTTON CHUTE.

slavery began with the plantations on the Ashley river, South Carolina being the only one of the thirteen colonies that was, from its beginning, a planting State with slave labor. In 1680, the capital was removed from old Charleston to where it now stands.

In 1694, the cultivation of rice began, the seed being brought from Madagascar. Cotton had been introduced as early as 1536, though it was not largely exported till 1770; but cotton, rice, and indigo early became the great staples of the State. In 1800, the export of cotton from South Carolina was over seven million bales, averaging in weight four hundred and forty pounds each. This immense increase of the cotton production was owing to the invention, by Whitney, of the "cotton gin," by the use of which the seed of the cotton was rapidly separated from the fibre, when before the work had been slowly done by hand. The cut shows how the huge bales of cotton are in some places loaded upon the steamers that bear them on their way to the manufactories or to foreign lands.

The government of the colony was in the hands of a governor sent out by the proprietors from England, though the people elected their own legislature. But when, in 1686, the royal governor oppressed the people, he was deposed by them and banished. The colony had difficulties with the Spanish possessions on the south, and also with the Indians, who were allies of the Spaniards. In 1706, the united fleet of the Spanish and French vessels attacked Charleston, but were repulsed with severe loss; and in 1715, there was war with the Indian tribes, who, swooping down on the frontier settlements, murdered large numbers of the inhabitants, but were driven back with great loss. These wars were a great expense to the people, and the proprietors in England not only refused to pay any part of the loss, but taxed the colonists severely, so that, in 1719, they threw off all allegiance to the proprietors and elected their own governor. For years there were quarrels between the people and their governors, the former insisting on their rights, as to which they were watchful and decided. In 1729, the king bought out the proprietors, and South Carolina was made a royal province, and so continued to the end of colonial times, being under royal governors, but electing their own Assemblies.

The planters of South Carolina were a wealthy and cultured class, and were early noted not only for affluence, but for their refined hospitality. The Huguenots, driven from France by persecution, added greatly to the population of the colony, as well as to its intelligence and moral worth. They were of high social position, and their descendants have always been conspicuous in the history of the State. Many of the young men of the colony were sent to England for education. Though the general spirit of the people was one of loyalty to the crown, they were always jealous of their liberties, and restless under the English laws of trade and restrictions on the industries of the colony; and taxation by England and the Stamp Act roused them to opposition and prepared them for the struggle with the mother country. Their delegates were sent to the Stamp Act Congress, which the prompt and decided measures of their colonial Assembly had aided to bring about, and the people of the State were active in forming the union of the States, of which South Carolina then became a part.

After the Revolution the State increased rapidly in population and wealth, and its political leaders gave it prominence and influence. The most important event in its history for seventy years was brought about by John C. Calhoun, who, with other leading men of the State, attempted to nullify certain acts of Congress which imposed a tariff on imported goods, which it was claimed bore unjustly against the interests of the State. For a time, this defiance of national authority threatened future trouble, but the prompt and decided action of President Jackson restored order. The desire to maintain State rights, however, was still held, and had much to do in bringing on the War of Secession.

South Carolina has little waste land; its soils are various, and adapted to every kind of agricultural products, as well as fruits and vegetables. Manufacturing establishments are numerous, and in the last few years have greatly multiplied. Provision is made by the State constitution for the compulsory attendance of all between six and sixteen years

SCENE IN SOUTH CAROLINA.

of age at schools, either public or private. The State has eight colleges, and numerous academies, seminaries, normal schools, &c., and, like most of the States, has numerous libraries in its different towns and cities. The population of the State in 1776 was 180,000; in 1880, 995,577, and in 1890, 1,147,161.

GEORGIA.

Georgia was the last of the colonies founded before the Declaration of Independence, and it was the only one that owed its existence to charity and the spirit of benevolence. Among all those who led the English race to the colonization of America, there were many men of striking character and most marked ability, but there was not

A PLANTER'S HOUSE IN GEORGIA.

one who displayed greater devotion to duty, or greater benevolence of spirit, than James Oglethorpe, who began the settlement of Georgia that it might be an asylum and refuge for the poor and oppressed. For himself and his associates he obtained from George II. a grant of the territory between the Savannah and the Altamaha rivers, to which, in honor of the king, he gave the name of Georgia. As a member of parliament his attention had been drawn to the condition of the prisons of debtors, where he found the greatest abuses and frightful suffering, a remedy for which he hoped to offer in his proposed colony. Leading a company of a hundred and twenty persons, he ascended the Savannah river in February, 1733, and began a settlement which he called Savannah, making friendship with the Indians, allotting land to individuals, and building a fort for defence.

Money was voted for his plans by parliament, and in the next two or three years large additions were made to the colony. Among the colonists were two young men who afterwards became quite noted in the world, Charles and John Wesley, the former being Oglethorpe's secretary, and the latter a missionary to the Indians. Their stay, however, was very short, Charles being dismissed for slandering Oglethorpe and for factious meddling in colonial affairs, and John embroiling the settlement by his zealous intolerance, and by a love affair in which he was disappointed, and leaving the colony under an indictment for libel. They were followed by George Whitefield, an equally distinguished leader in the great religious movement of the century, who did much as a missionary and a preacher, but came and went without leaving from this, his first visit, any enduring impressions or results.

Annoying as the Wesleys had been, there were two regulations which were sources of far greater trouble, one excluding rum from the colony, and the other prohibiting slavery. Both of these restrictions roused extended and great opposition, and neither could be enforced; for not only did South Carolina employ slaves, but it was thought that Georgia could not be successfully cultivated but by negro labor, and rum came in as freely as ever from the adjoining colony, so that law-breaking was added to drunkenness. Slaves, too, were smuggled in, and the prohibition of slavery became a grievance, great and growing as time went on. By these causes the growth of the colony was retarded, as it was also by the nearness and enmity of the Spaniards in Florida. Fearing danger from them, Oglethorpe went to England, and brought back with him, in addition to some regular troops, six hundred men, who, with their officers, were allowed to bring their families, as an inducement to settle in the province. In 1740, he invaded Florida, but without success; and two years later, the Spaniards, with thirty-six vessels and three thousand men, invaded Georgia, but were finally driven from the coast.

In 1743, Oglethorpe having returned to England, the government was left to a president and council. But trade languishing, in 1752, the charter was surrendered to the king, and Georgia became a royal province. The prohibitions spoken of were then removed, and Georgia rapidly advanced in population and wealth, and in all her institutions became like the other southern slaveholding colonies. She had no manufactures, but like other communities of the south, was dependent for them on the mother country and the more northern colonies. The English taxation policy and the Stamp Act roused deep and bitter opposition throughout the colony, though, through the governor's influence, delegates were not sent to the Stamp Act Congress. But Georgia took a decided part with the united colonies in the steps that led to and carried out the Revolution.

The area of Georgia is 58,000 square miles, about one-quarter of which is under cultivation, the diversity of soil and climate giving corresponding variety of production. The low grounds and islands on the coast are fertile in cotton of a superior quality, and rice, corn, and other cereals are easily cultivated, while valuable timber lands abound. Gold, silver, copper, iron, lead, marble, and some precious stones are found, and also coal, antimony, gypsum, slates, etc. Every variety of tree flourishes. Large tracts of land are valuable for pasturage. The State has eight universities or colleges, three collegiate institutions for agricultural instruction, several schools of law, medicine, and theology, and a system of common schools. Since the close of the War of Secession, the State has been greatly prospered, and is steadily growing in population and wealth. Its population in 1776 was about 50,000, of whom about one-half were slaves; in 1880, it was 1,542,180, and in 1890, 1,834,356.

SCENE IN A GEORGIA MEADOW.

PERIOD III.

CHAPTER I.

THE early colonies, the rise and progress of which have been traced, were not only governed and controlled by the English race, but, in every case, with the exception of New York and Delaware, that race laid the foundations of the future States. All had numerous traits in common, but in many things there were differences so marked as to be worthy of notice. Adventure brought men to Virginia; politics and religion, to New England; conscience and business, to Pennsylvania and New Jersey; philanthropy, to Georgia; trade and commerce, to New York; while the settlement of the other colonies was from mixed motives and aims. In many respects they may be spoken of as the New England, the Middle and the Southern Colonies.

THE NEW ENGLAND COLONIES.

The climate of the New England Colonies was one of extremes, with fine and warm summers, delightful autumns, severely cold winters, and harsh and inclement springs. The soil was greatly varied, the valleys being richly fertile, and the uplands more or less broken by rocky formations, demanding for culture incessant toil. There were vast forests, noble rivers, and safe and ample harbors, but nature gave so little that a bare subsistence and the limited comforts of life could be obtained only by constant labor on the land and daring adventure on the stormy and uncertain seas of the coast.

In this region the Pilgrims and Puritans made their homes, laid the foundations of powerful States, and gradually covered the land with prosperous villages and the coasts with thriving towns. The people who did this were almost entirely of the English race, some twenty thousand coming to New England between 1629 and 1639; and from these and a comparatively few Normans, Huguenots, and Scotch-Irish sprang the people of New England, of whom it was said that "God sifted a whole nation in order that he might send the choicest grain into the wilderness," or, as expressed by another, "God sifted three kingdoms that he might sow this land with the finest wheat."

At the time of the Revolution, the people of New England were, probably, the purest part of the Anglo-Saxon race, for, for one hundred and fifty years they had lived in the New World, receiving no infusion of fresh blood from any race but their own. Race, language, religious belief, manners, customs and habits of mind and thought were very much the same in all the New England settlements. And this community of so many traits was strengthened by community of class, for the settlers of New England were from the country gentlemen and substantial farmers and yeomanry of the Mother-land, the men of that famous "country party" in England, which sent Hampden and Pym and Cromwell to the House of Commons, and afterward fought the battles of the long Parliament and founded the Commonwealth. Many of them were men of wealth and highly educated in England, and all of them, with few exceptions, were men of property and influence in the country which they left for the New World. Not only their strength of character and their high intelligence, but their strong pride of race and origin, was to them, as in Virginia, one of the characteristics of a superior and dominant people, and one of the secrets of their practical wisdom and wonderful success.

ON THE NEW ENGLAND COAST.

At the outbreak of the Revolution, the population of New England was some 700,000, of whom about 15,000 were slaves. The people were occupied, chiefly, in agriculture and trade, their principal sources of profit being the whale and cod fisheries and their exports and coasting trade. Mechanical work gradually increased, and domestic manufactures soon sprang up. Paper, beaver hats, linens, and coarse woolens were made; the spinning-wheel and loom were in every family, and homespun and coarse linen, and on the frontier dressed deer-skins were worn. The governments of the different colonies, as we have seen, differed among themselves, but the main features of all were the extent of popular power, the practical independence of the Mother country and the common sense simplicity of the government and administration. Taxes were low; each person had an allotted share in the land; the village communities had charge of all local interests; every public measure was discussed and settled in the town meeting; the judicial system was simple, and admirably administered by men of high character and social and political prominence, in whom the absence of thorough legal training was supplied by a quick and strong common sense; law and medicine, as professions, were comparatively unknown; the army and navy had no existence, but the hardy fishermen had an intelligence and courage peculiarly their own, and from their class were manned the privateers which afterward inflicted such terrible injuries on the commerce of England, and so largely contributed to our success in the War of 1812. The English Puritan was essentially a brave and fighting man, and many of the early leaders had been trained to the art of war, both in Europe, and later under Cromwell, who said, "He that prays best will fight the best." Dangers from the Indians kept the warlike habit and feeling in full exercise, and the war with the Pequots, for effectiveness and success, has rarely been equalled in the history of any land. All adults were enrolled in the militia, and when the revolutionary troubles began the "lighting of the watch-fire on Beacon Hill would bring thousands of armed men to Boston in twenty-four hours," and Massachusetts alone furnished more men in the war for independence than all the colonies south of Delaware. Public spirit was a part of the New Englander's life, and "A coward and a Puritan never went together."

The clergy of New England were men of birth, education and culture. Many of them had filled leading pulpits in England, and all were men of the sternest courage and deepest convictions, having clear views of truth and broad ideas of what government and society should be. In every way they were leaders of the people, setting their mark indelibly upon the institutions of New England. In accordance with their views the laws were framed and the public policy shaped. For them the college was founded, and they of all others had the highest education. Though their congregations were made up of thinking and decided men, their influence from the pulpit, and in social life, was almost unbounded. They were profound scholars and their sermons were monuments of learning, and, personally, they were venerated and loved. Religion was the ruling force among the people: "He that made religion twelve and the world thirteen, had not the spirit of a true New England man."

Their church buildings, or "meeting-houses," as they were called, were like rude barns constructed of logs. Their churches were, each, self-sustaining and independent, the sovereign power resting with the congregation. Everybody attended the meeting on the Sabbath, all coming together at the beat of a drum or the sound of a horn. As a precaution against Indian attacks the men went armed to church, and sentinels kept watch at the door. Their worship was simple and purely spiritual. As has been said, they acknowledged no bishop, invoked no saints, raised no altar, bowed down to

7

ARMED CHURCH-GOERS IN THE EARLY COLONIES.

no crucifix, paid no tithes, and saw in the priest only a good man instructing and doing good to the people, and the lessons he inculcated in the pulpit they earnestly cherished in their thoughts and carried out in their daily life in the week. Their church was only a place for meeting; their graves were in unconsecrated earth; they married without a minister, and buried their dead without a prayer or remark. Their prayers were long and their sermons longer, often occupying two hours in delivery, and listened to with a patience and attention which made them an important means of intellectual training as well as of instruction in truth and duty. Their hymns, which were rude, both in language and versification, were given out line by line, and sung by the whole congregation, who, at the outside, did not know more than four or five tunes; and though singing by note was after a time introduced in the larger towns, in the country congregations it was almost unknown until about the time of the Revolution. "If you sing by note," said one of their leaders, "you will soon pray by rote, and then, as the next step, you'll become Roman Catholics." And what seems so strange to us, the bible was not allowed to be read from their pulpits on the Sabbath, for in the reaction from popery and high churchism, and in the fear lest the preachers might give their personal views of the interpretation of the Holy Word, and so trench on the right and duty of private interpretation, while the people were earnestly exhorted to "Search the Scriptures" at home, they were not read, as in modern times, as a part of the public worship of God till late in the seventeenth, or even the beginning of the eighteenth century.

Strict, and even severe, as the early Pilgrims and Puritans were in their religious opinions, and guided as they largely were by the teachings of the Old Testament, they were led to some views that seem to us strange and superstitious, though many such views were rather of the age than of any one country or people. They believed for a time in witchcraft; but where Scotland sacrificed scores to this delusion, there were but three victims in New England, and one of these was proved to be a murderess. They made religion a test of citizenship, and legislated as to everything connected, not only with the morals, but with the every-day life of the people,— with what they should eat, and drink, and wear. Long hair was abhorred as "worn by the sons of Belial," and rings were denounced as abominations. A minister's wife who was thought to dress too finely was reproved for "carnal-mindedness." A shoemaker was punished for making inferior shoes. Crime was comparatively rare, and though their penal codes seem to us to be severe, yet, for the age, and as compared with those of England, they were mild and humane. A crowd of offenses was banished from the catalogue of capital punishments, and the death penalty was rarely inflicted except for murder and arson. Fines were the mildest forms of penalty, and severe punishments, such as whipping, branding, cropping, the pillory and the stocks did not disappear till about the time of the Revolution. The burned scar was the worst mark, but letters of brilliant color sewed on the dress and worn for a length of time, indicating the kind of offence, were a device which at the same time might brand and punish. Scolds were gagged and set out, as an example and warning, at their own doors. Paupers were sold for support to the highest bidder, but they were kindly cared for. Divorce seems to have been unknown. Cruelty to animals was made a civil offence. One might be there for years and not see a drunkard, meet a beggar, or hear an oath. Good health was almost universal, and the average length of life, as compared with Europe, was greatly increased, some said, nearly doubled.

Strong social distinction existed, and an aristocracy of birth, ancestry, ability, education, and, to some extent, wealth, gave great prominence and influence to the leaders of the community. Even in the churches, people were seated according to their social standing. Though great estates were few, houses, large and costly for the times, were numerous. One is spoken of as having fifty-two rooms, endless paneling, carved mantelpieces, and expensive architectural ornaments from the old country. But the homes of the body of the people were of plain materials and simple construction; first the log hut, then the frame house in various forms, and now and then a dwelling of brick or stone. The houses were so cold that ink and wine often froze in the rooms where a fire was blazing on the hearth. The windows in these houses were generally of paper, which was oiled that the light might come through. Carpets were almost unknown, and the floors were often sanded. The furniture was plain. The sun-dial served instead of clocks, which were few and expensive. Pewter and wood took the place of china, and for a time the wooden "trencher" was on most tables. Wheat was abundant; fruit plentiful; tea was extensively used, but coffee rarely; cider was a common drink; or, if something stronger was desired, New England rum was abundant. A few of the better class of families had choice and handsome silver, which was more carefully kept than commonly used. The farms were well cultivated and productive.

Though amusements in most forms were frowned upon, yet, human nature would have its way, and neighbors would gather together to crack nuts, to chat and tell stories, frequently ending their meeting with a dance. A house-raising, in which all were ready to help, was frequently attended with feasting, drinking, and dancing, and there were quiltings, corn-huskings, and spinning bees, each ending with a simple supper and a dance. And as time went on, in their various seasons there were sleigh-rides, picnics, tea-parties, and supper parties, and dancing became common, while on great occasions, such as the ordination of a new minister, there was a grand ball, to which all were invited. One of the prominent ministers of Connecticut, at the time of his settlement as pastor of a leading church of the State, sent out invitations, in his own handwriting, to all the members of his church and congregation, to come to his house at night and dance at the ordination ball.

Post-offices, or anything like a postal system, were unknown to the early settlers, and even after a mail route was established between Boston and Philadelphia there was no post to the inland towns, which had to depend for news on chance visitors to or from the seaports. Letters were known to be weeks on the way from towns like Newport to Northampton or Hadley. No wheel carriages or public conveyances were known till about the time of the Revolution. Produce and supplies were carried on ox-sleds in winter, and on ox-carts in summer; and journeys for business or pleasure, to church, or for visiting, were made on horseback, the women and children riding on pillions behind the men. In the larger places, especially in Boston, the houses were larger and better, and there was more of gayety, dress, and amusement than in the smaller settlements; and on great occasions, such as the taking of Louisburg, there were public celebrations, the town being illuminated, bonfires lighted and the streets filled with people.

Marriage was treated merely as a civil contract, and was performed only by the magistrates. Weddings, for a time, were quietly celebrated at the house of the bride, but afterward became occasions of great festivity, the wedding-feasts, with dancing and

A PIONEER HOME IN WINTER.

merry-making, often lasting for two or three days. The banns of marriage were published from the pulpit or posted in some public place, and marriage sermons were often preached on the Sabbath before the marriage. At funerals in the early settlements, the dead were borne on the shoulders of bearers and silently laid in the earth without remark or prayer at the grave. But before the end of the seventeenth century such occasions came to be regarded as important, and were attended with much pomp and expense. Leading men became pall-bearers; long processions followed to the grave; scarfs, gloves and mourning rings were distributed, and the day was closed with a feast. At one funeral, of which an account is given, over twenty pounds were spent for scarfs, gloves, wine and tobacco; and at another, over a thousand scarfs and pairs of gloves were given away, and so extravagant became the expense of funeral gatherings that at length laws were passed to regulate such ceremonies and make them less costly.

One marked and distinguishing characteristic of the Puritans was their regard for education. One of the earliest acts of the New England colonists was to found a system of public schools. In many cases the towns and schools were founded almost at the same time; and as early as 1649 education was made compulsory everywhere except in Rhode Island. Instruction in these schools was simple and elementary, but it served as a beginning and led on to a universal system of public or common schools. These were soon followed by Latin schools, at which, and by the clergy, boys were fitted for college, the result being that at the time of the Revolution everybody could read and write, and illiteracy was almost unknown.

A college, too, was established within seven years from the time when Endicott and his followers landed at Salem. Its professors were men of character and learning, some of them eminent, and their instruction was excellent. At the beginning of the eighteenth century Yale College was founded in Connecticut; then Dartmouth, in New Hampshire; and then Brown, in Rhode Island, so that the number of thoroughly educated and

learned men among the new settlers, in proportion to the population, was very large, there being one Cambridge graduate to every hundred and fifty of the colonists.

As writers, the clergy largely predominated, but many laymen also became distinguished for their publications. A printing-press was established at Cambridge in 1639, within ten years after its settlement. The first newspaper appeared in Boston in 1690; and in 1775, the same city had five newspapers. Many persons had good private libraries, and at the time of the Revolution there was a subscription-library in almost every township.

Political discussion was intelligent and universal. The town meetings, and the various questions discussed in them as to their relation to the Mother country, trained every one to think, and kept up and cherished the patriotic spirit. The jealousy of external power never slept. The love of independence and self-government was a principle as well as a sentiment. The people were thoroughly loyal, but they knew, as by instinct, when their rights were invaded by unjust laws of trade and British taxation, and when the attempt was made to rule them in ways that they felt were unjust and oppressive, then began the resistance which led on to the Revolution.

Such was New England from its first settlement up to the time of the Revolution. The people were pure in race, industrious, frugal in their lives, enterprising and prosperous, a population of small land-holders, in a high degree educated and thoughtful; trained in the principles of liberty and self-government, thus laying the foundations of general intelligence and virtue, and of national prosperity and greatness. From this strong and vigorous race came, as in Virginia, many great leaders, both in civil and military life, but the great strength was in the body of the people. They were all possessed of the same general views and principles, and had the same intelligent and resolute purpose, the same shrewdness, perseverance, and force, and they carried their principles into the war for independence, and into the new national government to which it led.

Such were some of the prominent aspects of life in the New England Colonies. But the picture may be more complete, if we glance at four things which both expressed and shaped the character of the people, and moulded the future, not only of the New England States, but, more or less, that of the whole country. These were the voluntary principle, the practical views of education held by the colonists, the religious views and influences prevailing in their communities, and the town meetings of the people.

An early sermon of one of the leading preachers of the colonies was on the text, that for "*the soul to be without knowledge is not good*," and the sentiment, as well as the principle, was that of all the people, while in some of the other colonies education was practically regarded as the perquisite and privilege of the higher classes, and no public provision was made for the instruction of the great mass of the people. In the New England settlements education was looked upon as one of the necessaries of life, both for the individual and the family as well as for the State, and as a consequence, from the very first, schools and academies and then colleges were established, and the people freely taxed themselves for their support. The result was, as might have been expected, that a thoughtful intelligence pervaded the people, the power of which was felt for good in all the avenues of social, political and business life; and as emigrants in later years went forth to the new and rising States of the West, the same spirit went with them, and their school systems and school funds, and the general education of the people, may be traced to a great extent to the educational views and systems of the early New England colonists.

Another striking feature of colonial life in New England, shared also by the other colonies, was seen in the prevalence and workings of the voluntary principle, in civil and political matters as well as in religion. The laws of the people were not the edicts of superior and arbitrary power dictating to inferiors, as to servants or children, what they should or should not do; but were the self-suggested and just rules by which they freely bound themselves to what was reasonable and right, and so best for themselves and for the community. As in the Mayflower compact, and also in the civil laws of Moses, which though divinely given, were always proposed to the people, and were never regarded as binding until voluntarily assented to, and accepted by them, so it was with the civil laws and regulations of the early New England colonies. All the ancient and oriental policies, except those of Israel under Moses, were founded on force, but those of the Puritans, like those of the Jewish nation, rested only on the consent of the people, who themselves originated the laws by which they were self-governed. With the exception of the principle of *habeas corpus*, which was not in the Mosaic code, because imprisonment was unknown to the Hebrews, there is not a single fundamental principle which enters into the constitution of a free State, which was not found in the policy of the Hebrew commonwealth; and prominent among these was the voluntary principle which has shaped the destinies of our country in politics as well as in religion, resting government on the authority of the people, and making them the authors of their own laws, and the keepers of their own peace, prosperity and happiness.

The religion of a people both shows and shapes the character of their institutions, and also their personal, social and political life; and the religion of the Puritan settlers was that of Calvinistic Christianity, which De Tocqueville calls "a democratic and republican religion," because, while denying arbitrary and despotic power in the Church, it denies it also in the State, and thus brings to a people not only truth but liberty. It is of men holding these views that Hume, the historian, has said, "The precious spark of liberty was kindled and preserved by the Puritans alone, and it was to their sect that the English owe the whole freedom of their constitution"; that Taine says, "They founded the United States"; that Motley declares, "that to them, more than to any other class of men, the political liberties of Holland, England, and America are due"; and that Von Ranke, the historian of the Popes, speaks of Calvin as being, by his doctrines, "The founder of the free States of North America, as it was his doctrine that shaped the men who left home and country in order to preserve their religious freedom in the wilds of America"; and as their religion shaped their views of government, and gave them civil and religious liberty, so it established in their communities a higher standard of personal and public morality, and led to that industry, temperance and purity in social life which has made New England, in so many respects, a power for good to the entire land.

Our view of life in New England would still be incomplete without a distinct notice of one of the most striking features of its public policy — the town meetings. In these smaller and miniature republics every measure of importance was publicly discussed, and the people were trained to habits of thought and responsibility, and so the way was prepared for the larger republic of States and of the Union itself. The best developments of our later political life had, if not their origin, yet their steady and sure growth in these local assemblies, and there was cherished that spirit of independence and those intelligent views both of right and liberty which made each township a little independent State, and which, as the country increased, became the balance wheel to the immensity of our widespread territory.

When an American once asked a German what word or words in his language expressed the idea of *public spirit*, the reply was, "we have no word for it, for we have not the thing." In a country where the few rule and the great mass of people are treated as children or subjects, an intelligent public spirit cannot be expected and is never found. But in the town meeting where all are rulers, and at the same time voluntary subjects, and so rulers of themselves and of the public destiny, there an intelligent and true public spirit takes shape and goes forth in concert of action.

It was in the town meetings of the early colonies that the first note of independence was struck, that the people resolved they would not be taxed without representation, that resolutions of defiance were uttered against the most powerful nation of the world, and that the spirit of those resolutions, growing and burning till the whole country was on fire, carried us through an eight years' war, and brought us out with victory and independence.

The same spirit and custom of home rule, carried out in the town meetings and local gatherings of the various newer States, have been, and still are, the life of our free institutions. As the enterprising residents of the East have, in multitudes, left their old homes for the new States and territories, they have carried their town habits with them, and the village or town meeting is called, and a little republic is started, and as it lives and grows, it becomes the great city, or the new territory or State added to the Union, the township feeling pulsating as a life blood through every artery and vein of the country, giving to our widespread territory the unity of but a larger township, and to the varied parts of our vast commonwealth the unity of the one republic.

INDIAN BURIAL GROUND.

VIRGINIA.

Virginia, the earliest of the colonies, was marked by characteristics which it shared to some extent with the southern settlements, though it differed not a little from those of New England. It had a rich soil, a mild and genial climate, noble rivers, good harbors, and broad tracts of wild and uncultivated land. Its population in 1650 was estimated at 15,000 whites and 300 negroes; in 1671, at 40,000 persons, of whom 2,000 were negroes; and in 1750, at 250,000 whites, and a still larger proportion of negro slaves.

By nature the region had great attractiveness, and it is no wonder that the early settlers were delighted with the prospect that seemed to open for the future, and had they been as earnest and persevering as they should have been, the settlements might have entered at an earlier day on the prosperity which they afterward enjoyed. But the early entrance of slavery, and the troubles with the Indians that early arose, taxing the energies of the settlers in self-defence, as well as the fact that the early colonists expected results that could only be obtained by self-denying effort, all united to retard the growth of what might otherwise have been the most successful and prosperous of all the colonies of the New World.

The colony had no army or navy, but only a militia, made up of the able-bodied freemen between the ages of sixteen and sixty, but undisciplined and with no efficient organization. The judicial system was imperfect, and, judged by later standards, far from what was desirable. The judges were without legal training, yet, "being able and judicious persons," they administered substantial justice, and were respected and obeyed by the people. Trial by jury was established; and, as in all the colonies, so here, the common law was adopted except so far as modified by statutes; there were no educated lawyers; in 1646, the taking of fees was prohibited; and, as late as 1729, there was no formal pleading in the courts.

There were no towns as centers of population, as in New England, but the people were widely scattered. In 1716, Jamestown had only a church, a court-house, and three or four brick houses; and in 1732, Fredericksburg, in addition to its leading man, had only a merchant, a tailor, a tavern-keeper, and a woman who was both doctress and coffee-house keeper; and Richmond and Petersburg existed only on paper. Williamsburg, the capital, and the seat of the university, was a straggling village of some two hundred houses, of which the governor's was of brick and a handsome structure, while the college, as Jefferson said, "looked like a brick-kiln with a roof." The towns which have been mentioned were planted, in most cases, in the midst of the forests, and usually consisted of the little church, the court-house, the prison with its stocks, the pillory, the ducking-stool, and whipping-post, and one miserable inn, where the judges lodged when they came to hold court. The popular habits and occupations of the people explain the smallness of the few towns and the scattering of the population through the country.

In the early days of Virginia, the "professions" were at a low ebb. The so-called attorneys were, for the most part, pettifoggers and sharpers, or broken-down adventurers from London, and even indented servants who had been convicts. The only man in the seventeenth century who attained an honorable eminence as a lawyer was William Fitzhugh; and so late as 1734, only two men displayed ability in the profession, though a little later, Sir John Randolph was conspicuous as a learned advocate and attorney-general. It was not till the close of the colonial period that men of high position and real talent devoted themselves to the law, and it was at this period, in the rising conflicts of the Revolution, that such men as Patrick Henry, Thomas Jefferson James Madison, George Mason, and George Wythe studied law and came forward to the bar, of which John Marshall was the most distinguished member and the greatest name that has adorned the legal profession of the country. The profession of medicine was especially low in Virginia. The number of physicians was small, and, with a few honorable exceptions, the dispenser of drugs, the rude village surgeon or barber, or the unskillful apprentice were its chief representatives, and were without prominence or influence. The professedly learned class in the community was the clergy, but most of them were more noted for their failings than for their intelligence or virtues.

VIEW ON THE JAMES RIVER, VIRGINIA.

From the first settlement of Virginia the established church had been the Episcopal, and non-conformists were oppressed and driven from the colony. The Roman Catholics and Quakers were persecuted, and all separatist meetings were broken up. The Presbyterians were the first to make head against this intolerance, the conflict being carried on by Francis Makemie, supported by the large body of intelligent Scotch-Irish settlers. By the beginning of the eighteenth century the established church had lost, and the dissenters had rapidly gained ground. Though, before 1700, there were but few who were of "the sects," yet, by 1776, from half to two-thirds of the population were dissenters. Men like Madison and Jefferson strongly opposed the spirit of intolerance, and, as the dissenters in the rising conflict with the Mother country were all on the patriotic side, the powers and privileges of the old established church were swept away, and all denominations were fully tolerated.

This result was the more rapidly and easily brought about by the character of the Episcopal clergy. In the seventeenth century, the most of them, though not highly educated, were honest and zealous men and faithful in their various duties, but in the next century they rapidly declined in character and influence for good. For the most part, their morals were loose and their characters low. They were at the race-course and the cockpit, betting on the contending birds and horses; and marriages and funerals and christenings they often turned into revels. Bishop Meade, in his history of Virginia, and who speaks of it with deep sorrow, says: "There was not only defective preaching, but most evil living among them"; and he mentions one who received a stated sum for preaching annually four sermons against atheism, gambling, racing and swearing, though he was well known to be a gambler, a swearer and a horse-racer. The result, as might be expected, followed. The revival of the eighteenth century, with the earnest preaching and exemplary living of the dissenters—the Presbyterians, Baptists, Methodists, Moravians, and New Lights,—and the lukewarmness and indecision of the leaders of the established church in the contest with England, broke down the power of the Episcopal clergy and put all denominations on the same footing before the law.

The trade and business of the colony were for a long time depressed. Small shop-keepers were scattered about in the little towns. With the few who were merchants, business dragged heavily. Mechanics were few and incompetent; and most articles requiring skill in manufacture, or for domestic use, were brought from England. Shipping was in the hands of English merchants and the natives of the other colonies. The fisheries, from which much had been expected, were neglected, and the exports, except of tobacco, were limited in amount and value. The mineral wealth of the country was undeveloped, except as to iron, for the production and working of which there were mines and forges in various parts of the province. Tobacco was the great staple of the colony, which laid its foundation, gave it its wealth, and on which its prosperity rested for more than a century. It was used for a long time as the standard of values and as currency. By it taxes were paid and things bought and sold. Its cultivation made slaves profitable to their owners, and so fastened the curse of slavery on the province. Its exportation, which in 1750 was sixty thousand hogsheads, had risen, at the Revolution, to a hundred thousand, valued at nearly a million pounds sterling, and employing some three hundred vessels in its transportation.

Most of the early settlers of Virginia were mere adventurers, blindly hoping for speedy wealth in the New World, and to them were soon added indented servants, and even convicts from the Mother country. These, however, were not the controlling or relatively the important elements of the population. The leading Virginians sprang from a pure English stock, many of them being the sons of wealthy or noble families, or of the yeomanry and merchant class. There was also a small immigration of the excellent Huguenots, and also many of the Puritans with their characteristics of intelligence and strength, and later still of Scotch-Irish Presbyterians, and Germans from the middle colonies. These last named elements, however, were comparatively small, both in number and influence, and the population as a whole was essentially English. The entire community was made up of four classes: The slaves, who after a time formed nearly half the population; the indented servants and poor whites; the middle class of small farmers and planters and traders; and then, at the top, the great landlords or planters who ruled and represented Virginia.

In 1620, as we have seen, a Dutch trading vessel brought into James river twenty African negroes who were at once bought as slaves by the planters, but for fifty years afterward comparatively few more were imported. From this time on, however, as slave

A VIRGINIA SUMMER SCENE.

labor was found so profitable on the tobacco plantations, slavery rapidly increased. The slave laws were terribly severe, but in practice were greatly disregarded, and for the most part the slaves were well treated and cared for. By the great increase of negroes the indented white servants, who at first were the laboring class, came to be of little

importance, and as their terms of servitude expired, they came to be known as the
" poor whites," the lowest class in the community. They were ignorant, degraded, and
looked down upon, even by the negroes, for the most part were idle and shiftless, and
never worked except to gain a bare subsistence. The free negroes and those poor whites
formed the criminal class, hanging about taverns, drinking, fighting, and committing in
Virginia a larger proportion of small crimes than occurred in the other colonies.

The two remaining classes of Virginia society were in many respects alike, the
difference being one of degree rather than of kind. Both were of good sound English
stock. Both were land-owners and slaveholders, and with some exception as to a portion
of the middle class, they associated and intermarried with each other. The majority of
this middle class were yeomen and farmers. They were independent and men of
property, a sturdy and manly race, sadly deficient in education and knowledge of the
world, but generous and hospitable, often acquiring large fortunes, and if successful,
working their way up to the first positions. They gave strength, support and political
power to the great planters who represented and ruled Virginia, and gave tone and color
to the whole of her society.

The upper class, the great planters, regarded as the aristocracy, were country
gentlemen, not in the modern sense, but in that of the eighteenth century. Prominent
and wealthy as they were as a class, their advantages for education were lamentably
deficient. Public sentiment cared little for the instruction of the people, and many of
the early governors were decidedly opposed to it. It was as late as 1671 that Sir
William Berkeley "thanked God that there were no free schools in Virginia, and not
likely to be for a century to come." And when, in 1692, the attorney-general was
applied to for a charter for the college of William and Mary, which it was urged would
be "a means of the salvation of souls," his bluff reply was, "Damn your souls, grow
tobacco!" But though the college was chartered, the statutes of the colony show no
desire or effort to provide education for the people, and no system of anything like
public schools was attempted before 1776.

In this state of things the young Virginian was left to what instruction a parent
might give, or to the limited teachings of the parish minister or the freed servant. Some,
if their parents could afford it, were sent to the college of William and Mary, or to
England to be educated, but such cases were the exception, and the leading classes were
far from being well educated, but depended more on their mother wit, of which they had
an abundant portion, than on any acquired advantages or training for their success in life.
Their chief interest and employment was the cultivation of tobacco, the sale of the crop,
the importation of what was desired for the plantation or the family, and the bringing up
of their negroes for agricultural and other work; to these and their public duties their
time was given, and their sons were brought up to have the same aims, while the mothers
and daughters of the household were occupied with domestic matters, the training of
negro girls, the general charge of the family, and the interchanges of social life. The
style of living among the planters was one of generous profusion and unbounded
hospitality. Scattered as they were in the widely separated plantations, they were glad
to welcome any traveller or stranger whose visit would give variety to life and bring
the news which otherwise would not reach them.

The roads were miserable, and travelling was mostly on horseback. The houses of
the plainer classes were small and of wood, with wooden shutters as openings for light

and air; those of the middle classes were larger, and often of brick, with windows of oiled paper or small panes of glass; while those of the planters were spacious, with large, low rooms, panelled and wainscoted, handsomely furnished and hung with portaits or armorial bearings of the family connections. Located as they were in the midst of estates of great natural beauty, and surrounded by tobacco-houses and the huts of the negro quarters, while in the distance were seen the herds of the plantation grazing in the pastures, and the slaves toiling in the fields, they reminded one of the old manor houses of England, and testified to the independence and wealth of the proprietors. The houses of some of the richer planters were very expensive and elegant, and furnished not only with everything that could administer to comfort, but with all the luxuries that wealth could give; with choice libraries and works of taste and art brought from the old country.

About the second quarter of the eighteenth century, one of these planters writing to a friend in England, and suggesting that he send one of his sons to Virginia, says: "You may make a prince of him here for less money than you can make a private gentleman of him in England. We live here in health, in innocence and security, fearing no enemy from abroad nor robbers at home. Our government is so happily constituted that a governor must first outwit us before he can oppress us, and if ever he squeeze money out of us he must first take care to deserve it. Our negroes are not so numerous or so

enterprising as to give us any uneasiness or apprehension, nor indeed, is their labor any other than gardening, and less by far than what the poor people of other countries undergo. Nor are any cruelties exercised upon them, unless by great accident they fall into the hands of a brute, who always passes here for a monster. We all live securely with our doors unbarred, and can travel the whole country over without arms or guard; and all this not for want of money or rogues, but because we have no great city to shelter the thief, or pawnbrokers to receive what he steals."

The plantations were generally managed by overseers, and though they were largely profitable, yet the extravagance of the planters in living, and their generous and profuse hospitality led to self-indulgent and improvident habits, and brought not a

SUMMER ON THE RAPPAHANNOCK.

few to bankruptcy and ruin. The ladies of Virginia were highly accomplished in all that adorns society, and were notable housekeepers and good wives and mothers, managing the household, training the servants, overseeing and directing all domestic concerns, and diligently caring for their families.

The great event of the year was the annual visit to Williamsburg, the capital, where society was gay, and English fashions prevailed, and where in times of political excitement their leading orators were heard on the great questions of the day. Once a year, when the House of Burgesses met and the supreme court was in session, the fashionable world of Virginia assembled at Williamsburg, the ladies for acquaintance and social enjoyment, and the men for business and the amusements of the time, such as horse-racing, cock-fighting, card-playing, feasting and drinking. Prizes were offered for rough English sports, the very names of which now sound strangely; and athletic contests, hogshead races, greased poles, and bull-baiting amused the common people; while some of the largest estates were dissipated by the gambling which prevailed to a frightful extent. Intellectual pursuits found little place. It was not till 1736 that a newspaper was published, and this for many years was the only journal in the colony, and it was the middle of the eighteenth century before a mail from the north, once in two weeks, and another to the south, once in four weeks, both established by individuals, were thought necessary and convenient. Books were few, and reading limited to comparatively few, and in Governor Spottswood's time he said of two of the chairmen of committees of the House of Burgesses, that "They could not spell English, or write common sense." And even in the years just prior to the Revolution, Virginians read little and studied less, if we except the young and rising men who soon became noted in the stirring period then just commencing.

The subject of politics was always one of interest in Virginia. With brief exception, the right of voting was confined to freeholders. The leading class absorbed all the important offices of the State. The landed estates were entailed, the bulk of the property generally going to the eldest son, and it was not till the Revolution that primogeniture and entail, the foundation and support of the aristocracy, came to an end. Class distinctions were rigidly observed in the churches as well as in social life. Labor was looked upon as disgraceful, and for a young man to enter into trade or a counting-house was esteemed as shameful. The virtues and vices which are everywhere connected with an aristocracy were seen in the community, the lower classes being depressed and ignorant, while the governing classes were indolent, imperious, and sensitive to restraint, largely men of shrewdness and sense, and many of them men of liberal sentiments and enlightened understanding, knowing clearly their rights and determined to maintain them. And when the conflicts of the Revolution came on they proved themselves fine soldiers, sagacious politicians, and clear-sighted and able statesmen. At the call of the times, out of the self-indulgent, inert aristocracy came a set of high-minded and energetic men, who proved themselves worthy of the foremost places as leaders and patriots, and an honor to the American name. This ruling class were small numerically, but a body which in one generation produced such names as Washington, Marshall, Jefferson, and Madison, to say nothing of the Fairfaxes, the Lees, Fitzhughs, Pendletons, Randolphs, and many others, is one that may well take rank not only in the history of the United States, but in that of the English race, and of the world. Through the prompt action of such leaders, Virginia has the high honor of being first of all the colonies, in compliance with the recommendation of the Colonial Congress of May 15, 1776, to renounce the colonial name and condition, and to form herself into a free, independent, sovereign State. Her constitution was adopted the day after the Declaration of Independence.

8

UPPER AU SABLE LAKE

THE OTHER COLONIES.

In the different colonies of the New World there were, as we have seen, differences and contrasts in the character and aims of the colonists and in the manners and habits, and the social and business life of their peoples. The New England colonies are on one extreme, and the Virginia colonies on the other, while the remaining colonies may be considered as a third group, partaking more or less of the traits of the two mentioned above.

Maryland differed but slightly from Virginia, out of which her territory was originally taken, having the same climate and natural conformation, the same harbors and rivers, and the same fertile soil and noble forests. Except a large number of transported convicts, her early settlers had been of excellent character, the principle of religious freedom attracting not only gentlemen and substantial farmers from England, but many Puritans who had been exiled from Virginia by the established church party, as also many Scotch, Irish, German, and Dutch immigrants.

The chief occupations of the people were agriculture, and tobacco culture was the great interest till the close of the French war, when the planters began to turn from tobacco to grain, and a large export trade sprang up in wheat and flour. The mining and smelting of iron also became valuable. At first there was little foreign commerce and few shopkeepers in the small towns, but in the beginning of the eighteenth century Annapolis became a center of trade and fashion. One of the "paper towns" called Baltimore, had so grown, that by 1770 it was the first place in the province, and one of the five or six considerable towns of the colonies.

The early Catholic settlers established religious toleration, but before the Revolution they had become but a minority of the population, and the Church of England, which came into power, had all the vices of the early Virginia church without its safeguards and restraints, overthrowing the toleration policy and disgracing themselves by their conduct. As a result the dissenters greatly increased so as soon to include the majority of the people. The upper and middle classes differed little from each other, or from the same classes in Virginia, while the slaves and indented servants, many of whom were convicts and paupers, formed a low and degraded class of the population, being idle, shiftless and improvident. The planters and plantations, and the hospitality, fashions and amusements of the people were very much as in Virginia; though the children of the wealthy were sent abroad or to Pennsylvania for education. Among the common people education was almost entirely neglected, convicts and servants being almost the only teachers, and literary pursuits being scarcely known. The people, though indolent and illiterate, were not wanting in shrewdness and independence of spirit, and when the troubles of the Revolution came, under leaders like Carroll and Chase, they were faithful to the great work of establishing our independence.

North and South Carolina were at first one, but afterward were separated and became two States. The former was mainly an offshoot from Virginia, a refuge for the discontented and often thriftless adventurers from the latter, and was deficient in men of the ability and commanding character that made Virginia so distinguished. The coast was deficient in good harbors, and the soil light and sandy. There was almost a total absence of professional men, and the condition of religion, as of education, gave strong illustrations of the rudeness of society. At the time of the Revolution, there were in

North Carolina but six Episcopal churches, and as many more of the Presbyterians, and also of the Moravians. Besides those of these churches, there were no regular ministers, though there were not a few illiterate preachers.

In agriculture, North Carolina was the lowest of the English colonies. Lumber, tar and turpentine were produced, and in the southern portion rice, indigo and cotton, but tobacco was the great staple. There were no manufactures of any kind. At the time of independence there were but three villages large enough to be called towns. The slaves and indented servants were the lowest class. The bulk of the population above these consisted of "poor whites" and small farmers. There were a few large planters, like those of Virginia, but the great body of the men were slothful and inefficient. Society in its manners and amusements was like that of Virginia on a smaller and ruder scale. At the Revolution there were but two schools in the entire province, and printing was not introduced till 1764. Though the people were in many respects lawless, and averse to order and government, they were keenly alive to their own rights, and though among them there was a body of numerous and active Tories, the great body of the population fell in eagerly with the movement against England. They had no great leaders in the Revolution, but it is a strong proof of the vigor and soundness of the English race, that so lawless and apathetic a people raised themselves at last in the scale of civilization, and built up a strong and prosperous State.

In South Carolina the type of society was almost wholly like that of Virginia, differing, if at all, in the fact that it was intensified. The face of the country was much like that of North Carolina, but the soil of the whole province was good, while the lowlands along the river bottoms were extremely rich. The climate was variable, with great extremes of heat and cold. The sources of the population were various, the main element among the whites being English, but many of the Dutch came from New York, and a large number of Puritans from

A RIVER SCENE.

Massachusetts, and there was more or less emigration from Virginia, Pennsylvania and North Carolina. The Huguenots from France formed an excellent and influential element of the population. They were wealthy and of high social position, and their descendants were among the leading people of the State. A large emigration of thrifty and industrious Germans, and numbers of English and Scotch-Irish from the North of Ireland, who were Presbyterians, added excellent elements to the population, founding some of the most important families and producing some of the most distinguished leaders of South Carolina.

The charter of 1669, which provided for the support of the English church, guaranteed religious toleration to all. The majority of the people were dissenters, and the clergy of all denominations were men of excellent character, and devoted to their work, and while in Virginia three-quarters of the ministers were Tories, in South Carolina, as a rule, the ministers were patriotic, and sided with the opposition to England. The common law prevailed; the criminal laws were severe; and the profession of law, as well that as of divinity, was more advanced than in most of the southern colonies.

Almost all the whites were planters or farmers. Rice and indigo were for years the chief products, though later cotton became the great staple. Cattle multiplied rapidly, many planters having two or three thousand head, and beef was exported at great profit to the West Indies. Agriculture, exports, and traffic with the Indians were the chief industries, and the merchants who carried on all the trade, though a most respectable and prosperous class, were looked down upon by the planters who formed the leading part of the population and absolutely controlled the State. The poor whites and indented servants were few in number, and the planters and slaves were the two great classes, forming a pure and despotic aristocracy with its various dependents. The slaves, who far outnumbered all other classes of the population, were employed mostly on the plantations, and their condition, with the exception of those who were servants in families, was almost that of barbarism. The planters lived mostly in Charleston, leaving their estates in the charge of overseers. They were much the same country gentlemen as those of Virginia, but more polished, and of more refinement of manners and habits of life. The life of both sexes was one of greater luxury than in any other colony, and was self-indulgent and indolent. There were few very large fortunes, but little or no poverty. Those who were not large planters, were either self-supporting farmers, or traders, or hunters. There were no free and but few paid schools. For the great body of the people, general education was scarcely known till after the Revolution. The sons of the rich were educated in Europe or in Charleston, or in the schools and colleges of New England. In politics and commerce there was no lack of shrewdness and business tact, and the love of independence was strong and intelligent. The strongest and best of the planters were active and decided in the patriot cause, and notwithstanding a bitter Tory influence they carried the colony safely through the struggle for independence, and gave the State a strong position in the country, and a place second only to that of Virginia in the southern group of colonies.

Georgia was founded from benevolent motives, and being started by Oglethorpe and his associates as a field for philanthropic experiments, its population at first was a strange mixture of rude and unformed elements, the great body of its immigrants being from debtors' prisons or shiftless and bankrupt adventurers and servants of a low class, such as would be an injury to any society, especially to one just founded and struggling for existence. It had some men of standing and good substance, but the great mass of the colonists were of the former character. Gradually better elements came in, Puritans from South Carolina, emigrants from Scotland, and, in 1763, a large body of Quakers and other settlers, attracted by the profits expected from trade and agriculture. Land was given out in but small quantities, and under unwise restrictions, and slavery and the importation of negroes were prohibited, as was also the introduction of rum, which greatly injured trade with the West Indies. But both prohibitions were more or less evaded, and so law was brought into contempt, trade stagnated, and general discontent prevailed.

Under the royal government in 1752, the restrictions above mentioned were removed, and the colony then became prosperous, so that just before the Revolution it had a population of over 150,000, of whom half, at least, were slaves. There was very little of town life; almost every one was a farmer or planter, and large estates were few. Some of the plantations had large and handsome houses, the owners living easy and self-indulgent lives, giving much time to amusements and social life. Horse-racing and gambling prevailed, and gambling and drinking brawls, with all their excesses, became so common with the lower classes as to call for severe laws for their repression.

Speaking chiefly of these classes, the historian tells us that "No pastimes could flourish among them that did not partake of danger or risk. They formed hunting clubs which met once a fortnight. They gambled and bet, and gathered in crowds to see cocks cut each other to pieces with spurs made of steel. They came from all parts to enter their horses for races. At such times the men of the lower caste played faro, wrestled, and seldom went home without a quarrel, or perhaps a brutal fight. We are told by those who beheld these scenes, that the fighting was rarely in hot blood, that the preliminaries were cooly arranged, and each combatant agreed, before he began, whether it would be fair to bite off an ear, to gouge out an eye, or to maim his opponent in a more terrible way. Gouging was always permissible; every bully grew a long thumb or finger-nail for that very purpose, and when he had his opponent down would surely use it, unless the unfortunate man cried out 'enough'. If the gouger took out the eye of but one man, his punishment might be a few hours in the pillory, or a few lashes of the whip. If he repeated the offence, he might, the law declared, be put to death. Yet the practice was a favorite one, and common as far north as the Maryland border."

A COTTON FIELD.

The early history of religion in Georgia is one of confusion and wrangling. Later, under the royal government, toleration was allowed, and the Puritan influence was felt; but the clergy had but little influence for good. Education was at a lower ebb than in any colony, the few teachers being of a low class, and too ignorant themselves to be of much benefit to others. There was no native literature. Georgia played but an

THE CASCADES.

insignificant part in the difficulties with England and in the war of the Revolution, and produced but few able men to compare in influence with those of Virginia and New England.

Pennsylvania and Delaware may be treated together, as for a long time they were under the same government, and both had much the same climate, and the same rich, though varied soil. At the Revolution the population of both colonies was some 400,000, of whom nearly a third were negroes. The people were varied; their employment chiefly agriculture. Their exports were grain, flour, timber, and the produce of farms; and saw mills and grist mills were numerous. Ships were built at Philadelphia, and before the eighteenth century there were manufactures of paper, glass, drugget and stockings; and the mining and smelting of iron were extensively carried on. There was thrift and enterprise in all kinds of business, and a rich and growing prosperity among the people. The judicial system was above that of most of the colonies. The bar was exceptionally good, and the medical profession was marked by education, and was highly respected. With one trifling exception, religious freedom was enjoyed from the beginning. The Swedish Lutherans in Delaware formed the earliest churches, but the Quakers were for a long time the prevailing denomination.

In 1750 Philadelphia was second only to Boston in size and importance, and at the Revolution it was the first city in America in population. The social and political system of the southern colonies was unknown in Pennsylvania, and though the descendants of Penn's followers were long the leading men, they could hardly be deemed an aristocracy. African slaves were never numerous, but there were many indented white servants and redemptioners, and still more of transported convicts, who finally became so numerous and troublesome that laws were passed forbidding their importation. Crimes were no more common than in the other colonies, but pauperism abounded, for the liberal spirit of the founders drew many of a low class who brought crime and poverty with them.

The curse of pirates and smugglers, who infested the American coasts, fell heavily on Pennsylvania. Murder at first was the only capital offence, and every form of immorality was forbidden, but in the second generation morals had become so relaxed that in 1738 criminal legislation was made more severe, work-houses and jails were established, and the number of capital offences was increased from one to fourteen. Every felony except larceny was made capital on a second offence, and the pillory and whipping-post were punishments for most smaller offences. In Philadelphia was the only lunatic asylum in the colonies; and a hospital, a reform school, a soldiers' home, and many societies for the care of the poor, and aged, and infirm, as well as a watchful regard for the health and morals of the people, show that Pennsylvania had made greater progress in social improvement than any of the colonies.

The manners and habits of the people and their modes of life differed greatly. In the outlying country districts their log houses were small, their clothing of the plainest kind, and their amusements as rude as their means of comfort. The farming class was one of great prosperity. The houses were good and well furnished. Luxury was unknown, but solid comfort abounded in all their dwellings. Weddings and funerals, which at first were attended with feasting and drinking, gradually became more quiet and simple in their observances. The amusements and relaxations of the people were found at seed time and harvest, in corn-husking and cider-pressing, in house-raising, shooting matches, and Christmas sports, all of which were times or occasions of social gatherings, and were enjoyed to the full. The inns were poor, but their deficiencies were made up by the hospitality of the people, at whose homes every traveller was sure of a welcome.

In the rural districts, the condition of education was wretched, only the barest rudiments being taught, and those badly and for small fees. There was little learning, less order, and much whipping in the schools everywhere. In the towns the case was somewhat better, and in Philadelphia a public school was opened in 1689; and in 1740 a plan for extended education was adopted, and charity schools were opened. In 1755 a college was added, which was well attended and became the foundation of the great university of Pennsylvania. Philadelphia also, greatly through the influence of Franklin, became noted for literature, arts, and sciences, and was a center of more literary activity than any place except Boston. Newspapers were published, and the city had two public libraries; a post office was early established, and here originated the postal system of Franklin. The style of living from the first was plain, but in every way most comfortable, but at a later date luxury in dress and habits appeared as prosperity and wealth increased. The general intelligence and force of character which marked the leading colonists of Virginia and Massachusetts were lacking in Pennsylvania, as they were in the middle provinces. The people, as a whole, were conservative and slow in action, and were not prompt to come forward in the work of the Revolution.

New Jersey, with its low, flat country, and shut in by the great provinces of New York and Pennsylvania, had, from the outset, little to check its growth. Its population, which was about 100,000 at the Revolution, with but few negroes, was mainly of English stock, with some Quakers and Scotch Presbyterians. The chief occupation was farming. Social life was simple, and the modes of living plain. Paupers and criminals were few, and thefts and robberies uncommon. Except in the case of some wealthy and gentlemen farmers, the houses were plain, the poorest farmers living well and their children finding ready employment. There were few amusements, the Puritan views having great influence. The professions, though their numbers were small, were respectable, and their members active and influential. The Church of England had a nominal but no real establishment. Its members were but a fraction of the population. The energetic and powerful sects were the Scotch Presbyterians and the New England Congregationalists, their ministers being active and earnest, and many of them men of learning.

THE ALLEGHANY MOUNTAINS

Through these two denominations the interests of education were greatly advanced, the towns taxing themselves for the support of teachers, and a college being founded in 1746 which grew to be the present university at Princeton. The professions of law and medicine included men of character and ability. The early system of courts was simple, one of the early governors, it is said, sitting on a stump in the meadow while he gave his decisions; but afterwards, courts of various grades were established, and the administration of justice became more dignified as well as efficient. The government, at first proprietary, and then transferred to the crown, was much like that of the ordinary royal government in the colonies, and there was the usual jealousy of the governor which was common to all the colonies. As a whole the people were conservative, thrifty and peaceable, being saved by their situation from the evils of the Indian and French wars. They were pure in race, and partook socially and politically of the traits and qualities which marked New England and Pennsylvania.

A COAST SCENE.

New York was founded by the Dutch only for trade. At the time of the Revolution the population of the province was about 170,000, of whom 20,000 were negroes. The whites were mostly descendants of the original settlers, but many New Englanders had come in, and a large number of French Huguenots had, in 1652, added greatly to the numbers in the city of New York. The chief staples of the colony were farm products, and the trade in furs with the Indians was extensive and profitable. The annual imports and exports were nearly a million pounds in value, and employed some five hundred vessels. There were few manufactures, but with its rich soil and the extensive and growing trade the province was greatly prospered. The French war brought heavy debt and burdensome taxation.

At the beginning of the eighteenth century, the condition of both the bench and bar was very bad, the chief justice having little knowledge of law, and the lawyers being often of scandalous character; and even at the Revolution matters were little better, trained lawyers being very few. The profession of medicine was even worse than that of law, but in 1776 a medical school was founded, and the profession began to attract men

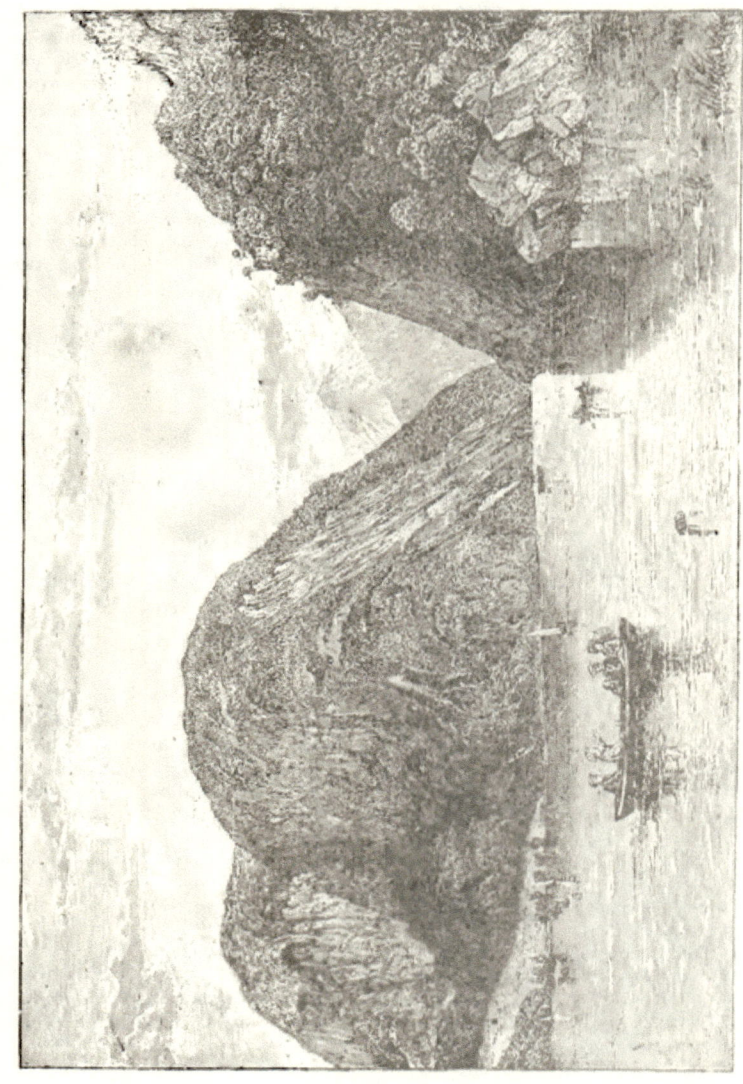

ROGER'S SLIDE, LAKE GEORGE.

of character and ability. The clergy stood far higher in character and influence than the men in either of the other professions, and were for a long time the only learned men in the colony. The general policy under the Dutch rule was one of toleration, to which the Quakers and Roman Catholics were the only exception; but when the English came into power, the Episcopal was made the established church, taxing all for its support, though

A DUTCH HOUSEHOLD

it had but a small part of the population. At the Revolution the negroes were about a sixth of the population. They were mostly employed as domestic servants, and were properly clothed and fed. Crimes were rare, capital offences few, and for lesser offences there were the stocks, the pillory, and the whipping-post. Of pauperism there was even less than of crime, and the few paupers in town were sold at auction to those who would support them for their labor. Education was as general and as good as in the other middle provinces, and better than in those of the South. The best schools were in the Long Island towns and in New York, and were kept some nine months in the year, and in the middle of the eighteenth century, Kings College (now Columbia) was established in New York.

The trading habits of the people drew men of all nations to New York, so that even in the seventeenth century sixteen languages were spoken in the province, but one and all gave way before the English. Besides the social distinctions caused by wealth, there was in New York an upper class, stronger and better defined than in any of the northern provinces, and reminding one of the ruling class in Virginia. It was composed of the proprietors of the large landed estates, or manors, who, in many cases, were entitled

EARLY SETTLERS ASCENDING THE HUDSON.

to representation in the Assembly, and to many feudal privileges which gave them a position more like that of the Old World nobility than any one else in the American colonies. Most of these manors descended, without will, to the eldest sons, and the influence of their families outside of the town of New York was immense. From the mouth of the Hudson to Albany, and far up the Mohawk Valley, the farmers were mostly Dutch, but further south the mixture was with other races. The farm buildings were small and their furniture plain, with abundance of good living. The only amusements were picnics in the woods, and corn huskings and spinning bees, and in the winter skating and coasting while in the southern parts and on Long Island there were tavern parties, bull-baitings, and horse races.

Albany was the great center of the fur trade for the northern colonies. In the earliest times each dwelling was a trading house with a store-room for furs in the second story. The houses were low, with peaked roofs, and gable ends to the street; and in the doorways the old Dutchmen passed much of their time peacefully, smoking and chatting about business and their neighbors. Their amusements were few; their women worked hard, and were neat and notable housewives. Life was quiet and uneventful, and the chief defect of the people was their grasping spirit in trade, which was such that it was said that even a Jew could not make a living among them.

New York became at an early day a great center for trade from all parts of the world, and many years before the Revolution the better streets were lighted, paved, and kept fairly clean. The houses, for the time, were large and handsome, the furniture of mahogany; china was rare, pewter and copper taking its place, but almost every family of standing had its massive silver. The society was mixed, and more polished and hospitable than in most of the colonies. The wealthy class was fashionable in dress and manners, their tables displaying great luxury, and their balls, concerts, private theatricals, and clubs furnishing their varied amusements. The Dutch had great liking for holidays, and made much of Christmas, New Years', Passover, Whit-suntide, St. Nicholas, and St. Valentine's days, and the English had their celebration of the gunpowder plot, and of the birthday and coronation of the king, when there were bonfires, feasting, and great rejoicing.

Literature in New York had a feebler existence and less influence than in any of the northern colonies. There were many good private libraries, but in most houses there were no books except of a religious kind, and the few booksellers had little, except bibles, prayer books and spelling books in their stock. As in most of the colonies, people married very young, and weddings were occasions of feasting and drinking. Funerals were attended with much pomp and ceremony, and funeral feasts were often marked by great expense and excessive indulgences.

In local politics there was more of real excitement than in any of the colonies. Candidates kept open houses and feasted their supporters, and on election days bands of half drunken electors went through the city, stopping at every house to demand votes. Questions as to the relations with the mother country were discussed and fought over with unusual violence. Impressment was a sore point; and in 1744 fishermen, who had suffered from the press-gang, burnt the boats of an English man-of-war. Matters of church policy kept up a constant struggle between the dissenters and the government. The Tory influence was strong and active, but the New England spirit was still more active and powerful, and took a most decided and efficient part in the steps that led to and carried on the Revolution.

Thus we come to the end or the middle group of the colonies. From the south, Virginia influence acted on Delaware and Pennsylvania; and on the north, New York was strongly influenced by the colonies of New England, where, as in Virginia, were some of the great social and political forces that aided so strongly in shaping the movement of the Revolution and the character of the future United States.

CHAPTER II.

THE FRENCH AND INDIAN WARS.

WITHIN a few years after the discoveries of Columbus and the Cabots, the Spanish, Dutch, and French also made discoveries, explorations and settlements in various parts of North America; and each of these nations, by right of discovery and possession, claimed parts of what is now the United States. The French, especially, were increasing in numbers on the St. Lawrence, and had established numerous missions, trading-posts and forts along the great lakes, and on down the Ohio river. And, finally, they claimed all the region from the source of the Mississippi to its mouth in the Gulf of Mexico, saying it was a part of New France. Between 1609 and 1616 Champlain had discovered and named Lakes Champlain and Huron. In 1668 the mission of St. Mary's was established on the outlet of Lake Superior. In 1673, Marquette, a Jesuit, and Joliet, a trader, went west to reach the Mississippi, and sailed down to the mouth of the Arkansas river. In 1679, La Salle sailed through the great lakes as far as Green Bay; and three years later he went down the Mississippi to the Gulf of Mexico, formally taking possession of the country for France, and giving it the name of Louisiana. These and other French settlements led, of course, to rival claims between the French and English settlers, and brought on the contests known as the French Wars. Of these there were four in number, those of 1689, or " King William's War"; of 1702, or "Queen Anne's War"; of 1745, or " King George's War"; and of 1754, the last and most important, known as the " French and Indian War," though all of them were French and Indian wars, as the Indians were greatly influenced by the French, and were generally their allies in the conflicts with the English.

In 1689, the war between England and France extended to the American colonies, and brought on the *first*, or what is known as King William's War, in which the Indians, who were allies of the French, fell upon the settlements in New Hampshire and Maine, destroying Dover, and carrying many people off as prisoners to Canada. They also captured Fort Pemaquid in Maine, and massacred most of the inhabitants of Salmon Falls and Casco Bay. Northern New York was also attacked by a war party of French and Indians from Montreal, who burned Schenectady, and killed or took captive many of the people.

In return the colonists resolved to invade Canada; and a fleet and army were sent from Boston to attack Quebec; while nine hundred men from New York and Connecticut marched against Montreal. Both expeditions, however, were failures, though, in 1690, Port Royal was captured by forces from Massachusetts under Sir William Phipps. The war was prolonged for several years, chiefly by hostile invasions and Indian conflicts, in which New England suffered much from the Indians, Haverhill being attacked by them

Quebec.

and forty persons being killed or taken captive. But in 1697 the war was ended by the treaty of Ryswick, leaving the various bounds and territories the same as before it began.

The *second*, or "Queen Anne's War," was brought on by the war between England on the one side and France and Spain on the other, in 1702, and this also involved the colonies. In it, as before, New England was the principal sufferer; the French from Canada, with their Indian allies, ravaging the frontier settlements, and in 1704 burning Deerfield, and slaughtering its inhabitants, or carrying them as prisoners into Canada. As in the previous war, the colonists, in 1707, invaded Acadia unsuccessfully, and again successfully in 1710, when Port Royal was taken, and Acadia, being conquered, became a British province under the name of Nova Scotia. In 1711, an English fleet, with New England forces, sailing to attack Quebec, was wrecked at the mouth of the St. Lawrence, and a column of troops which had started to attack Montreal, hearing of the failure of the fleet, abandoned the expedition, the whole plan being a failure. In 1713, this second French and Indian war was brought to an end by the Treaty of Utrecht.

The French, in the meantime, had been extending their settlements in the southwest. In 1699, Iberville made a settlement at Biloxi, in Mississippi, which, in 1702, he moved to Mobile, now in Alabama, making Mobile the capital of Louisiana. In 1712, Crozat established a colony at what is now Natchez. In 1716, Louisiana was put under control of the "Mississippi Company," to which Bienville, who was made governor, brought several thousand French settlers, and founding New Orleans, made it the capital. At the same time, the French were establishing themselves in the northwest, having built Fort Niagara in 1728; Crown Point, in 1731, and a post at Vincennes, soon afterwards; so that by 1750 they had control of all the water routes from the great lakes to the valley of the Mississippi, with more than sixty military stations between Lake Ontario and New Orleans.

This progress of the French, however, was interrupted in 1744 by the *third* French and Indian war, known as "King George's War," the only important event of which was the capture of Louisburg, a very strong fort, which controlled the entrance to the Gulf of St. Lawrence. A force of 3,200 men, under Sir William Pepperell, sailed from Boston in April, 1745, and when they were just ready for a combined land and naval attack, the fort was surrendered, June, 17, 1745. In 1748, this war was brought to a close by the treaty of Aix La Chappelle, when Louisburg was ceded back to the French.

The first three French wars had grown out of wars in Europe, in which, as colonies of Great Britain, the Americans were involved. But the *fourth* and last, the "French and Indian War," which was greater than all the others, grew out of the question whether the French or English should be supreme on the American continent. The former had the grand design of forming a French empire in the rich territory watered by the St. Lawrence, the great lakes, and the Mississippi river, hoping to confine the English to the Atlantic coast, while they were intending to hold all west of the Alleghanies, and so to control the rich traffic with the Indians. They claimed by the right of French discovery and settlement; while the English claimed by the right of the discovery by the Cabots.

Up to 1752, the English had made no settlements west of the Alleghanies, but in that year the Ohio Company, under a grant from the King, established a trading-post on the Monongahela. The French at once made prisoners of the traders, and began building their own forts on the disputed territory. Washington, though only twenty-one years old, but even then spoken of as a person of distinction, was sent by direction of the British government to demand an explanation of the outrages. The answer to the demand was a letter from the French commandant, refusing to withdraw the French from their position. And as this reply was unsatisfactory, in 1754 a regiment was sent to the disputed territory, under Colonel Frye, with Washington as second in command. While these troops were on their way, the French had driven off the English and completed their fort, which they named Du Quesne. Washington, hastening forward, met the French at Great Meadows, and attacked and defeated them, and there built a fort called "Fort Necessity." While here, Colonel Frye died, and Washington became

WASHINGTON'S ATTACK ON THE FRENCH.

chief commander. His fort being attacked by a strong body of French, he was compelled to surrender, but was allowed, with his troops, to go back to Virginia.

The struggle being thus commenced, both France and England prepared for war, and the colonies, acting with England, did the same. Delegates from the various colonies met at Albany, and by a treaty of peace secured the alliance of the Six Nations, or Iroquois. In the spring of 1755, the British government sent out two regiments, under General Braddock as commander-in-chief, and he, with the colonial governors, planned three campaigns: one, under Braddock, against Fort Du Quesne; a second, under Shirley, against Fort Niagara, and a third against the fort at Crown Point, on Lake Champlain. Nearly all the colonies raised troops and voted money and supplies for these campaigns. While these preparations were going on, it was determined to attack the French in Nova Scotia, including Acadia, which was now a British province and ruled by an English governor. The French community, a peaceful, happy and innocent people, wished to remain neutral during the war; but the English, fearing that they might be led to side with the French, sent an expedition and captured the two forts at the head of the Bay of Funday, and kidnapping the French settlers to the number of 7,000, forced them on board ships and exiled them to the various colonies. It was a most sad and cruelly barbarous deed, which no plea of necessity could ever justify, and which brought great suffering to the poor Acadians.

Braddock's column of 2,500 troops marched to attack Fort Du Quesne, but when some ten miles from it they were attacked in the woods by the French and Indians, and the whole column was thrown into confusion and fled, and Braddock himself was killed. Washington, who was his aid-de-camp, with his little band of Virginians, covered the retreat, and the expedition was given up, the whole force returning to Philadelphia. The second column, under Shirley, marched as far as Oswego, where a fort was built; but storms, sickness, and the desertion of the Indians caused the enterprise to be abandoned. The third column, under Johnson, after building Fort Edward on the Hudson, moved to Lake George, and after a skirmish of part of his forces with the French, in which the former were defeated, the main bodies joined battle, and the French, under Dieskau, were badly beaten, and he was taken prisoner in the battle of Lake George. Not feeling strong enough to attack Crown Point, Johnson built and garrisoned Fort William Henry, and then disbanded his forces.

In 1756, Lord Loudon was sent from England as commander of the English forces, and the Marquis of Montcalm was made successor of Dieskau. In August, Montcalm captured the fort at Oswego, taking 1,400 prisoners and a quantity of stores, and then returned to Canada, and as a result of this heavy loss, the English plans of campaign for the year were given up. In July, 1757, Montcalm besieged Fort William Henry, which was defended by 2,000 troops. General Webb, with 4,000 troops, was at Fort Edward, only fifteen miles off, but as he sent no assistance, Fort William Henry was surrendered August 9th, and a number of prisoners were killed in cold blood by the Indian allies of the French.

In 1758, that great man, William Pitt, was at the head of colonial affairs; and determining to carry on the war with vigor, he sent Abercrombie to take the place of Loudon, with an army of 22,000 regular troops, and 28,000 of the colonial forces; and three expeditions were planned by Abercrombie; one against Louisburg, one against Ticonderoga and Crown Point, and one against Fort Du Quesne. In June, the English, with a large fleet and 12,000 troops under General Amherst, attacked Louisburg, which, after a vigorous resistance, was obliged to surrender, and the whole of Cape Breton Island, with 6,000 prisoners and a large amount of ammunition was taken. In the second expedition, Abercrombie led 15,000 men against Ticonderoga, which was held by Montcalm with 4,000 troops, but he was forced to retreat, and his place was supplied by General Amherst. The capture of Fort Frontenac was the only success of this expedition. The third movement of the campaign against Fort Du Quesne, in

WOLFE'S COVE.

November, under General Forbes, with 9,000 troops, was successful. The French abandoned the fort, and the name was changed to Fort Pitt, now Pittsburg.

The great object of the next campaign, in 1759, was the capture of Quebec, though operations were planned against Fort Niagara, and also against Ticonderoga and Crown Point. For the attack on Quebec, General Wolfe, with a fleet carrying 8,000 troops, sailed up the St. Lawrence to Orleans Island, a few miles below the city, and landing, began preparations for an attack. This move led Montcalm to weaken the garrisons at Ticonderoga and Crown Point, the result of which was that Amherst

NIGHT ATTACK ON COLONIAL SCHOONER.

captured Ticonderoga in July, and Crown Point in August, and Johnson took Fort
Niagara in July. Wolfe, after some preliminary movements, which were unsuccessful,
scaled the "Heights of Abraham," where, on the 13th of September, was fought the
battle which decided the war. Wolfe, though twice wounded, still led on his troops, till,
by a third wound, he was killed, as Montcalm also was. After hours of stubborn
fighting, the English carried all before them, and five days afterward, Quebec

was surrendered, and in
September of the next year,
Montcalm was also taken,
and soon all Canada was
given up, thus closing the
contest in America for English supremacy in 1760.

The war between France
and England still continued
elsewhere till 1763, and
through these three years
the Indians kept up their
hostility, especially in the

ATTACK ON THE FORT AT PRESQUE ISLE.

northwest, where all the forts west of Oswego, except Fort Niagara, Fort Pitt, and Detroit, were captured by them, and hundreds of persons were massacred or driven from their homes.

The seige of Detroit was marked by many thrilling occurrences. One of the schooners was returning from Niagara with despatches, having a crew of only a dozen men, when, on the night of August 4th, she was attacked in the Detroit river by fully three hundred Indians, who were not discovered until they were climbing the sides of the vessel. Rushing to the gunwales, the crew fought desperately with spears and hatchets; but the savages could not be beaten back. The mate, seeing that all was lost, shouted an order to fire the magazine and blow up the boat. Several Indians understood the command, and the next moment the entire party had leaped overboard and were swimming frantically for shore. The captain was killed and several of the crew disabled.

There was also hard fighting at Fort Presque Isle, which stood near the present site of Erie, Pa., and was under the command of Ensign Christie, with a courageous garrison. Early on June 15th, it was surrounded by two hundred Indians, most of them from the neighborhood of Detroit. The garrison immediately withdrew to the block-house, prepared to fight as long as the last hope remained. Burning arrows rained upon the roof, which repeatedly caught fire, but was often extinguished by the cool daring of the soldiers. The assailants threw up a rude but strong breastwork on the ridge commanding the fort, and for two days and a half the desperate fight continued. A number of the Indians, with unusual daring, attempted to run from behind their breastworks and shelter themselves close to the walls of the fort, but the watchful garrison picked off every one of them.

In the meantime, they began a mine, and, there being no way of checking them, they succeeded in reaching and firing the house of the commanding officer. The smoke and heat almost stifled the garrison, but they held out bravely, and whenever they could catch sight of a dusky figure, they riddled it with bullets. All that night and through the next day the heroes fought and labored with unsurpassed courage. Meanwhile, the assailants pushed their mining operations until the sound of their digging was heard under the edge of the block-house itself. Further resistance could avail nothing. Ensign Christie agreed to surrender under pledge that he and his exhausted men should be allowed to depart unmolested. The promise was given, but broken. All were bound and taken as prisoners to Pontiac's camp.

The colonists, at length, rose in force and subdued the savages. The war between France and England was ended by the "Treaty of Paris" in 1763, when France gave up to England all her American possessions east of the Mississippi, except New Orleans, as she gave those west of the Mississippi to Spain; and Spain gave Florida to England in exchange for Havana, which England had taken in 1762. These various conflicts resulted in the full establishment of English supremacy over North America as then known.

MEETING OF WASHINGTON AND ROCHAMBEAU.

PERIOD IV.

CHAPTER I.

CAUSES OF THE REVOLUTION.

WHEN the question is asked, "What led the colonies to revolution and so to independence of Great Britain?" the usual answer is, that it was the attempt of England to impose taxes on them without their consent or representation. This, however, is but part of the truth. The imposition of taxes, and the passage of unjust and oppressive laws, were the *occasion* of the uprising of the colonies; but the *causes* of it are to be found far back in English history, and in the character and training of the colonists themselves.

Before the thirteenth century, and as influenced by the Norman invasion, the idea of personal rights had found lodgement in the minds and hearts of the English people. And in the Magna Charta, wrested by the Barons from King John at Runnymede in 1215, and still more in the Barons' War in 1263–67, and in the meeting of the first House of Commons in 1265, we see the early germs of that personal and political freedom which has been gradually but steadily growing to the present day.

The Protestant reformation was the world's recoil from arbitrary authority, and so the suggestion of individual and personal rights in the doctrines of Calvin, which were the outgrowth of that reformation, was generally received by the early settlers, and teaching, as they did, the individuality of man before God, they impressed the idea of personal responsibility, and with this came the sense of personal rights. "In this view," says Bancroft, "Calvin held a foremost rank among the champions of modern democracy," and "the promulgation of his theology was one of the longest steps that mankind have taken toward personal freedom." Ranke says of him, in reference to his views of personal responsibility, "We may consider him the founder of the free States of North America, as it was his doctrine that shaped the men who left home and country to preserve their religious freedom in the wilds of America." In the religious views of the Puritans was the foundation of their political principles; and "the rights of Englishmen" was an expression full of meaning to the early settlers of the colonies.

So early as 1638, Mr. Hooker, in opening the session of the general court, in a sermon of wonderful power, maintained "that the foundation of authority is laid in the

free consent of the people," and in the following year,
the freemen, assembled at Hartford, adopted a written
constitution which acknowledged no
government outside of Connecticut
itself. This was the first written constitution known to history, and the first
that created a government, "marking
the beginnings of American democracy,
of which Thomas Hooker, more than
any other man, deserves to be called the
father." In it "all the attributes of
sovereignty, not expressly granted to the
general court, remained, as of original
right, in the towns." In the same spirit
the elder Winthrop said, that "The
safety of the commonwealth was the supreme law, and
if, in the interests of that safety, it should be found
necessary to renounce the authority of Parliament, the
colonists would be justified in doing so."

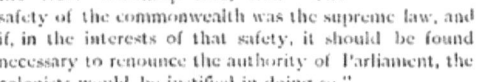

In all these things we find the germ idea of personal
independence, and of allowing no government without consent
and representation by the people, an idea to which the discussions of the
early town meetings of New England and the colonial legislatures gave the
stability of a principle intelligently understood and firmly held. It is true that
the colonists had various grievances of which they reasonably complained, such
as unsatisfactory charters, bad governors, navigation laws, and trade regulations which
bore heavily on their industry and commerce. But in the very origin of the colonies, and
in the spirit which the colonists brought with them from England, were the elements of
personal independence and future freedom. They had left their homes for the New
World, not only in the spirit of self-reliance and independent enterprise, but with a
knowledge of their personal and political rights, and from the high and strong motives
of civil and religious liberty. And in opposing the arbitrary acts of the English
authorities, and in managing the affairs of the early settlements, they were ever ready to
assert their right to the "liberties of Englishmen." More than once they drove out or
imprisoned the royal governors, and refused the supplies they demanded. When a clerk
of the Virginia Council had betrayed their secrets, they cut off his ears, and sent him to
the pillory, and when the charters of the colonies were recalled, in many cases the
demand was refused or evaded, and in Connecticut, at the demand of Andros, the charter
was brought in and laid upon the table, yet before it could be taken, the lights were
suddenly blown out and it was spirited away and hidden in the hollow of the tree, which
for a hundred and seventy years was known through New England as the famous
"Charter Oak."

The spirit of freedom had, from the first, been steadily growing in the colonies, and
they insisted on the right of controlling their own internal affairs. They admitted that
England might regulate commerce, as in the "Navigation Acts," but denied her right to
tax the colonies without their consent. But in 1764 Parliament asserted its right of

taxation, and in the following year passed the "Stamp Act," by which all deeds, notes, bills and other legal documents had to be on stamped paper which the British revenue officers were to furnish at fixed rates. The news of the passage of this Act reached America in April, 1765, and at once roused both indignation and alarm. The legislature of Virginia, which was in session, led by the eloquent Patrick Henry and his able associates, passed resolutions which claimed for the people all the rights of British subjects, and their action was everywhere discussed, and in all the other colonies had great effect. Associations called "Sons of Liberty" were formed. The stamps that came from England were unpacked, or seized and burned; the stamp officers were compelled to resign; and the Act itself was everywhere denounced, and taxation without representation was boldly declared to be tyranny. The people were everywhere aroused. The merchants agreed to import no more goods from Great Britain till the Stamp Act was repealed. The people denied themselves all luxuries from England, and the trade with that country was almost entirely stopped. The very children in the streets caught the spirit of the times, and learned the cry " Liberty, property, and no stamps!"

Massachusetts, at the suggestion of that sterling patriot, Samuel Adams, proposed the calling of a convention or congress from all the colonies, and it met in New York, October 7, 1765, a month before the Stamp Act was to have gone into effect. Nine colonies were represented in it by twenty-eight delegates. After full deliberation, the Congress agreed on a statement of grievances and a declaration of rights, claiming in strong terms the right of being free from all taxes not laid, or assented to, by themselves, and a petition on the subject was sent to the king and Parliament; and these proceedings were heartily and strongly approved by the various colonial Assemblies.

When the first of November, the day fixed for the Stamp Act to take effect, came, the stamp officers had been compelled to resign, and not a stamp was anywhere to be seen. The colonists, by their united and firm stand, had made the law of no effect. The great question now was, "would England endeavor, by force, to compel the colonies to obedience?" It did not, for several reasons. *First*, some of her ablest statesmen, among whom were William Pitt and Edmund Burke, took sides with the colonies, believing them to be right; and, *second*, because the British merchants, finding their business greatly suffering from the loss of the American trade, petitioned Parliament for the repeal of the Stamp Act; and it was accordingly repealed, February 22, 1766. All now might have been well, but that Parliament, while repealing the Stamp Act, passed another bill asserting its supreme power over the colonies in all things, which of course implied the right of taxation. And they went on to lay taxes in the shape of import duties on various articles, among which was tea. Other Acts also remained, and among them the Act requiring quarters to be provided for the English troops, which the colonists refused to do.

When the news of these measures reached America the ill-feeling broke out afresh, and the press, the pulpit, and the legislatures everywhere denounced the Acts of Parliament. In Boston, a sloop belonging to John Hancock being seized for the evasion of the revenue laws, the seizure resulted in a riot; and in New York, a conflict took place between the British troops and the "Sons of Liberty," in which one citizen was killed, and several were wounded, January 17, 1770, this being the first blood that was shed in the rising revolution. In Boston, on March 5th, the soldiers, being provoked by the taunts and jeers of the crowd, fired upon them and killed three persons and wounded several others. This was called the Boston massacre, and it raised tremendous excitement, not only in that region but through all the colonies.

The attempt to raise a revenue by taxes having failed, Parliament took off the duty on most articles, but to assert and carry out the principle that they had a right to tax the colonies, they still kept the tax on tea. The tax was but trifling, only three pence on the pound, and it was thought that to so small a duty the Americans would not object; but it was not the amount, but the principle to which they objected, and when the tea arrived at various ports, it was either sent back or locked up. When a cargo of tea reached Boston, the people would not allow it to land, and the governor would not allow

BUILDING IN BOSTON WHERE THE TEA PLOT IS SUPPOSED TO HAVE BEEN HATCHED.

it to be sent back; and the great question as to what should be done was publicly discussed in a great gathering of seven thousand men. And, as night came on, Samuel Adams, rising in the dimly lighted church, said solemnly, "This meeting can do nothing more to save the country." As arranged beforehand, at once there was a wild war-whoop outside, and a band of men, disguised as Indians, rushed to and boarded the ships, and emptied the entire cargo of tea into Boston Harbor, December 16, 1773. And in every colony the news of this bold and decisive act was welcomed with the warmest approval.

When the news of these doings reached England, the king and people were alike determined to punish the rebellious colonists, and Parliament passed what was called "The Boston Port Bill," which closed the port of Boston, and they sent General Gage as civil governor with four regiments to carry out the provisions of that bill, and to arrest

BUILDING IN PHILADELPHIA WHERE THE FIRST CONGRESSES WERE HELD.

and bring to trial the patriot leaders, of whom Samuel Adams was the foremost. They also passed a second Act, called "The Charter Act," annulling the charter of Massachusetts, forbidding the town meetings and public gatherings, a measure far graver and more offensive than the Port Bill, and one that struck at the political life of every colony alike. They also transferred the trial of certain officers from the colonies to

England, provided for quartering the troops in Boston, and so changed the borders of the old colonies as to threaten the territories of Virginia and Pennsylvania, thus rousing the anger of all the colonies alike.

Now, for the first time, the colonies began to think of armed resistance, but wisely seeking mutual consultation, the first Continental Congress was called, and met in Philadelphia, September 5, 1774. At the north, New York moved first, led by the wise counsel of John Jay and his associates; and at the south, Virginia, aroused by the eloquence of such patriots as Patrick Henry and Richard Henry Lee, voted for the Congress; and this action of the great southern province brought in all the other southern provinces, except Georgia, whose governor prevented the election of delegates. Of this Congress, Peyton Randolph, of Virginia, was chosen president, and Charles Thomson, secretary. Among its members were George Washington, Patrick Henry, John and Samuel Adams, John Jay, Christopher Gadsen, and John Rutledge. The Congress voted to sustain Massachusetts in her resistance to England; signed an agreement not to export or import to or from England; passed resolutions against the slave trade; appointed a second Congress; set forth to the world a declaration of rights, and prepared addresses both to the king and the people of Great Britain.

The issues involving the right of taxation, and the question of retaining the charters were firmly and strongly met, and the way was fairly open for the adjustment of all difficulty with England if that country had but acted with wisdom. But the king and his ministers, sustained by the Parliament, rejected the proposals of Congress. Massachusetts was declared to be in rebellion, and preparations were made for war. Lord Howe was sent out with a fleet, and made proposals of compromise which were rejected. Gage attempted to seize the public stores at Salem, but was prevented from doing it. Dunsmore, who had seized powder in Virginia, was forced by the people, led by Patrick Henry, to give it up. In September, 1774, Gage fortified Boston Neck, and seized the ammunition and stores in the arsenals at Cambridge and Charlestown. The "Minute Men" were organized in Massachusetts, as a "Committee of Safety," under John Hancock. Washington organized the militia of Virginia. And Patrick Henry, reviewing the situation of the colonies, and their duty to themselves and their principles, had declared in thunder tones, "We must fight! I repeat it, sir, we must fight!"

CHAPTER II.

THE WAR OF THE REVOLUTION.

IN April, 1775, when Parliament had declared the colonies were in rebellion, Gates had sent some of his troops to Concord to seize some military supplies there, and on their way, at Lexington, they found a small body of militia, whom the English officer commanded as "rebels" to disperse. As the Americans did not obey, he ordered his soldiers to fire. They did so, and eight Americans were killed and several wounded, while the others, without firing, dispersed. The British marched on and destroyed the stores at Concord. But at once the militia around Concord and Lexington hastily gathered, and attacked the British troops as they were returning, killing two and wounding several; and as the British, after firing, moved on, the "Minute Men" poured in their deadly fire from the woods and rocks and fences, till the retreat became a rout, and the whole British force would have been destroyed but for reinforcements sent to their aid, under the cover of which they made their way to Charlestown as a place of safety, having lost, in killed and wounded, about two hundred and eighty, while the loss of the Americans was only ninety.

The news spread like wildfire. From every part of New England the militia hastened to Boston, and the King's army was soon besieged by twenty thousand men, and fortifications were raised confining the British to the Boston peninsula. In May, the bold and hardy Vermonters, under Ethan Allen, surprised and captured Ticonderoga and Crown Point, securing military stores of great value to the Americans. In June, the leaders of the forces around Boston, anticipating the supposed plans of the British, took possession of the high grounds near Charlestown, thus commanding Boston and the shipping in the harbor. On the night of the 16th, Colonel Prescott, with about a thousand men, crossed the Charlestown Neck, and between midnight and sunrise threw up an earthwork on Breed's Hill. At day-break, the British men-of-war in the harbor opened fire on the redoubt, and the batteries on Copp's Hill followed; and by noon some three thousand English troops, under General Howe, were on their way to storm the rude earthworks, behind which were the American forces, some fifteen hundred in number.

In the afternoon the battle of Bunker Hill began. Setting fire to Charlestown, and under cover of a heavy cannonade, the British advanced against the intrenchments. Twice they were driven back with slaughter, mowed down by the heavy and sure fire of the Americans. Rallying a third time with difficulty, they were received with another deadly volley, but the powder of the Americans being exhausted, their fire slackened and ceased. Having no bayonets, the Americans fought with clubbed muskets, yielding inch by inch, till at last Prescott gave the word to retreat, when the Americans fell back, leaving the British in possession of the field. The loss of the English, in killed and wounded, was over a thousand, of whom eighty-three were officers, while the American loss was less than five hundred. Covered by the rude intrenchments, the colonists had twice repulsed with slaughter the English troops, fully equipped and thoroughly disciplined as they were. They had completely crippled Gage, and the British, as the result of the conflict, had merely the ground on which they stood. The idea that the Americans would not fight was at an end, and the defeat of Bunker Hill was of more value to the colonists than many victories. On the ground where the hottest of the battle was fought, a granite monument 220 feet in height has been erected, at a cost of $100,000. This sum was raised by popular subscription. The corner-stone was laid by Lafayette, on his visit to this country in 1825. The monument was completed in 1842, and at its dedication Daniel Webster delivered one of his best addresses.

Before the battle of Bunker Hill, the second Continental Congress had met in Philadelphia, May 10, 1775. It took control of the general government of the now United States; voted to raise an army of twenty

THE MONUMENT ON BUNKER HILL.

thousand men; authorized the issue of $3,000,000 of paper money, and appointed George Washington commander-in-chief of the continental army. On the third of July, he took command at Cambridge, where he found some 14,000 militia, brave and patriotic, but poorly armed and unorganized, and wanting in almost everything needful for war. In the face of almost inconceivable difficulties, he gave order and unity and strength to his forces, and though winter set in with great severity, he moved steadily onward, drawing his lines closer and closer around Boston, till, at last, from Dorchester Heights the bombardment began, and the British, who had come in the full confidence of victory, were compelled to evacuate Boston, which was entered by American troops March 17, 1776.

In the meantime, the excitement had spread through the other colonies, in every one of which the power of the royal governors was destroyed; and in North Carolina, the patriots met at Charleston in May, 1775, and issued the celebrated "Mecklenburg

STATUE OF JEFFERSON.

Declaration," declaring their independence of Great Britain, thus, as some suppose, anticipating the well known Declaration of Independence. In carrying on the war, the invasion of Canada was planned, and St. Johns, and then Montreal was taken in November. An attack was also made on Quebec, which was unsuccessful, and in it the gallant Montgomery was killed, and Benedict Arnold was wounded. As spring advanced, the British forces were increased, and the American forces were driven back, so that the Canada invasion was a failure.

THE PRISON SHIP "JERSEY."

Meanwhile, the British government was preparing to push hostilities with force. Their army was raised to over 40,000 men, including some 17,000 mercenary Hessians, hired from the petty German princes, and preparations were made to assail the colonies at various points. The first attack was upon Charleston, South Carolina, the harbor of which was protected by a rude fort, garrisoned by 400 men under Colonel Moultrie. General Gadsden defended the approach by land. The attack was made by the British fleet, under Sir Peter Parker, and for twelve hours they poured their shot and shell upon the fort, but in vain; while the land attack, led by Clinton and Cornwallis, was also repulsed, the attack being a complete failure and the British losses so severe that their plan of capture was abandoned, and their forces returned to New York. This victory, at Charleston, gave safety to the whole southern coast.

In the early history of the difficulties with the mother country, the colonists had still been loyal to England, but the opening of the war changed all this, and though there were numerous Tories in the colonies the great body of the people were now for entire independence of Great Britain. Accordingly, on the 7th of June, 1776, Richard Henry Lee, of Virginia, offered in Congress the resolution, which was seconded by John Adams, that "The United Colonies are, and ought to be, free and independent States." This resolution was adopted on the 2d of July, and a committee was appointed to prepare a "Declaration of Independence." This was written by Thomas Jefferson, and was adopted July 4, 1776, so that the thirteen colonies became the United States of America.

With the declaration of independence the colonial system came to an end, and the colonies became States. But six dreary years of warfare were to pass before actual independence was achieved.

Washington at this time had moved his forces from Massachusetts to New York, where Howe, reinforced by Clinton, had 30,000 troops. Howe's plan was to take Brooklyn, and then to capture New York; and at the end of August the British landed on Long Island, which was defended by General Putnam, with 5,000 men. In the battle of Long Island, August 27th, the Americans were defeated with heavy loss, after which they retreated to the fort at Brooklyn, and while the British delayed attacking them, Washington, with great skill, and under cover of a fog at night, withdrew his forces to New York; and later, in September, evacuated that city and moved to Harlem, on the way to which they had a skirmish with Howe's troops, after which Washington fell back to a strong position on North Castle Heights, and Howe retraced his steps, taking Fort Washington, while Fort Lee being found untenable, the Hudson was open to the British.

Leaving Lee to hold the position at North Castle, Washington retreated to New Jersey, and on the 8th of December crossed the Delaware. The British, under Cornwallis, followed and took possession of New Brunswick, Trenton and Princeton. By desertion, and by the expiration of the term of service, the American army was now reduced to about 3,000, and Charles Lee, who was afterward proved to be a traitor, disobeying orders, failed to bring his forces to Washington's aid, and luckily was himself captured by the British. Sullivan, who succeeded Lee, joined Washington on the 20th of December. The British forces were approaching in strength, the army was greatly weakened, New Jersey and Pennsylvania were full of panic and fear; and Congress, in alarm, had left Philadelphia. Many of the loyalists were coming in and

WASHINGTON CROSSING THE DELAWARE.—(*From a painting by Lutz.*)

accepting the pardon offered by Howe, and the prospect for the future was dark and discouraging. It was the supreme moment of the Revolution, and the fate of the colonies seemed trembling in the balance. The great conflict, with all its tremendous issues, was centered on one man, and he at the head of a small, dispirited and neglected army.

Washington saw and felt the full gravity of the situation, and knew that for moral effect, far more than for any military gain, a victory must be won. Crossing the Delaware on Christmas night, he fell unexpectedly on a body of 1,500 Hessians, at Trenton, capturing 1,000 men, with guns, cannon and flags, while he lost but four men. This bold and decisive stroke encouraged the army greatly, and it was soon increased in numbers and moved over the river to Trenton. Here Cornwallis was preparing to attack them, when Washington, leaving his fires burning, marched back by another road, in the very direction by which Cornwallis had just come, and entering Princeton, routed the regiments left there by Cornwallis, thus regaining nearly the whole of New Jersey, and confining the British to New Brunswick and Amboy. He then marched to Morristown, and both armies, in these positions, went into winter quarters. On December 8th of this year, the British fleet, under Sir Peter Parker, took possession of the island of Rhode Island, and by military force held that State.

In 1777, there were several raids and surprises on both sides, the British burning Danbury, in Connecticut, but being driven back to their vessels with loss; and the American militia attacking the British at Sag Harbor, burning several of their ships and destroying supplies. But the most important and encouraging event was the despatch of supplies from France, through the efforts of Beaumarchais, and with the connivance of the French government.

During the winter, Washington had greatly recruited his army, and had now some 10,000 men. About the end of July, the English army and fleet sailed from New York for Chesapeake Bay and landed at Elkton, intending to march from there to Philadelphia, and Washington, hastening south to meet them was joined by Lafayette, De Kalb, and a few other French officers. The opposing forces soon met at the river Brandywine, but the Americans, under Sullivan and Wayne, were repulsed, and were forced to retreat; and a few days later, Wayne's command was surprised at Paoli, and suffered severely. The British pressed on. The news of their advance compelled Congress to flee from Philadelphia to Lancaster, and afterwards to York, and on the 20th of August, Howe, with his forces took possession of the city.

The English forces were now somewhat divided, some troops having been sent against the forts on the Delaware, Cornwallis being in Philadelphia, and the main body being at Germantown. Here they were attacked by Washington, but at the Chew house, which was occupied by the enemy, he met with stubborn resistance, and was repulsed with heavy loss. The British now held Philadelphia, but as the Delaware was not open to them, owing to Forts Mifflin and Mercer at its mouth, in October, they besieged these forts, their first attack being repulsed with heavy loss, but their next effort, aided by the fleet, being successful, so that their vessels now sailed to Philadelphia. After some heavy skirmishing, in which the advantage was with the Americans, both armies went into winter quarters, the British in Philadelphia, and Washington, with his bare-footed, ragged and suffering soldiers, at Valley Forge.

ATTACK ON CHEW'S HOUSE.

While Washington, though defeated, had still been holding the enemy in check in Pennsylvania, the Americans had a series of brilliant successes in the north, which aided greatly in deciding the fate of the Revolution. Burgoyne, with 7,000 regular troops from Europe, and a large body of Indians, and with heavy artillery, invaded northern New York from Canada, expecting Clinton from below to join him, so that, holding the Hudson river, he might cut off New England from the other colonies. He besieged Ticonderoga, which he took on the 2d of July, and forced Schuyler to abandon Fort Edward and fall back to the mouth of the Mohawk, and though Washington sent troops, including Morgan and his Virginia riflemen, to aid Schuyler, the whole country was alarmed at Burgoyne's rapid success.

The alarm was most fortunate, for it aroused the people to arms. Burgoyne was delayed after his victories over Schuyler, by the latter having torn up bridges and obstructed the roads, so that the tide began turning against him. Determined, however, to strike right and left, as well as in front, he sent Colonel Bawm with 500 men to capture a quantity of stores at Bennington, but the forces sent were signally defeated by John Stark with 400 "Green Mountain Boys" and the New Hampshire militia; and a fresh body of the British that came up were also defeated by Colonel Warren, the English loss being 700 men while the Americans lost less than 100. Burgoyne had also sent a body of troops under St. Leger to capture Fort Schuyler (now Rome), and then to join him at Albany; but St. Leger was forced to retreat into Canada, and Burgoyne never got to Albany, but remained at Fort Edward, while the American army was at the mouth of the Mohawk.

In August, the American forces were put under the command of Gates, who moved to Stillwater, where they were attacked by the British on the 19th of September, and as this engagement was not decisive, another took place on the 7th of October, in which the Americans had the advantage, and Burgoyne attempted to retreat to Fort Edward. The Americans, however, advanced so rapidly, that they cut off his retreat, and surrounded his forces at Saratoga, and Burgoyne was obliged to surrender his whole army, October 17, 1777, over 5,000 men laying down their arms, and being sent as prisoners to Boston.

These battles of New York, which deservedly take rank among the decisive battles of the world, led to three important results. The first was a wretched intrigue, known as the "Conway Cabal," to supersede Washington and put Gates at the head of the armies. While Washington was struggling through the dreary winter at Valley Forge, overcoming every kind of obstacle, encouraging and training the army, and devoting himself entirely to the welfare of the country, this miserable faction was at work against him, and not without hope of success, for, dazzled by the northern victories, Congress did not comprehend the great services of Washington, even in defeat. But the whole conspiracy came to light and was crushed and ruined by the overwhelming popular support of Washington. Gates was sent to the north; Mifflin put on trial for mismanagement, and Conway was forced to resign, his place being filled by Baron Steuben, who did excellent work in discipline and organization of the troops. The second result of Burgoyne's surrender, was the recognition of the colonies by France, on the 6th of February, 1778, and a treaty of alliance with that power, brought about by Franklin, and ratified by Congress in May of the same year. The third result was the offer of Lord North to abandon the right of taxation and recognize Congress,

without yielding independence, while the opposition in Parliament were for making
peace at all hazards. But the king obstinately opposed the views of the latter, and
North's proposals, like all the rest of his policy, were too late.

In November, 1777, Congress adopted
the "Articles of Confederation," which were
to form the constitution or general government for the United States, when approved
by all the States. Before this there had been
various flags, one in Massachusetts, with a
field of white with a pine tree on it, and the
motto "An appeal to Heaven"; another

SURRENDER OF BURGOYNE.

with a rattlesnake coiled, and the motto "Don't tread on me" and still another, a union flag, with a red field, "The liberties of America" on one side, and "No Popery" on the other. But now the Stars and Stripes were adopted, at first with the intention of adding a new stripe for each new State, but as that would soon make the flag too large, the design as at present was adopted, of thirteen stripes for the original thirteen States, and a new star for each State that should be added.

In 1778, the British made an attempt to capture Lafayette, but were foiled. Besides Lafayette, Kosciusko and Pulaski, two Polish patriots, and two distinguished Germans, De Kalb and Steuben, had come over to serve

WASHINGTON REPROVING LEE AT MONMOUTH.

in the American cause, in which as able officers they rendered great service. In April, a French fleet, under Count D'Estaing, left for America, bringing 4,000 troops; and on its arrival, by Washington's advice, it sailed, in July, to Rhode Island to attack the British fleet, an American force, under Sullivan, being sent to co-operate in reducing

Newport. But a storm arising, so damaged the French vessels that they had to put into Boston for repairs, and Sullivan's force had to retire from Rhode Island. In June, the British army left Philadelphia for New York, and being followed by Washington, a battle took place on the 28th, at Monmouth, in which, owing to the bad conduct of Charles Lee, nothing was gained, and Lee was dismissed from the service.

No account of the battle of Monmouth is complete without the story of Molly Pitcher, who, we are told, was a powerful woman dressed in the skirts of her own sex and an artilleryman's cloak, cocked hat and feather. Molly's husband was a cannoneer who suffered so much from thirst during the fight that his wife was kept busy bringing him water from a neighboring spring. While thus engaged, she saw her husband fall. The officer ordered the gun removed, because, as he said, he could not fill the post with so brave a man as he had lost. Molly's patriotism outweighed her fears, and she asked to be allowed to take her husband's place. Her request was granted, and she handled the gun with such skill and courage that all who saw her were filled with admiration. Washington conferred on her the rank of lieutenant, and she was granted half-pay during life.

Clinton marched on to New York, and Washington following took up position at White Plains. In July, Wyoming, in Pennsylvania, was attacked by a force of Tories and Indians, the settlers massacred, their houses burned, and their beautiful valley left in desolation. In November, Cherry Valley, in New York, experienced the same dreadful fate.

Through the north, the gain on the whole was with the Americans, the British having been driven from New England. For two years the middle colonies had suffered the horrors of war with but little gain to the English, who, as they had so far failed at the north, determined to carry the war to the southern provinces. Late in the fall of 1778, Colonel Campbell landed in Georgia with 2,000 men, and surprising and capturing Robert Howe in command of the American forces, captured Savannah; and General Provost, coming with additional forces from Florida, Augusta was also captured, and Georgia restored to England. The Tories, who were strong and numerous at the south, sided with the English, but quite a body of these renegades marching to unite with the British army, were met and totally defeated at Kettle Creek by Colonel Pickens in 1779. In March, General Lincoln, who now had command of the southern troops, sent 2,000 men, under General Ash, against the British in Georgia, but this force was surprised and defeated by Provost. In April, Lincoln with 5,000 men marched into Georgia, and a conflict took place at Eton's Ferry, but without important results, and the summer heats hindered further operations till September.

In the north, Clinton remained inactive; Matthews with a small force plundered and ravaged a part of Virginia; and Tryon made a second raid in Connecticut, burning, destroying and killing in the villages. Other movements of this sort were checked or prevented by Wayne's brilliant assault on Stony Point, capturing the fort and 500 men, with cannon and supplies, and destroying the works, thus keeping Clinton quiet and watchful for the defense of New York. An attempt was made from Massachusetts against a British post on the Penobscot, but it ended in defeat and disaster. To avenge the massacres of Wyoming and Cherry Valley, Washington sent General Sullivan with a large force to attack the Indians on the frontiers of Pennsylvania and New York, by which the savages were everywhere defeated, and forty of their villages were burned. In the autumn, both Clinton and Washington went into quarters for the winter.

In 1779, the center of the war was at the south. In September, the French fleet, under D'Estaing, with 6,000 troops, and with the co-operation of the American forces under Lincoln, assaulted the British works at Savannah, but were repulsed with the loss of 1,000 men in killed and wounded. D'Estaing was among the wounded, and Pulaski was slain. In December, Clinton, with increased forces attacked Charleston, where Lincoln was now in command, and the town and army fell into the hands of the British. The city was plundered, and both officers and soldiers enriched themselves with the spoils. Not only

ARNOLD AT NEW LONDON.

was confiscation threatened to all who did not submit, but all who would not take up arms for the king were treated as rebels, and the brutish severity of Clinton in killing and hanging, and the ill-treatment of the prisoners, favored and carried out by the Tories, gave the war in the south a character for barbarity and bitterness elsewhere unknown.

Clinton soon left Cornwallis in command, and returned to New York, where he sought by base treachery, through the well known treason of Arnold, to gain the ends he failed to secure by force; but the plot by which he sought to gain West Point and the control of the Hudson, miserably failed, and Major Andre, acting as a spy, suffered death on the gallows, while the chief traitor and criminal, the disgraced and dishonored Arnold, escaped to the enemy, and afterward went to England, where, though rewarded for his treason, he was treated with deserved contempt. Before his escape to England, and while in the service of the British, he went with a force to attack New London, where, it is said that he watched the flames kindled

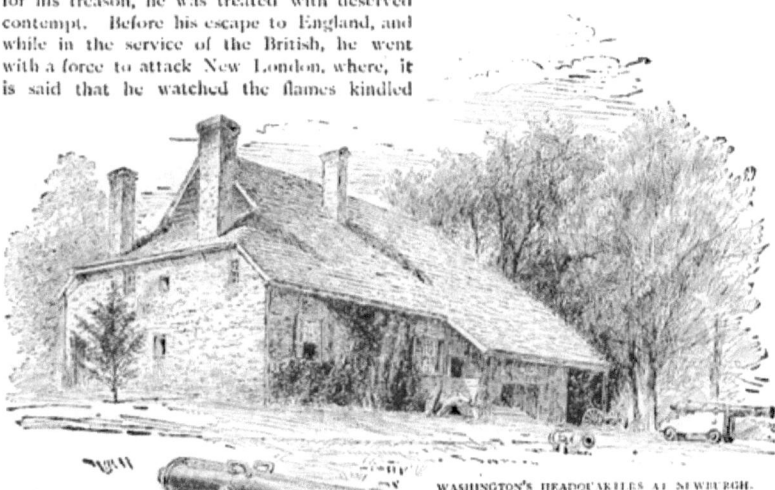

WASHINGTON'S HEADQUARTERS AT NEWBURGH.

on the dwellings. A woman, roused by his villainy, fired a ball from her musket, which barely missed its aim, and came near ending the career of the traitor to his country.

During the summer of this year, the noted Paul Jones was furnished with a squadron by the American commissioners in Paris, and in September he attacked and took two British frigates convoying a fleet of merchant vessels, which caused great rejoicing. At the close of the year there was much despondency through the country. No important victories had been gained. The paper currency, which had been largely issued, had so depreciated that it took thirty paper dollars to make one of specie, as it afterward took fifty, and even sixty. To purchase provisions and supplies for the army with this currency was almost impossible, and Washington had to take supplies for his suffering soldiers from the surrounding country, and but for the fact that the people were fighting for a principle and liberty, the prospects of the country would have been desperate.

EXPLOIT OF ARNOLD.

At the opening of 1780, everything at the south seemed to be in favor of the British forces, but at the darkest hour the tide began to turn, and the patriotism and courage of the people rose for the defense of their homes. While Cornwallis was carrying out his policy of brutal punishments, a body of patriots, led by Sumter, fell upon a party of British raiders, and routed them; they also defeated some regiments of English at Hanging Rock. Gates, joining De Kalb on Deep river, led their united forces in attacking

ATTACK BY THE BRITISH ON THE BLOCK HOUSE AT
TOM'S RIVER, 1782.

Cornwallis, but was badly defeated, and De Kalb was killed. Cornwallis, now flushed with victory, and expecting everywhere to conquer, began his march through North Carolina and Virginia. A large body of regulars and loyalists, led by Ferguson, formed part of his forces, but they were attacked by a strong band of the "Ninety-six" and backwoodsmen led by Servier and Shelby, who killed or made prisoners of the whole body, some 1,100 men, while the patriots lost only twenty. The effect of this victory was electrical. The Tory rising was checked. The patriots, led by Marion and Sumter, everywhere took up arms, and increased in numbers and activity, and Nathaniel Greene, one of the ablest of the American generals, was sent to take the place of Gates in commanding at the south.

In January, 1781, Greene sent Morgan with a force of 1,000 men to hold the British in check in South Carolina. Here he joined battle with Tarleton, the English cavalry leader, at Cowpens, January 17th, gaining a signal victory with a loss of but seventy men, while the British lost 700, with all their artillery. This was a heavy blow to the British, and Cornwallis pressed on, hoping to attack and conquer Greene, and then to carry out his intended scheme of ending the war on the Chesapeake. Greene, uniting his forces with Morgan, by the middle of March engaged the enemy at Guilford Court House, the British losing 500, and the Americans some 300 men; and Cornwallis, crippled by this victory, marched on to Virginia.

Greene now turned back to Carolina, and though not successful in an attack on the British under Rawdon, still kept harassing the enemy. Marion and Lee compelled the British to leave Camden, and their outlying posts fell, one after another, into the hands of Marion and Sumter. After several engagements, which were not of decisive importance, the Americans withdrew for the hot months to the hills of the Santee. Coming down in September, Greene attacked the British, at first carrying all before him, but later suffering defeat, though he lost only 500, while the British loss was over 1500 men. Though failing several times of complete victory, yet in less than one year, and with raw troops and no supplies, he had taken two States from the British and shut them up in Charleston. This campaign was a masterwork of skill and persevering fortitude, placing him next to Washington as one of the leaders of the Revolution.

Early in 1781, Cornwallis had moved from the south and taken command of the British forces in Virginia, and in June, by direction of Clinton, he took up a strong position at Yorktown, where he fortified himself,—a position in which he would be near New York, in case that place should be attacked by Washington.

Washington had intended attacking New York, but with his usual sagacity, he saw that a decisive blow might now be struck, as he was able to unite all the allied forces. De Grasse arriving in the Chesapeake with 4,000 men; Barras, with his fleet and transports and ordnance, joining them from Newport, and Rochambeau coming from Rhode Island. Washington continued to act as if planning only to attack New York, and Clinton, supposing this to be his design, arranged his defenses accordingly; but suddenly, in September, when everything was ready, Washington appeared before Yorktown and began its siege, De Grasse blocking up the James and York rivers to prevent the escape of the British by water, as Washington cut off their escape by land.

The siege was pushed with all possible vigor, a hundred pieces of artillery doing terrible execution. The British fell back from their outposts, and in October, two advanced redoubts were assailed and carried by the Americans. For three weeks the siege continued, the British losing over 500 men during the bombardment. Finding his situation hopeless, Cornwallis was obliged to surrender, and on the 19th 7,000 British soldiers laid down their arms and gave up Yorktown, with ships, cannon and supplies to the conquerors. The news of this great victory filled the land with exultation and joy. Patriotic demonstrations abounded everywhere, and Congress appointed the 13th of December as a day of public thanksgiving. From the retreat at Lexington, April 19, 1775, to the surrender at Yorktown, October 19, 1781, in twenty-four main engagements, the British losses were not less than 25,000 men, while those of the Americans were between 8,000 and 9,000.

The war had lasted nearly seven years. It had cost Great Britain $500,000,000, and the lives of 50,000 men, besides the loss of the colonies. It was a war of which William Pitt, the great English statesman, said, "It was conceived in injustice, nurtured in folly, and whose footsteps were marked with slaughter and devastation." It had cost the Americans great and widespread suffering and immense expense, but it left them a free and independent nation, growing to this day in extent, population and prosperity. The country rejoiced in the issue of the war, and felt that the losses and sufferings of the people were more than repaid by the results to the nation.

THE HOUSE WHERE CORNWALLIS SURRENDERED.

As Congress appointed a day of public thanksgiving after the victory at Yorktown, which brought the war to a close, so the King of Great Britain appointed a day of thanksgiving after the war was ended and our independence was assured. Proposing the appointment of the day, he was asked by one of the bishops why he wished to appoint it. "Is it, your Majesty, for the loss of the thousands of your brave soldiers who have perished in the conflict?" "No," was the reply, "not for that." "Is it for the vast amount of treasures which have been sunk and expended in vain?" "No, not for that." "Is it, then, for the loss of those thirteen prosperous colonies, which might have been the glory of the Empire?" "No, not for that." "What, then, is there, your Majesty, for which to be thankful?" "We may well be thankful," was the reply, "that matters are not worse!"

The surrender at Yorktown was the real close of the war, and was so recognized both in this country and in Europe. It crushed in Europe the last hope of ever subjugating the colonies. In the British Parliament resolutions for terminating the conflict were introduced, and in the spring of 1782 the British ministry offered to treat with the Americans. John Adams, Benjamin Franklin, Henry Laurens, and John Jay were sent as commissioners for the United States, and concluded a preliminary treaty of peace, which was signed at Paris on the 30th day of November, and the final treaty, the "Treaty of Paris," was signed on the 3d day of September, 1783. By this treaty, Great Britain acknowledged the independence of the United States, the boundaries of which were agreed upon as extending to the great lakes on the north and to the Mississippi on the west. On the 3d of November the army was disbanded, the patriot soldiers returning with honors to their homes, and by the close of the year the last British soldier had left the United States, and the country was rejoicing in peace and independence. On the 4th of December, Washington bade farewell to his officers at New York. On the 23d, at Annapolis, he resigned his commission to Congress, and retired to his farm at Mount Vernon, carrying with him the deep gratitude and love of the whole country, as his entire course, before and afterward, has made him the admiration of the world.

The government of the States at the close of the war was not, as now, under a constitution binding on all, but only a *confederation*, or league of the different States, the articles of which had been agreed upon by Congress in 1777, and ratified by the last of the States in 1781. This confederation, however, was little more than a name. Of its Congress, the seat of its power, Jay, one of the wisest of men, said that "They might declare war, but had no power to raise money or men to carry it on; might make peace, but had no power to see its terms observed; might form alliances, but without the ability to comply with their own stipulations; might enter into treaties of commerce, but without power to enforce them; might borrow money, but without means to repay it; might regulate commerce, but without authority to enforce their ordinances; might appoint ministers and other officers of trust, but without power to try or punish them for misdemeanors; might resolve, but could not execute, either with despatch or secrecy." In a word, he says, "they may consult and deliberate, recommend and make requisitions, and only those who please may regard them." Trade was depressed, the currency was depreciated, rioting was threatened in many States, and rebellion, under Shay, existed in Massachusetts, so that not a few of the most thoughtful men were more apprehensive of danger than even in the war itself.

So great and extended were these troubles and dangers, that the feeling became general that a new constitution should be formed,—one that should make the United States one great nation, and which, instead of leaving all powers in the hands of Congress, should forever separate the three great departments of sovereignty (the legislative, the judicial, and the executive), so that each should be a check on the others. This principle, so strongly urged by Jay, and advocated in the " Federalist," became the corner-stone of the present federal constitution.

A convention of all the States was called, and met in Philadelphia in May, 1787, and Washington was made its presiding officer. After four months' deliberation, they agreed upon a constitution which was signed September 17, 1787, and adopted by the people of eleven States in 1788. The remaining two States adopted it soon afterward. It went into operation March 4, 1789.

11

WASHINGTON SURRENDERING HIS COMMISSION

Its provisions were, in the main, those of the present Constitution of the United States; *first*, the *Legislative*, or law-making department, called Congress, consisting of the Senate, in which each State has two members, and the House of Representatives, in which the representation for each State is in proportion to its population; *second*, the *Executive*, consisting of a president and vice-president, appointed for four years, and those appointed by the former as secretaries, and associated with him; and *third*, the *Judicial* department, consisting of the supreme court and such lower courts as Congress may establish. The judges were to be appointed by the President, with the advice and consent of

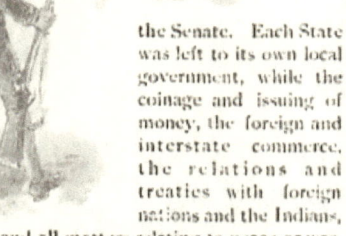

the Senate. Each State was left to its own local government, while the coinage and issuing of money, the foreign and interstate commerce, the relations and treaties with foreign nations and the Indians, and all matters relating to peace or war, were left to the general government. There is no religious establishment, all being free to worship in their own way; and the constitution provides that there shall be no interference with the freedom of opinion or speech, or of the press. Under this constitution the people of the United States elected members of the first National Congress, and Washington was chosen the first President of the United States.

ATTACK ON THE RIOTERS.

PERIOD V.

CHAPTER I.

THE NEW STATES.

THE Constitutional Period extends from March 4th, 1789, when the new government went into operation to the present time. The Union at first consisted of thirteen States, to which Vermont and Maine, the territories of which were then included in the other States of New England, were afterward added, and of which the brief history has already been given. Besides these thirteen, thirty-one other States, including Maine and Vermont, have since been added, making in all forty-four States beside the territories. An account of the founding and growth of these newer States may now be given.

KENTUCKY.

Kentucky was the first of those newer States, and was admitted to the Union in 1792. It had been partially explored in 1760 by Thomas Walker of Virginia, of which State it was made a county in 1776. In 1769, Daniel Boone, a bold and successful pioneer and trapper, went from North Carolina into Kentucky, where he had many exciting adventures with the Indians, and by whom he was at one time taken captive, though he soon escaped. In 1775, he built a fort on the site of what is now Boonsborough. This place and other small settlements suffered greatly from the Indians, from the bloody wars with whom came the name of the State, which, in the Indian language, signifies "the dark and bloody ground."

After the Revolution large numbers of emigrants, especially from Virginia and New England, entered the region, and Louisville, Lexington and other places were settled, and the population increased to some thirty thousand. The area of the State is 37,680 square miles. The country is rolling, the soil for the most part is fertile, giving some of the finest agricultural regions in America, and producing all the grains and fruits of the warmer temperate regions. Herds of cattle find the best of pasture, and uncounted swine fatten in the woods. Coal, lead, iron, salt and beautiful marbles are found. The State is well watered, and the hills and valleys are well wooded. From the beginning, Kentucky was a slave State. The limestone region abounds in caves, of which the great

MAMMOTH CAVE, KENTUCKY.

Mammoth cave, in Edmonson county, is one of the wonders of the world. It has been explored for more than ten miles. The chief industries of the State are agricultural and manufacturing. It has numerous railroads, many public libraries, fourteen colleges, eight or ten institutions for the instruction of women, a system of common schools, and numerous academies, seminaries and private schools. The population of the State in 1880 was 1,648,690, and in 1890, 1,854,486.

TENNESSEE.

The next State added to the Union was Tennessee, which was admitted in 1796. Its name signifies "the river of the great bend." Its territory was originally a part of North Carolina, which claimed westward to the Mississippi; and in 1777 it was made a county of that State. In 1790, having been ceded to the United States, it was organized as the Southwest Territory, and so remained till admitted to the Union. At that time it had but few settlers, but after the removal of the Indians in 1819, its growth rapidly increased. During the rebellion of 1861-5, the whole State was a battle-ground, and important conflicts occurred at several places—at Nashville, Chickamauga, Lookout Mountain, Missionary Ridge, Knoxville, Franklin, and other places; but in April, 1865, the legislature of the State ratified the Thirteenth Amendment to the Constitution, and reorganized the State government, and in the next year it was again received into the Union.

The area of the State is 45,000 square miles. The climate is temperate, and for the most part healthful. The soil is extremely fertile, producing all the grains and fruits of the temperate regions. The State is richly wooded with pine, oak, hickory, cedar and black walnut, and the woods abound in wild game. The State has twenty colleges, a large common school fund, many private schools and academies, asylums for the deaf and dumb, and for the insane, numerous railroads, extensive iron mines, a number of caves, mostly unexplored, and several important rivers, giving water power to the entire State. Until 1783 the educational interests of the State were greatly neglected, but since that

LOOK-OUT MOUNTAIN, TENNESSEE.

time laws have been passed establishing public schools and providing for their support, and aid to education has been given from the Peabody fund. In 1880, the population was 1,542,359, of which 403,342 were colored; in 1890, 1,763,723.

OHIO.

Ohio was the third of the new States, coming into the Union in 1802. The region now forming the State was visited by La Salle in 1669-70, but no settlement followed his visit for nearly a hundred years. Its name, Ohio, is said to have come from an Indian word signifying "the river of blood." The territory was part of the region which was ceded to the English by the French in 1763. Virginia claimed all the territory ceded by the French under grants from the crown; and Connecticut, New York and other colonies also claimed parts of it under conflicting grants. Virginia finally ceded her claim to the general government in 1787, and Connecticut obtained recognition of her claim in the grant of 3,686,921 acres, which were set off to her on the south side of Lake Erie, known as the "Western Reserve" or "New Connecticut," and which laid the foundation of the great school fund of that State.

In 1787, a company of New England settlers, under the lead of General Rufus Putnam was organized in Boston, and in 1788 a company of educated and estimable families founded the town of Marietta. A similar settlement was made at Cincinnati in the next year, and other settlements soon followed on the Western Reserve. For a time the Indians were troublesome, killing and wounding the settlers, but after the victory over them at Tippacanoe and Presque Isle, in 1794, emigration rapidly increased. In

RED-MILL FALLS, NEAR ELYRIA, OHIO.

1800, a territorial government was established, and in 1802 Ohio became one of the United States. "No State," said Washington, "was ever settled under such favorable auspices, and never were men better fitted to promote the welfare of such a community."

Ohio contains 39,964 square miles, and no State in the Union has less waste land in its borders. The broken hills of the southeast part are noted for their production of coal and iron. Every production of the temperate zones may be cultivated in some parts of the State, and every species of domestic animal is as profitably raised there as anywhere. In the production of wool, flax, butter and cheese it is one of the leading States. The fisheries of the State are profitable, and in manufactures the State ranks fourth in the Union. The farms occupy more than four-fifths of the State. Over six hundred companies are engaged in coal and iron mining, and in the packing business the State is surpassed only by Illinois. The State has over sixty different railroads, connecting every part of the State with the other States. It has an excellent common school system, six colleges, and universities, numerous academies and private schools, public libraries in ever part of the State, public charities and asylums of almost every kind,— for the insane, the blind, the deaf and dumb, for the orphans of soldiers and sailors, for inebriates, and for the reformation of juvenile offenders. The population of the State in 1880 was 3,198,062, and in 1890, 3,666,719.

A MISSISSIPPI RIVER BOAT.

LOUISIANA.

Louisiana was the fourth of the new States, and was admitted to the Union in 1812. The region was visited by De Soto in 1541, and in 1673 by Marquette and his Canadian followers, who descended the Mississippi to its mouth, but founded no settlement. In 1682, La Salle, descending the river, took possession of it in the name of Louis XIV., in whose honor he named it Louisiana. But no colony was founded till 1699, when Iberville settled in Biloxi, which is now in Alabama, for the name Louisiana was then applied almost indefinitely to a widely extended region supposed to extend to the Pacific ocean. Bienville, after the death of Iberville, led the colonists to the present site of New Orleans, where they made a stand and unfurled the French flag. In 1712, Louis XIV. gave to Anthony Crozat the privilege for fifteen years of exclusive trading in all this vast region. In 1717, the province came into the hands of John Law, the noted speculator, and in 1723 New Orleans was made the capital of the colony, which remained under the French crown till 1762, when it was transferred to Spain, but in 1800 was restored to France.

The name Louisiana was originally given to the vast possessions of France in the valley of the Mississippi, which were larger than all the original thirteen States of the Union. Bonaparte had intended to make this territory a great French colony, and had

LOADING A COTTON STEAMER ON THE MISSISSIPPI.

even designated one of his generals to be its governor. But in the prospect of war with England he sold it to the United States in 1802 for $15,000,000. It embraced at that time nearly all the present States of Louisiana, Arkansas, Missouri, Iowa, Minnesota, Dakota, most of Kansas and the Indian Territory, part of Colorado, most of Wyoming, and the whole of Montana, Idaho, Oregon and Washington. In 1804, the southern part of this vast territory was organized as the "Territory of Orleans," and in 1812, with some additions, it was admitted to the Union with its present name.

Louisiana has an area of 41,346 square miles. Its surface is mostly low and level. The land along the Mississippi, below New Orleans, and for a hundred and twenty miles above, is below the high-water level of the river, and is protected from inundation by high embankments, called *levees*. The river bottoms are exceedingly fertile, the alluvial lands are heavily timbered, the forest trees are various, and the State abounds in all kinds of tropical fruits. The chief agricultural staples, however, are cotton, sugar, rice and corn. The mineral productions of the State are unimportant. The State has several rivers. Almost all kinds of wild animals are found in its borders. In foreign and domestic commerce, Louisiana ranks next to New York. The State has a large school fund, and supports a good system of common schools. It has ten colleges, and numerous seminaries and academies, as well as private schools. The State was one of the first seceding States and was the scene of several battles, and for three years was under military occupation by the United States forces. But in 1868 it was readmitted to the Union. The population of the State in 1880 was 939,946, and in 1890, 1,116,828.

INDIANA.

Indiana, the fifth of the new States, was added to the Union in 1816. It was originally a part of the great Northwestern Territory, but in 1800 was made the "Territory of Indiana," and William H. Harrison, who afterward was the ninth President of the United States, was its first governor. As early as 1702, settlements were made at Vincennes, Congdon and other places by emigrants from Canada and some of the older colonies. For several years the Indians were hostile and greatly troublesome, and when Harrison was governor, under the lead of the noted Tecumseh, who had unbounded influence with his people, they attacked the settlements, but were signally defeated by Harrison in a desperate battle at Tippecanoe in 1811, after which they sued for peace. But in the war of 1812 they again rallied to attack the whites, but were speedily conquered and never afterward gave trouble.

The State has an area of 33,809 square miles. It has no mountains, but is mostly level or undulating on its surface. The soil is wonderfully fertile. The table lands of the interior are many of them like vast prairies, interspersed with groves of hickory, beech, black walnut, ash and other trees. The staple productions are wheat, maize, cattle, swine, tobacco, fruits, &c. Coal, iron and valuable building stone are also found. The celebrated block coal, and also cannel coal and peat are abundant.

After coming into the Union the growth of the State, both in population and wealth, was rapid. Its constitution was formed with great care and wisdom. The State has a large number of public charitable institutions; fourteen colleges, a large school fund of about $9,000,000, the school revenues from which and from other sources are, annually, between two and three million dollars. The State has several beautiful lakes, and the great Wyandotte cave is almost as wonderful as the Mammoth cave of Kentucky. As an agricultural State, Indiana stands high. It has numerous and valuable manufacturing interests, and there are large and valuable libraries in several parts of the State. The population of the State in 1880 was 1,978,301, and in 1890, 2,189,030.

MISSISSIPPI.

Mississippi, being the sixth of the new States was admitted to the Union in 1817. Its name, like that of its great river, signifies "The Father of Waters." The region was early visited by De Soto, in 1539; by Joliet and Marquette, in 1673, and by La Salle and Tonti, in 1682. But it was not till 1699 that the first attempt to establish a colony was made by Iberville. After various changes the region was ceded by France to England in 1763, and in 1798 came into possession of the United States. In 1800, it was organized as the "Territory of Mississippi"; and in 1817 the western part of this State was made a State of the Union. In 1861, the State seceded from the Union, but in 1869 it assented to the United States Constitution, and again became one of the United States.

The State contains 47,156 square miles; the surface is undulating and the soil generally fertile, especially in the river bottoms. The sea coast is sandy, but well timbered with live oak, magnolia, and pine trees. The climate is semi-tropical, and the chief productions are cotton, sugar, maize, wheat, and the various fruits. In the forests are found deer, bear, wolf, wildcat, and wild fowl; and in the rivers, alligators and fish. The State is well provided with railways, and has great wealth and resources. It is well watered, and has no mountains. Its mineral deposits are not valuable. Much of the State is covered with primitive forests. The great agricultural staples are cotton and corn. Excellent pasturage is found in the lowlands and river valleys. The State has a number of manufacturing establishments, a system of common schools, many private schools and academies, five colleges, and nine collegiate seminaries for the instruction of young women. Population in 1880, 1,131,597, and in 1890, 1,284,887.

ILLINOIS.

Illinois, which takes its name from an Indian tribe, was the seventh of the new States, and was admitted to the Union in 1818. The first white settlements within its borders were made in 1682 by French traders and missionaries from Canada. It was originally part of the great Northwestern territory, but in 1809 was made a separate territory, embracing what is now Wisconsin and part of Minnesota. The Indians were for a long time troublesome, which impeded the progress of settlement, but after the war of 1812 their hostilities ceased, immigration from the Eastern States set in, and important public improvements were made. In 1840 the Mormons settled at Nauvoo, intending to make it their great "Jerusalem"; but their doctrines and practices led to an uprising of the people, in which Joseph Smith, the founder of the sect, and his brother were killed, and the Mormons soon afterward removed to Utah.

The State has an area of 55,410 square miles. It is generally level, having no mountains, and is nearly covered with fertile prairies, while the soil of the river bottoms are so rich as to have produced abundant crops for many successive years without manuring. The whole State is of limestone formation, with rich deposits of lead and coal. As an agricultural State Illinois stands in the first rank, producing in abundance all the grains and every kind of fruit. In manufactures it ranks as the sixth of the States. Its railroads are more numerous and of greater extent of track than in any

VIEW ON THE MISSISSIPPI.

A NOOK, FOX LAKE, ILLINOIS.

other State in the Union. It has many charitable institutions, twenty-seven colleges, an organized and efficient system of common schools, a school fund of some $8,000,000, two law, and two medical, and nine theological schools, and great numbers of excellent academies and private seminaries or schools. In 1831, Chicago was an insignificant trading station, amid wigwams of the Indians; now it is one of the largest grain ports in the world, and the second city in the United States, having over a million of inhabitants. Population in 1880, 3,077,877, and in 1890, 3,818,536.

ALABAMA.

Alabama, signifying "here we rest," so named after the river of the same name, was the eighth of the new States, and was admitted to the Union in 1819. The celebrated exploring expedition of De Soto had to fight its way through the Indian tribes which at that time inhabited the region, who were less savage and more numerous than the Northern tribes, and in their mode of living were in advance of the latter. In one instance, it is said, that the house of a chieftain was 120 feet by 40, and included small buildings like offices. And on the Savannah river was found a remarkable temple 100 feet long by 40 wide, and of proportionate height.

Early in the eighteenth century the French built a fort on Mobile Bay, but the city of that name was not commenced till 1711. In 1763, when all the French possessions came into possession of the English, Alabama was first with Georgia, and afterward, in 1802, with the Mississippi territory, but finally, in 1819, it became one of the United States. During the war of 1812, the Creek Indians, a powerful tribe, gave the whites a great deal of trouble, in one instance taking a fort and killing some four hundred persons, but being opposed by a strong force under General Jackson, in less than two years they lost 2,000 of their warriors and were glad to make peace.

Alabama has an area of 50,722 square miles. The country is neither mountainous nor level, but rugged and broken, having many picturesque views and wild romantic gorges. The State has three large bays and several large rivers. The climate is tropical, and the soil fertile, yielding large crops of cotton. Rice, maize, wool, oats, wheat, rye, tobacco and flax are abundantly raised. Wild deer and turkeys, and wild geese and ducks frequent the muscle shoals in immense numbers. Trees are numerous, and iron, marble and limestone are abundant, and also bituminous coal of a superior quality. Education is making satisfactory progress. The State has several colleges, a small school fund, normal, agricultural and mechanical schools, several collegiate schools for the education of young women, and numerous libraries in the different towns of the State. It was one of the first States to secede, but in 1866 it adopted a new constitution and was received back into the Union. Population in 1880, 1,262,505, and in 1890, 1,508,073.

SCENE ON THE MISSISSIPPI RIVER BELOW ST. LOUIS.

MISSOURI.

Missouri, the ninth of the new States admitted to the Union in 1821, is so called after the river of the same name, the word signifying the "muddy river." It was formerly part of the vast territory of the French Louisiana, and was first settled in 1755, though before this, as early as 1720, attention had been drawn to its valuable lead mines, which have been so successfully worked. St. Louis, which was at first a fur trade station, and other small settlements grew very slowly till Louisiana passed into the possession of the United States in the time of Jefferson's administration. It was made a territory in 1812.

Applying for admission to the Union in 1817, the application led to fierce excitement in Congress and throughout the country ; the question being whether it should be a slave State or free. The question was settled by what is known as the "Missouri Compromise," which forever excluded slavery from all the country lying north of 36° 30', and Missouri came in as a slave State.

From that time on the growth of the State was rapid, though the people were always greatly divided in their views of the slave system. In 1861, at the opening of the war of secession, a convention declared for the United States government, while the governor, by proclamation, declared the State out of the Union. During the war several important battles took place in its borders. And in 1865 a new constitution was formed, and in 1869 the State was readmitted to the Union.

The area of Missouri is 67,380 square miles. Its main rivers are the Mississippi and the Missouri. The State has immense coal measures, and vast beds of iron, and also valuable lead deposits. The climate is varied. Much of the land is very fertile, producing wheat, maize, hemp, tobacco, and various kinds of fruits. Cotton is grown in the southern counties. A large German population has introduced wine-making. The chief manufactures are in ironworks, distilleries and breweries, and the State has a large and profitable trade supplying the more western regions. The State has an excellent school system, and a school fund of over $3,000,000, and its school expenditures are over $2,000,000 annually. It has also several normal schools, and academies and private schools of a high order, nineteen colleges, four theological schools, and two law and five medical schools. Its forests are extensive, and wild

CATHEDRAL SPIRES ON THE MEERIMAC.

animals are numerous, and birds of almost every kind are found. The commerce of the State is extensive, and its mining and manufacturing interests are highly valuable. Population in 1880, 2,168,389, and in 1890, 2,677,080.

ARKANSAS,

So called from the river of the same name, was the tenth of the new States admitted to the Union, which it entered in 1836. It contains 52,198 square miles, of which but a small part is under cultivation. Though nominally colonized by the French in 1685, it was virtually a wilderness till the time of the Louisiana Purchase by the United States, and it was not till 1819 that it became a territory, and not till seventeen years later that it was made a State.

In climate and production the State occupies an intermediate position between the eastern and western States. It is rich in minerals, particularly in manganese and zinc, having also lead ores which are said to contain a large proportion of silver. It also contains the principal varieties of coal—anthracite, cannel, and bituminous. Mineral and medicinal springs are numerous. There are large forests of cypress, oak, pine, cedar, black walnut, maple, and other valuable trees. All the cereals are easily grown,

HOT SPRINGS, ARKANSAS.—LOOKING WESTWARD.

and bring large returns, but cotton raising is the leading business, and cotton is grown in every part of the State. Game is abundant and fish are plentiful in the streams and bayous. There are four colleges in the State and normal and industrial schools, and the State has a small school fund. Population in 1880, 892,523, and in 1890, 1,125,365.

MICHIGAN.

Michigan, so called from the Indian word signifying the "lake country," was the eleventh of the new States, and was admitted to the Union in 1837. The French missionaries and fur traders visited Detroit as early as 1610; and the first settlement by the Europeans was at the Sault Ste. Marie in 1668. In 1763, this region, with other French possessions, fell into the hands of the English. After this the Indian chief Pontiac organized a conspiracy to exterminate the whites, and the garrison at Mackinaw was butchered, and Detroit for a long time was besieged. It was not till 1796 that the United States took actual possession of this region, then part of the Northwestern territory.

In 1705, it was made a separate territory. During the war of 1812 it suffered greatly from the British and their Indian allies, and Hull, its governor and commander, in a most cowardly manner, surrendered his forces and the whole territory to the British, for which he was dismissed from the army, and being tried by a court martial, was condemned to death, though the sentence was remitted; and facts afterward came to light which partially, if not wholly, relieved him from blame.

DETROIT RIVER SCENES.

But the victories of Perry on Lake Erie, and of Harrison on the land, restored the territory to the United States in 1814, and peace was then made with the Indians. In 1818, the sale of the public lands brought a large emigration to Michigan, which since that time has greatly prospered.

Michigan has an area of 56,243 square miles. It is comprised in two peninsulas, of irregular shape, separated from each other by the strait of Mackinac which connects

12

Lakes Michigan and Huron. The upper peninsula, containing about one-third of the area of the State, is rugged and mountainous, and is said to be richer in mineral productions than any part of the United States. Its northwestern part is celebrated for its extensive deposits of iron and copper, the mines of which are some of the most productive in the world. Michigan alone, chiefly from its northern peninsula, produces ores of copper and iron of greater value than all the gold and silver products of the States of the great West. In 1890 it mined and sent to market some 10,000,000 tons of iron and 200,000 tons of copper, and its mines of both these metals are being steadily and profitably developed.

SCENES ON THE ST. MARY RIVER.

The commerce that passes through the great lakes and waters of Michigan is greater than all that enters the harbor of New York, both in the number of tons and the value of the merchandise. The commerce that passes annually through the canal at the Sault Ste. Marie is greater than that which passes through the Suez canal, though for five months in the year the former is closed by the ice of winter. Some fifteen of the great Western States pour the great body of their agricultural products and of their general commerce through this canal to the eastern and foreign markets, while the return commerce of the East comes back through the great lakes and through the canal to them. So greatly has this commerce increased that the great canal at the Sault, which is 615 feet long and 80 feet wide, is not large enough to accommodate it, and the United

GOVERNMENT CANAL AND LOCKS, SAULT STE. MARIE, MICH.

States government has entered on the work of a new and far larger canal, with the needful and enlarged lockage, the excavation for which is completed, so that the work of construction is now under way. The walls of the new lock are 1,200 feet long and 100 feet wide throughout, with 21 feet depth of water on the sills and a lift for vessels of 18 feet. The length between the gates, that is the length available for lockage, is 800 feet, and in the two and a half years in which the excavations have been going on, 242,000 cubic yards of material have been dug up and removed, of which some 100,000 cubic yards were of stone. The cost of these excavations alone has been about $230,-000. The cost of the entire work when completed is estimated at not less than $4,585,865, and the work itself will be the largest of the kind in the world. When it is finished vessels loaded to the depth of nineteen feet can pass on their way, which, at a freight of but $1.00 per ton—a low estimate—would mean a profit of $1,800.00 on a single down trip of a vessel loaded with iron ore. Lake ship building and the carrying industry will have a new life from the completion of this great work, and the direct commerce between the great West and foreign countries will be greatly increased.

The southern or lower peninsula is, in almost everything, a contrast to the upper. The surface is generally level, and for the most part fertile. Where vast forests once stood their place has been taken by the broad farms of the people and by the flourishing cities and villages that are scattered throughout the State. The manufacturing, lumber, salt, iron, and railroad interests of the State are extensive, and are highly profitable. Some of the largest stove factories of the country, and also large manufactories of freight cars for railroads are carried on in the State.

Throughout its borders there are numerous islands, some of the largest of which are favorite summer resorts. Mackinac Island, especially, is noted for its beautiful situation, its pure and healthful atmosphere, the many points of interest in and near it, and the abundant provision made for the comfort of its summer visitors. It was here that Father Marquette, during his early voyages, founded a college for the education of Indian youths in 1671. Cadillac, who afterward founded Detroit, built a small fort here in 1695. And here it was that the fur trade opened in 1809, when John Jacob Astor organized the American Fur Company, with a capital of $2,000,000, so that for forty years Mackinac, the great central market for the fur trade, was the gayest and busiest place on the lakes, her streets being crowded with people, and her warehouses filled with merchandise. Here, too, for a long time, the United States government made its annual payments to the Indian tribes, who assembled in thousands to receive their promised stipend.

As an agricultural, and also as a manufacturing State, Michigan stands high. The waters of the State are well stocked with fish of various kinds, and the soil produces all kinds of grain and fruits. Shipbuilding is carried on extensively and profitably, and in no part of the country are there so many facilities for delightful summer excursions as on her vast lakes and broad rivers.

The State has numerous charitable, reformatory and penal institutions, and it takes high rank in all that pertains to education. The annual income of its school funds is nearly $5,000,000. Its State university is one of the foremost in the country, and there are nine other colleges and several professional schools and various seminaries of a high order. Population in 1880, 1,636,937; and in 1890, 2,089,792.

FLORIDA.

Florida, the twelfth of the new States, said to have been so called from the flowers which everywhere cover the country, was purchased from Spain in 1824 for $5,000,000; was soon afterward organized as a Territory, with Andrew Jackson as its governor, and was admitted to the Union in 1845. Ponce de Leon, in search of the "fountain of youth," was the first European to visit it. It was visited in 1528 by De Narvaez with a large force, but being strongly resisted by the Indians, no permanent settlement was made. De Soto, and afterward a band of French Huguenots attempted settlements, but were unsuccessful, and after various changes it was purchased by the United States.

The State has an area of 60,000 square miles. Much of it is sandy and marshy, yielding such productions as cotton, sugar, rice, and various kinds of tropical fruits. It has inexhaustible forests of timber, much of it valuable for shipbuilding. Its waters swarm with fish, and as a winter resort it is extensively visited by northern people.

AMELIA ISLAND, FLORIDA.

For years the State suffered from conflicts with the Indians, but in 1842 their migration to reservations took place. The State seceded in 1861, but after the war repealed the ordinance of secession, and in 1868 was readmitted to the Union. Live oak, hickory and pine trees thrive well. Phosphate in immense quantities has recently been discovered. All kinds of grain, cotton, sugar cane, tobacco, rice, coffee, and all the fruits of the tropical regions are raised, especially oranges, which are sent in abundance to every part of the country. The State has a small school fund. Population in 1880 was 269,493, and in 1890, 390,435.

TEXAS.

Texas, the thirteenth of the new States, was admitted to the Union in 1845. The region had been explored and a fort erected by La Salle in 1687. In 1715, it was settled by Spaniards, and several missions were established, but the warlike Indians greatly hindered the progress of the country. In 1803, when

Louisiana was bought by the United States, Texas was claimed by both this country and Spain; but when Florida was bought from Spain, in 1819, Texas was given up to that country.

In 1820, Moses Austin, an American, obtained from Mexico the grant of an extensive tract of land in Texas, and began a settlement which rapidly increased, but in 1830 Mexico forbade further emigration from the United States, because the new comers had given trouble to her government. In 1833 a convention of settlers, who were now some twenty thousand in number, was called, with the intention of forming an independent State, but the attempt was unsuccessful. In 1835, however, they organized a provisional government, and General Sam Houston, who had come to Texas, was chosen commander-in-chief.

Both the character and career of General Houston were so remarkable as to be worthy of more particular notice. He was born in Virginia in 1793; enlisted as a common soldier in the war of 1812; was chosen ensign, and fought under Jackson with such courage and success as to win his warm and lasting friendship; in 1823 was chosen a member of Congress, and in 1827 was made governor of Tennessee. In 1829 he married the daughter of an ex-governor of the State, and the day after the marriage, to the surprise of every one, and for reasons that were never known till after his death, he resigned his office as governor of the State, abandoned his wife, his country and civilization, and joined himself to the Cherokee Indians beyond the Mississippi, and by them was made a chief of their nation. Removing to Texas, where, as stated, he was made commander-in-chief, the Mexicans were soon driven out of the province, and in consequence the Mexican army of 7,500 men, under Santa Anna, at once invaded the country. The Americans at first sustained some severe defeats, and were obliged to retreat before the Mexicans for nearly three hundred miles. But suddenly turning on his pursuers, Houston fought the remarkable and decisive battle of San Jacinto, April 21, 1836, and at one blow annihilated the Mexican army and achieved the independence of Texas. He was elected first president of the new republic, and was re-elected in 1841. In 1837, the independence of Texas was acknowledged by the United States, as it also was in 1840 by England, France and Belgium. During the presidency of Van Buren, Texas applied for admission to the United States, but the application, though urgently favored by the South, was strongly opposed by the people of the North, because if admitted it would add another slave State to the Union, and so it was refused. In 1844, the slavery question was hotly debated, both in Congress and throughout the country, and the bill for the admission of Texas was passed by Congress, was approved by President Tyler March 1, 1845, and being also approved by Texas, that State, on the 4th of July, 1845, was admitted as one of the United States. Its independence was not acknowledged by Mexico, and its admission to the United States was soon followed by the war with Mexico, an account of which is elsewhere given.

In 1859, Houston was elected governor of Texas. With the spirit of an independent and true patriot, he opposed the secession of the State, but finding opposition useless, he retired to private life, and died in 1862. It was not till after his death that the secret of his leaving his new wife, resigning his high office as governor of Tennessee, and retiring to the wilds of Arkansas and to life with the Indians was made known. It was that he discovered on the part of his wife a prior attachment to another, and that she had been coerced or over-persuaded to her marriage with him and that with the natural nobility of his nature he had promptly sacrificed himself, his

SAM HOUSTON.

social position and all his political prospects, that the woman he truly loved might be made happy. His bride, after his departure, as arranged between them, soon obtained a divorce on the ground of desertion, and married the man of her choice.

Not only did Houston resist secession from the first, but it shows his true spirit, and belongs to his history and to the history of the country, that on the day of Lincoln's inauguration as President, he rode fully armed close beside the carriage of the President-elect, to guard him against the possibility of assassination, which, even then, had been threatened, as afterward it was consummated. The picture of this resolute and stalwart old patriot, then nearly threescore and ten years old, guarding the person of Abraham Lincoln, is well worthy of preservation as connected with the life of one who added the largest of all the States to the Union.

In 1861, Texas joined in the secession movement and in the war that followed, but in 1870 it was re-admitted to the Union, and in 1876 its new constitution was adopted by the people.

Texas is far the largest State in the Union, its area being 274,356 square miles, nearly six times as large as the great State of New York. It has fine marbles, and some deposits of lead and copper, and the coast produces the finest cotton and sugar, as the interior does all kinds of grain and abundant pasturage, making it one of the finest cattle countries in the world. Vegetation is of the greatest variety, and the forests abound in wild animals. The chief exports are cotton, sugar, tobacco, cattle and wool. The school fund of the State is about $3,000,000. The State has ten colleges and several first-class seminaries, and public and private schools which are well sustained. Its deaf and dumb, orphan, blind and lunatic asylums have large endowments. The rapid growth and development of the State is largely due to the Missouri Pacific Railroad, which, on account of the picturesque scenery through which it passes, has become the favorite route to the southwest. Population in 1880, 1,531,749, and in 1890, 2,222,220.

IOWA.

Iowa, so named from an Indian word signifying "the beautiful country," was the fourteenth of the new States, and was admitted to the Union in 1846. The first white settlement within its borders was in 1788, by Julian Dubuque, a Frenchman from Canada, who obtained a grant of a large tract, including the city that now bears his name, and also the rich mineral lands around it. He built a fort and carried on mining and trading with the Indians till his death in 1810. In 1834, it was part of Michigan, and in 1836, part of Wisconsin; but in 1838 it was made a separate Territory, embracing part of what is now Minnesota, and all of Dakota; but in 1840, with its boundaries contracted, it was made a State.

The State has an area of 55,045 square miles. It is the most purely agricultural of all the States. In proportion to the extent of its territory its grain production is said to exceed that of any one of the States of the Union. The beauty of its scenery, the richness of its soil, and its naturally good drainage, have attracted the best class of farmers and business emigrants from the more eastern States, giving it a population of thrift, energy and intelligence. Its wealth and population are distributed with great uniformity. The chief productions are wheat, maize,

A NOOK ON MUD LAKE, IOWA.

tobacco, cattle, horses and hogs. It has little foreign commerce, but trades extensively with the interior and with the Atlantic and Gulf towns. Its lead mines are valuable, and other metals are found in abundance. The prairies are extensive, and of great fertility and beauty.

Coal, peat and building stone are abundant. The State has numerous manufactories. It abounds in fruit trees, and some experiments have been made in tea culture. In 1873 its expenditures for schools were over $4,000,000. It has nineteen colleges and several important public institutions sustained by the State, and numerous and excellent private schools and academies. Population in 1880, 1,624,611; and in 1890, 1,906,729.

WISCONSIN.

Wisconsin, the fifteenth of the new States, was admitted to the Union in 1848. Its history dates from 1639, when settlement was made by the French at Green Bay. During the next forty years other settlements were made, but conflicts with the Indians greatly retarded their progress. Up to 1796 it had been under British control, but it was then ceded to the United States and annexed to the great Northwestern territory. In 1836 it was made a distinct territory, covering what is now Iowa, Minnesota, and part of Dakota, and so remained until, with these regions set off, it was admitted to the Union as a State. Since the Civil War, in which it took an active and efficient part, its population and wealth have rapidly increased.

The State contains 53,924 square miles. The country is a high rolling prairie. The lakes and rivers abound in fish; the minerals found are iron, lead, copper, zinc, plumbago, fine marbles, coal, and so forth. In the State are curious earthworks in the form of men and animals, and ancient fortifications made by the prehistoric people that have now utterly disappeared. The chief manufactures are of iron, lumber, and agricultural implements, flour, and so forth. Wheat is one of the chief productions. The State has a school fund, nine colleges, several State and numerous town libraries, and is one of the most prosperous of the States. Population in 1880, 1,315,493; and in 1890, 1,683,697.

CALIFORNIA.

California was the sixteenth of the new States, being admitted to the Union in 1850. The name was at first applied to a peninsula on the west side of New Mexico, but was gradually extended as far north as 42°, the original California and its northern increase being distinguished from each other as the old and the new, or upper and lower. It was first explored by the Spaniards, and in 1507 was visited by Sir Francis Drake, and though claimed by him for England, it remained a Spanish possession, the Spaniards having numerous missions at or near the coast, including at one time some thirty Indian tribes under their care and influence.

In 1822, when Mexico threw off the Spanish rule and became independent, upper California was made a Mexican province, and for some twenty years had but a small population, mostly Spaniards, Mexicans and Indians. When the war between the United States and Mexico took place, in 1846, the Americans in California asserted their independence of Mexico, and had several encounters with the Mexican authorities,

ON THE BRULE RIVER, WISCONSIN.

in which they were successful. Monterey was taken by Commodore Sloat, who, by proclamation, claimed California for the United States, and a little later Commodore Stockton, who had superseded Sloat, took San Diego, and, aided by Fremont, captured Los Angeles. In 1847, the battle of San Gabriel took place, in which General Kearney, with strong forces, overthrew the Spanish power and established the authority of the United States in California. And at the close of the war of 1848, by the treaty of Guadaloupe Hidalgo, the United States acquired New Mexico and California, paying to Mexico fifteen million of dollars, and

BIG TREES OF CALIFORNIA.

assuming some three million dollars of debts due to Americans. In 1849, the people of California adopted a constitution forever excluding slavery, and the next year the State was admitted to the Union.

Just before the treaty with Mexico was concluded, gold was discovered in California on a fork of the Sacramento river. The water washing through the raceway of a sawmill built by a new settler, deposited particles of gold. The news at once spread throughout the land and led to a rush of emigration unparalleled in modern times. In 1849, some forty thousand emigrants arrived in San Francisco; by 1850, California had a population of one hundred thousand; and in 1860, over three hundred thousand. The amount of gold taken from the mines was enormous, averaging, from 1849 to 1875, some fifteen million dollars per year. Up to 1860, the great object of the emigrants was to make a fortune and return home. But after that time the population ceased to be exclusively of the mining class, but began to develop the other rich resources of the State, when it was soon found that the agricultural products were almost unlimited, the exports of wheat and fruit being more than equal to the value of the gold taken from the mines. Its agricultural and fruit products, as well as its business enterprise, are more and more becoming prominent. The orange orchards have so increased and been found so productive that from fifty to seventy carloads of oranges in 1890 were daily sent to eastern markets, and the prospect is that California will become the greatest orange producing country in the world. All kinds of tropical fruits are easily and abundantly cultivated, and extensive arrangements have been made for

YOSEMITE FALLS.

the new industries of camphor production and for the manufacture of olive oil. Table fruits in the greatest abundance are raised and sent forth to every part of the land. Wine making, sugar beet production, and rich harvests of the various grains, are making California as noted for her agricultural and manufacturing prosperity as at first she was for her mines of gold.

As such facts make plain, the later progress of California has been both rapid and healthful. Her wonderful scenery, her immense trees of the giant red-wood, her rich

THREE BROTHERS, YOSEMITE VALLEY.

soil, fine climate and varied productions are attractions drawing not only settlers for business, but thousands of visitors for health and pleasure. The great trees of California are the wonders of the world. The most celebrated grove of these trees is in Mariposa county, which is said to contain about four hundred of them; the largest of which are some thirty feet in diameter and three hundred feet high. There are seven groves of these trees in different parts of the State. One of the trees, which has fallen, is estimated to have been four hundred and fifty feet high and forty feet in diameter. The hollow trunk of one of them, which is seventy-five feet long, is named the "Horseback Ride," from the fact that one might ride through it, upright, on horseback. On the stump of one of these trees, which has been levelled, thirty persons, it is said, stood sociably at one time, and one tree in the Tulare grove is two hundred and seventy-six feet high and one hundred and six feet in circumference at the base. In the State there are two thousand six hundred and seventy-five of these giant trees.

The scenery in the Yosemite Valley is remarkable for its sublimity. It is formed by a gorge in the Sierra Nevadas, which is from eight to ten miles long and about two miles wide. The walls are of solid granite, varying in height from two to five thousand feet.

In some places it is filled with noble oaks, and in others opens out into broad, grassy fields. On account of the great depression of the valley the streams from the surrounding mountains find their way into it and form marvelous cataracts as they dash down its perpendicular sides. In the spring, when the snow melts, these streams are innumerable; and even in the dry season there is an abundant supply of water in the valley, keeping its vegetation fresh and green.

The Bridal Veil, formed by a stream which enters the Valley from the South, is one of the most beautiful water falls in the world. About a mile above the Bridal Veil Falls the wall rises to a height of 3,300 feet and is called El Capitan, the Indian name being Tu-tock-a-nu-la, which means Great Chief of the Valley.

On the northern side of the valley, a short distance from the Three Brothers, is the great Yosemite Fall, formed by a stream of the same name. It falls, in three great leaps, a distance of 2,550 feet. Further on we come to the Yosemite Falls proper, the upper part of which is the highest water fall in the world, being sixteen hundred feet in height. Below the falls are the two huge mountains of bare granite, called the North and South Domes. East of these, in a valley which branches off from the main one, is a beautiful sheet of water about a mile in circumference, called Mirror Lake on account of its wonderful transparency. The descent into the valley is about three miles in length and very steep, but the grandeur of the scenery compensates for any difficulties which may be met in reaching it.

MIRROR LAKE AND MOUNT WATKINS.

Railroads connect California with all the other States, and her splendid steamers reach out to the shores of Asia. Her vast and growing commerce, her mines, her agricultural advantages, and her wonderful abundance of the richest fruits, make sure her great prosperity and substantial and steady growth. She has a State university, twelve colleges, numerous seminaries of various kinds, a noble school system on which is expended some three million of dollars a year. And she is soon to have the most richly endowed university in the world—that established and endowed by Mr. Stanford. Population in 1880, 864,694, and in 1890, 1,204,002.

MINNESOTA.

Minnesota was the seventeenth of the new States, and was admitted to the Union in 1858. Its name signifies the "cloudy water." It was first settled in 1680 by the French, who ascended as far as the Falls of St. Anthony. In 1763, the territory was ceded to Great Britain. In 1776, the region was explored by Jonathan Carver, from Connecticut, and in 1783 it became part of the United States, and was included in the great Northwestern Territory. But it was not till 1838 that the Indian title was extinguished, after which settlements were made at and near Stillwater in 1842. In 1849, it was organized as a Territory, at which time it was comparatively a wilderness, over which the Dakotas or Sioux Indians roamed. But in 1851, when the lands were ceded to the

THE FALLS OF ST. ANTHONY.

United States, the growth of the Territory in population, wealth and intelligence began. At the breaking out of the Rebellion, the Indians attacked the settlements, murdering families, burning villages, and killing about one thousand of the inhabitants; but they were speedily and effectually suppressed, and were banished from the State.

The area of Minnesota is 83,581 square miles. It is abundantly watered by its great rivers, which are navigable, and the State abounds in lakes and ponds. It is one of the most beautiful, fertile and salubrious of the States, and has extensive and valuable forests. The Falls of St. Anthony afford abundant water power which drives the machinery of some of the largest flouring mills in the world. The State is rich in minerals, including iron, copper, coal, and lead. Gold also has been found. The surface of the country is for the most part undulating, with no mountain ranges. Three-fourths of the State are rolling prairies. The northern portion of the State is one of the finest wheat producing regions in the world. The forest growths are oak, beech, elm, maple, spruce, and pine. More than twenty millions of forest trees have been planted on the prairies.

LAKE OF THE WOODS.—(Rat Portage, Manitoba, in the distance.)

The hardier fruits grow readily, though the season is too short for peaches and the tenderer kinds of grapes. The winters are long, but the air is dry, the temperature even, and the climate healthful. Most of the early settlers of the State were from New England, and the school system of their native States they carried with them to their new home. The school fund is between three and four million dollars. The State university has seven departments. There are in the State six colleges, three normal schools, three theological seminaries, several business colleges, numerous seminaries and academies of a high order, and various charitable and reform institutions, hospitals, asylums, and so forth. Population in 1880, 780,773, and in 1890, 1,300,017.

13

OREGON.

Oregon was the eighteenth of the new States, and was admitted to the Union in 1859. It was originally discovered in 1592 by the Greek navigator De Fuca; and in 1640 was visited by the Spanish admiral, Fonte, on the ground of whose visit Spain claimed it, but in 1790 ceded it to England. In 1788, it was visited by Captains Kendrick and Gray, in two trading-ships from Boston. In 1804, it was explored by Lewis and Clark, who were sent out by Jefferson, an exploration which led John Jacob Astor to plan a settlement on its coast for fur trading. He sent out two parties, one by water and another overland, and in 1811 Astoria was established at the mouth of the Columbia river, by the "American Pacific Fur Company," of which Mr. Astor was the director. In 1812, its property was merged in the Northwest Fur Company, and afterward in the Hudson Bay Company, depots for trade being established at Fort Vancouver.

PORTLAND, OREGON, AND WILLAMETTE RIVER.

Up to 1834, but few American settlers were in Oregon, but in that year a missionary colony, led by Messrs. Whitman and Spaulding, established themselves in the valley of the Willamette, and were soon followed by others. A treaty with Great Britain, in 1846, settled a disputed boundary, and in 1849, the gold excitement in California added to the emigration, which had somewhat increased in 1848, when Congress organized the territory. In 1850, Congress passed a law giving land to settlers, and from that time the country began to fill up with emigrants.

Oregon has an area of 95,274 square miles. The Cascade mountains divide the State into two unequal parts. The western third has a mild, equable and moist climate, with valleys of great fertility, where pines grow to the height of from two hundred to three hundred feet, and fir trees are from four to ten feet in diameter. East of the mountains the climate is dry and variable, and the soil less fertile. Gold and silver are found in the Cascade mountains, and also copper, platinum, iridium and osmium. Coal is found in many parts of the State. The Mammoth Cave of Kentucky has a world-wide reputation, and was supposed to be unequalled. But an enormous cavern has been discovered in Oregon, about forty miles from the coast, the passages of which have been explored for miles underground. The walls of the cave are of great beauty, containing semi-transparent stalactites and giant pillars of milk-white and crystallized limestone, while within the cave are pools and streams of pure, clear water, and a small stream flows from the main opening of the cave, which, on further examination, may be found as extensive and remarkable as the great cave of Kentucky. The chief agricultural productions are wheat, oats, vegetables and fruits. The forests abound in wild animals, and the rivers swarm with salmon. The seashore is three hundred miles in extent, and has five bays and good harbors. The ship canal around the Cascade Falls, a mile and a half in length, with locks three hundred feet long and fifty feet wide, each overcoming a fall of twenty-six feet, is the work of the United States government. Above the falls there is steamboat navigation for nearly three hundred miles. More than any State except Texas, Oregon is a primary market for live stock. Its timber is unsurpassed by that of any State except California. Its wood crop is very valuable, its manufactures are numerous, and its various foundries, machine shops, rolling, crushing, wood and paper mills, tanneries, canning establishments, etc., show the prosperity of the State. Oregon has a good system of common schools, a State university, five colleges, and several public institutions of State charity, as for the deaf and dumb, the blind, the insane, etc. Population in 1880, 174,768; and in 1890, 312,490.

KANSAS.

Kansas, the nineteenth of the new States, was admitted to the Union in 1861. It was originally part of the "Louisiana Purchase." When, in 1854, it was proposed to organize the territories of Kansas and Nebraska, the advocates of slavery brought into Congress a bill known as the "Kansas-Nebraska Bill," which provided that the question whether these territories should be slaveholding or free, should be determined by the vote of the inhabitants. This was called "popular sovereignty," and the bill was nicknamed the "Squatter Sovereignty Bill." It was strongly opposed and denounced as a violation of the "Missouri Compromise," but was finally passed, its object being to introduce slavery into these new territories, and so prepare the way for making them slave States.

Here was the beginning of a series of events which led directly to secession and the great rebellion, and to the war between the North and South. The excitement caused by this law was intense throughout the country. The slave and free States each sent into the new territory emigrants favoring their own views. Large parties of "free soil" men poured into Kansas from the North and East, and the friends of slavery came in numbers form the South, especially from Missouri, from which came bands of armed men, known to the anti-slavery party as "border ruffians." Each side strove for the mastery, and for years there were conflicts and bloodshed and lawless violence, till at

A KANSAS HARVEST SCENE.

last, in 1859, the anti-slavery party triumphed, and a constitution prohibiting slavery was ratified by the people, 10,421 voting for, and 5,530 against it, and the question being thus settled, Kansas came into the Union as a free State.

From that time on its growth and prosperity have been singularly rapid. Emigrants have poured in from every part of the land. Railroads have opened the fertile prairies for hundreds of miles, and the vast buffalo ranges have all given way to corn-fields and settlements. From 1875 to 1880, nearly a hundred thousand were annually added to the population, and flourishing cities have sprung up and increased.

Kansas is mainly an agricultural State. The soil is fertile, producing all the cereals, and also cotton, tobacco, hemp and various kinds of fruits. The prairies have abundance of game; the rivers abound in fish. Iron, coal, lignite, marble, kaoline, and salt are among its minerals. Manufactures are extensively carried on. The fossils in the west part of the State are of great geological interest. The east part of the State is well wooded with oak, hickory, black walnut, cotton-wood, elm, ash, and other trees. The State has a large school fund, and the value of its school property is some six million dollars, while over two million are annually expended for common school education. Some of its public institutions are for the insane, the blind, and the deaf and dumb. There are two colleges, and many excellent academies and private schools. Population in 1880, 956,090, and in 1890, 1,423,485.

WEST VIRGINIA.

West Virginia, the twentieth of the newly created States, was a part of the old State of Virginia, but was separated from it during the War of Secession, and was admitted to the Union in 1862. Its early history is that of the State from which it was taken. Its area is 23,000 square miles, in 16,000 of which the coal measures are found, containing every quality of cannel, splint, coking and bituminous coal yet discovered. Salt is found in springs of great strength and purity. Building limestones, fire-clay, glass-sand, barytes and saltpeter abound, and zinc, copper, and lead are found in limited quantities. Half the State is covered with forests, giving various kinds of valuable timber. The climate is free from extremes of heat and cold, and the air is pure and healthful. The State has many kinds of manufactures, and large numbers of mining establishments. Its free school system is in efficient operation. It has four colleges, and numerous good academies and private schools. Population in 1880, 618,457, and in 1890, 760,448.

NEVADA.

Nevada, the twenty-first of the new States, was admitted to the Union in 1864. It was a part of the territory acquired from Mexico by the United States, under the treaty of Guadaloupe Hidalgo in 1848. Before this it was inhabited only by Indians, there being no settlement, and not even a mission within its borders. Its first white settlements were made by a few Mormons, when it was a part of what was then Utah Territory; but the population was very small till the silver discoveries of 1859, which brought in great numbers of settlers and led to the founding of several towns, among which Carson and Virginia City took the lead. It was made a Territory in 1861, and so remained until it was taken into the Union as a State.

The area of the State is 104,125 square miles. Its surface is rough and mountainous, and its soil for the most part sterile and unfitted for agriculture. Its great wealth is in its mines and mineral resources which are various and abundant. Its silver mines are said to be the richest in the world, the great Comstock lode being probably the largest deposit of the precious metal ever known. So far back as 1874 there were two hundred and forty-three mines in thirteen counties of the State, the yield from which was over $35,000,000. The educational interests of the State are not old enough to have made much progress. But the State has a school system, and a small but increasing school fund. A State university has been organized, and its preparatory departments have been opened, and much has been done in the way of academies and private schools. Population in 1880, 44,327, and in 1890, 62,266.

NEBRASKA.

Nebraska, so named from an Indian word signifying the "water valley," was the twenty-second of the new States, and was admitted to the Union in 1867. For a time it formed a part of Missouri territory, but was made a separate territory in 1854. Its early history is much the same as that of Kansas. Up to 1854, it had few residents except the soldiers at forts, a few missionaries, and the fur traders, but after the building of the Pacific railroad the population increased rapidly.

The State has an area of 75,995 square miles. It is a vast plain, rising gradually toward the Rocky Mountains, with numerous prairies, which formerly had immense herds of Buffalo, and in which are fertile and well timbered bottom lands. In the mountainous parts are mines of lead, gold, silver, copper and cinnabar. The climate is dry and healthful, with abundance of bright, sunny days. The country produces wheat, maize, hemp, tobacco and fruits in abundance, while the rolling prairies afford the best of pasturage. The manufactures of the State are in their infancy, but are rapidly increasing, and the enterprise of the people is seen in car works, foundries, gas works, flouring mills, carriage, wagon and implement factories, pork packeries, &c. The State has numerous railroads. Its educational interests are well managed. For public school interests the government has devoted 2,700,000 acres of land, and 400,000 for a State university; and the annual expenditures for public schools are between one and two million dollars. The State university has six departments — the college, agriculture, law, medicine, and practical science, including mining, engineering and mechanics, and the fine arts. Besides this, there are two colleges and many private seminaries. The population in 1880 was 452,496, and in 1890, 1,056,792.

COLORADO.

Colorado, the twenty-third of the new States was admitted to the Union in 1876. Its name signifies the "red waters." A portion of its territory was a part of the "Louisiana Purchase," and the remainder came from the Mexican territory that was ceded to the United States after our war with that country. The region it occupies was explored by Pike in 1806, by Colonel Long, of the United States engineers, in 1820, and by Fremont in 1848, but no permanent settlements were made till the discovery of gold on the river Platte in 1858. Then the tide of immigration set in, and settlements and towns sprung up as if by magic, and since then its growth has been rapid and substantial.

The State has an area of 106,400 square miles. Its surface is irregular, and broken by high mountains and vast intervening valleys, which are spoken of as "parks." The famous South Park, for example, covers 1,200 square miles, and has a general elevation of 8,000 feet, rising in places to 10,000. It is surrounded by mountains, and probably was once the bed of a vast lake. San Luis, the largest of the so-called parks, is in the central part of the State, and is exceedingly fertile, and this, and three other such openings or parks, extends as in a line through the middle of the State. All these parks are walled by high mountain ridges, are of varied surface, are exceedingly fertile, and have dense pine forests, where the elk, bear, deer, and other wild animals are found. Here also are mineral springs, and in Middle Park are hot, sulphur and other springs, which are remedially valuable.

The climate of Colorado is remarkably regular and healthful. The cold, except on the heights, is seldom severe. The atmosphere is remarkably pure, and the summers are

BASALTIC PINNACLES, COLORADO RIVER.

almost rainless. The State is rich in minerals, gold and silver being the most important. Coal is found in abundance. Agriculture is advancing rapidly, about half the land, except the mountains, being available for cultivation, and producing corn, wheat, rye and oats, as well as all kinds of vegetables. The school lands amount to 3,740,000 acres, and in time will give ample provision for common schools. There is a State university, with a normal department; and there are three colleges, a school of mines, and an institute for agricultural instruction. The State is rapidly advancing in enterprise and wealth. Population in 1880, 194,327, and in 1890, 410,975.

WASHINGTON.

Washington, the twenty-fourth of the new States, was admitted to the Union in 1889. The region was visited by De Fuca, a Greek navigator, in 1592; by Spaniards, in 1775; by Cook, in 1778; by Berkley, in 1787; by Gray, an American, in 1791; and by Vancouver, in 1792. Lewis and Clark, who were sent out by Jefferson, explored the region during his administration, and trading-posts were established in it by the Hudson Bay Company in 1828. The first American settlers entered the territory, which was then a part of Oregon, in 1845. In 1853 it was made a separate Territory. Wars with the Indians in 1855, and again in 1858, retarded immigration, but the discovery of gold at Fraser's river in the latter year attracted many who became permanent settlers.

THE CASCADES.

The State has an area of 69,994 square miles. It is divided by the Cascade mountains and the Columbia river, into Western Washington, lying west of the mountains, Central Washington, lying between the mountains and the Columbia river; and Eastern Washington, east of the river. Western Washington, comprising two-fifths of the State, is a densely timbered region with a few fertile prairies and some rough mountain land. The climate is relatively warm in winter and cool in summer, and the amount of rainfall is large. The regions about the river valleys in the central part are fertile. In the eastern part the summers are warmer and the winters cooler than west of the mountains. On the Pacific, the coast line of the State is 180 miles long. Coal, both anthracite and bituminous, is found in various parts of the State, and it is said to exceed in volume all that is in the Atlantic States combined. The known workable coal strata cover an area of over one million acres. An area of 16,000 acres is being worked, with an output in 1889 of 1,750,000 tons, and of some 2,250,000 tons in 1891. Sixty other veins covering about 30,000 acres are being opened, and will add to the output in 1892. The coal ranges in character from a true cannel, showing 88 per cent., to a semi-anthracite of 91 per cent. carbon. The lignite measures cover 800,000 acres, with an output of about 1,000,000 tons in 1890. The gold mines, which at first gave promise of extensive production, have for several years been declining. The vegetable and animal productions of the State are the same as in Oregon. Fish are very abundant, a dozen kinds of salmon filling the rivers, while other fish, such as halibut, cod, herrings and sardines, are in great quantities. The water and mountain scenery is perhaps the finest on the continent. The chief product is timber. Wheat, barley, oats, and the hardier fruits and vegetables are produced in abundance. The schools are supported mainly by taxation, which in 1890 was nearly $350,000; and some two million acres of land have been set apart as a permanent school fund, the estimated value of which is $20,000,000. And for a scientific school, and for charitable, penal, and reformatory institutions large appropriations of land have been made by the State. The State university and another college are the main institutions for higher education. Population in 1880, 75,116, and in 1890, 349,516.

NORTH DAKOTA.

North Dakota, the twenty-fifth State, was admitted to the Union in 1889. It was named from an Indian word which signifies "allied" or "leagued," referring to the confederate tribes of the Dakotas or Sioux, who so long roamed over the region. The Territory of Dakota was organized in 1861, and it was the northern part of this Territory which, in the division of the territory by the Act of Congress, which made two States, became North Dakota. The State has an area of 70,715 square miles. It is well watered, and includes open, grassy plains and high, rolling prairies. It abounds in game as well as furnishes valuable furs. The land is fertile and well timbered, and is rich in coal and other minerals. In the basin of the Red River of the North there are vast plains covered with grass, affording pasturage in summer and feed in the winter in abundance. In the Black Hills are extensive forests of pine and other valuable timber. A century ago these regions were the resort of fur traders, trappers and hunters, but the immigration of great numbers of settlers is rapidly changing the condition of the

State. There are three colleges, and several excellent academies, as well as private schools, in the State. The population of the State in 1880 was 36,906, and in 1890, 182,425.

SOUTH DAKOTA.

South Dakota, the twenty-sixth of the new States, was admitted to the Union in 1889. Like North Dakota, it was made by dividing the Territory of the same name. What has been said of Northern Dakota applies in most respects to this State, as both are in the same region, and both formed the Territory. The area of the State is 77,650 square miles, and this State has been more rapidly settled than North Dakota, and is rapidly filling up with emigrants from other States, whose enterprise and numbers give promise of steady and substantial growth. The Indian reservations in both States take up some 60,000 square miles. Educational interests are receiving attention. Population in 1880, 98,282; and in 1890, 327,848.

MONTANA.

Montana, the twenty-seventh of the new States, was admitted to the Union in 1889. As a Territory it was formed, in 1864, from parts of Dakota and Idaho. Its area is 143,776 square miles, but a small part of which is under cultivation. It has great mineral wealth, including gold, silver, copper, galena, coal, and some kinds of precious stones. Its surface is rough and mountainous, the main range of the Rocky Mountains entering the west part of the State from the north, and passing through toward the west boundary. The mountainous regions constitute two-fifths of the State, and in some parts rise 11,000 feet above the level of the sea, and are covered with perpetual snow.

The State has extensive prairies and bottom lands, which are rich in soil, but to a great extent are not cultivated or tilled. The climate is subject to great variations. Wild animals are numerous. Fish of every kind abound in the streams. In the large towns manufactures are rapidly increasing. The State has comparatively few schools. It is exceedingly well watered, and well adapted for grazing, and when the Indian reservations which take up so large a portion of the State are open to settlers, the white population will greatly increase.

The Yellowstone region was formerly a great resort of buffaloes, of which it is said that in 1880 five hundred thousand were seen in a single day, though now they have almost entirely disappeared. The great "National Park," with its varied and wonderful scenery, is partly in this State, and contains numerous hot and mineral springs. The geysers have their name from an Icelandic word signifying "to burst forth violently," as is expressed by the English word "gush," and some of these eruptive springs, as they suddenly send up their powerful jets, make a great noise, and fill the air with clouds of steam. These geysers are hundreds—and, counting the smaller ones, thousands,—in number, and some of them throw up immense columns of water to the height of from 20 to 200, and in one case, 250 feet. The giant geyser is one of the most remarkable. At intervals it throws up a column of water some five feet in diameter to the height of

130 feet, continuing its active period for about an hour and a half, and then subsiding. The schools of Montana, both public and private, are as yet few in number, but are steadily increasing and improving. Population in 1880, 39,159, and in 1890, 131,769.

WYOMING.

Wyoming, the twenty-eighth of the new States, was admitted to the Union in 1890. As a Territory it was organized in 1868, out of parts of Dakota, Idaho and Utah. The area of the State is 97,883 square miles. It is very mountainous, and is elevated from 2,500 to 3,000 feet above the sea level. It has several important rivers. The soil of the valleys is moderately fertile, and there is good pasturage. The State is rich in minerals, including iron, copper, lead, coal, silver and gold. The most notable feature of the State is the valley of the Yellowstone river, in the northwest corner of which 3,525 square miles have been reserved as a grand National Park. The region was first explored by parties from the United States in 1870-71. It is one of the most wonderful and remarkable

MOUNT STEPHENSON, NEAR THE SUMMIT OF THE ROCKIES.

regions on the face of the earth. Here and in Montana are found the largest and most numerous geysers or spouting, intermittent, thermal springs in the world, being thousands in number, and some fifty of them throwing up water 200 or more feet high, the temperature of the water ranging from 160 to 200 degrees of heat. The "Tower Falls," another of the wonders of this region, have a sheer descent of 400 feet, and the "Grand Canon," another curiosity, is a fearful abyss, 3,000 feet in perpendicular depth, and from its bottom the stars are visible at mid-day. Gold, iron deposits and coal beds are found in the State, and there are profitable mines of copper, lead and gypsum. The growth of Wyoming has been slow, as the Indians have been

VIEW IN GRAND CAÑON.

troublesome, and the proportion of land adapted to agriculture is comparatively small. Mining interests, however, are steadily increasing. Educational progress is encouraging. Women can vote in the State and sit on juries, and are eligible to public office. Population in 1880, 20,789, and in 1890, 60,589.

IDAHO.

Idaho, the twenty-ninth of the new States was admitted to the Union in 1890. In 1863 it was organized as a Territory, with an area three times as large as its present limit, having then within its boundaries a large part of Wyoming and the whole of Montana. It was first explored by Lewis and Clark in the early part of the eighteenth century, before which time, it is said, no white man had ever set foot within its borders. After that it was traversed only by hunters and trappers till 1852, when the discovery of gold near the northern boundary drew great numbers to the region.

ROCKY MOUNTAIN SCENE.

The area of the State is 86,294 square miles. The surface is generally elevated, about one third of it being suitable for agriculture. The mountain, timber and mineral lands cover more than half, while the lakes and streams take about a tenth of the State. Gold, silver and lead are found near the sources of most of the rivers, the region on the Boise river proving one of the richest gold fields ever known. Up to 1874 the product of the precious metals was nearly $80,000,000. The Custer mine is said to be remarkable for exhibiting the greatest mass of ore on the surface that has ever been discovered.

The climate of Idaho is varied, though generally delightful during the summer and autumn. In the mountains the winters are extremely cold and the snows heavy, but in the lower valleys and plains cattle sometimes winter without shelter. In the western part of the State the temperature is like that of central Illinois, and in the eastern part much like that of northern New England. The forests of Idaho are confined to the northwestern parts and to the sheltered valleys of the mountains. Noble pines, cedars and spruces are found, and the red cedars are of larger size and in greater abundance than in any part of the world. The long-leaved pine, which is abundant, attains a height of from 120 to 170 feet, and a diameter of from four to seven feet, and serves for saw logs to the very top.

Agriculture is as yet but little developed, and grazing lands are not extensive. The great fish of the State is the salmon which comes up from the Columbia river in immense numbers to spawn in the Salmon and other rivers, where it attains great size, sometimes being from forty to fifty pounds in weight. The red fish, one of the rarest and most beautiful of all fishes, and said by Humboldt to be found in only five lakes in the world, are found in the lakes of the Saw-tooth mountains. Some interesting fossils have been found in the State. The remains of the mastodon, and of the elephant and tapir families have been found, and also of bears, monkeys, crocodiles, alligators, and other saurians, and of genera allied to the horse. The schools and school interests of Idaho, like those of all sparsely settled communities with greatly mixed populations, are but little developed, but are slowly improving. A branch of the Yellowstone Park is in progress in Idaho. Population in 1880, 32,610; and in 1890, 84,229.

CHAPTER II.

THE TERRITORIES.

TERRITORIES, in the United States, are those public lands set off by Congress, and still under its direct authority, which have the capacity of becoming States when so authorized by Congress. Each Territory has a governor, a judiciary system and proper administrative officers appointed by the President, and also a territorial legislature of limited powers, the action of which is subject to Congressional revision. In addition to the forty-four States of the Union, there are four Territories included in the property and under the jurisdiction of the United States, or seven, if we include the District of Columbia, the Indian Territory and Oklahoma, and also Alaska, the territorial government of which is not yet fully organized.

NEW MEXICO.

New Mexico was formerly a State of Mexico, but coming into possession of the United States by treaty and purchase, it was organized as a Territory in 1850. Three years later what was called the "Gadsden Purchase," which was also obtained from Mexico was annexed to it, the Territory then containing the whole of what is now Arizona and parts of Colorado and Nevada, which were afterward set off from it. The capital, Santa Fe, is, next to St. Augustine, the oldest town in the United States.

The area of the Territory is 121,201 square miles. Two great chains of the Rocky Mountains cross the eastern part of the Territory from north to south, while in the western part the mountain ranges rise to an elevation of 12,000 feet. The climate is cold in the elevated regions, and hot in the plains. Heavy rains fall in July and August, but the rest of the year is dry. The productions are wheat, maize, oats, tobacco, and various fruits; and pasturage is abundant. There are in the Territory numerous mines of gold, silver, copper, iron, and salt. The Indian population has been very large, but is decreasing, several of the tribes having been removed to reservations. Stock-raising and wool-growing have for many years been important occupations. Manufactures are slowly increasing. Schools are but few in number; not till 1812 was there any established system of common school instruction, and then comparatively few of the schools were above the grade of primary teaching. Population in 1880, 119,565, and in 1890, 144,862.

UTAH.

Utah was originally part of Upper California, and was acquired by the United States from Mexico in 1848, at the close of the war with that country. Its name is from an Indian word signifying "dwellers in the mountains," as the region is traversed by high mountain ranges, rising thousands of feet in elevation. The Mormons, who had

MOUNTAIN SCENERY, UTAH.

been driven from Illinois and Missouri, emigrated to Utah in 1847-8, and established themselves in what was then an almost unknown region, which they called Deseret. Under the superintendence and leadership of their high priest, Brigham Young, Salt Lake City was founded, and in 1850 a territorial government was formed, of which Young was appointed governor. In 1857, however, he set at defiance the authority of the Federal government, and from that time to this there has always been more or less difficulty in controlling the Territory.

The Mormon system started from what its founders pretended was a revelation set forth in some golden plates which they said were dug up near Palmyra, in the State of New York, and from which they pretended to have copied the book of

WHITE CLIFFS, UTAH.

Mormon. But for the doctrine of polygamy, which is not taught in the Mormon bible or in the book of Mormon, the leaders claimed they had special revelations and directions, as they seem conveniently to have had for other of their views and customs.

In 1862, the Mormons formed a State constitution, and demanded admission to the Union as the State of Deseret. This was refused, as it has been ever since, on account of the system and practice of polygamy, which the Mormons claim is enjoined by their religion. Severe laws have been passed against this system by Congress; and in all probability Utah will never be admitted as a State till the system is entirely abandoned.

Most of the Mormons are from the lower classes in England and the north of Europe, but there is a large and growing class of the "gentiles" or non-Mormon people,

14

who are steadily gaining in numbers and power, and it is to be hoped that through their influence and the legislation of Congress, the objectionable features of Mormonism may be brought to an end.

Utah has an area of 84,476 square miles. It is an immense basin 4,000 to 5,000 feet above the level of the sea, surrounded by mountains which, at some points, rise to the height of from 8,000 to 13,000 feet. Several of the rivers of the Territory flow into the Great Salt Lake on its northern part, and in the Territory there are numerous lakes and also warm and salt springs. Iron is abundant, and gold, silver, copper, lead, zinc and marble of various kinds have been found. The climate is bleak, the soil, as a whole, is barren,

COLORED CLIFFS NEAR KANAB, UTAH.

with spots of great fertility; and where irrigated, as it is in some sections, it is very productive. The chief crops are wheat, oats, barley, maize, flax, hemp, and fruits; and cattle and sheep are abundant. The chief manufactures are those required in a new country, such as farming implements, furniture, carriages, woolen goods, leather, steam-engines, cutlery, machinery, etc. The great Mormon temple is a vast structure, and many of the public buildings are expensive. Besides the common schools, there are many private schools and academies. The university at Salt Lake City has medical, collegiate, normal and preparatory departments. The constitution grants the right of suffrage to women. Population in 1880, 143,963, and in 1890, 205,498.

MARBLE CAÑON OF THE COLORADO.

ARIZONA.

Arizona was formerly a part of New Mexico, including what was known as the "Gadsden Purchase," but was made a separate Territory in 1863. It is a rough and elevated country of broad plateaus some seven thousand or more feet above the level of the sea, and the peaks of some of its mountains are from twelve thousand to fourteen thousand feet high. Its grazing lands cover three-fourths of the Territory, but its chief wealth is in its mineral resources, which are of great value and are being rapidly developed. The rivers, flowing southward, have worn enormous gullies or cañons in their course. The great cañon of the Colorado is the largest in the world, being four hundred miles long, with walls perpendicular, and from fifteen hundred to six thousand feet high, while at the bottom of this vast chasm the river plunges and roars in cataracts and whirlpools that make extended navigation impossible, and render even exploration difficult and dangerous. The illustration on page 213 gives a view of Moqui, one of the stone cities of Arizona, inhabited by the Pueblos or Moquis Indians. These towns are numerous along the Colorado river. They are built upon commanding eminences, and can be reached only through narrow defiles in the rocks on which they stand. Many of them are without population, and are but deserted relics of a once numerous people — perhaps of a civilization.

CLIFF DWELLINGS, ARIZONA.

The Territory has an area of 114,000 square miles. In the northern part the climate is cold, but in the southern part it is delightful. Of the Indians, who are numerous, some five thousand are settled on reservations, engaged in agriculture and cattle-raising. In the northern part are the Pueblo or "Town Indians," supposed to be the remains of the once powerful Aztecs, or of even some earlier race. They are a quiet, inoffensive people, dwelling in rude stone houses, and having many of the arts of civilaiztion. Educational interests are but little developed. Population in 1880, 40,404, and in 1890, 59,691.

THE INDIAN TERRITORY.

The Indian Territory is not like the regularly organized Territories which have been described, but is the region set apart as the home of the civilized, or partly civilized remnants of the once powerful tribes of Indians, who, from time to time, have been removed by the government from different parts of the Union, and are now upon separate reservations, under forms of government established by themselves, living

DISTANT VIEW OF MOQUI, WITH SHEEP-PENS IN THE FOREGROUND.

at peace with each other and with the United States. In 1830, Congress passed an Act setting apart all that part of the United States west of the Mississippi, and not within Missouri, Louisiana or Arkansas, to be known as "the Indian country."

Parts of it have since been organized into new States and Territories, and to the remainder has been added a strip of land from Texas, the whole making the "Indian Territory."

The area of the Territory is 74,127 square miles, of which somewhat more than two-thirds are assigned to the Indians, and on which are twenty different reservations occupied by as many tribes of Indians. These reservations occupy some 47,000 square miles of the Territory, and some 22,000 square miles are as yet unassigned. Agents representing the United States live among the various tribes, having an oversight of their affairs and interests, and protecting them from encroachments by the whites. The occupations of the Indians are agricultural. There are over two hundred common schools and ten high schools in the Territory. Nearly all the tribes have abandoned their pagan religion. The traffic in ardent spirits is absolutely prohibited, and no other Territory of the United States has as many houses of worship, or so many Sunday schools, or so good attendance at both in proportion to its population, as are found in this. The population does not appear in the census of 1880, but it is reported to be about 75,000, exclusive of whites.

OKLAHOMA.

Oklahoma is the last organized of the Territories. It consists of the southern part of the Indian Territory, the Cherokee country, and the small region which has long been known as "No Man's Land." It was made a Territory in 1890, and has an area of 39,030 square miles. As to soil, climate and productions, it is like the southern part of the Indian Territory, having rich lands and giving fine openings for settlers, who rushed in in large numbers as soon as the region was open for occupation. It is still, as with all new Territories when first open for immigrants, in comparatively an unorganized state as to society and public works, but is rapidly taking shape and gives promise of great progress and prosperity. Population in 1890, 60,834.

ALASKA.

Alaska, the word signifying "the great land," is the name given to the whole of what was Russian America in the northwest corner of North America, including all the islands in the Aleutian Archipelago, except Copper and Behring Islands on the coast of Kamtchatka. Its area, including that of the islands, is 580,170 square miles in extent. It was purchased from Russia by the United States, in 1867, for $7,200,000.

Such is the statement generally received, but it is said to have been publicly stated by General Sherman that the real history of its possession by the United States is as follows: In the War of Secession, when there was apparently danger that the Southern Confederacy might be recognized by England or some other European power, several Russian war vessels made their appearance on our coast. These vessels, it is said, had been privately engaged by our government to aid in protecting our ports if it was found that protection was needed. Alaska, it was claimed, was a burden on Russia, protected and cared for at great expense and giving no satisfactory returns, so that Russia would willingly have given it to our government without compensation. And the payment apparently made for its purchase, was, it is said, actual payment for the

presence of the Russian vessels, which, if need be, would have been actively engaged
on the side of our nation, while it was understood by the public that the price paid was
only for Alaska, the whole of which might have been obtained at a far lower rate, if not
gratuitously, from Russia, to which it was a useless region.

Such is the story as publicly given by General Sherman, who must have been
informed as to the secret history of the war and its connected public movements, a
story which, it is believed, has never been denied. But whether it be correct or not,
Alaska at the time mentioned came into possession of the United States. The region
was long the headquarters of the Russian American Fur Company; and its fisheries and
fur trade were and are its leading industries, being unsurpassed in value in any part of
the world. The capture of seals is especially important, 160,000 of them having been,

SITKA, ALASKA.

for years, annually taken in Alaskan waters. They have been killed in such numbers as
to endanger their entire destruction, and the American and British governments have
now united in staying their slaughter, till by arbitration, the extent of control over the
seal producing regions can be settled to the satisfaction of both nations.

Besides the seals, the principle fur-bearing animals of Alaska are the fox, martin,
mink, otter, lynx, black bear, and wolverine. There are also the coarser furs of the
reindeer, mountain sheep, goat, wolf, muskrat, and ermine. There are also large
deposits of coal, copper, sulphur, amber, gold and silver, the last two being of great

value. The lumber of Alaska is varied, and almost unlimited in extent. The forests of yellow cedar, white pine, hemlock, and balsam fir are enough to supply the world.

The climate, of course, varies with the vast extent of the country, in some places being that of the extreme Arctic regions, while the influence of the great Gulf Stream of the Pacific makes the southern coast and the adjacent islands as mild in winter as in New York. The Yukon river is a wonderful stream, two thousand miles long, and navigable for fifteen hundred miles from its mouth, and a thousand miles above its mouth it is, in places, twenty miles wide, including the intervening islands. Polygamy and sorcery are common with the natives, as well as many of the gross and cruel practices of heathenism. They believe in the transmigration of souls from one body to another, but not to an animal; and the wish is often expressed that in the next change they may be born into this or that powerful family. If slaves are sacrificed at their burial, it is supposed to relieve their owners from work in the next world. Strong efforts are being made to civilize and christianize the people.

SCENES IN THE INLAND PASSAGE.

The census of 1890 reports the population of Alaska to be 31,000, of whom 4,800 are whites. The native population is several thousand less than it was ten years ago, the agent saying: "They have learned the use of intoxicating liquor from the whalers, and it is killing them off rapidly."

THE DISTRICT OF COLUMBIA.

The District of Columbia is neither a State nor a Territory, but has an organization peculiar to itself. It is a small territory between Maryland and Virginia, or rather bounded on three sides by Maryland, and on the west by the Potomac river, selected by Congress in 1790 as the place where the national capital of the United States should be permanently located.

The old Continental Congress had, at various times, met in different places: in 1774-6, at Philadelphia; in 1776, at Baltimore; in 1777, at Philadelphia; and in the same year at York, and then at Lancaster; in 1778-83, at Philadelphia; in 1783, at Princeton; and in the same year at Annapolis; in 1784, at Trenton; and in 1785-89, at New York. These various changes were caused by the exigencies of the war. But the first Congress of the United States under the Constitution was held in New York in 1790, the general government having been organized in that city, March 4, 1789; and there Congress continued to hold its sessions till 1791, after which the " Federal Town " was to be Philadelphia till the year 1800.

The question of the location of the capital had been somewhat discussed in the convention at Philadelphia in 1787, but it was not till the summer of 1790 that it was finally decided at the meeting of Congress in New York. The discussion of the question was long and earnest. New York, Philadelphia, Baltimore, Harrisburg, Trenton, and several other places urged their claims to be made the capital city, and for a time it seemed almost impossible to make a selection. Maryland and Virginia had offered the territory needful for the Federal District, and after many votes had been taken, Congress, in July, gave to President Washington the sole power of selecting a " Federal Territory," not exceeding ten miles square, on the Potomac, to be "the permanent seat of the government of the United States."

The final adoption of the present site was brought about by a stroke of policy, or a legislative bargain, "which," says another, "in the mildest slang of to-day would be called a log-rolling job." Hamilton's bill for the assumption by the general government of the debts incurred by the States during the Revolutionary War, amounting to some $20,000,000, had been defeated in Congress, and if not reconsidered and passed, it was feared that the Eastern or creditor States might secede from the Union, and it was through the influence of Jefferson and Hamilton that the bill was reconsidered and passed, the Southern States, which had strongly opposed it, agreeing to its passage on condition the seat of government was fixed where it now is, on the Potomac.

The territory, ten miles square, on both sides of the Potomac, was ceded by Maryland and Virginia, on condition that Congress, or the United States authorities, should have exclusive control over it forever. Maryland gave sixty-four square miles and Virginia thirty-six; but in 1846, the Virginia portion was returned to that State, no part of the government buildings having been erected on that side of the river and no public use made of that part of the grant.

The government title to the territory thus taken was perfected, suitable buildings for the time were erected, and in December, 1800, the capital was fixed at the new federal city which was named " Washington." The formal transfer of the government from Philadelphia to Washington took place in October. And that it was indeed a day

WASHINGTON.—1: FROM STATE, WAR, AND NAVY BUILDINGS.   2: FROM SMITHSONIAN INSTITUTE.

of small things is evident when, as we read, "a single packet sloop brought all the office furniture of the departments, beside seven large and five small boxes, containing all the archives of the government." The officials numbered fifty-four persons, including President Adams, the secretaries and all the clerks of the departments. The crudeness and discomfort of Washington seem to have dissatisfied and even disgusted them all. Mrs. Adams spoke of it as "a wilderness city," and Secretary Wolcott, in a letter to his wife, said: "There are but few houses, and most of them are small and miserable huts. The people are poor, and as far as I can judge, live like fishes, by eating each other." A member of Congress, in a letter at the time, says: "Pennsylvania avenue is a deep morass covered with elder bushes, which are cut through to the president's house." There seemed to be only two really comfortable habitations within the bounds of the city, and the roads in every direction were muddy and unimproved. Newspapers and

WASHINGTON IN 1810 — THE OLD CAPITOL.

satirists everywhere cracked their jokes at the infant city. The capitol was called "the palace in the wilderness," and Pennsylvania avenue, "the great Serbonian Bog;" Georgetown was said to be "a city of houses without streets," and Washington "a city of streets without houses." And when there was some talk of removing the capital to another place a clever Scotch artist made a good deal of sport by the caricature of a congressman, with the capitol strapped on his back, ready to start as soon as it was decided where to go.

For years afterward Washington was but the skeleton of a town, and from its greatly extended but incomplete plans, it was nicknamed "the city of magnificent distances." The appearance of the city, even so late as 1810, with the comparatively small capitol building, may be seen in the engraving (p. 219), though at that time there were no sidewalks, and the broad avenues were but thoroughfares cut through the woods or farms of the region then almost unoccupied. Of the contrast to the present appearance some idea may be formed from the second engraving, on page 221.

During the war of 1812, the British fleet, sailing up Chesapeake Bay, landed some 4,500 men, who began their march for Washington. At Bladensburg, five miles from the city, they were opposed by a large body of raw militia and a few hundred seamen, but overcoming these forces, they continued their march, and on the 24th of August, 1814, they reached the city, and soon entered the hall of the House of Representatives, where the soldiers formed around the Speaker's chair, in which Cockburn, seating himself, derisively called the assemblage to order, crying out, "Shall this harbor of Yankee democracy be burned? All in favor of it, say Aye!" As all at once cried out in the affirmative, he gave orders to fire the building, which soon was in flames. Leaving the fire burning furiously, the soldiers marched on to set fire to other public edifices, but a severe rain setting in, extinguished the flames on the capitol, so that though the inside was burned the walls were left standing. Afterwards the building was restored, or rather rebuilt, and greatly enlarged, and in 1827 was reported to Congress as finished, covering then about one and a half acres, and being 352 feet long, and 145 feet high to the top of the dome, its construction having cost $2,433,814. In 1851, and several following years, a new dome and other improvements were added at a cost of $1,250,000, making the total expenditures on the building nearly $13,000,000. It now covers an area of over three and a half acres, and the grounds around it comprise forty-two acres. Its total length is 751 feet, and its greatest breadth 324 feet. Its basement is devoted to the committee-rooms of Congress, the law library, and the document and folding-rooms, the Congressional post office, and the Senate and House restaurants and offices. The principal story contains the Rotunda, the Statuary Hall, the Supreme Court room, the library of Congress and the halls of both Houses of Congress, with various rooms for the members and public officers.

The drenching rain, which extinguished the fire at the capitol, saved the White House and other public buildings from total destruction, and the enemy left the city late that night, fearing an attack under cover of the darkness; and taking to their fleet, which had come as far as Alexandria, sailed down the Potomac. The damage done by their invasion was estimated at $1,000,000. Seventy-five Americans were killed

THE CAPITOL.—EAST VIEW.

1.—THE BARTHOLDI FOUNTAIN IN THE BOTANICAL GARDEN. 2.—STATUE OF
GENERAL SCOTT AT THE SOLDIERS' HOME. 3.—MILLS' STATUE OF GENERAL
WASHINGTON. 4.—MARBLE GROUP ON THE PORTICO OF THE CAPITOL.
5.—STATUE OF GENERAL GREENE. 6.—MILLS' STATUE OF GENERAL JACKSON.

or wounded in the
conflict at Bladensburg,
and the British suffered
the loss of several
hundred men.

At this period
Washington was com-
paratively a scattered
village in the midst of
farms or plantations.
Nearly all the domestic
and field labor, in and
around it, was performed
by slaves, who were
generally treated with
kindness and well
clothed and fed, and
many of whom had neat
and comfortable homes.
On many plantations
they were allowed good
pay for extra labor, and
so not a few of them
saved money enough by
industry to purchase
their freedom. The
chief culture was that
of tobacco, which made
many of the planters
very wealthy. The
tobacco was largely
shipped to Europe, and
it was generally brought
to the place of shipment
in hogsheads. Through
these hogsheads a hole
was bored and an axle
was placed in it from
end to end. To this
axle a shaft was
attached, like the shaft
or thills of a cart, and
horses or mules were
hitched to it. The
hogshead was then
drawn along the streets,

up hill and down, rolling and bumping over stones and rough places till it reached the place of shipment. The total annual cost of supporting a slave was about $98, but the annual earnings of his labor amounted to hundreds of dollars.

From 1825 to 1829, during the administration of John Quincy Adams, the population of Washington was about 20,000, but it was a sprawling, slow-going, uninteresting city, with very few signs of promise; and even so late as 1840, the French minister said: "It is neither a city, nor a village, nor the country, but a building-yard, in a desolate spot, where living is unbearable." "There were no public schools," says another, "and stray cows and pigs were the statuary that adorned the squares and parks.

In 1870, however, Washington was roused from its lethargy by an earnest effort which was made to remove the capital to St. Louis, which offered to expend millions to make a Federal city worthy of the name. At this juncture an energetic and strong man, Alexander R. Shepperd, came into leadership, and soon turned the tide that was setting for removal. He was favored by the strong friendship of President Grant, and was noted for his immense energy and invincible resolution. His aim was to make Washington the cleanest and most beautiful city in America, if not in the world, and to accomplish this end the old municipal government was abolished, and in its place a territorial government with a legislature and an active board of public works was established. Eighty miles of the half-made streets and avenues were improved, and nearly all of the more settled streets were

1.—THE NAVAL STATUE, OR MONUMENT OF PEACE. 2.—GREENOUGH'S STATUE OF WASHINGTON. 3.—BROWN'S STATUE OF GENERAL SCOTT.

paved with wood or concrete. A general and costly system of sewers was begun. Scores of new parks were graded, fenced, and set with trees and fountains. From $15,000,000 to $20,000,000 were expended in the great undertaking. Over a thousand new buildings were erected. In ten years the city was transformed. Fifty thousand shade trees were planted. The streets were covered with smooth and almost noiseless pavements. Squares and circles were adorned with statues of heroes and distinguished men. Market buildings, splendid school houses, and elegant churches were erected, and water works and sewers were constructed on a scale unsurpassed in the country. Washington was gradually made one of the most healthful, attractive, and elegant cities in the country. In 1880, the population was 147,624, and in 1890, 229,796; and beside this there is a floating population in the winter months which is estimated at 50,000, composed of congressmen and their families, people of means, students and professional men from

1.—STATUE OF GENERAL RAWLINS. 2.—WARD'S STATUE OF GENERAL THOMAS.
3.—STATUE OF EMANCIPATION. 4.—STATUE OF GENERAL McPHERSON.
5.—STATUE OF ADMIRAL FARRAGUT.

WASHINGTON MONUMENT.

various parts of the land, so that year by year the capital is rapidly increasing in prosperity and importance.

The public buildings of the city are numerous, and some of them imposing and elegant. The number of persons employed in them in the public service is some 20,000, and as the country grows this number is steadily increasing. Tourists from every part of the world, in great numbers, visit the city, while from all parts of the land hundreds of persons arrive for business with the public departments. The extensive libraries and scientific collections attract many students and those engaged in special researches. The vast collections of natural history in the Smithsonian Institute and the National Museum, the great law library of the government, and the libraries of the Patent office, and of the State, War, and Navy departments are largely sought and used by professional persons from every part of the States. The statues and monuments in various parts of the city add greatly to its attractiveness.

The Washington Monument has been called "the world's greatest cenotaph," and has cost about $1,200,000. It rises 572 feet above the surrounding ground, and at its base is 55 feet and at its top about 30 feet square. In the interior lining of the obelisk are numerous blocks of stone presented by the cities and States of the Union, by foreign countries, and by various societies and associations. The ascent to the top is made by an elevator and also by a spiral staircase, and the interior of the shaft is lighted by electricity, as the only openings, except the entrance doors, are the small windows at the top. The shaft is the largest structure of the kind in the world, and is higher than any of the cathedral spires or monuments of Europe or the East. The prospect from the top is sublime beyond description.

The Executive Mansion, commonly known as the "White House," is another of the noted buildings of Washington. It stands in the center of an enclosed plat of twenty acres, which slopes gradually to the river bank, giving a far-reaching view over the Potomac and the blue hills of Virginia. It is built of free-stone painted white. After the burning of the building by the British, in 1814, the house was reconstructed, and was re-opened in 1818, more beautiful than before it was set on fire by the enemy. The building itself may be seen in the engraving.

THE WHITE HOUSE, FROM PENNSYLVANIA AVENUE.

Some of the other noted buildings of Washington are the Smithsonian Institute the buildings of the various departments of the government, the Naval Observatory, the Soldiers' Home, the Army and Medical Museum, the Hospital for the Insane, the Howard and Columbian Universities, the Corcoran Gallery, the Deaf and Dumb Institute, and so forth.

Other objects of interest, as associated with the city and the history of the country, are Mount Vernon, so long the home of Washington, and Arlington, formerly belonging to Daniel Parke Custis, whose widow became the wife of Washington, and which through her descended to General Robert E. Lee, and after the War of Secession was bought by the United States government for $150,000. It consists of 1,160 acres, two hundred acres of which are now the National Military Cemetery, where are buried 16,264 soldiers who lost their lives in the War of Secession, 11,915 of whom were identified, and 4,349 were unknown. In it is also a vault containing the remains of 2,911 unknown Union soldiers, gathered from various battle-fields after the war was over. Mount Vernon is also seen in the distance, standing on the brow of a sloping hill, a hundred and twenty-four feet above the river, which at this point is two miles in width. In Washington's time the estate comprised 8,000 acres, but since his death portions of it have from time to time been sold by the heirs, till now only 200 acres with the house have been retained. It is now in the charge of an

MOUNT VERNON, FROM THE POTOMAC RIVER.

association, and is visited by thousands of people every year. In 1876, the Centennial year, it was visited by 45,000 persons.

Until 1871, the District was governed directly by Congress, but since that time, by an Act of Congress, it has had the right of self-government as an organized Territory, having a governor and secretary appointed by the President and Senate, and also a Council and House of Delegates, and the right to send a representative to Congress. The city has numerous hospitals, and charitable houses for various classes of the unfortunate and needy; for orphans, sailors, soldiers, the insane, for the freedmen, etc. In the city are several colleges or universities, and excellent schools of every kind.

Beside the city of Washington, Georgetown is a large city within the limits of the District and separated from it only by a bridge, over which street cars and travel in general are passing continually.

DEC. 26, 1776

THE DEFENDER OF THE MOTHERS
WILL BE
THE PROTECTOR OF THE DAUGHTERS.

WASHINGTON'S RECEPTION AT TRENTON.

CHAPTER III.

WASHINGTON'S ADMINISTRATION — 1789 TO 1797.

INDEPENDENCE having been declared and acknowledged, the Constitution adopted, and the government under it established, Washington was chosen President, and John Adams, Vice-President. The inauguration took place in New York, April 30, 1789. As Washington was on his way to that city, which was then the seat of government he was everywhere met and greeted by crowds of admiring people. At Trenton, for example, where he had fought several battles, a triumphal arch, supported by thirteen pillars, was thrown over a bridge he was to pass, and on it was the inscription, "The defender of the mothers will be the protector of the daughters." Beneath the arch stood a party of young girls with baskets of flowers, who, as he drew near, sang:

> Welcome, mighty chief, once more;
> Welcome to this grateful shore.
> Now no mercenary foe
> Aims again the fatal blow,—
> Aims at thee the fatal blow.
>
> Virgins fair, and matrons grave,
> Those thy conquering arm did save,
> Raise for thee triumphal bowers,
> Strew for thee the way with flowers,—
> Strew our hero's way with flowers.

And as Washington rode on, they strewed the flowers in profusion in his way. All the march to New York was a triumphal procession. The inauguration was on the balcony of "Federal Hall."

The government, as we have seen, consisted of three branches—the *Legislative*, to make laws; the *Executive*, to see them executed, and the *Judicial*, to interpret them. The *Executive* began with four departments, that of the State having charge of foreign affairs; that of the Treasury; that of War; and that of Law or Justice. The officers of the first three were called Secretaries, and the last, Attorney-General. All were appointed by the President as members of his Cabinet, and had to be confirmed by the Senate. Other departments have since been added, viz.: the Secretary of the Navy, the Postmaster-General, and the Secretary of the Interior. Besides these there are several "Commissioners," as of Patents, the Land Office, Pensions, Agriculture, Education, Labor, the Indians, Railroads, and the Civil Service.

In the first year of Washington's administration, Benjamin Franklin, one of the grandest men ever born in this country, died in Philadelphia, aged eighty-four years. Congress was organized on the 4th of March. At its first session it submitted

GEORGE WASHINGTON.

to the States several amendments to the Constitution, ten of which were ratified in 1791. To provide a revenue for the support of the government a tonnage tax was laid on merchantships, and duties were levied on certain imported goods, making what is known as the "Tariff." Provision was also made for the public debt incurred by the Revolutionary War, which was now some $75,000,-000. Congress also established the Bank of the United States, chartered for twenty years, with a capital of $10,000,000, and located at Philadelphia, with branches in other places. The presidential term had been fixed by the Constitution at four years, and the first term expired in 1793. Washington was a second time elected, with John Adams as Vice-President.

At this time, the French Revolution had run its course of violence, the king had been executed, a republic had been established, and war had followed between France and England. Genet, sent by the French government, had demanded that the United States should form an alliance with France against Great Britain, but Washington had already issued his famous proclamation of non-interference with European politics and quarrels, in which he was supported by Hamilton and the Federalists, while the Republicans, led by Jefferson and others, were in favor of war to aid France in her conflict with England. Genet, emboldened by the Republican feeling, impudently threatened to appeal to the people against Washington, and confident of success had already fitted out privateers to prey upon English commerce. But Washington was firm, and at once demanded the recall of Genet, who was accordingly called back to France.

The feelings of the people against Great Britain were still bitter, not merely from memories of the Revolution, but because England had not yet surrendered some Western forts as agreed by the treaty of 1783, and had allowed the capture of neutral vessels, and also had impressed into British service seamen known to be Americans. To preserve peace and a friendly policy, John Jay, the chief justice, was sent by Washington to England, where he concluded a treaty, which, though strongly objected to by the Republicans, was ratified in 1795, and doubtless through the wise policy of Washington, saved the Nation from the evils of another war.

During this administration, Jefferson and Hamilton, leaders of the two great political parties, so differed that both resigned office as Secretaries of State and of the

FRANKLIN'S GRAVE AT PHILADELPHIA.

Treasury. There had been troubles, too, in the West with the Indians, who, however, were completely routed by General Wayne, in 1794, and forced to relinquish their claims to Ohio. In the same year, what is known as the "Whiskey Rebellion," occurred in Western Pennsylvania, the people rising to resist the tax imposed by Congress on distilled spirits, a rebellion which was broken up by troops sent by Washington. In 1795, a treaty with Spain settled the boundaries between the Spanish possessions and Louisiana and Florida, and secured to the United States the free navigation of the Mississippi; a large sum was paid for the liberation of persons who had been taken captive by the Bey of Algiers; and the work of preparing a navy was begun. In 1791, Vermont, and in 1792, Kentucky, were admitted to the Union, and the "Territory south of the Ohio" was organized. At the close of his second administration, which ended March 4th, 1797, Washington, who had refused re-election, published his "Farewell Address," a paper eminently marked by wise counsel and devoted patriotism, and then retired to his estates at Mt. Vernon.

Two candidates were now brought forward for the office of president. John Adams by the Federal party, and Thomas Jefferson by the Republicans. Adams received the highest number of votes, thus making him president, and Jefferson the next highest number, making him vice-president.

As Washington was the first one to hold the high office of president of the United States, there were several matters of interest as to his important position and his

VIEW OF WASHINGTON'S HOUSE, MT. VERNON.

relations to the public; but the first question that arose was as to what should be the official title of the president. Washington himself was in favor of the words, "His High Mightiness," the title of the Stadtholder of Holland, which at that time was a republic. Other titles were suggested and discussed, but finally it was agreed that he should be addressed as "His Excellency." In going to the sessions of Congress he was driven in a State coach, the body of which was a hemisphere, cream-colored and ornamented with festoons of flowers supported by figures of cupid. On great occasions the coach was drawn by six horses; at ordinary times by four, and on Sundays by two. The driver and postillions were in liveries of scarlet and white.

The levees or public receptions of the president were held once every two weeks, in his own house, on the afternoon of the day, when, with the members of his cabinet and other leading men, he received visitors. At these levees he was usually dressed in black velvet, with light-colored waistcoat, yellow gloves, and silver buckles at his knees and on his shoes. His hair was powdered and gathered in a silk bag behind. He held his cocked hat in his hand, and wore a long sword, the scabbard of which was of polished white leather. He never shook hands with those who called, but bowed to each one and had brief conversation with them.

Mrs. Washington, who was always addressed as Lady Washington, also had her levees, which were held in the evening, and at which all appeared in full dress. The birthday of the President was celebrated by dinners and public meetings in all the cities and large towns of the nation, as the birthdays of the kings of England had been in colonial days.

WASHINGTON'S BED-CHAMBER.

Such formality and care for costume and ceremony was not confined to the President, but extended to those who were prominent in public office. The judges of the supreme court in winter wore robes of scarlet faced with velvet, and in summer had black silk robes, such as are worn by the judges of that court at the present day. Clergymen wore wigs with gowns and bands in the pulpit, and cocked hats in the street. Ladies wore elegant silks and brocades, and had their hair dressed with powder and pomatum, and often built up high above the head, and on great occasions the hairdressers were kept incessantly busy from early morning till night. The clothes of gentlemen were of various colors and of rich materials, such as are now used only by ladies; and the wig, the white stock, the satin embroidered vest, the black satin breeches, the white silk stockings, and a fine broadcloth or velvet coat was the dress when going to entertainments. At home, a velvet or linen cap took the place of the wig, while a dressing gown lined with silk took the place of the coat, and the feet were supplied with slippers of some fancy color.

The ceremony and formality of Washington's receptions, as well as his style of living, were thought by many to give dignity and importance to the office of president, but others disliked and opposed it as ostentatious and savoring too much of the customs

JOHN ADAMS.

of monarchy. Less ceremony and plainer tastes gradually prevailed, so that when Jefferson was President he went to the other extreme, often walking to the doors of Congress, or riding by himself without attendants and tying his horse to a post, while he was attending to public business.

ADAMS' ADMINISTRATION—1797 TO 1801.

The second President of the United States, John Adams, of Massachusetts, was inaugurated March 4, 1797, with Thomas Jefferson, of Virginia, as Vice-President. Mr. Adams was born in October, 1735, in that part of Braintree which is now Quincy, Massachusetts. He was graduated at Harvard College, and taking up the profession of law, soon rose to a distinguished position in the State and Nation. He was a prominent member of several of the colonial Congresses, was employed in several important negotiations with European powers, and especially in the commission for settling the conditions of peace with England in 1782. In 1785, he went to London as the first ambassador from the United States; and when George III. expressed his pleasure in receiving an ambassador who had no prejudices in favor of France, his prompt reply was "I have no prejudices except in favor of my native land."

In all internal affairs the United States were now prospering, and the agricultural and commercial wealth of the country had greatly increased. But there was trouble with France, and that nation being dissatisfied with our treaty with England, had given orders to prey on our commerce, and had ordered Pinckney, our minister, to leave the country. War being thus threatened, Congress was called together, and John Marshall and Elbridge Gerry were appointed envoys to France, that, with Pinckney, they might attempt a reconciliation with that country. To these gentlemen it was intimated by the French agents, that unless they paid large sums of money they would not be allowed even a favorable hearing. This is said to have brought forth from Pinckney the memorable expression, "Millions for defense, but not one cent for tribute," an expression which was re-echoed through the United States. Marshall and Pinckney were ordered to leave France, and Gerry was soon recalled. Measures were at once taken to prepare for war. The navy and army were increased, and Washington was appointed commander-in-chief of the latter, with Hamilton as active commander, and the conflict beginning, Commodore Truxton, with the ship Constellation, in 1799 gained one or two victories over French men-of-war. But though hostilities had actually begun on the ocean, change of circumstances in France prevented further conflict. In 1799 Bonaparte overthrew the existing government in France, and taking control into his own hands, made peace with the United States in 1800.

MARTHA WASHINGTON'S BED-CHAMBER.

During 1798 the disturbed state of foreign affairs had led to great excitement and heated discussion throughout the country and what were known as the "Alien and Sedition Laws" were passed by Congress. The first increased to fourteen years the period of naturalization for foreigners, and empowered the President to send out of the United States any foreigner whose presence he thought dangerous to the public welfare. The other punished with a fine and imprisonment the uttering of "any false, scandalous or malicious statements" concerning the President or Congress. These laws were bitterly denounced, and though the first was never carried into effect, they made the administration unpopular, and prepared the way for the defeat of the Federal party in the next national election.

On the 14th of December, 1799, Washington died, the sad tidings of his death filling the land with sorrow, and wakening afresh the universal admiration felt for his character. In the next year the capital was removed to the city of Washington, and the Northwestern Territory was divided into the Territories of Ohio and Indiana, of the latter of which General William H. Harrison was made governor. At the presidential election in the fall of the year, the candidates of the Federal party were John Adams and Charles C. Pinckney, and those of the Republicans, Thomas Jefferson and Aaron Burr, the two last named being elected. As the law then was, it devolved on the House of Representatives to decide, in view of the votes given, which of the two

WASHINGTON'S GRAVE, MOUNT VERNON.

should be the chief magistrate, and on the thirty-sixth ballot Jefferson was made President, and Burr Vice-President. The votes in all the previous balloting had been forty-six for Jefferson and forty-six for Burr. Then Bayard, of the Federal party, proposed to Burr that he would vote for and make him President if he would agree to carry out certain views and measures of the Federal party, which Burr positively refused to do. The same, or a similar offer was then made to Jefferson, and he assented to the proposal. The Bayard vote was then cast for him, and made him President, giving the Vice-Presidency to Burr.

JEFFERSON'S ADMINISTRATION — 1801 TO 1809.

The third President of the United States, Thomas Jefferson, of Virginia, was inaugurated March 4, 1801, with Aaron Burr, of New York, as Vice-President. Mr. Jefferson was born in Albermarle county, Virginia, April 2, 1743. After studying at

THOMAS JEFFERSON.

the college of William and Mary, he entered on the practice of law, and early took an active and prominent part in the measures that led to the calling of the Continental Congress, of which he was a member, and for which he drew up the celebrated Declaration of Independence. He was chosen governor of Virginia in 1779, and in 1784 was made minister to France, and he was also Secretary of State under Washington.

The bills to establish religious freedom, to abolish entails, and to put an end to the right of primogeniture, were some of the reforms he effected in Virginia, and to him we owe the system of decimal coinage and currency. He also advocated the abolition of slavery after the year 1800, but to this Congress would not agree. He was chiefly instrumental in establishing the college out of which grew the University of Virginia, in which he took so much pride that he wrote as a part of his own epitaph, "Father of the University of Virginia."

Elected by the Republican or Democratic party, Jefferson acted in public on the principles of democratic simplicity. He rode to the capital on horseback, and delivered in person his first inaugural address to Congress, though afterward his messages were sent by a secretary, which has since continued to be the custom. He also began the custom of giving the most important offices to men of his own party, thus laying the foundation of the political maxim of a later day, that "to the victors belong the spoils."

The "Alien and Sedition" laws had expired by their own limitation, and Jefferson granted pardon to all who had been imprisoned under the latter, and Congress, at his suggestion, abolished internal taxes, reduced both the army and navy, and introduced other economical reforms. But the most important event of his administration was the "Louisiana purchase," which added to the United States a territory larger than all the thirteen original States, and opened to navigation and commerce the great water ways of the Mississippi, from its mouth to its distant sources and tributaries, extending to the great regions of the North and West. This vast region, including all from the west of the Mississippi to the Rocky Mountains, and north to the British possessions, had been ceded by Spain to France, and Bonaparte had intended making it an immense French colony, and had even appointed a governor to carry out his plans of French sovereignty. But needing funds for his expected war with Great Britain, he offered to sell the entire territory for some $15,000,000, and his offer was accepted, and the purchase was made in 1803.

The purchase at the time was unauthorized, but was afterward ratified by Congress. It is not strange that Livingston, who, with James Monroe, was one of the commissioners making the purchase, afterward said, "We have lived long, but this is the noblest work of our whole lives." Napoleon also, who, while he felt the necessity of the sale, saw the vast importance of the region, is reported to have said: "I have just given to England a maritime rival that will sooner or later humble her pride." In 1804, the northern part of this region was explored by Captains Lewis and Clark, who brought back detailed accounts of its geography and resources. A part of it was organized as the "Territory of Orleans," the other portions retaining the name of the Territory of Louisiana. In 1805, a part of the Northwestern Territory was organized as a separate territory, under the name of Michigan.

For a long time before this the Barbary States had been interfering with our commerce, and had taken and held in captivity not a few of our people. In 1803, Commodore Preble, with a squadron, was sent against them, and in the summer of the next year he bombarded Tripoli, and with the help of a deposed sovereign of Tripoli, captured the seaport of Derne, and secured a treaty of peace, effecting the liberation of many sailors who had been held as captives. Before this, when the frigate Philadelphia had been run aground in the harbor, Lieutenant Decatur, with less than sixty men, had boarded that vessel, under the very guns of the enemy, and killed or forced overboard every one of her defenders, set fire to the vessel, and returned with not a man killed and only four wounded.

In the meantime a most sad and tragic event occurred at home. Aaron Burr, the vice-president, seeing he would not again be likely to be nominated for the presidency, sought to be governor of New York, but was defeated mainly through the opposition of Alexander Hamilton, who thus incurred his bitter enmity and was challenged by Burr to a duel, in which he was killed, the country thus losing one of the most brilliant and useful men of its early history. Burr afterward was accused of plotting, with Blenerhasset and others, to separate the Southern and Western States from the Union, and organize another government of which he was to be the head. He always denied this, and in his later years is reported to have said that his only plan was to seize Mexico, and hold it as a separate government till it might possibly become a State of the Union, thus doing for Mexico what forty years later was done by General Sam

Houston for Texas. But political feeling was bitter against him and he was arrested and tried for treason, but was acquitted. He afterward went abroad, and later came back to New York, to engage in the practice of law, but he was generally neglected, and died in poverty in 1836.

In 1804, Jefferson was re-elected, with George Clinton as Vice-President, but by a twelfth amendment to the Constitution, the president and vice-president were henceforth to be voted for separately by the electors, so that it could never again be left to the House of Representatives, as in the case of Jefferson and Burr, to decide which of two men having the same number of votes should be president. During Jefferson's second term of office, war was going on between France and England, and the latter, by

DUEL BETWEEN BURR AND HAMILTON.

her powerful navy, having swept from the seas most of the vessels of France and her allies, the Americans found profitable employment in carrying in their vessels goods for France and other European nations. To put a stop to this, England, in 1806, declared a blockade of the coast of Europe, thus shutting out American and other vessels; in retaliation for which Bonaparte declared a blockade of the British Islands. American vessels on their way to their different ports were captured by the English or French, and as a consequence, American commerce was seriously injured; and later still, the famous "orders in council" of the British, and the "Milan Decree" by Napoleon, worked ruinously to our shipping and commerce.

As a further step in their arrogance and injury, the British asserted their right to search American vessels, and to take from them any sailors whom they claimed as having been British subjects, and pressing them into the English service; and in carrying out this insolent claim they frequently seized and forced into the British navy, Americans, under pretense that they were deserters. In 1807, the American frigate Chesapeake refusing to give up men thus claimed, was fired upon by the British frigate Leopard. The Chesapeake was unable to make any resistance, and the officers tendered their swords, but the English officers declined to receive them, and demanded the muster-roll of the ship. Four of her crew, three of whom were Americans, were picked out as deserters, and carried off and impressed by the British; and though the act was

THE OFFICERS OF THE CHESAPEAKE OFFERING THEIR SWORDS.

afterward disavowed by the English government no reparation was made. This outrage brought out Jefferson's proclamation forbidding British vessels from entering our ports; and in 1807, Congress passed the "Embargo Act," prohibiting all exportation from our ports. The intended object of this measure was to force England and France to acknowledge our rights as neutrals, but in actual effect it caused great distress and was ruinous to our commerce; and the act being violently opposed, after about fourteen months was repealed. In this state of affairs Jefferson, having declined a nomination for a third term of office, retired from the presidency, and James Madison and George Clinton were nominated and elected as president and vice-president.

MADISON'S ADMINISTRATION — 1809 TO 1817.

The fourth President of the United States, James Madison of Virginia, was inaugurated March 4, 1809, with George Clinton of New York, as Vice-President.

He was born in King George's county, Virginia, March 16, 1751; was graduated

with high honor from Princeton College in 1771, and soon after entered on the practice of law. In 1776, he was a member of the Virginia Convention, and from this time on his life was devoted to politics, and he became one of the most eminent, accomplished, and respected of American statesmen. He was not regarded as an orator, but so extensive was his information, so luminous and discriminating his mind, and so uniformly sound his judgment, that Jefferson said of him that he was "first in every assembly of which he was a member;" and Chief Justice Marshall, when once asked, who of all the public speakers he had heard,

JAMES MADISON.

he thought the most eloquent, replied: "If eloquence includes persuasion by convincing, then Mr. Madison is the most eloquent man I ever heard."

Madison was from the beginning, intelligent and active in all that prepared the way for independence. He was one of the leading members of the convention that met in Philadelphia in 1787, for framing the Constitution of the United States; and next to Hamilton, he was the leading writer of the *Federalist*, of which Judge Story said: "It was an incomparable commentary on the Constitution." So successful was he in fixing his own views of government in that remarkable instrument, that he was often called the "Father of the Constitution." On coming to the presidency, Madison, who had favored a peace policy, found that war was inevitable. In 1809, the "Embargo Act" was repealed, and the "Non-Intercourse Act" was passed, forbidding trading with

16

Great Britain and France. France, in 1810, repealed the "Milan Decree"; in 1810, Madison, by proclamation, declared that commerce with France was free, but was prohibited to Great Britain. The right of search by the latter country was still insisted on, and six thousand seamen, who were not Englishmen, it is said, were pressed into the British service.

In 1811, the American frigate "President" hailing the British sloop of war "Little Belt," instead of a satisfactory answer received a shot in return. An action followed in which the British vessel was disabled and silenced, having eleven men killed and twenty-one wounded. Within seven or eight years the British had captured some nine hundred American vessels for violating their unjust regulations, and the indignant feelings of the American people had so increased that on the 19th of June, 1812, war was declared against England, and Henry Dearborn of Massachusetts, was appointed commander-in-chief, and the president was authorized to borrow $11,000,000.

The first aggressive movement was against Canada, led by General Hull, governor of Michigan, who crossed to Sandwich, but hearing that the British had taken Mackinaw, he returned to Detroit, where in turn he was attacked by General Brock and the British forces. The Americans were prepared and eager for battle, but Hull, who was both incompetent and cowardly, surrendered without an effort all his forces and the territory to the enemy, for which he was dismissed from the army and afterward court-martialed and sentenced to be shot, but was finally pardoned by the President. The day before this disgraceful surrender, Fort Dearborn, where Chicago now stands, was surrendered to the Indians, and though the garrison was promised safety, many of them were cruelly massacred, and the fort was burned.

On the 13th of October another detachment of Americans crossed from Lewiston into Canada, and attacked the British on Queenstown Heights, but were overpowered, chiefly from the failure of the New York militia to come to their aid, as had been expected. A hundred and sixty of the Americans were killed, and a large number taken prisoners.

The failure of the Americans by land was offset by their success in several brilliant naval engagements. The first was on the 9th of August, when Captain Dacres, of the British frigate Guerriere, was forced to surrender to the Constitution, called "Old Ironsides," commanded by Captain Hull, the Guerriere being so badly battered that she had to be destroyed. In October, the sloop of war Wasp attacked and took the British brig Frolic, which was convoying a fleet of merchant vessels; but the Wasp was soon after captured by the much heavier British vessel Poictiers. In the same year the frigate United States, Commodore Decatur, captured the British frigate Macedonia, the Americans suffering little loss, and inflicting much. And the Constitution, Commodore Bainbridge, after a fierce engagement, captured the British frigate Java, which was so riddled and shattered that she had to be burned. Beside these victories, which caused the greatest enthusiasm in the United States, and equal dismay in England, American privateers had captured during the year some three hundred merchant vessels and taken over three thousand prisoners.

Madison was re-elected President, entering on his second term in 1813, with Elbridge Gerry as Vice-President, Clinton having died in the previous year. In 1813 the American forces were divided into three departments, that of the West under General Harrison, that of the Center under General Dearborn, and that of the North

PERRY'S VICTORY ON LAKE ERIE.

under General Wade Hampton. The object of the first was to recover Detroit and Michigan from the English, and in January the forces under General Winchester took Frenchtown, repulsing the British, but were in turn attacked and obliged to surrender to a much larger force of British and Indians under General Proctor, who promised them safety. But when Proctor had departed, the Indians, maddened by liquor, fell upon the Americans with savage ferocity, murdering many, setting fire to houses that were filled with the wounded, and carrying away numerous captives whom they held for ransom. General Harrison, who was now in command, built Fort Meigs, where, in May, he was besieged by Proctor and his Indians, but General Clay coming from Kentucky with twelve hundred men, the assailants were defeated, and the siege raised. The Indians acted with their usual ferocity toward some prisoners they had taken. Tecumseh on one occasion saved one of the captains from their brutality, and even rebuked Proctor, who had said he could not restrain the Indians, sternly saying to him, "Go and put on petticoats; you are not fit to command men!" In July, the British and Indians, 40,000 in number, attacked Fort Meigs, but after a fierce conflict, in which they suffered severely, the siege was abandoned.

During the summer of this year, a fleet of nine American vessels, carrying fifty-four guns, was placed on Lake Erie, under command of Commodore Perry, where they were opposed by six English vessels, carrying sixty-three guns, under Commodore Barclay. A battle between these two opposing forces took place in September, lasting three hours, and resulting in a brilliant victory for the Americans. It was reported by Perry in a brief and modest despatch, saying, "We have met the enemy and they are ours. Two ships, two brigs, one schooner and one sloop." Harrison's forces now crossed into Canada, where, after taking Malden, they pursued the British forces to a strong point on the river Thames, where, on the 5th of October, a battle was fought, in which the British were defeated. The Indians fought bravely under Tecumseh, till a bullet ended his life, when they fled, and the victory of the Americans was complete, so that Michigan was recovered, Lake Erie was in possession of the Americans, Ohio was safe, the Indian confederacy was broken, and Harrison's army was now able to join the army of the Center.

The invasion of Canada now being the leading object, General Dearborn crossed Lake Ontario and attacked York, now Toronto, which the British abandoned, blowing up the magazine, thus killing or wounding some two hundred Americans. General Dearborn then took Fort George, which gave the Americans possession of all the Canada side of the Niagara river. The British soon afterward, after being repulsed from Sackett's Harbor, recaptured Fort George, took Fort Niagara, and made several plundering excursions into northern New York, setting fire to Buffalo, Lewiston, and some other villages. During the year several battles at sea had taken place. In February, the sloop of war Hornet, Captain James Lawrence, had a short, but severe, battle with the British brig Peacock, in which the latter, having surrendered, sunk almost immediately. Lawrence was then put in command of the Chesapeake, which had a bloody engagement with the British frigate Shannon, in which every one of the American officers were killed or wounded, and Lawrence himself received a mortal shot. His last expression was, "Don't give up the ship;" and he was afterward buried with all the honors of war. In August, the American brig Argus took as prizes some twenty merchant vessels, but was herself captured by the British brig Pelican. The British brig Boxer' was captured by the American vessel Enterprise. During the year the British squadron on the New England coast bombarded Lewiston, and the English vessels in Delaware and Chesapeake bays burned Frenchtown, Georgetown, Havre de Grace, and Frederick, and attempted to capture Norfolk, but were repulsed with heavy loss.

In 1814, the Northern campaign was on the Niagara frontier, where, on the 30th of July, General Brown, assisted by Generals Scott and Ripley crossed the river, took Fort Erie, and advancing to Chippewa, defeated the British under General Riall. On the 25th, the two armies met at Lundy's Lane, where, in an action that was not decisive each side lost about eight hundred men. The Americans then fell back to Fort Erie, where they were attacked by the British, five thousand strong, who were repulsed with a loss of one

THE BURNING OF WASHINGTON

thousand men, and afterward were so badly beaten that they gave up the siege of the fort, which after some time was blown up by the Americans as they withdrew from the Canada shore, going into winter quarters in Buffalo.

England, having now successfully concluded her war with France, sent large numbers of her veterans to join her forces in this country, and, in September, Sir George Provost, with fourteen thousand troops, attempted to invade the United States by way of Lake Champlain, and advanced on Plattsburg, where General Macomb was stationed with less than two thousand men. The American squadron, under Commodore McDonough, was lying in the harbor, and on the 11th of September the British land forces, supported by the fleet under Commodore Downie, began the attack. After a contest of two hours, some of the British vessels struck their colors, and those that could sailed away. On the shore, the overwhelming forces of the British had well-nigh gained a footing, when the Americans, inspired by the victory on the lake, rallied and drove them back, and the day was won. The British having lost two thousand five hundred men, retired to Canada, the victory of the Americans being complete.

While these events were taking place at the North, the British fleet, bearing some four thousand soldiers, arrived on the coast of Virginia, and General Ross and his forces began their march to Washington, forty miles away. On the 24th of August, they entered the city, which had been deserted by the President and other officials, burned the President's house, the magnificent but unfinished capitol, and other buildings, doing damage to the amount of $2,000,000. General Ross offered to spare the city for a large sum of money, but unfortunately there was no one within reach who was authorized to make such a bargain. The burning of Washington was a disgrace and crime for which no excuse can be given. Part of the British squadron sailed up the Potomac to Alexandria and there captured twenty-one vessels and large quantities of flour and tobacco. Ross now sailed to attack Baltimore, but landing at North Point, they were met by the Americans, and in a skirmish Ross was killed. The British fleet then sailed up the Patapsco, and all day and night bombarded Fort McHenry, but producing little effect, the troops were re-embarked and the fleet sailed away. It was during this bombardment that the noted piece, "The Star-Spangled Banner," was composed by Francis Key.

In August, Commodore Hardy bombarded Stonington, Connecticut, but the gathering of the militia prevented his forces from landing, and this was one of the last assaults of the British, as the war was now drawing to its close. The last great conflict was at New Orleans, which was defended by General Jackson, after he had repulsed the British at Pensacola and taken that town. In December, 1814, a powerful British fleet carrying some twelve thousand soldiers and also marines, under General Packenham, entered Lake Borgne to the northeast of New Orleans and began their march to the city, four miles below where Jackson had taken up a strong position, using bales of cotton and sand-bags to add to the strength of his works. There, with about six thousand men, he awaited the enemy's attack. On the 8th of January the assault was made, the enemy charging across the open space under a terrible fire from cannon, and the still more terrible fire of the sharpshooters of Tennessee and Kentucky, who, safe behind their intrenchments, mowed the enemy down with their sure and deadly shots. Packenham was killed, the second in command mortally wounded, and the British troops were recalled, two thousand of their army having been killed, wounded, or captured, while the American loss was only seven killed and six wounded. The British then withdrew to their ships.

On the 20th of February, Captain Charles Stewart, while cruising off Cape St. Vincent, in the Constitution, fell in with two British brigs, the Cyane and Levant.

CAPTURE OF THE CYANE AND LEVANT.

The British vessels maneuvered to get the better position, but Stewart held them, as may be said, each at a corner of a triangle, while he kept the third corner, firing his forward guns into one, and his after guns into the other. Both vessels were captured.

These were the closing battles of the war of 1812, for news soon came that a treaty of peace had been signed in Great Britain before the battle of New Orleans. In the summer of 1814, commissioners had been sent from this country to meet others from Great Britain, and the treaty had been signed on the 24th of December, though the news did not reach this country till February, on the 18th of which it was ratified by the United States Senate, and the President proclaimed peace. The treaty was little more than an agreement to stop all hostilities, but though there were no formal assurances that the grievances which had led to the war should cease, yet this was the practical result of the war, the many American victories of which had given a lesson as to the power of the United States that was not likely to be forgotten. Both nations rejoiced at the return of peace. Hundreds of vessels and thousands of lives had been lost on both sides; and at the close of the war our public debt was $100,000,000. The charter of the United States Bank was now renewed, a heavy duty was laid on imported merchandise, public credit was restored, shipbuilding again commenced, factories were re-opened, commerce revived, and prosperity returned to the nation.

During the eight years of Madison's administration Louisiana was admitted, as the seventeenth State, to the Union in 1812; and Mississippi, as the eighteenth, in 1817. The famous "Hartford Convention" was also held in 1814. Its deliberations were secret, and it was charged by some with having treasonable aims, but all that came of it was the recommendation of some changes in the Constitution.

There was war also, during this administration, with the Indians of the Northwest, led by the famous Tecumseh. General Harrison marching against them, was met near their town of Tippecanoe by a proposal for a conference the next day, to which he assented, but knowing the treacherous nature of the Indians, he ordered his soldiers to remain armed and watchful through the night. Before sunrise the next day, November 7, 1811, the savages, creeping along the ground, rushed suddenly upon the camp. But the soldiers, being fully prepared, sprang to their arms, and after a fierce conflict utterly overwhelmed the enemy and burned their town. Tecumseh, finding his people subdued, departed for Canada, where, as we have seen, he joined the British, fighting with whom against the Americans he was killed in 1813.

There was trouble also with the Creek Indians in Alabama, who in 1813 surprised Fort Mimms, and murdered four hundred men, women and children. But they were defeated in several battles by Generals Jackson and Coffee, six hundred of them being killed in the last of the conflicts in 1814, when all that remained were glad to submit. During the war, too, Algiers had repeated her former outrages on American vessels, and after peace was declared Commodore Decatur was sent with nine vessels to right our wrongs. He captured two of the Algerine vessels, compelled the Bey to release all American captives, and then going to Tunis and Tripoli, obliged them to give pledges of good behavior for the future, thus ending our trouble with the Barbary States.

JAMES MONROE.

and was present in several battles, but afterward commenced the study of law. In 1782 he was elected to the Assembly of Virginia, and the next year to Congress, where he took an active part in preparing the new Constitution. In 1799 he was made governor of Virginia, and in 1803 was sent by Jefferson as minister to France, where, with others, he effected the "Louisiana Purchase," which added so immensely to the territory of the United States. He had been Secretary of State under Madison, and had been employed in diplomatic services both in England and Spain. He was an able statesman, but not a speaker, nor a man of brilliant talents.

His biographer says of him: "The one idea he represents consistently from the beginning to the end of his career, is this, that America is for Americans. He resists the British sovereignty in his early youth; he insists on the importance of free navigation in the Mississippi; he negotiates the purchase of Louisiana and Florida; he gives a vigorous impulse to the prosecution of the second war with Great Britain, when neutral rights were endangered; and, finally, he announces the Monroe Doctrine."

His election was not regarded as a triumph of either the Federal or Republican party, but as a result in which people of both parties were united. In September, a treaty was made with the Indians north of the Ohio river, by which their claims to the country were purchased for certain sums of money and promised annuities, so that the

region was thus opened to white settlers.
The Indians were by arrangement located
on reservations, a plan which has since
been carried out with most of the larger
Indian tribes, in the hope that so they
might be led to the industries and habits
of civilization. The government also
suppressed and dispersed the bands of
freebooters who were engaged in
privateering, and also in the slave trade on
the coasts of Florida and Texas.

Before the close of the year the
Seminole Indians, encouraged by the

A SCENE IN THE EARLY SETTLEMENT OF OHIO.

Spanish authorities of Florida, began hostilities in Georgia. General Jackson was sent against them, and with a thousand riflemen from Tennessee he laid waste their country, and then marching to Florida, captured the Fort of St. Marks, took Pensacola, and seized and executed two Englishmen who had incited the Indians to war. This act, which excited great indignation in England, was approved by the government, and was afterward admitted by England to have been just. And out of these proceedings came negotiations with Spain which resulted in the purchase of Florida in 1819 for $5,000,000, and which also led to fixing the boundary of Mexico at the Sabine river.

During Monroe's administration the famous "Missouri Compromise," fixing the dividing line between the slave and free States, was passed, largely through the influence of Henry Clay. It went into effect in February, 1821, and for years settled the agitating question of the limits of slavery. In the fall of 1820 President Monroe and Vice-President Tompkins were re-elected, and a second time were inaugurated, March 4, 1821. In the next year, the President, in a message to Congress, recommended the recognition of the South American republics, which had been struggling against Spain for their independence. In 1823 he announced the noted "Monroe Doctrine," in which he asserted that the American continents "are not henceforth to be considered as subjects for future colonization by any European power," and declared the American policy of neither entangling ourselves in the broils of Europe, nor suffering the powers of the Old World to interfere with the affairs of the New, and that "any attempt to extend their system to any portion of this hemisphere would be dangerous to our peace and safety," a doctrine heartily endorsed by the American people.

The great popular event of Monroe's administration was the visit of Lafayette to the United States. He had come to this country in the days of the Revolution and fought with our armies to secure our independence; and now that a mighty nation had taken the place of the colonies, he was everywhere received with the highest honors and congratulations, and travelled as in triumph through the length and breadth of the land. While in Boston, on the 17th of June, 1825,—that being the fiftieth anniversary of the battle of Bunker Hill,—he laid the corner-stone of the monument then about to be raised. He returned to France after about a year, in the frigate Brandywine, so named in honor of the first battle in which the French had fought side by side with the Americans.

During this administration, Mississippi, Alabama, Illinois, Maine, and Missouri were admitted to the Union as States, and Arkansas was made a Territory. The work of piracy in the West Indies, from which our commerce had suffered, was suppressed. Monroe was an honorable and able statesman, though not a speaker nor a man of brilliant talents. Like his predecessors, Adams and Jefferson, he died on the 4th of July.

ADMINISTRATION OF JOHN QUINCY ADAMS — 1825 TO 1829.

The sixth President of the United States was John Quincy Adams, of Massachusetts. He was inaugurated with John C. Calhoun, of South Carolina, as Vice-President, March 4, 1825. There were several candidates for the office, but no one having a majority of votes, the election was thrown into the House of Representatives, when Mr. Adams was chosen. Mr. Adams was a son of John Adams, the second President of the United States. He was born in Massachusetts, July 11, 1767; was graduated from Harvard college in 1788, and after studying law, entered on its practice in 1791. In 1794 he was appointed by Washington minister to the Hague, and afterward was

JOHN Q. ADAMS.

appointed by his father minister to Berlin. In 1809 he was appointed by Madison minister to Russia, and while there was appointed associate judge of the United States Supreme Court, but declined the appointment. After retiring from the presidency, for seventeen years he was in Congress, where in the House of Representatives he was always at his post and always at work, and distinguished not only for his knowledge and wise statesmanship, but as the uniform champion of the right of petition. He was one of the most thoroughly educated and most remarkable men of his time, independent, patriotic, and eminently faithful in the many public offices he was called to fill.

His administration was marked by few notable events. It was a time of peace, and the nation was steadily growing in population, wealth and power. The party lines which in early years had divided the country, had for the most part disappeared, and new parties were soon to arise, based on new issues.

During the first year of his administration a difficulty arose, which was settled, with the authorities of Georgia. When that State had ceded her claims to the Territory of Mississippi, the national government had agreed to purchase and give to her the lands held by the Creek Indians within her limits, but had never done it. Georgia being dissatisfied, her governor was about to remove the Indians and take possession of their lands. The danger of conflict with the general government for a time was serious, but finally the President made a treaty with the Creeks, purchasing their lands, and they removed to a reservation west of the Mississippi.

In 1825 the Erie Canal was formally opened. At that time it was the most extensive public improvement ever undertaken in the United States. The canal,

extending from Albany to Buffalo, was 363 miles in length, and its first cost was
$7,600,000. Its completion, which took eight years, has greatly contributed to the
prosperity of New York, the "Empire State," as well as to all the great and growing
States of the West.

The question of tariff, or duties on imported goods, was one which began to assume
importance during this administration. One party insisted that such duties should be
levied "only for revenue," that is, to provide means for the expenses of the government.

EARLY DAYS ON THE DELAWARE & HUDSON CANAL RAILROAD.

Others advocated a protective tariff, or what was called the "American system," that is, a
system of duties that should especially protect and encourage American manufactures.
A tariff of the last mentioned kind was enacted in 1828, mainly through the influence of
Henry Clay. The "Tariff Question" has ever since been a source of divided opinion
and political action.

Another event occurred in 1826 in New York which caused great excitement,
and led to the formation of a new political party. William Morgan, a Freemason, in

western New York, announcing he would reveal the secrets of Freemasonry, suddenly disappeared, and was never seen or heard of again. It was said, and by multitudes believed, that he had been murdered by the Masons, and the great and widespread

ANDREW JACKSON.

excitement caused by his disappearance led to the formation of the "Anti-Masonic Party," which was strongest in New York, but spread to some extent throughout the country. In 1832 it nominated William Wirt for the presidency, but after his defeat the party soon declined and disappeared. It was a singular coincidence that on the 4th of July, 1826, the fiftieth anniversary of the Declaration of Independence, John Adams and Thomas Jefferson both died. Each had signed the Declaration of Independence, each had faithfully served the country, and each had been elected to its highest office, the presidency.

John Quincy Adams was one of the ablest and most accomplished statesmen the country has ever produced.

JACKSON'S ADMINISTRATION—1829 TO 1837.

The seventh President of the United States was Andrew Jackson, of Tennessee. He was inaugurated March 4, 1829, with John C. Calhoun, who had been re-elected Vice-President. His election was a victory for the Anti-Federal party, which now took the name "Democratic."

Mr. Jackson was born in Waxhaw county, South Carolina, March 15, 1767. When the Revolution broke out he went to the field, being only thirteen years old, and remained with the army till the end of the war. Though he studied law, and was rising in his profession, he was soon called off from its practice to lead in the conflicts with the Indians, whom he fought with such bravery and success as to be named by them "Sharp Knife" and "Pointed Arrows." He was in the Legislature and then in the

Senate of Tennessee, and was appointed judge of its supreme court, and also major-general of its militia. In several conflicts with the Indian tribes he was so energetic and successful, that he was appointed major-general of the United States army. As such, in the War of 1812 he defended New Orleans, and, as we have seen, defeated the British forces under General Packenham in 1814, which gave him wonderful popularity. He was a man of strong character and iron will, unpolished, but thoroughly honest and incorruptible, aiming always at what he thought right and best for the country, and allowing nothing to turn him from his intended course. These traits, which

A NEGRO VILLAGE.

gave character to his administration, gained him the name of "Old Hickory," and he was loved as warmly by one party as he was decidedly opposed by the other.

The charter of the United States Bank having expired, Jackson opposed its renewal, and when Congress renewed the charter, he vetoed the act, and before the expiration of the charter he removed from the bank the government deposits of some $10,000,000, distributing the funds among the different State banks. There was a fierce discussion in Congress over this act, and the Senate took the unusual course of passing a vote of censure on the President, which stood on its records for four years till it was finally expunged by a vote of the Senate. The bank was afterward chartered by the State of Pennsylvania, its chief office being in Philadelphia.

The tariff question came into threatening prominence in 1832, from the fact that Congress in that year passed a bill laying heavy duties on a large number of important articles. This met with strong opposition, especially in South Carolina, where a State convention declared the act null and void, advising that the collection of duties at Charleston should be resisted if need be by force. This was called " Nullification," of which John C. Calhoun was a decided supporter. Open opposition to the government by force seemed impending, but Jackson, acting

SCENE IN FLORIDA NEAR ROCK LEDGE.

with his usual energy and promptness, issued a proclamation warning the people that the law would be enforced, and followed this up by sending a man-of-war to Charleston, and ordering General Scott there with troops, saying he "would hang Calhoun as high as Haman, if he resisted the law." These steps prevented the threatened danger, and in the spring of 1833, a bill, proposed and carried through Congress by Mr. Clay, so modified the duties of the tariff that the trouble for the time came to an end.

In 1832, Jackson was re-elected President, and Martin Van Buren, of New York, Vice-President. In this year the western Indians, led by the noted Black Hawk, began war against the people of Illinois, but after several battles they were defeated. Black Hawk was taken captive, and the Indians were removed further west. There was trouble also, as in the previous administration, with the Creeks in Georgia, as they were

SCENE ON ST. CLAIR RIVER, MICHIGAN.

still on the lands claimed by that State. The United States court declared in their favor, but the President refused to interfere, and the difficulty was finally ended by the Indians going west to a reservation.

A graver difficulty arose with the Seminoles of Florida, whose hostilities began in 1835, two of their chiefs refusing to recognize a treaty made by some other chiefs. The struggle lasted for several years, over a hundred men under General Dade being ambushed and murdered, only four escaping, and General Thompson and several of his friends being surprised and killed. Later, in 1836 and 1837, the Indians were defeated in several engagements by Generals Scott and Taylor, but they carried on an intermittent warfare from the swamps and everglades till 1842, when peace was established.

In 1834, there was trouble with France, which had persistently delayed the payment of some $5,000,000 which they had agreed to pay to satisfy claims for injuries done to American commerce during the time of Napoleon. In view of this continued neglect, the President

17

ordered the American minister to leave France, and was preparing for still more decided steps, when France, seeing his decision and the danger of war, fulfilled her promise and paid the amount. Portugal, by the same decided course, was made to pay up similar claims.

MARTIN VAN BUREN.

In 1830 the first locomotive was built in the United States, and the first passenger railroad, the Baltimore and Ohio, was opened for fifteen miles. In 1835 an immense fire took place in New York, destroying between five and six hundred buildings, and causing a loss of millions of dollars. In 1836 Arkansas, and in 1837 Michigan, were admitted as States into the Union. Jackson removed more officials in one month than his predecessors had in forty years, and he used the veto power more freely than any President had ever done. The Whig party had become a successor of the Federal, and the Anti-Federal, a republican party, had now become known as the Democratic.

VAN BUREN'S ADMINISTRATION — 1837 TO 1841.

The eighth President of the United States was Martin Van Buren, of New York, who was inaugurated March 4, 1837, with Richard M. Johnson, of Kentucky, as Vice-President. This election was a triumph of the Democratic party, and implied a continuance of the policy of Jackson's administration.

Mr. Van Buren was born at Kinderhook, New York, in December, 1782. He was both a lawyer and a politician before he was of age. In 1812 he was in the State Senate, three years later was appointed attorney-general of the State, and was afterward made United States senator, to which office he was re-elected, but resigned to become governor of the State of New York.

In 1837, the first year of Van Buren's adminstration, occurred what was known as the "Panic of '37," in which most of the banks of the country suspended payment, causing an immense number of failures and great commercial suffering. The distribution of the national funds among the various State banks had led to a large increase of paper currency, and to a corresponding increase of loans, and this had led on to widespread speculation, especially in real estate; and the fact that the government would receive only coin for its public lands drew large quantities of specie from the banks, and forced many of them to suspend specie payment. Congress, too, had authorized the distribution to the States of some $40,000,000 of its surplus funds, and this amount being drawn from the banks of deposit, greatly increased the evil. In March and April the failures in New York city were for more than $100,000,000. An extra session of Congress was called, but little was done except to issue some $10,000,000 of Treasury notes, and though after a time business began to revive, for a long time the effects of the panic were felt throughout the country.

The Seminole war still continued in the South, costing many lives and adding largely to the national debt; and in 1837 there was trouble, also, with Canada. In 1791, the English parliament had divided Canada into an upper and a lower province. Each was constituted with a governor, an executive council nominated by the crown, a legislative council appointed for life in the same way, and a representative assembly elected for four years by popular vote. The powers of the State were ill-adjusted, and the assemblies of the two provinces became bitterly opposed to their governors and councils. For five years no provision had been made by the legislature of Lower Canada to pay for administering the government in the province. During four years the payments in arrears amounted to a large sum, the legislature refused to provide for it, and demanded an elected legislative council, and complete control over all branches of the government. The British parliament was willing to make some concessions, but not to the extent demanded. A rebellion followed, in which many Americans joined. Seven hundred men from New York seized and fortified Navy Island against the Canadian royalists, and the latter set fire to the Caroline, a vessel belonging to New Yorkers, and sent it burning over the Niagara Falls. But the President issued a proclamation of neutrality, and sent General Scott to the region of the trouble with a strong force, so that after some time the disturbance was quieted.

In 1840, Congress passed the "Sub-Treasury Bill," the object of which was to provide for the safe keeping of the public funds of the country. Van Buren's administration had been held responsible for the financial depression that marked its commencement, but the foundation of the trouble was laid while Jackson was President.

The next election was one of great excitement, General Harrison being nominated for the Presidency; and as a Democratic paper had sneeringly said that "Harrison would be satisfied with a log-cabin and a barrel of hard cider," the expression was caught up as a party watchword through the land. Log cabins were everywhere erected, and as Harrison had gained the great victory of Tippecanoe in the war of 1812, the campaign cry of "Tippecanoe and Tyler too" rang through the land, and the result was a sweeping victory for Harrison and Tyler.

ADMINISTRATIONS OF HARRISON AND TYLER—1841 TO 1845.

The ninth President of the United States was William H. Harrison, of Ohio, who was inaugurated March 4th, 1841, with John Tyler, of Virginia, as Vice-President. He was a son of Benjamin Harrison, one of the signers of the Declaration of Independence,

WILLIAM H. HARRISON.

and was born in Virginia, February 9, 1773. In 1792, he joined the army which Wayne was leading against the Indians. In 1801, he was made a governor of Indiana, and afterward represented that State in Congress. In 1811, in the war with the Indians, which soon became a war with the English in Canada, as Commander-in-Chief he showed great military promptness and talent. He defeated the Indians in the famous battle of Tippecanoe, and aided by the victory of Perry on Lake Erie, was enabled to pursue the British invaders into Canada, where he totally routed them in the battle of the Thames, October 5, 1813. He was elected to Congress in 1816, and in 1824 to the United States Senate. He was afterward ambassador to Columbia. He selected an able Cabinet and called an extra session of Congress to legislate on matters of finance, but before Congress assembled he sickened and died on the 4th of April, just one month after taking office. According to the Constitution, Tyler then became President, and took the oath of office on the 6th of April. He retained the cabinet which had been appointed by Harrison.

When Congress met, the sub-treasury bill was repealed, and a bankrupt law was passed. A bill was also passed renewing the charter of the United States Bank, but it was vetoed by Tyler, who, on this point, held the views of Jackson. Congress then passed a modified bill for a bank, and that, also, was vetoed by Tyler, when at once all his cabinet resigned except the Secretary of State, Daniel Webster. He remained in office to complete negotiations with Lord Ashburton, who had been sent by Great Britain to settle some of the Northern and Northeastern boundaries of the United States which had been left unsettled by the treaty of 1783. By them the Northeastern boundary was definitely fixed, and the Northern also as far west as the Rocky Mountains. The boundary beyond that was not settled till four years later.

JOHN TYLER.

In the same year there was trouble in Rhode Island from the disturbance known as "Dorr's Rebellion." Under a new Constitution, which it was claimed was not ratified by the people, Thomas W. Dorr was chosen governor, and attempted to assume that office. But the "Law and Order" party, led by Governor King, denied his claims. Both sides took up arms and the Dorr party was twice dispersed, though without bloodshed, by the aid of national troops. A new Constitution was then formed which was ratified by the people, and went into effect in 1843. Dorr was convicted of treason, but was afterward pardoned and restored to citizenship. There was also trouble for some years in New York, with the anti-renters, who refused to pay the rents which had always been paid to the Patroon estate at and near Albany, but this at last was quieted, and in 1846 the State constitution abolished all feudal tenures.

Some years before this the Mormon religion had been started by Joseph Smith, who pretended he had found some golden plates near Palmyra, New York, on which was written the revelation which was the foundation of his system. Gathering a company of followers he went to Ohio, and when driven out from that State he went to Missouri, and from there to Illinois, where he founded the town of Nauvoo. Here the numbers of the Mormons increased to some thousands, and defying the laws, Smith and his brother were arrested and imprisoned and afterward killed by a mob. In 1846, the great body of the Mormons went still further West, and in 1848, laid the foundation of their city at Salt Lake, in Utah.

During the last year of Tyler's administration the country was agitated by the proposed annexation of Texas, which had been part of Mexico, but in 1835 had declared itself independent. The South favored annexation, intending to make Texas a slave State; and the North, for that reason, strongly opposed it. The question was

SALT LAKE CITY.

hotly debated in Congress and throughout the country, and finally Texas was annexed in 1845. Florida was also admitted to the Union in 1845. In 1844, the first electric telegraph line in the world was established between Washington and Baltimore. Professor Samuel F. B. Morse had invented the telegraphic system thirteen years before, but not till this year did he obtain from Congress an appropriation of $30,000, which enabled him to bring his wonderful invention into practical use.

ADMINISTRATION OF POLK—1845 to 1849.

The eleventh President of the United States was James K. Polk, of Tennessee, who was inaugurated March 4, 1845, with George M. Dallas, of Pennsylvania, as Vice-President. Mr. Polk was born in Mecklenburg county, North Carolina, November 2, 1795. He was educated at the university of North Carolina; was admitted to the bar in 1820; was a member of Congress, and speaker of the House of Representatives for five sessions, and in 1839, was made governor of Tennessee. He was devoted to the principles of the Jackson democracy, to State rights, to an independent treasury, to a tariff only for revenue, and to a strict construction of the Constitution.

JAMES K. POLK.

The most important event of his administration was the Mexican war, originating in the annexation of Texas, which Mexico still claimed as part of her territory; and besides this the southwestern boundary of Texas was still unsettled, that State claiming to the Rio Grande, and Mexico denying the claim, and preparing to enforce by arms her asserted rights. Proposals for a peaceful settlement of the question made by our government had been rejected by Mexico, and General Taylor was sent to the disputed territory, where he built Fort Brown. The Mexican forces demanded Taylor's withdrawal, but as he remained and strengthened his defenses, hostilities commenced. The Mexicans, after surprising and capturing a body of dragoon, who had been sent to reconnoitre, with a force of six thousand men attacked Fort Brown, and in a battle that took place were defeated by Taylor, who the next day attacked and defeated another body of Mexicans, their loss being a thousand, while that of the Americans was but little more than a hundred. On the 18th of May, Taylor crossed the Rio Grande and took possession of Matamoras.

When the news of these things reached Washington, Congress declared war with Mexico, placing $10,000,000 at the disposal of the President, and authorizing him to accept 50,000 volunteers for the army. General Wool had charge of the new recruits; a fleet was to be sent to attack Mexico on the Pacific coast; a column was to invade that country from the North; and still others were to invade and conquer New Mexico and California. In September, 1846, Taylor, with six thousand troops, marched against Monterey, which was defended by nine thousand Mexicans, and the place was

THE CITY OF MEXICO.

surrendered on the 24th. He then advanced and occupied Saltillo, while Tampico was taken by our naval forces. Part of his forces now went to the aid of General Scott, who was to invade Mexico by way of Vera Cruz. Santa Anna, who had been recalled from exile and made president and commander of the Mexican forces, now marched with twenty thousand men to attack Taylor, and in the battle of Buena Vista he was badly defeated by the Americans, February 23, 1847, thus securing the frontier of the Rio Grande, and leaving our forces free to act against Vera Cruz.

While these events were occurring in the South, General Kearney, with the army of the West, marching one thousand miles overland, took possession of Santa Fe, and

THE CITY OF VERA CRUZ.

continuing his march to California, was met with the news that that country was already in possession of Fremont, who, before the opening of the war, had been sent with an exploring party to seek a new route to Oregon further south than the one usually taken by emigrants. While in California, Fremont learned that the Mexican commander was raising a force to expel the American settlers from the province, and a message was sent him from Washington to protect the Americans and their interests. The Americans had had several conflicts with the Mexicans in which the latter were beaten, and by the advice of Fremont the Americans declared their independence of Mexico, July 5, 1846. Just at this time Commander Sloat on the Pacific seized Monterey, and Commodore Stockton a little later took San Diego; and the united land and naval forces captured Los Angeles on the 17th of August. Thus by Fremont and Stockton the Mexican authority in California was overturned. Meanwhile Colonel Doniphan, in New Mexico, with less than a thousand men, marching southward, had subdued some hostile Indians;

A WOODLAND SCENE.

gained two successive victories over superior Mexican forces, and taken possession of Chihuahua, a city of forty thousand inhabitants, after which he joined General Wool at Saltillo in May.

In the beginning of 1847, General Scott, who was now commander-in-chief in Mexico, with an army of twelve thousand men, began the siege of Vera Cruz, which was guarded by the strong castle of San Juan De Ulloa, and after a furious bombardment of four days the city was surrendered on the 27th of March, with five thousand prisoners, and five hundred pieces of artillery. Scott now began an advance on the city of Mexico, but was met by Santa Anna with fresh troops at the pass of Cerro Gordo, and in a battle which took place the Mexicans were defeated, and the Americans continuing their advance, took Pueblo, where they waited some three months for reinforcements.

In August, with his army now numbering about ten thousand men, Scott resumed his march towards the city of Mexico which was defended by thirty thousand Mexicans under Santa Anna, as well as by strong fortifications. On the 20th of August, in assaults by five different detachments five victories were gained by the United States troops with a loss of eleven hundred men, while the loss of the Mexicans was four thousand, killed and wounded, and three thousand taken prisoners. The next day the Mexicans asked for an armistice, which Scott granted in hope of making peace, but his proposals being rejected by Santa Anna hostilities were renewed, and the Mexicans were defeated in several engagements, their whole army being routed. On the 14th of September, Scott entered the city, and by the fall of the capital the war was practically at an end. Santa Anna made one or two other attacks on our forces, but in each case was defeated and soon became a fugitive, and the power of Mexico was thoroughly broken. The war was formally ended by the treaty of Guadaloupe Hidalgo, February 2, 1848, and peace was proclaimed on the 4th of July following. This treaty ceded to the United States, New Mexico, California and Utah; and Mexico received for the ceded territory a compensation of $15,000,000; and the debts due to American citizens from Mexico, to the amount of $3,000,000, were assumed by the United States.

In the Mexican war the Mexican forces were nearly four times as many as our own, and yet within about a year our armies had fought and won thirty battles, taken one thousand cannon, carried ten fortified places, and completed the conquest of Mexico and California without the loss of a single battle.

About this time gold was discovered in California, an account of which is given in the history of that State. During this administration our Northwest boundary was settled by treaty with England, in June, 1846. In 1846, Iowa, and in 1848, Wisconsin was admitted to the Union; and in 1846, David Wilmot, of Pennsylvania, proposed a bill in Congress prohibiting slavery in all the territory that might be gained from Mexico. This "Wilmot Proviso," as it was called, was defeated, but it laid the foundation of the noted "free-soil" party, which decided the fate of the next Presidential campaign.

ADMINISTRATION OF TAYLOR AND FILLMORE—1849 TO 1853.

The twelfth President was Zachary Taylor, of Kentucky, with Millard Fillmore, of New York, as Vice-President. As the 4th of March came on Sunday, the inauguration was on the following day, March 5th, 1849.

Mr. Taylor was born in Orange county, Virginia, November 24th, 1784. Going early into Kentucky he had few advantages of education. He entered the army, and in 1812, as captain, with only fifty men, he made a gallant defense of Fort Harrison

against the Indians led by the famous Tecumseh, for which he was made a major-general. He gained several victories over the Indians who were allies of Great Britain in 1812; and in the Mexican war he won a decided victory over Santa Anna, who had four times the forces of the Americans, a result which excited the greatest enthusiasm through the country, and led to his nomination to the presidency.

He had scarcely entered on his office when the slavery question again excited sharp and bitter discussion, both in Congress and throughout the country. It came up in Congress on the application of California to be admitted to the Union as a free State,

ZACHARY TAYLOR.

the South wishing it to be open to slavery, while the North insisted on slavery being prohibited. Other connected questions added to the excitement of feeling and debate, the South desiring efficient laws for the return of fugitive slaves, while the North insisted on the abolition of the slave trade in the District of Columbia. The violent debates in Congress, with threats of secession by the South, led to a Compromise Act, proposed by Clay, which embraced so many different measures that it was called the "Omnibus Bill." It proposed that California should come in as a free State; that Utah and New Mexico should be made territories without any mention of slavery; that $10,000,000 should be paid to Texas in satisfaction of her claims to the latter territory; that the slave trade should be abolished in the District of Columbia; and finally, that rigorous laws should be passed for the return of slaves who might have escaped from their masters to the free States. The discussions on this measure lasted till September, before which time President Taylor died, on the 9th of July, 1850, leaving Fillmore as President. The bill was passed on the 9th of September, and signed by the President. It was generally opposed at the North, the fugitive slave law

MILLARD FILLMORE.

being everywhere bitterly denounced, and its enforcement not only evaded but resisted, while Mr. Fillmore was bitterly assailed by his own party for giving it his approval.

In the same year, 1850, General Lopez, a native of Cuba, in violation of our neutrality laws, organized in the United States an expedition to aid the people of that island in a revolt against Spain. In the following year, landing in Cuba with four hundred and eighty followers, he was attacked, his forces dispersed, and he and several of his followers were executed. France and England, getting the impression that the United States favored the annexation of Cuba, proposed that both those countries and this should, by treaty, bind themselves never to attempt the acquisition of that island. The Secretary of State, Mr. Everett, in a masterly paper, disavowed any such intention on the part of this country, but in accordance with the "Monroe Doctrine," said decidedly that the question was purely an American one, in which interference by any foreign government would not be regarded with indifference.

Another event of interest was the fitting out, in 1850, of two vessels by Mr. Henry Grinnell, of New York, for an expedition to the Arctic Ocean, for the discovery, if possible, of Sir John Franklin, who, six years before, had sailed for that region and of whom no tidings had ever been received. In 1853, our government sent out Dr. Elisha Kane with a party on a similar search. They suffered severely and had to abandon their ships, but were finally brought home in 1855. Franklin was never found.

FRANKLIN'S EXPEDITION IN THE POLAR REGIONS.

In 1852, difficulties arose with England as to the Newfoundland fisheries, and both that government and ours sent armed vessels to the region; but in 1854 the question was settled favorably to our claims by negotiation. During this administration

FRANKLIN PIERCE.

three of our greatest statesmen died: John C. Calhoun in 1850, and Henry Clay and Daniel Webster in 1852.

PIERCE'S ADMINISTRA-TION—1853 TO 1857.

The fourteenth President was Franklin Pierce, of New Hampshire, who was inaugurated March 4, 1853, with William King, of Alabama, as Vice-President. Mr. King took the oath of office in Cuba, where he had gone for his health, but on returning home he died on the 18th of April, 1853. Mr. Pierce was born in Hillsborough, New Hampshire, November 23, 1804. He was educated at Bowdoin college; after studying law, was admitted to the bar in 1827; was elected to the thirty-third Congress, and in 1837 to the United States Senate. He took an active part in the Mexican war and led his brigade in two important battles.

This administration was marked by several events of interest, and by one of great importance connected with the matter of slave and free territory. As to one of the first mentioned events, a dispute had arisen with Mexico as to the boundaries of New Mexico, and Santa Anna, who was now President, sent an armed force to the disputed region. The matter was settled by what is known as the "Gadsden Purchase," by which the United States secured what are now parts of Arizona and New Mexico. This was in 1853, in which year engineers were sent to explore a route for railroad communication with the Pacific regions. In this year, too, Commodore Perry sailed with a squadron to Japan, and in the next year closed a treaty with that nation, by which two ports were opened to American vessels.

In 1853, the Crystal Palace was opened in New York for the "World's Fair," which had exhibits of all kinds from almost every civilized nation. There were also several "fillibustering" expeditions, led by General William Walker, against the governments of Central America; and also in the same year, against Lower California; in the next year, against Sonora in Mexico; and in 1855, against Nicaragua, where he made himself for a time president, but from which he was driven out in 1857. His last expedition was against Honduras, in 1860, where he was captured and shot.

MOUNT HOOD.

Some difficulties again arising with Cuba, the President directed our ambassadors at London, Paris, and Madrid, to consult as to the best way of settling matters, and their advice, known as the "Ostend Manifesto," was to purchase the island, if possible, and if not, then to take it by force; but nothing further was done in the matter. With Austria, too, there was a difficulty as to one Martin Kotszta, who, having taken steps to become a citizen of the United States, was seized and put on board of an Austrian man-of-war. The American consul then demanded his release, and when this was refused, Captain Ingraham, of the American sloop-of-war, cleared his vessel for action, and was about to open fire, when Kotszta was given up to the French consul and finally released and came back to his adopted home.

JAMES BUCHANAN.

The great question, however, of this administration was connected with the matter of slavery. In 1854, Stephen A. Douglas, of Illinois, brought into the Senate a bill to organize the Territories of Kansas and Nebraska, containing the provision that the people in them should decide for themselves whether slavery should be prohibited or not. It was, and was intended to be, a practical repeal of the Missouri Compromise of 1820, which had forever prohibited slavery in that region. But it passed Congress, and became a law May 31, 1854. The story of the struggle which followed is given in the history of Kansas, and the final result, which was not reached till 1861, was that Kansas was then admitted to the Union as a free State. The discussions connected with this subject led to the party lines of the next presidential election, the Republican supplanting the old Whig party, while the American or "Know-Nothing" party also arose, having for its main feature opposition to all foreign influence in the affairs of this country.

BUCHANAN'S ADMINISTRATION — 1857 TO 1861.

The fifteenth President of the United States was James Buchanan, of Pennsylvania. He was inaugurated March 4, 1857, with John C. Breckinridge, of Kentucky, as Vice-President.

Mr. Buchanan was born in Franklin county, Pennsylvania, in April, 1791. He was educated at Dickinson college; adopted the profession of law; in 1820 was elected to

18

Congress, where he served for five terms, when he was appointed ambassador to Russia. In 1833 he was elected to the United States Senate, and in 1853 was sent as minister to England. He filled many important positions with ability, but at the outbreak of the war seemed irresolute and vacillating, when a decided policy might have led much earlier to the final result.

In the first year of this administration the Mormons in Utah, under Brigham Young, their governor, opposed the federal courts and drove away the United States officials, and later in the year they attacked and destroyed a supply train of the United States troops, but an armed force being sent into their territory, and a new governor

HARPER'S FERRY, VIRGINIA.

appointed, order was the next year restored. In 1858, the first Atlantic cable was successfully laid, and Minnesota became a State, as Oregon did in 1859, and Kansas, as a free State, in 1861.

The great events of the administration, however, were connected with the questions of slavery and State rights, which led on to the War of Secession. The Dred Scott decision by the supreme court, denying freedom to one who, as a slave, had been taken by his master to a free State, and, asserting that such a person was not a citizen, and also that the Missouri Compromise was unconstitutional and void, was the cause of intense excitement. It was welcomed at the South, but was most bitterly denounced at the North, and greatly increased the opposition between the two sections of the country. The bitter feeling it excited was intensified by the noted raid of John Brown, who seized the United States arsenal at Harper's Ferry, expecting to rouse the slaves of the Southern States to insurrection, but who was captured and hung in 1859. The struggle in Kansas was still in progress, and the violent attack in the Senate on Senator Sumner, of Massachusetts, by Butler, of South Carolina, after the former, in 1856, had made a strong anti-slavery speech, carried the public excitement at the North to the highest pitch. In this state of feeling, when the Democratic convention met in Charleston, in 1860, to nominate a candidate for the coming presidential election, its delegates were divided, and part of them withdrawing and adjourning to Baltimore, nominated Stephen A. Douglas for the Presidency. The Republican convention, assembled in Chicago, took strong ground against the extension of slavery, and nominated as their candidate, Abraham Lincoln.

The canvass that followed was one of intense earnestness and excitement, and resulted in the election of Lincoln, with Hamlin, of Maine, as Vice-President. The

A SKIRMISHER.

result of this election had been expected, for the South had proclaimed that if Lincoln was elected it would withdraw from the Union. Some members of Buchanan's cabinet were open friends of the Southern cause, and Buchanan himself, with a vacillation that was as weak as it was mischievous, while denying the right of secession, still said he had no constitutional authority or power to prevent it, thus virtually saying that the enemies of the Union would not be opposed by force.

Encouraged by these views of the chief magistrate of the nation, it has constantly been said that "the Southern States took immediate action for secession from the Union." But in point of fact *not a single State, as a State, ever seceded.* The political leaders of eleven Southern States, gathered in convention between December 20, 1860, and June 3, 1861, adopted ordinances of secession, declaring their States no longer in the Union. Each State was proclaimed to be a sovereign, and their papers referred to items of intelligence from the Northern States as "Foreign News."

In February, 1861, delegates chosen in six States, by *conventions, not* by votes of the people, met at Montgomery, Alabama, and formed the league of the "Confederate States of America," which was a misnomer, as no States, *as States*, had withdrawn from the Union. *The people — those who really composed the State — had never in any State been permitted to vote on the calling of conventions, or on the ratification of any ordinance of secession, or as to the formation of a Confederacy.* As has well been said, "the leaders in the great insurrection dared not submit the question to the arbitrament of the people." The league formed at Montgomery was simply a compact between usurpers of popular rights, who were in no sense representatives of States. And it was against the usurpers and their willing and unwilling instruments in making war on the republic, that the national government put forth its strength, and drew to its support the loyal citizens from every State in the Union. It was not a war between States, but a war against the enemies of the United States, who were in rebellion against it.

Jefferson Davis, of Mississippi, was made President, and Alexander H. Stephens, of Georgia, Vice-President of the Confederacy thus formed, and the South at once began securing the national forts and arsenals within its borders. Major Anderson with his forces had gone from Fort Moultrie to Fort Sumter, where Buchanan's administration made a weak attempt to reinforce him with men and provisions. On the morning of January 9, the Star of the West approached Fort Sumter in an attempt to deliver the supplies. A masked battery on Morris Island opened on her, and she ran up the stars-and-stripes. The battery paid no heed, but continued its fire several minutes longer, Fort Moultrie also sending in a few shots. The captain, seeing his danger, put to sea, and returned to New York.

The admission of Kansas at this time, and the nearness of the new administration, increased the existing excitement. Threats were made that Mr. Lincoln would be assassinated on his way to the capital; but he passed through Baltimore, where violence had been feared, in the night, and arrived at Washington on the 23d of February, where he remained till his inauguration.

GENERAL ROBERT E. LEE'S OLD HOME, ARLINGTON.

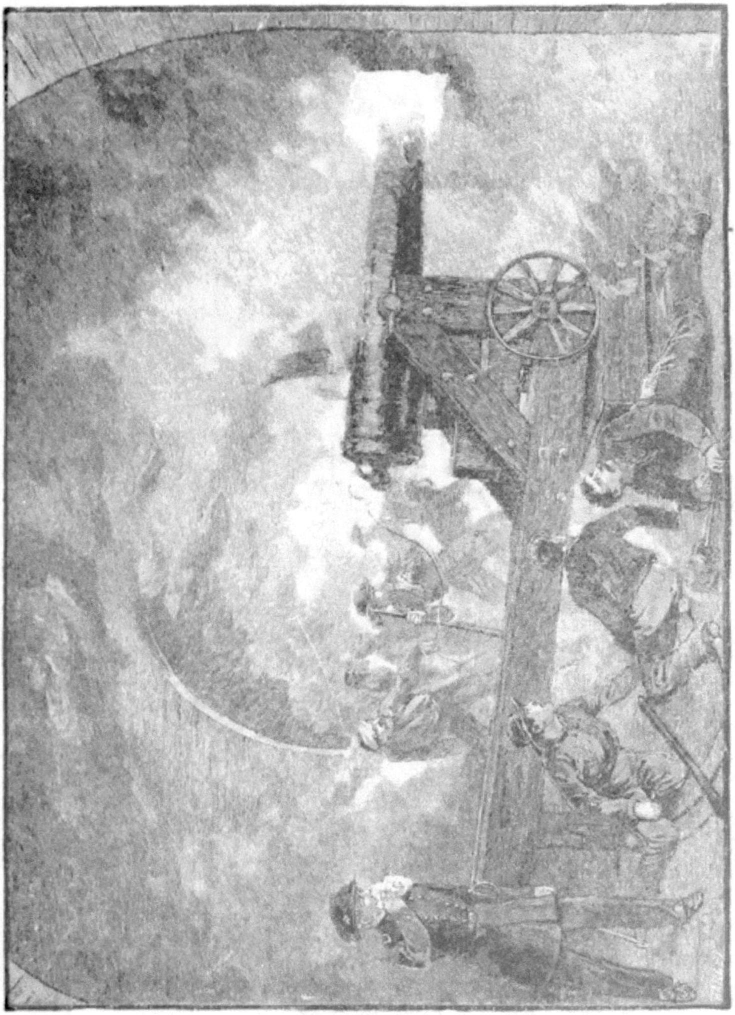

DEFENSE OF FORT SUMTER, APRIL 13, 1861.

CHAPTER IV.

THE CIVIL WAR AND EMANCIPATION.

THE CAUSES OF THE WAR.

THE Civil War, or War of the Secession, began with the firing on Fort Sumter in April, 1861, and closed with the surrender of the Southern army in April, 1865, having lasted four years. The seeds of the conflict had been sown at an early day, in the views and occupations of the people, but the full fruit was slowly and at last fully developed. In a debate in the United States Senate, during the session of 1829-30, Senator Hayne, of South Carolina, who became involved in a warm discussion with Senator Webster on the question of nullification, or whether a State had a right to annul an act of the general government, speaking of his own section, said, "They will look to the constitution; and when called upon by the sovereign authority of the State to preserve and protect the rights secured to them by the charter of their liberties, they will succeed in defending them, or perish in the last ditch." To which Webster replied, "When my eyes shall be turned to behold for the last time the sun in Heaven, may I not see him shining on the broken and disfigured fragments of a once glorious Union; on States dissevered, discordant, belligerent; on a land rent with civil feuds, or drenched, it may be, in fraternal blood. Let their last feeble and lingering glance, rather, behold the gorgeous ensign of the Republic, now known and honored throughout the earth. * * * * * Liberty and union, now and forever, one and inseparable." Thus two great minds anticipated our Civil War thirty years in advance of its coming.

Almost from the origin of the government, one class of statesmen had looked upon the Union as only a league or confederation, in which the States were bound together only by their own wishes and interests, while another class regarded it as one national government which could not be dissolved. One party exalted State rights, as if each State were a sovereign. The other gave supreme power to the Union, leaving to the States control over their State interests, while all the States were regarded as but parts of the one great Union. This, indeed, was a wide difference of opinion, but so great was the love of country and the benefits of Union that probably it would never have led to the idea of separation but for questions connected with the business interests and material prosperities of the country.

Such questions did arise and grew in importance as the country grew and prospered. The South having the advantage of slave labor, and raising crops which to a large extent were exported, and having comparatively few manufacturing industries, wished for free trade with foreign countries. But the North being largely engaged in manufacturing, desired a protective tariff to enable them to compete successfully with foreign manufactures, and so to encourage and build up the manufacturing interests of this country. Connected with these different views was the great question of slavery. From an early day there had been slaves in the Northern States, the census of 1790 showing that there were 158 slaves in New Hampshire, 17 in Vermont, 952 in Rhode Island, 2,759 in Connecticut, 21,324 in New York, 11,423 in New Jersey and 3,737 in Pennsylvania; but the number was comparatively small and was steadily decreasing. In the South the cultivation of tobacco and rice had early made slave labor profitable, and the invention of the cotton gin by Whitney, in 1793, which soon made cotton the chief staple of the South, greatly increased the demand for slave labor, and so of

A RAILROAD BATTERY.

course added steadily to the number of slaves. In 1860, the negroes of the South numbered some 4,000,000, while in the North, where slave labor was not profitable, slavery had gradually died out; and as the new States of the Northwest filled up with free settlers the Northern opposition to slavery steadily increased. Washington, Jefferson, Hamilton, Franklin and Madison all saw and lamented the evils of the system, and Jefferson was the first one to bring forward the proposition that slavery should be prohibited in the great Northwestern territory. After 1808 the importation of slaves was forbidden, but as the value of slave labor increased the slaves also increased in numbers, and the South strongly advocated and maintained slavery, while in the North the abolition doctrine was steadily growing.

These opposing interests and sentiments on the subject of slavery led to a long political struggle, the rapid increase of the population of the North tending to decrease the power of the South in Congress, and leading to the effort of the latter so to extend the borders of slavery as to hold their controlling political influence. The Missouri Compromise of 1820, the discussion of which agitated the whole country, had for a while settled the excitement, but after a time it proved unsatisfactory to both North and South, the former objecting to any increase of slaves and to the slave trade, and the latter being bent on extending its political influence by extending the system to the new territories which would soon become States. And then in addition to all this, what was known as the "fugitive slave law," which was enacted in 1850, wakened not only the opposition, but the deep indignation of the North. This was followed by the repeal of the "Missouri Compromise" in 1854. Then the Republican party was formed, then came the Kansas and Nebraska struggle; then the political campaign of

EARLY HOME OF ABRAHAM LINCOLN, GENTRYVILLE, INDIANA.

1856, where the question of slavery was the avowed issue; then in 1857, the "Dred Scott" decision; and then the John Brown raid; of each of which events an account has been given; and then the Presidential election of 1860, in which there were four candidates, and as the result of which Lincoln was elected. The election of Mr. Lincoln was the signal for action by the secessionists, South Carolina leading the movement. A convention in that State passed an ordinance of secession, December 20, 1860, and this action was followed in January, 1861, by Mississippi, Alabama, Florida, Georgia and Louisiana, and in February by Texas; and by the 15th of February the Confederate government was fully organized at Montgomery, Alabama, by the election of Jefferson Davis, of Mississippi, as President, and Alexander H. Stephens, of Georgia, as Vice-President. Here was the beginning of the great and terrible contest, which for four years convulsed the country, piled up a national debt of $2,749,000,000, and sent to the grave, or left as wounded and crippled, on both sides, more than one million of men.

LINCOLN'S ADMINISTRATION — 1861 TO 1865.

The sixteenth President was Abraham Lincoln, of Illinois, who was inaugurated March 4, 1861, with Hannibal Hamlin, of Maine, as Vice-President.

Mr. Lincoln was born in Kentucky, February 12, 1809, but when about seven years of age, went with his father to Indiana. In the rude life of that then comparatively unsettled country, he had almost no advantages for education. In 1830, he removed to Illinois, where he was at various times a boatman, a farmer, and clerk in a store. At that time he was known as thoughtful and intelligent, and in 1834, was elected to the

Legislature of the State. At this period, he acted for a time as a surveyor, occupying what leisure he could get in searching the few books within his reach, often studying far into the night by the light of burning chips from the shop of a cooper. Three times he was elected to the Legislature. In 1836, he was admitted to the practice of law. In 1846, he was chosen a member of Congress. In 1854, he had become a recognized leader of the Republican party, and by his political speeches, and especially by his public debates through the State, with Stephen A. Douglas as an opponent, had excited great interest not only in Illinois, but throughout the country.

ABRAHAM LINCOLN
[From first photograph taken after his nomination for President.]

He was original in thought, of quick and searching discernment, and most genial in nature, and many curious and amusing anecdotes are related of his story-telling, his energy, his oddities, his generosity, his thorough honesty and independence, and his power as a debater. He was noted for his clear intellect, his sound judgment, and his unwavering will in all that he believed to be right. With all his fondness for comical anecdotes and stories, there was in his character a deep underlying seriousness, tinged with a sadness that was manifest to all who knew him. As to all his public duties, his feeling as well as purpose clearly was, as he once said, with regard to emancipation, "It is my earnest desire to know the will of Providence in this matter, and if I can learn what that is, I will do it."

When he was chosen as President, to the friends who accompanied him to the depot as he left for Washington, he said, "I know not when I shall see you again. A duty devolves upon me greater than has devolved upon any man since the days of

Washington. He never would have succeeded but for the aid of divine Providence, upon which he at all times relied. I feel that I cannot succeed without the same divine aid which sustained him, and on the same Almighty Being I place my reliance for support. And I hope you, my friends, will pray that I may receive that divine assistance, without which I cannot succeed, but with which success is certain."

Of his well known and great speech at the Cooper Institute in the spring of 1860, Horace Greeley said, "It is the very best political address to which I ever listened, and I heard some of Daniel Webster's grandest. As a literary effort it would not of course bear comparison with many of Webster's speeches, but regarded simply as an effort to convince the largest possible number, that they ought to be on the speaker's side, and not on the other, I do not hesitate to pronounce it unsurpassed."

FEDERAL IRON-CLAD RIVER GUN-BOAT.

In his inaugural address, Mr. Lincoln declared that no State could withdraw from the Union, disavowed any intention to interfere with slavery, and proclaimed his intention to enforce the laws of the country and to retake and hold the public property, meaning the forts, arsenals, etc., that had been seized by the Confederates. This was taken by the secessionists to be a declaration of war, and they at once began organizing an army.

Many Southern born officers of the army and navy of the United States, joined the Confederate service. General Beauregard was placed in command of the Southern forces, numbering about 4,000 men, who were then investing Fort Sumter in Charleston Harbor. That fort was at the time garrisoned by eighty men, under Major Anderson, and early in April, Lincoln resolved to send a fleet with supplies to them. As soon as this became known, Beauregard was ordered to demand the evacuation of the fort, and if the demand was not complied with, then to reduce it by force. The demand was made, and when refused by Major Anderson, fire was opened on the fort from batteries which had been erected, and the bombardment was kept up vigorously for thirty-four hours, at the end of which time the fort was surrendered and the garrison came out with the honors of war on the 14th of April.

THE SWAMP ANGEL.

The attack on Fort Sumter produced the most intense excitement in every part of the country. It roused the North as by an electric shock, uniting all parties in the stern determination to uphold the supremacy of the government and the interests of the Union. The President at once issued a call for seventy-five thousand volunteer troops to serve for three months, and they were promptly raised at the North. And on the 19th of April one of the first raised regiments, the Sixth Massachusetts, passing through Baltimore, where the disunion sentiment was strong, was attacked and fired on by the mob, and three of its members were killed and several wounded. The soldiers returned the fire, killing and wounding several of the assailants. This was the first bloodshed of the war, and it tremendously increased the excitement of both the North and the South.

The secession authorities in the meantime had called for thirty-five thousand additional troops, which were promptly raised. At the surrender of Fort Sumter, only seven of the Southern States had been declared in secession, and eight other slave States, Virginia, Maryland, Delaware, North Carolina, Kentucky, Tennessee, Missouri and Arkansas had not joined the secession movement, but were still hoping for peace. On these States the President called for its proportion of troops, but from all of them came defiant replies and refusal to respond to the call, and Virginia, Arkansas, North Carolina and Tennessee were soon declared to be in secession. In Delaware, Maryland, Kentucky and Missouri, there was strong opposition to the secession movement, and these States were still kept in the Union. The Confederate government was removed from Montgomery to Richmond. And war was now fully begun.

CAMPAIGNS OF 1861.

On the 18th of April the national forces at Harper's Ferry, finding superior Confederate forces approaching, evacuated the armory at that place, and on the 20th, when Norfolk was threatened, the Union troops withdrew, after setting fire to the buildings and ships; and the Confederates secured some two thousand cannon. Elated by this success, their cry was, "On to Washington," where they hoped to be able to take the capital. On the 3d of May the President called for 83,000 more soldiers to serve through the war. On the 23d, General Scott, as commander-in-chief, took possession of Arlington Heights and Alexandria. General Butler, with 12,000 troops, was at Fortress Monroe; General Patterson was at Harper's Ferry, and General McClellan, with a large body of troops, was in West Virginia. A blockade of the Southern ports had been declared by the President, and vessels were sent to enforce it. At this time the principal army of the Confederates was at Manassas Junction, under General Beauregard, and there were also forces at and near Yorktown, under General Magruder, to hold Butler in check; and a force in the Shenandoah Valley, under General Johnston, was confronting the corps under Patterson, while there was also a Confederate force in West Virginia, to prevent or resist the advance of McClellan.

The first conflict took place in West Virginia on June 3, and in it McClellan's forces were successful, the Confederates being driven back. On the 11th of July the Confederates were again defeated by Rosecrans at Rich Mountain and at Cheat River; and again on the 10th of August at Carnifex Ferry; and on the 14th at Cheat Mountain, results which secured West Virginia to the Union, and gave to the North control of the Baltimore and Ohio Railroad. These successes, though not of great magnitude or importance, encouraged the North and led to the appointment of McClellan as commander of the main army in Virginia.

The Union forces now in West Virginia were about 30,000, and those of the Confederates about 10,000. General Butler in the meantime had attacked General Magruder and was repulsed at Big Bethel on the 10th of June. General Lew Wallace successfully attacked the Confederates at Romney in West Virginia, and the movement being supported by General Patterson, the Confederates retired to Winchester, and the Union troops again took possession of Harper's Ferry.

The two main armies now were the Northern, called the Army of the Potomac, of about 35,000 men, commanded by General McDowell, as General Scott was too infirm to take the field, and the Southern, called the Army of North Virginia, under General Beauregard. On the morning of Sunday, July 21, the Confederates were drawn up in three lines along the southern bank of Bull Run, watching the eight fords over which they expected the Unionists to come.

Long before daylight on the hot Sunday morning, the Union army was astir, but the forenoon was half gone before the army was fairly started. Tyler's division

ON THE BALTIMORE AND OHIO RAILROAD.

followed the main road to the stone bridge, while Hunter and Heintzelman turned to the right and crossed the stream at Sudley Ford.

Colonel Evans, holding the extreme Confederate left, had become suspicious, and marched up the stream with half a brigade, with which he confronted the Union advance while the turning column was beyond the turnpike. Instead of overwhelming this small force, McDowell sent detached regiments and brigades against it. Colonel Evans was thus enabled to hold his ground until heavily re-enforced, when he took a stronger position a short distance back. Hunter, re-enforced also, pressed Evans so hard that Generals Beauregard and Johnston hurriedly rode toward the scene of conflict to direct the movements of the troops. They ordered up all the reserves and formed a new line of battle, with six thousand five hundred men, two companies of cavalry and thirteen guns. Near the center the Federal brigade, under Colonel Richardson, opened fire against Generals Jones and Longstreet at Blackburn's Ford, with a view of preventing them from re-enforcing the Confederate left, where Unionists were pushing hard. Longstreet, under orders from Beauregard, crossed the stream and assailed the Federals, thus preventing them from joining in the fight on the left.

Although the fierce fighting at the center was for a time without any marked success on either side, it was on the whole favorable to the Unionists. Late in the afternoon, however, the Confederates were re-enforced by four thousand men, under General E. Kirby Smith, and Beauregard, who now found himself with more men than

DESTRUCTION OF FORT OCRACOKE.

the Unionists, directed an advance of the whole line, feeling sure of victory. The re-enforcements were placed in a position to the left of the Confederate line and swept like a cyclone against the exhausted Federals. Thus the seeming victory was turned into an utter rout, and a panic seizing the Union troops they fled, a discouraged mass, back to Washington, the Confederates losing in killed and wounded 1,900, and the Union forces in killed, wounded and prisoners, over 3,000 men. This first great battle of the war filled the South with enthusiasm and greatly disheartened the North. President Lincoln now called out half a million troops, and General Scott retiring from service, General McClellan was made commander-in-chief. By the fall of the year the Army of the Potomac numbered over 150,000 men, and the Southern army had larger additions, but the main armies did not again meet during the year. The only

BULL RUN.—STAND OF THE UNION TROOPS AT THE HENRY HOUSE, 3 P. M.

operation in the East was an encounter of the opposing forces at Ball's Bluff, where the
Union forces were repulsed with the loss of 1,000 men, and General Baker, their
commander, was killed.

At the West, military operations were chiefly confined to Missouri, where the
Confederates, in two engagements, at Carthage and Wilson's Creek, were successful
against the Union forces, and where, at Belmont, General Grant in November destroyed
a secessionist camp, but was forced back to Cairo. In June, General Lyon gained a
victory over the Confederates at Boonville, and in August, Generals Lyon and Sigel,
with about 5,000 men, attacked a much larger force of the Confederates near Springfield
and drove them from the field, but Lyon was mortally wounded in the conflict. The

FORT PENSACOLA.

Confederates, under General Price, with 25,000 men, laid siege to Lexington, which was
garrisoned by less than three thousand Union men, and the place was taken by the
Confederates, but soon was retaken by the Federal forces. Meanwhile General
Fremont, who had been placed in command in Missouri, proclaimed martial law, and
issued an order freeing the slaves of all who were in arms against the United States;
but he was not sustained in this course by the President, who thought the step was
premature, and he was superseded by General Hunter, who in turn was soon superseded
by General Wallace.

To keep up the blockade of the Atlantic coast and the Southern ports, several
expeditions were undertaken during the year. The first was under General Butler and
Commodore Stringham, who, acting together, in August took the forts at Hatteras Inlet

CAPTURE OF NEW ORLEANS.

19

on the coast of North Carolina. In June, a gun-boat expedition under Commander J. H. Ward, was repulsed at Matthias Point with severe loss.

In October, a small expedition in row boats, under Lieutenant Harrill, left the Potomac at 2 A. M., and under cover of darkness proceeded up Quantico Creek, where it succeeded in burning a large schooner belonging to the enemy, and narrowly escaped under a heavy fire. Another small expedition from the frigate Colorado entered Pensacola harbor, and after a desperate fight, in which several men were killed and wounded, destroyed a large armed schooner.

A second expedition under General Sherman and Commodore Dupont captured the works commanding Port Royal in South Carolina in November. The blockade was so vigorously enforced that it was difficult for any Confederates or any unfriendly vessel to enter or leave the Southern ports.

A blockade-runner that did elude the United States vessels, had taken James M. Mason and John Slidell, who were on their way as Confederate ambassadors to England and France, both of which nations had in May recognized the Confederates as belligerents, not as insurgents. The British mail steamer on which they sailed was stopped, on the 8th of November, by the United States steamer San Jacinto, and Lieutenant Fairfax was sent on board with a demand to see the papers of the British steamer. Captain Moir refused to show them, or to allow his passenger list to be examined. Mr. Mason, however, was recognized, and Lieutenant Fairfax ordered a part of the crew of one of his armed boats to come aboard. Messrs. Mason and Slidell were then requested to accompany the Lieutenant back to the San Jacinto. They refused, and were forcibly taken away. The San Jacinto then proceeded on her way to the United States, and Mason and Slidell were imprisoned in Fort Warren.

The greatest excitement was caused by the news of the occurrence, both in the United States and England. The British government demanded the surrender of these envoys, and in so doing virtually admitted the doctrine always asserted by the United States as to neutral vessels, the violation of which by England had been the chief cause of the War of 1812. The seizure of the envoys by Captain Wilkes was disavowed, and so a war with Great Britain was prevented, and the hopes of the Confederates that such a war might take place were disappointed.

CAMPAIGNS OF 1862.

The military operations of 1862 began at the West, where the Confederate forces were under General Johnston, and those of the Union under General Halleck. In January, General Thomas successfully attacked the enemy at Mill Spring. In the next month General Grant left Cairo with about 17,000 men, in two divisions, accompanied by Commodore Foote with a naval fleet of seven gun-boats, four of which were iron-clads, for the purpose of reducing Fort Henry, a strong fortification of the enemy situated on the east bank of the Tennessee River, about sixty-five miles from its mouth. Foote began the bombardment of the fort on the afternoon of the 6th, Grant landing his troops for the purpose of investment and capture of the garrison, which numbered 2,700 men; but General Tilghman had already sent the garrison to Fort Donelson, which was only twelve miles away on the west bank of the Cumberland.

Tilghman himself remained with his artillerists, and defended the fort for about one hour, when, satisfied that his troops had escaped, he surrendered with 100 men and twenty pieces of artillery.

February 12, General Grant put his army, now called the Army of the Tennessee, in motion for Fort Donelson, which was garrisoned by about 21,000 men, commanded by Jno. B. Floyd. After several severe engagements the fort was surrendered with about 9,000 men and a large quantity of stores on the 16th of February. When General Buckner, who, by the flight of Floyd and Pillow, had been left in command of the fort, asked what terms would be granted if he surrendered, General Grant replied, "Only an unconditional surrender can be accepted. I propose to move immediately on

BAILEY'S DAM ON THE RED RIVER.

your works," and the surrender was made. The loss of these forts was a severe blow to the South, not only in the loss of men and guns, but because it opened up the Cumberland and Tennessee rivers and destroyed the whole defensive line of the Confederates. It compelled Johnston to abandon Kentucky and a large part of Tennessee, and as he retired to Murfreesboro, the Union army, under Buell, followed, and on the 23d took possession of Nashville. The capture of Fort Donelson not only broke the center of the defensive line of the Confederates, but also endangered its left, the stronghold at Columbus. This also they had to abandon, and it was occupied by the Union army on the 22d of March. These brilliant successes greatly encouraged the North.

Johnston now united all his forces at Corinth intending to strike a blow at Grant, who had moved to Pittsburg Landing on the Tennessee river, where he was attacked by the Southern forces. The result was a severe battle at Shiloh, which lasted two days. At the opening of the battle, Grant was on the opposite side of the river in consultation with Buell. Hastening back, he came upon a field that appeared to be hopelessly lost. By noon the entire Union army had been driven out of their camps, and were huddled together on the verge of the bluff above the landing, where it looked as if there was no possible escape.

Before the Confederates could reach that part of the plateau where the Federals were, it was necessary for them to cross a deep ravine. A few unimportant earth works had been hastily thrown up on the opposite brink, and about fifty guns got into position.

U. S. MILITARY TELEGRAPH WAGON.

Two gun-boats were also stationed so that their fire swept the ravine. The Confederates charged down the bank and tried hard to dash up the other side, but the fire in front and from gun-boats swept them away like leaves from the path of a tornado. The attempt was finally given up and Grant was left master at that point. Still, the Confederates held the field.

On the morning of the 7th the Federals moved forward to the attack and the battle opened all along the line. The enemy resisted in desperation but were continually driven back, and by 2 P. M. the Federals had recaptured their camps. The Confederates retreated to Corinth, and the Union victory was complete.

The Union loss was nearly 15,000, and that of the Confederates 10,699 in killed, wounded and missing. The Northern forces pressing on, Corinth was evacuated by Beauregard, and was occupied by the Union army on the 30th of May. The Confederates thus retreating, several of their strong points on the Mississippi fell into the hands of the Union forces; Island No. 10 on the 7th of April; Fort Pillow on the 4th, and the city of Memphis on the 6th of June.

After the capture of Corinth, Grant's forces remained quiet for some time, and an army under Buell was sent to take Chattanooga, but his forces were attacked by the main Confederate army of the southwest, now under General Bragg, and obliged to retreat to Louisville. A column also under General Kirby Smith joined Bragg's army in

FORT PILLOW.

Kentucky, the joint forces overrunning the State and gathering vast quantities of supplies, but the Union army being largely re-enforced, Bragg and Smith retreated toward Chattanooga at the end of September. Buell's army pursued Bragg and an action was fought on the 8th of October without important results. Near the close of December, General Rosecrans, coming from Nashville, attacked Bragg at Murfreesboro, the action beginning in the morning and continuing with intermissions, for three successive days, the Union army holding the field and Bragg retiring to Duck river; the Union loss being some 14,000 and that of the Confederates over 10,000. While Bragg and Buell were thus in Tennessee, Grant was attacked at Corinth and Iuka by Price and Van Dorn, but as he was very strongly fortified their attack was in vain. Still earlier in

THE "DESTROYER," TORPEDO-VESSEL OF CAPTAIN ERICSSON.

the year a severe battle was fought at Pea Ridge in Arkansas, in which the Southern army under Van Dorn was defeated, March 7th and 8th, by the Union forces under General Curtis.

Turning now to the Virginia campaigns, in the spring of 1862; McClellan was in chief command near Washington with 200,000 men; and the Southern army under General Johnston, was still at Manassas Junction. On the 4th of April, the Army of the Potomac moving from Fortress Monroe, was brought to a stand by the fortifications at Yorktown, and in the delay Johnston with his army entered that place, but after a month spent by McClellan in erecting batteries before it, Johnston retired, going toward Richmond, and McClellan, after taking possession on the 4th, followed the retreating army, and an action took place at Williamsburg, from which Johnston made good his retreat.

McClellan now advanced to the Chickahominy, where, on the last day of May, he was attacked by the enemy in the battle of Fair Oaks, when the advantage was with McClellan; and the Confederates retreating, and Johnston being wounded, General R. E. Lee took command of the army.

McDowell's force was now at Fredericksburg, Fremont's was in southwestern Virginia, and Banks' in the Shenandoah Valley. Stonewall Jackson now struck a blow at Fremont causing him to retreat, and then at Banks, inflicting severe injury, thus obliging McDowell to leave Fredericksburg to oppose him. Jackson, then, on the 25th of June, moved upon the right flank of the Union army at Mechanicsville, and on the next day Lee, uniting with Jackson, attacked McClellan's army on the north side of the Chickahominy at Gaines' Mill, June 27, when the Union troops were driven from their position with heavy loss. McClellan's retreat was marked by three engagements at Savage's Station, June 29; at Glendale, June 30, and at Malvern Hill, July 1, in the last of which Lee's army was repulsed. In these movements McClellan failed of his object, which had been to capture Richmond, but Lee's losses were about 20,000 in killed, wounded and missing, while McClellan's were only about 18,000. In July of this year, Lincoln called for 300,000 men, and in August for 300,000 more.

McClellan having withdrawn to Harrison's Landing on the James river, Lee began moving toward Washington. Between him and the Potomac were about 50,000 men, made up of the forces that had been under Fremont, Banks, and McDowell, but all now united under General Pope. Lee pressed heavily on this force, and in the bloody second battle of Manassas, August 29th and 30th, it was entirely defeated. McClellan was now called back to Washington, and the broken army of Pope was united with his forces and all put under his command. Lee now marched to Frederick, and from there westward, leaving a force at South Mountain to hold the passes of the hills, and sending Jackson to capture the Union garrison at Harper's Ferry. McClellan, after a vigorous fight, carried the passes, September 14th, but before he could reach Harper's Ferry the garrison of 12,000 men had been surrendered to Jackson, September 15th. Lee, on learning of McClellan's presence before the passes of South Mountain, had sent for Jackson. Knowing he would be assailed by the powerful army of McClellan, his purpose was to concentrate his forces and await the shock of battle.

Jackson's division was so worn out that hundreds fell out by the wayside, so that only a part joined Lee on the 16th. His men had been pushed beyond their power of endurance, and he was forced to stop and wait for them to come up. His force at

BATTLE OF MALVERN HILL.—LEE'S ATTACK.

Antietam, when about to give battle, was less than forty thousand muskets. When McClellan reached the other bank of the Antietam he had 70,000 men. But McClellan was so tardy in his movements that he gave the enemy much advantage. Instead of attacking at once, he decided to wait till next day, and when the next day came, he thought best to wait until all his divisions had come up.

After waiting until Lee had gained every advantage, McClellan prepared to attack him. The conflict raged all day, both armies being terribly shattered, but the Union army held its ground, and Lee was driven back and retreated up the Shenandoah Valley, and McClellan did nothing till November, when he moved to the east side of the blue ridge.

ANTIETAM BRIDGE.

McClellan was now superseded by General Burnside, who, with an army numbering about 110,000 men, moved to the Rappahannock opposite Fredericksburg, and at once began the construction of bridges at that point, and also lower down, toward the enemy's right, opposite Smithfield. Lee could not stop the Federals, and all his dispositions were with a view of attacking them after they had crossed. He so placed several regiments, however, as to harass them while making their way over. By daylight on the 13th, the Army of the Potomac was on the southern shore, and at the same hour the Army of Northern Virginia was gathered on the heights behind Fredericksburg. The fighting, which soon opened, lasted through the day, and ended with a loss of about 11,000 Union men and a Confederate loss of about 5,000. The Federal army had exhibited great valor in this battle, advancing and retiring under the most terrible fire known in the war up to this time, and only fell back when it was found utterly impossible to proceed farther. On the morning of the 16th, when the enemy discovered the disappearance of the Federal army, they again extended their outposts to the town of Fredericksburg.

Thus far in the year the results of the war in and about Virginia, were, on the whole, highly favorable to the Confederates, while at the West they were equally favorable to the Union army.

The war was now waged on an enormous scale. Hundreds of thousands of men were on the field on both sides, North and South, carrying on the deadly conflict, on the one hand for the Union, on the other for the Confederate States.

SINKING OF THE ALABAMA.

In 1862, there were several important naval actions and events; one of which took place in Hampton Roads, where the steam frigates Minnesota and Roanoke, and the sailing frigates Congress, Cumberland and St. Lawrence lay at anchor. On the 8th of March the iron-clad Merrimac was sighted, and the Minnesota and Roanoke at once advanced to meet her, the former meaning to run her down, but both got aground. The Cumberland swung herself across the channel so as to bring her broadsides to bear; the Congress opened fire also, but with no effect; the Merrimac moved straight on, firing as she approached, and striking the Cumberland a hard blow with her prow,

FIGHT BETWEEN THE MONITOR AND MERRIMAC.

opened a large hole in the side of the frigate. The crew of the Cumberland worked at the guns till the water was knee deep on her deck. She sank to her cross-trees in fifty-four feet of water, the stars-and-stripes still floating from her top-mast; 121 lives were lost.

The Merrimac now turned her attention to the Congress, but could not approach within a considerable distance on account of shallow water. The field artillery and the infantry on shore took part in the fight, the artillery availing nothing; but the sharpshooters did some injury by firing at the port-holes of the Merrimac. The conflict continued for two hours, when the Congress was set on fire and her crew compelled to abandon her, having suffered a loss of 100 men.

At daylight the next morning the Merrimac steamed out, anxious to finish the work, but before she reached the helpless vessels the Monitor came out from behind the Minnesota and boldly advanced, firing the first shot when the Merrimac was only a hundred yards away. Many of the shots from the Merrimac passed over the low deck of the Monitor. The battle lasted four hours and ended in the defeat of the Merrimac, a shot from the Monitor having struck her below the water line and opened a bad leak. The Merrimac was compelled to retire to Norfolk, where two months afterward she was destroyed by the Confederates, to prevent her falling into the hands of the Union forces, who had then taken that city.

On the Atlantic coast, too, Roanoke Island was captured by the Federal forces on the 8th of February. Newbern, by the Federal forces, under General Burnside and Commodore Goldsborough, was captured on the 14th of March, and St. Augustine, Fernandina and other places in Florida in the same month. In April, Fort Pulaski, at the mouth of the Savannah river, was taken by General Gilmore; and on the 21st of April, Fort Mason, in North Carolina, was surrendered to Commodore Goldsborough. In 1862, the commerce of the North suffered greatly from the Florida and Alabama, two Confederate cruisers, which had been built in Great Britain, and which had been suffered by the British authorities to be let loose for their destructive work.

CAMPAIGNS OF 1863.

The first day of 1863 was forever made memorable by President Lincoln's emancipation proclamation, which declared freedom to all the slaves in the Confederate States. When the war began, it was with no thought on the part of the North of destroying slavery, though not a few thoughtful men foresaw what the end might be. But as the conflict went on, it came to be viewed as "a military necessity," as it certainly was a most effective blow to the power of the Confederate government.

Lee's army was now at Fredericksburg, and the Army of the Potomac, now under General Hooker, was on the north side of the Rappahannock. In April, Hooker began his movement. A column of 36,000 marched thirty miles up the Rappahannock and crossed at Kelly's Ford, without opposition. The four corps took different roads to Chancellorsville. Sickels, with 18,000 more, was but a short distance behind. An excellent beginning had been made, and General Lee was taken by surprise. He did not know from what point the attack was likely to come, and it was not until the afternoon of the 30th that he was satisfied that the decisive struggle would be at

THE "NASHVILLE" DESTROYING THE "MERCHANTMAN."

Chancellorsville. Stonewall Jackson, who was twenty miles away, was ordered up, and before noon on May 1, the Confederate army was drawn up in battle-line in front of the Wilderness.

Hooker had ordered an advance from the neighborhood of Chancellorsville toward Fredericksburg, but learning directly after this that Lee was moving with his whole army against him, he posted himself in a line of felled trees and earthworks which he hurriedly strengthened during the night. His purpose was to choose his own fighting-ground, but Lee was too wary to be drawn into the trap. Hooker was trying to flank Lee, who resolved in turn that Hooker himself should be flanked. To do this, Lee was compelled to take desperate chances. He sent Jackson with 30,000 men to pass around the right rear of the Federal army, while Lee with only 20,000 masked the movement by keeping up noisy demonstrations in front. By thus dividing his army he so weakened it that it would have been easy to crush each division in detail.

Hooker did not realize the danger, and his weak intrenchments in the rear were unguarded. Howard's corps had stacked their arms, and were getting their suppers ready. Suddenly Jackson's men burst from the woods like a cyclone, sweeping everything before them. The whole corps broke in the wildest panic and fled toward Chancellorsville. At the same time, Lee was fiercely attacking the front, and it looked for a time as if the whole Union army would be stampeded. Hooker's plans had been so damaged that it was doubtful whether they could be rearranged.

The battle was resumed on the 3d, the Federals being compelled to withdraw a mile toward the river.

Hooker had been out-generaled and defeated on the 2d and 3d of May. On the 5th, a violent storm set in. The Rapidan and Rappahannock rose rapidly and threatened the bridges at the fords, which were the only means of retreat left open to the Federals. Hooker decided to go back over the Rappahannock while he was yet able to do so, and preparations for the retreat were begun. On the morning of the 6th, the whole Army of the Potomac was across the Rappahannock and on its way to its old camp at Falmouth, having lost over 17,000 in killed and wounded. It was in this battle that Stonewall Jackson was mortally wounded, through mistake, in the darkness, by one of his own soldiers.

Lee, being now successful, resolved, for the second time, to invade the North, and calling in forces from the South so as now to have some 70,000 men, he moved to Harper's Ferry, crossed the Potomac, and advanced North on the Cumberland Valley, the Union army in the meantime marching to Frederick in Maryland, where Hooker had been superseded by General Meade. Lee's army took York and Carlisle, and the Union army marching against them the two armies met July 1, in the tremendous battle of Gettysburg, the greatest conflict of the war, lasting through three successive days. Gettysburg lies in the middle of a small valley formed by several ranges of hills. To the north the country is not very rugged, but to the south, east, and west, the hills are steep and high. About a mile to the westward is a ridge fringing the east bank of Willoughby's Run; and a quarter of a mile distant is another elevation called Seminary Ridge. The opening battle took place between these ridges.

The Federal line of battle followed the ridge in the form of a horse-shoe, the convexity turning toward Gettysburg. The position was an extremely good one, and was

BATTLE OF CHANCELLORSVILLE — JACKSON'S ATTACK ON THE RIGHT WING,

held by a hundred thousand veterans and two hundred guns. The Confederates occupied Gettysburg and the country to the east and west. At the end of the second day matters were in an unsatisfactory shape for both sides. Lee had not failed, nor had he met with the success on which he had counted. He had gained some important advantages, but the Union line was substantially unbroken. The losses were fearful, amounting to more than twenty thousand on each side.

On the morning of July 3, Meade opened a heavy fire, and sent a strong body of infantry against the Confederates. The latter, though outnumbered, held their ground for four hours, when they were driven out and the Federal line re-established. This disaster forced Lee

to change his plan of battle. He hurriedly massed his artillery and made ready for a grand attack. By noon he had one hundred and forty-five

VIEW FROM GETTYSBURG — WEST.

cannon on Seminary Ridge, while Meade lined the crest of Cemetery Hill with eighty pieces of artillery. The cannonade lasted for two hours, during which the mountains and valleys seemed to sway with the most tremendous outburst that ever took place on the American continent. The Union fire gradually slackened, and the troops grasped their muskets for the more deadly shock which they knew was close at hand. From Seminary Ridge, a mile away, was seen to issue a column of five thousand men, marching with the steady and firm tread of a dress parade. They were the flower of the Southern army, under the lead of Major-General Pickett, and all had been tried in the fire of many battles. Half the distance between the two armies was passed when the Union artillery burst

PICKETT'S CHARGE AT GETTYSBURG

2·

forth and swept away scores, but the lines instantly closed up. The Federals then waited until the gray coats were within short musket range, when the crest of the hill became one sheet of flame, and a hurricane of bullets flew in the very faces of the Confederates. Pettigrew's division which was supporting Pickett, was driven backward, leaving two thousand prisoners and fifteen standards with the Union army. Wilcox's supporting brigade had fallen behind. Pickett and his heroes rushed up the crest of Cemetery Ridge and captured the works at the point of the bayonet; but a converging fire was poured upon them and they were attacked in front

GETTYSBURG FROM LITTLE ROUND-TOP — EAST.

and flank. Looking around for his supports, Pickett saw that he was alone, and that a few minutes more would be enough for the destruction of his command. The order was given to fall back, and "all that was left of them" withdrew. Of the five thousand who advanced with such proud bearing upon that wonderful charge, thirty-five hundred were killed, wounded, or prisoners in the hands of the Union army.

General Lee now realized that he had begun a task he could not perform. The Union forces were too strong to be defeated, and nothing remained for him but to leave the country where nothing could be gained and all might be lost. By the morning of the 5th, he was on his way back to Virginia.

GUN-BOATS PASSING BEFORE VICKSBURG.

The battle of Gettysburg was the life and death struggle of the Southern Confederacy; it had been fought, and the Confederacy was defeated, and was now doomed. It never could be so strong as it was before Gettysburg; its utmost resources had been drawn upon, while those of the North were strong as ever.

In the West, at the beginning of the year, there were two Union armies; one, the Army of the Cumberland, under Rosecrans, opposed by the Confederates under Bragg, near Murfreesboro, and the other, the Army of the Tennessee, under Grant, at Memphis and Corinth, opposed by the Confederates under Pemberton, holding the line of the Tallahatchee. The great object of Grant, was fully to open the Mississippi river, which could be effected if Vicksburg and Port Hudson could be taken. In 1862, Sherman had assaulted the works north of Vicksburg, but they had proved too strong to be taken. Grant now crossed the river to the north of city, and adopted the bold plan of marching below Vicksburg, and then crossing the river to attack the city in the rear, which he successfully carried out. In making this movement, he five times met and defeated the Confederates under Pemberton, who then retreated to his works in Vicksburg, to which

LONGSTREET'S ARRIVAL AT BRAGG'S HEADQUARTERS

Grant now laid siege. The siege lasted for six weeks, at the end of which time Pemberton surrendered on the 4th of July, with 27,000 troops, who were thus taken prisoners.

By the surrender of Vicksburg, the Confederacy lost the services of more than 20,000 men, nearly a hundred pieces of artillery, and 40,000 small arms. In his report, Grant thus summed up the results of the campaign: "The defeat of the enemy in five battles outside of Vicksburg, the occupation of Jackson, the capital of Mississippi, and the capture of Vicksburg, its garrison and munition of war; a loss to the enemy of 37,000 prisoners, at least 10,000 killed and wounded, and hundreds, perhaps thousands, who can never be collected and re-organized. Arms and munitions of war for an army of 60,000

FEDERAL LINES AT CHATTANOOGA.

men have fallen into our hands, beside a large amount of other public property, and much that was destroyed to prevent our capturing it."

While Grant was thus engaged at Vicksburg, Banks, who had succeeded Butler in command of the Army of the Gulf, laid siege to Port Hudson, and as that could not hold out after Vicksburg was taken, it was surrendered on the 9th of July, and so the Mississippi was opened through its entire length. These successes, taking place at the same time as the decisive battle of Gettysburg, caused great rejoicing at the North, and gave encouraging promise of final success to the Union armies. The Army of the Cumberland, which had remained at Murfreesboro till June, then moving south, had several partial and successful actions with Bragg's forces, and then after taking possession of Chattanooga, engaged the Confederates in the great battle of Chickamauga, which was fought on the 19th and 20th of September. The Union forces were beaten, but under General Thomas they fought so stubbornly that in retiring they fortified themselves in Chattanooga. There they were besieged by Bragg's forces, and in danger of being starved into surrendering, when Sherman from Vicksburg, and Hooker from Virginia, came to their aid, and Grant, being put in command of all the forces, moved to Chattanooga, the siege of which was raised by the great battle of November 23–25, at Lookout Mountain and on Missionary Ridge.

On the evening of the 23d, the Confederate picket lines were driven back, and a good position gained by the Federals. The next morning Hooker was sent to assail the position on Lookout Mountain. The Union flag was carried to the crest, and by two o'clock the mountain swarmed with Federal soldiers. The Confederates retreated toward Missionary Ridge, having lost 2,000 prisoners.

The heavy fog lying below the soldiers gave this engagement the name of the "Battle above the Clouds." The next morning Grant ordered a general movement on the left center of the Confederates. The resistance here was of the most determined character, but it was the one weak point, and a whole

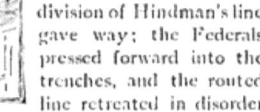

division of Hindman's line gave way; the Federals pressed forward into the trenches, and the routed line retreated in disorder toward Ringgold. A vast number of prisoners and an enormous amount of supplies were taken.

As the next step, Sherman was sent by Grant to East Tennessee, where Longstreet had succeeded in shutting up Burnside's army in Knoxville. As the result of this movement, Longstreet retreated to Virginia and East Tennessee, the population of which was largely Unionist, and was afterward held permanently for the Union cause.

MOIST WEATHER AT THE FRONT.

ATTACK ON CHARLESTON.

There were several other operations this year, not on a large scale, and not ensuring very important results. On the 8th of January the Confederates attacked Springfield in Missouri, and were repulsed. On the 11th, they were defeated at Hartsville; in April, they were driven back from Cape Girardeau; and in July, they were repulsed with heavy loss from Helena, Arkansas. In August, a band of guerillas fell upon Lawrence in Kansas, and murdered a hundred and forty people. In September, the Union forces took Little Rock, from which the Confederates were obliged to retreat; and in June of this year, the Confederates, under General Morgan, with 3,000 men, started from Tennessee, raiding Kentucky, Indiana and Ohio nearly to Pennsylvania, where at New Lisbon they were captured by the Union forces and scattered or taken prisoners.

FAIRFAX COURT HOUSE.

As to naval matters, in April, Admiral Dupont, with a fleet of iron-clads, made an unsuccessful attempt to capture Fort Sumter and Charleston, but his vessels were so damaged by heavy shot that he was obliged to retire. In June, the attempt was renewed by General Gilmore and Admiral Dahlgreen, but without success; and an attack in July on Fort Wagner was repulsed with severe loss. But afterward, in September, Gilmore, with very heavy guns, battered Fort Sumter into ruins, and threw shells into Charleston, after which the national forces were able to keep a closer blockade on the harbor.

In June, of this year, the President had called for 100,000 men, and in October, he called for 300,000 under the Conscription Act, which had been passed by Congress in

March. This act led to the great riot in New York, commencing on the 13th of July and lasting three days, in which over 200 lives were lost, some $2,000,000 worth of property destroyed, and the city kept in terror for several days. At the close of the year the Union forces held possession of the Mississippi river, of Missouri, Arkansas, Kentucky, and Tennessee, and of large parts of Mississippi, Louisiana, and Florida. West Virginia, which had repudiated the secession, which extended to the rest of Virginia, was admitted to the Union this year, as a new State, on the 20th of June.

CAMPAIGNS OF 1864.

The two main campaigns of 1864 were by Grant in the East, and Sherman in the West. Grant having been made lieutenant-general and commander of all the armies, transferred his headquarters to the Army of the Potomac, which was still under Meade, while Sheridan was in command of the cavalry. Lee, with some 70,000 men, was still at the Rapidan, and on the 4th of May the Army of the Potomac of 140,000 men, crossing the river, met the Confederates in the bloody battle of the Wilderness, which lasted three days without decided victory on either side, and a loss on both of some 25,000 men, in killed, wounded and prisoners.

Grant now moved toward Spottsylvania Court House, but Lee moving more rapidly planted his forces there behind earthworks. For two weeks Grant tried to carry these works, the fighting beginning on the 9th and continuing to the 12th of the month, with great slaughter on both sides; though the Confederates, protected by their earthworks, lost far less than the Nationals. The only important success of the latter was by General Hancock, who took part of the Confederate lines and captured some 4,000 prisoners. It was from the scene of this fierce and continued conflict that Grant sent to Washington his famous dispatch, "I propose to fight it out on this line, if it takes all summer."

Grant, now, by a first and then a second movement, brought his forces to Cold Harbor, twelve miles from Richmond, and here made several attacks on the Confederate intrenchments, the severest assault being on the 3d of June, when the Nationals were repulsed with the loss of 7,000 men. Grant then made a change of base, crossing James river and moving on Petersburg. Lee also fell back within the intrenchments of Richmond and Petersburg. These various movements and engagements, making what is known as the "Overland Campaign," occupied six weeks, and cost the Union army 60,000 men, while the Confederate loss was only about a third of that number, the Union forces being brought up against the strong works of Richmond and Petersburg.

While all this was going on in Virginia, two co-operative movements were begun, one by Sigel in connection with Hunter, down the Shenandoah Valley, where they met the Confederate forces and were defeated; after which Hunter marched against Lynchburg, but failed to take it, and then retreated to West Virginia.

The other was a column led by Butler, in transports, up the James river to City Point and Bermuda Hundred, his object being to join Grant and take Petersburg before it should be strongly fortified. Accordingly, the place was assaulted on the 18th of June, but the attack was repulsed, as were several other attacks made within a few days. Lee's lines now extended some thirty miles from the southwest of Petersburg to the

northeast of Richmond, and Grant preparing an elaborate system of works, sat down
for a long siege, which lasted from June 1864 to April 1865, in which time there were a
number of actions and several important battles, but without any great and decisive
combat. One operation from which much had been expected, was the explosion of a
vast mine of powder which had secretly been excavated under the forts of the enemy.

It was fired on the 30th of July, carrying
all the works over it into the air, and
destroying several thousand men,
after which a storming column rushed
on to attack Petersburg, but was
repulsed with great slaughter.

In July, Lee sent a column under
General Early, to threaten,
and if possible
capture Wash-
ington, hoping

EXPLOSION OF MINE BEFORE PETERSBURG.

thus to divert Grant from
the siege of Petersburg.
Early crossed the Poto-
mac and defeated the
Nationals under Lew
Wallace at Monocacy, but
finding that additional
troops had been thrown
into Washington, he went
back to Virginia, taking
much booty from Mary-
land and Pennsylvania, and having
burned Chambersburg on the 30th of
July. A force of some 30,000 had,
in August, been sent by Grant to

follow Early into the Shenandoah Valley; and to command it, he sent Sheridan, who, in the battle of Winchester, defeated the Confederates on the 19th of September, and again, in three days after, at Fisher's Hill. The National forces, after ravaging the valley, took a position on Cedar Creek, and Sheridan left for a time, being called to Washington. Early, being reinforced, fell suddenly on the Union camp, on the 19th of October, and had driven them as far as Middletown, when Sheridan, who, on his way back had heard the fighting, rode rapidly to the front, rallied the retreating forces, and led them back to victory in one of the most brilliant actions of the war, in which Early's army was scattered with great losses.

In May, Sherman, commanding the western army, began a march from Chattanooga to Atlanta in Georgia, and as he advanced, Johnston, who was at Dalton, was obliged to leave position after position, finally retiring within the works of Atlanta, in July. During this march, several actions took place between the two forces,—at Resaca, May 14

GENERAL SHERMAN'S SCOUTS.

and 15; at Dallas, May 25–28; and at Kenesaw Mountain, June 22 to July 3.
Johnston's retreating policy greatly dissatisfied the Confederate authorities, and he was
superseded by General Hood. Hood made three vigorous assaults on Sherman's
forces, July 20, 22, and 28, but they were not successful, and Sherman getting between
Hood and Atlanta, occupied that city, September 2. Hood now endeavored to cut off
Sherman's supplies, that he might compel him to move back, but Sherman sent
Thomas with a large force to oppose Hood, while he himself, in the meantime, was
preparing for his intended march southward and eastward to the sea.

Hood now advanced his forces,
hoping to capture Nashville, on his
way to which place he
encountered the forces of

DEATH OF GENERAL POLK

Schofield, and
an action took
place, Novem-
ber 30, in
which Hood
was severely repulsed with a loss
of several of his officers. The
Confederate forces now laid siege to
Nashville, where they were attacked
by Thomas, December 15 and 16,
Thomas gaining the victory, and
Hood's forces suffering severely.

In the meantime, Sherman, cutting off his
communications with the North, and burning
Atlanta, began his celebrated march through

Georgia, intending by moving through the interior of the Confederacy to destroy their supplies and so cut off the means of sustaining their armies. Starting from Atlanta in the middle of November, he pressed on, three hundred miles, through a hostile country, meeting with no serious resistance, and in a month reached the sea coast near Savannah. For thirty miles on each side of his course he wasted the country, carried off what supplies he wished, and destroyed what he could not use. He tore up the railroads, proclaimed liberty to the slaves, many of whom joined his forces, and made the Confederates feel that their power was rapidly declining. The only obstacle of importance in his way was Fort McAllister, which he took by assault, December 13;

SAVANNAH.

and marching on, he put the army in communication with the fleet off the coast, and took Savannah, December 31, thus ending this important campaign.

Beside the two main campaigns of the year, there were other operations of the opposing forces. Seymour making an expedition from Port Royal to Florida, was defeated, February 20, by the Confederates at Olustee; and Sherman, before he went to Chattanooga, going from Vicksburg to destroy the railroads in northern Mississippi, was but partly successful. Forest defeated his cavalry column, and then attacked and captured Fort Pillow, which was garrisoned mostly by negro troops, many of whom were massacred. Banks, in March, led an expedition from New Orleans into the Red River region, in Louisiana, being aided by the fleet under Admiral Porter. Two actions were the result, one at the Sabine Cross Roads, April 8, in which the

Confederates were victors, and the other at Pleasant Hill, which was indecisive, after which the expedition was given up.

In naval operations in July a powerful fleet under Admiral Farragut, with a land force under General Granger, was sent against Mobile, which was defended by Forts Morgan and Gaines, and by a Confederate fleet. Farragut passed the forts with the loss of only one vessel, and engaged and captured the Confederate iron-clad, the Tennessee; and the combined Union forces afterward took the forts, and so got control of Mobile Bay, though the city itself was not taken till the spring of the next year. A similar expedition was made against Fort Fisher at the entrance to Wilmington, North Carolina, Admiral Porter with the fleet, and General Butler with the land forces, attacking the fort in December. The assault was a failure, and the land forces returned to Fortress Monroe. But the fleet remained and the Fort was taken by General Terry on the 15th of the next month.

Immense loss was this year caused to American commerce by Confederate cruisers, which had been built in England, and were now acting as privateers against the North. The most destructive of these vessels was the Alabama, commanded by Captain Simms, which captured and destroyed over sixty northern vessels and $10,000,000 worth of property. In a naval battle off Cherbourg, France, the Alabama was captured by the United States vessel Kearsarge, Captain Winslow, and was sunk in June. In October, Lieutenant Cushing, with a party of volunteers, by a daring and brilliant exploit, attacked the Confederate iron-clad Albemarle, in the Roanoke river, and destroyed her. He fastened a torpedo to the Albemarle, which exploded and sunk her, but only he and a single companion escaped with their lives.

James I. Waddell, captain of the Shenandoah, was the only sailor who carried the flag of the "Lost Cause" around the world. In 1864, he made nine captures in the Atlantic and then sailed for the sea of Okhotsk. He ran down the Abigail, a whaling brig owned in New Bedford, and then steered for a fleet of New England whalers in the Behring Sea. For six months the steamer was dodging the icebergs, battling the sleet and snow, and burning the whaling vessels to the water's edge. At the end of that period the Shenandoah had made thirty-eight captures, wrecked the New England fleet, taken 1,053 prisoners, and inflicted damages to the amount of a million and a half dollars,

In those far-off waters no news could reach Waddell from home, and it was not until August 2, that he learned that the Confederacy had been dead for months, during which time he had been wrecking right and left in the face of the proclamation that all found in arms against the United States would be treated as outlaws. He sailed for Liverpool, and after escaping several times by a hair's breadth the Federal cruisers that were hunting for him, he ran into the Mersey, and surrendered to the Queen, November 5, 1865.

He settled near London for a time, but afterward accepted a captaincy under the Pacific Mail Company. After several year's service he took a contract from the State of Maryland to suppress the pirates on her oyster beds. With a small police boat, manned by a crew of ten men and two howitzers, he steamed after his game. He fell in with a fleet of the oyster thieves, above the mouth of the Honga river. When he called on them to surrender, they laughed at him. He sank one boat, drove three ashore, captured three, and the rest escaped by flight, thus ending the oyster war in less than half an hour.

OPENING OF THE FIGHT BETWEEN THE KEARSARGE AND ALABAMA.

During the year five different calls were made by the President for additional troops; in February, for 200,000; in March, for 200,000; in April, for 85,000; in July, for 500,000; and in December, for 300,000. In the fall of the year Abraham Lincoln was

END OF THE OYSTER WAR.

re-elected President, and Andrew Johnson was elected Vice-President. In October, of this year, Nevada was admitted as a State into the Union, and on the 1st of November the "Money Order" system was established in connection with the post office department of the government. The year was one of marked success for the Union cause, and the end of the war was manifestly drawing near.

THE FINAL CAMPAIGN — 1865.

Such was the situation at the opening of 1865, that it was believed the war must soon come to an end. A strict blockade shut out the South from the markets of Europe. Her supplies of arms and ammunitions were running low, and even if she could find men enough to resist the North, she could not equip or fully provide for them. Food was becoming scarce. In Lee's army the pangs of hunger had been felt, and elsewhere through the South there was not a little suffering with those who had once been rich.

THE PEACE COMMISSIONERS.

The soldiers were insufficiently supplied with clothing, and as winter came on, so many of them deserted and left for home that punishment was impossible. The North had a million of men in the field, and nearly six hundred vessels of war, seventy-five of which were iron-clads, and she had full command of everything that could give comfort and efficiency to her soldiers, while the rolls of the Southern army showed only four hundred thousand men, and from desertion and other causes, large numbers of these were not actually in the ranks.

While the money resources and credit of the North seemed almost unlimited, in the South it had become impossible to borrow at home, and the supply by loan from abroad was as nothing to the great and increasing need. Confederate notes or promises to pay were printed as fast as machinery could do it, but they steadily fell in value, three paper dollars being required in 1863 to purchase one of gold, while after the battle of

RAISING THE FLAG OVER FORT SUMTER.

Gettysburg it took twenty, and somewhat later sixty to obtain one in coin. A loaf of bread cost three dollars, and it took a month's pay to buy the soldier a pair of stockings. A touching weakness appeared in the fact that the government appealed to the people for jewelry and plate, and that the Richmond papers published lists of gold rings, silver spoons, and tea-pots, which, in the hopeful enthusiasm of the givers, were sent in aid of the depleted treasury. And when iron-clad ships were needed, and iron was scarce, an association of ladies, it is said, was formed to collect old pots and pans to be used for their construction. Brave as their soldiers were, and skillful and tireless as their leaders might be, it seemed hopeless for the South to think of success against the resources and resolute determination of the North.

Mr. Lincoln, as we have seen, was re-elected, and by the largest vote ever known in a presidential election. "It is not in my nature," he said, "to triumph over any one, but I give thanks to Almighty God for this evidence of the people's resolution to stand by free government and the rights of humanity." He was inaugurated on the 4th of March, and his address was brief, but high toned and most serious, and one that probably produced a deeper impression on the American people than any State paper ever delivered.

DESTRUCTION OF THE NASHVILLE.

In closing it, he uttered these memorable words, which have almost the ring of one of the old prophets of Israel: "Fondly do we hope, fervently do we pray, that this mighty scourge of war may speedily pass away; yet if God wills that it continue until all the wealth piled by the bondsman's two hundred and fifty years of unrequited toil shall be sunk, and until every drop of blood drawn with the lash shall be paid by another drawn with the sword — as was said three thousand years ago — so still it must be said 'The judgments of the Lord are true and righteous altogether.' With malice towards none, with charity for all, with firmness in the right, as God gives us to see the right, let us finish the work we are in, to bind up the Nation's wounds, to

care for him who shall have borne brunt of the battle, and for his widow and his
orphans; to do all which may achieve and cherish a just and lasting peace among
ourselves, and with all nations."

Sherman had now almost destroyed the Western army of the Confederates, and by
his triumphal march and success at the South he had paralyzed opposition in that
quarter. The only formidable army of the Confederates now was that of Lee with his
veterans, but this consisted of less than forty thousand men, while Grant's army was
one hundred thousand strong. To join Grant, Sherman had turned north from
Savannah, February 1, and on the 17th captured Columbia, which was set on fire by the
Confederates before they left it. On the next day he entered Charleston, which had
been evacuated by General Hardy after setting fire to its buildings, and though the
flames were checked by the Federal troops after they entered, it was not till great
damage had been done and an explosion of a large quantity of powder had killed two
hundred men.

SUNSET OVER ATLANTA.

Advancing north, General Sherman was joined by General Slocum, and on the
11th of March he occupied Fayetteville. On the 16th, he had an engagement at
Averasboro with the Confederate forces of forty thousand men under General
Hardee, which resulted in a Federal victory. On the 19th, he had a severe conflict at
Bentonville which was not decisive. On the 23d, he entered Goldsboro, where he was
re-inforced by Generals Schofield and Terry with their troops. On the 13th of April, he
engaged Johnston at Raleigh, taking and entering that city; and on the 26th, Johnston,
who had heard of Lee's surrender, finding that further resistance was hopeless,
surrendered his army to the Federal forces.

General Wilson in the meantime, with a cavalry column had captured Selma and
Montgomery in Alabama, and also Columbus and Macon in Georgia, taking many
prisoners and cannon, and doing great damage to Confederate property; and General
Stoneman, in Virginia and North Carolina, had torn up miles of railroads and captured
many prisoners and valuable military stores.

The main armies of the North and South were still at Petersburg and Richmond, where Sheridan, after capturing most of Earley's remaining force in the Shenandoah Valley, had swept down to the James river, tearing up railroads and destroying the canal, and then joining Grant's forces. Lee, though now surrounded by overwhelming numbers, planned an assault on the Union lines, in which, on March 25, he took Fort Steadman, from which, however, he was soon driven out. Grant now assailed the right flank of the Confederates, which brought on the battle of Five Forks, April 1, in which the Confederates were defeated. An attack was then made, April 2, along the whole line

ON PICKET — "WHO GOES THERE?"

of the Confederates, in which the Nationals
were successful, and Lee, in the night,
abandoned Petersburg and Richmond, which
were entered by the Union forces on the
3d of April.

Lee now retreated westward hoping to
join Johnston in North Carolina, but he was
at once pursued by Grant's forces,
and all hope of retreat being cut
off and his army being completely
surrounded at Appomattox Court
House, he was
obliged to sur-
render, which
he did on the
9th of April.

RETREAT OF LEE'S ARMY.

He had strug-
gled bravely but
in vain against
overwhelming
numbers and
forces, and the
last hope of success for the
Confederates was overthrown.
Appreciating the desperate
condition of affairs, Lee saw
that there was but one possible course before him, and
accordingly the two great leaders met, and Grant received
from Lee the surrender of the
army under his command.

By the terms of surrender
Lee's officers and men were
paroled and were not to
take up arms again unless
exchanged, and the arms,
ammunition and supplies of
the Confederates were also
given up to the conquerors.
This was the conclusive act
of the war, and there were no
more important engagements.
When Grant asked if these

SURRENDER OF GENERAL LEE.

terms were satisfactory, Lee replied that they were, adding that "his position was such that any terms must be satisfactory;" and as showing the sad condition of his forces, he then said that for two days his men had been without food, when Grant, generously eager at once to relieve their wants, sent to them a large drove of oxen and a train of provision wagons, which were received with cheers by those who appreciated the noble spirit of the giver. By the end of May all the Confederate forces had surrendered, and the war of secession was at an end.

The President and cabinet of the Confederate government had before this retired from Richmond, and Jefferson Davis had fled south by a special train, but he was

THE HOUSE WHERE GENERAL LEE SURRENDERED.

captured and imprisoned in Fortress Monroe till May, 1867, when he was indicted on the charge of treason; but bail being given, he was never brought to trial, but was afterward included in the general amnesty of December 25, 1868, the nation thus showing its desire that the antagonisms of the war should come to an end, and the country again be at peace as one people. When Richmond was abandoned, just before Lee's surrender, the evacuating Confederates, plundering as they went, blew up the gun-boats, broke down the bridges, and set fire to the great warehouses, so that by the flames thus kindled a third part of the city was destroyed. The next morning when the Northern troops came in, the first to enter the capital of the former slave owners was a regiment of negro cavalry.

The surrender of Lee and the end of the rebellion caused the greatest joy throughout the North, but in the midst of it a most sad and terrible event occurred. President Lincoln was assassinated in the theater at Washington on the evening of April 14, by John Wilkes Booth, a fanatical adherent of the Confederacy, who, entering the box where Mr. Lincoln was seated, with the wild cry "The South is avenged!" fired

THE CAPTURE OF BOOTH.

a pistol shot into the President's brain, and then escaped by a back entrance before the startled audience fully realized what had been done. Mr. Lincoln died the next morning.

The same night another villain entered the sick-room of Mr. Seward, the Secretary of State, and stabbed, and would have killed him had he not been prevented, the different attacks giving the impression that a plot had been formed to murder the leaders of the administration in the hope of helping or avenging the lost cause of the South. The conspirators were hunted down. Booth was shot in Maryland; four others connected with the conspiracy were tried and hung, and some others were imprisoned. The grief of the country for its murdered President was intense and bitter. No man was ever more sincerely and deeply mourned. All business was suspended, and crowds gathered in silent sadness as his funeral train passed through the different States to the place of burial at Springfield, where a splendid monument marks the last resting place of one whose name, like that of Washington, will ever be held in the highest honor and esteem by the nation that he saved. As Washington was well called "the father of his country," so Lincoln was its savior. The one was the founder of a republic, the other the preserver of the nation and the liberator of a long enslaved race.

At the end of May, a two days' review of the armies of Grant and Sherman took place at Washington. These armies numbered about 200,000 men. The disbanding of all the forces, both North and South, was begun, and nearly 1,000,000 men retired quietly from the camps and pursuits of war to the occupations of private life.

The expenses of the war had been enormous, the national debt in 1860 amounting to $65,000,000, and in 1866 to over $2,800,000,000, and the Confederate debt to over $2,000,000,000, which was never paid. At one time the expenses of the national government reached the vast sum of $3,500,000 a day. To meet these immense

LINCOLN'S GRAVE.

expenditures, the government in 1862 issued $150,000,000 of legal tender notes, known as *greenbacks*, from the color of the paper on which they were printed, and also United States bonds bearing interest; and they also levied internal revenue taxes, and greatly increased the duties on imported goods. National banks were also established in 1863, having the national bonds as security for their currency, and as a guarantee for its redemption, thus providing for the expenditures of the war. The expenses and losses by the

REVIEW OF THE UNION TROOPS AT WASHINGTON.

war, both North and South, including the value of property destroyed, have been estimated at $9,000,000,000.

The number of troops called for at the North was 2,942,748, and the total number obtained and actually in service was 2,690,401. The terms of service varied. Some were called for three months, some for six months, and others for one, two, or three years, or to the end of the war. On the Union side it is estimated that over 290,000 were killed in battle or died from disease in the field, and 400,000 more were disabled or crippled for life; and on both sides it is believed that nearly or quite 1,000,000 men were killed or received wounds. The Christian Commission and the Sanitary Commission were charitable associations, organized at the North, for the relief of the sick and wounded soldiers, and to carry to the camps the instructions and consolations of religion, and they did their work of benevolence on a most liberal scale, millions of dollars being contributed to their funds, and provision in various forms being made in every part of the country for the comfort and aid of the soldiers.

THE LINCOLN MONUMENT.

As the results of the war, the Nation has been freed from the curse of slavery, which had so long hindered the progress of the fairest section of the country and kept up a constant antagonism between the North and South, and the South has entered on a course of prosperity far greater than ever before known. The death blow has been given to the idea that States may at any time secede and be independent, and the claim of the United States to be one great nation, and not a mere confederacy, has been established forever. Republican institutions were on trial, and the end has shown that a free people can safely guide their own destinies in war as well as in peace. And terrible as the conflict and its sufferings have been, the generations to come may reap advantages that otherwise could never have been known, and the world may have received a lesson that shall yet be fraught with blessings to governments and to mankind.

REVIEW OF CAMPAIGNS.

So important were the movements and events of the War of Secession, that a tabulated view of the various engagements and their results cannot but be of interest, especially for reference. Below are the principal events of each of the annual campaigns.

CAMPAIGNS OF 1861.

Fort Sumter surrendered,	April 13.
McClellan's *West Virginia* campaign (successful),	June and July.
Butler's repulse at *Big Bethel*,	June.
Action at *Carthage*, Missouri, Confederate victory,	July 5.
Bull Run, Confederate victory,	July 21.
Action at *Wilson's Creek*, Confederate victory,	August 10.
Ball's Bluff, Confederate victory,	October 21.
Action at *Belmont*, Missouri, Confederate victory,	November 7.

CAMPAIGNS OF 1862.

In the West.

Capture of *Fort Henry*, Union victory,	February 6.
Capture of *Fort Donelson*, Union victory,	February 16.
Occupation of *Nashville*, Union victory,	February 23.
Occupation of *Columbus*, by Union fleet,	March 22.
Battle of *Shiloh*, Confederate victory,	April 6.
Battle of *Shiloh*, Union victory,	April 7.
Capture of *Island No. 10*, Union victory,	April 7.
Capture of *Corinth*, Union victory,	May 30.
Capture of *Memphis*, Union victory,	June 6.
Invasion of *Kentucky*, Confederate success,	August and September.
Battle of *Perryville*, Union victory,	October 8.
Battle of *Murfreesboro*,	December 31.
Battle of *Murfreesboro*,	January 1.
Corinth and *Iuka*, Union success,	September and October.
Pea Ridge, Arkansas, Union success,	March 7, 8.

In the East.

Capture of *Yorktown*, Union victory,	May 4
Action at *Williamsburg*, Union victory,	May 5.
Battle of *Fair Oaks*, Indecisive,	May 31.
Battle of *Fair Oaks*, Indecisive,	June 1.
Jackson's Raid, Diving Creek, Union forces,	May and June.
Battle of *Gaines' Mill*, Confederate victory,	June 27.
Seven days' skirmishing at *Malvern Hill*,	July 1.
Lee's *Invasion of the North*, Confederate victory,	August and September.
Fight at *South Mountain*, Union victory,	September 14.
Harper's Ferry taken by Confederates,	September 15.
Battle of *Antietam*, Union victory,	September 17.
Battle of *Fredericksburg*, Confederate victory,	December 13.
Capture of *New Orleans*, Union victory,	April 28.

CAMPAIGNS OF 1863.

In the East.

Battle of *Chancellorsville*, Confederate victory,	May 2, 3.
Lee's *Invasion of Pennsylvania*,	June.
Battle of *Gettysburg*, Union victory,	July 1, 2, 3.

In the West.

Vicksburg taken, Union victory,	July 4.
Port Hudson taken, Union victory,	July 9.
Advance through *Tennessee*, Union victory,	June, July and August.

Battle of *Chickamauga*, Confederate victory,   September 19, 20.
Battle of *Missionary Ridge*, Union victory,   November 23, 24, 25.
Action in *East Tennessee*, Union success,   .   .   .   November.
Attack on *Fort Sumter*, Confederate victory,   .   .   April 8.

CAMPAIGNS OF 1864.

In the East.

Grant's *Overland Campaign* begun in May; battles of *Wilderness, Spottsylvania, North Anna,*
    Cold Harbor, indecisive ; terrible loss of Union Army, but Lee compelled to retreat.
Attack on *Petersburg*, Confederate success, ...   June 18.
Movements in *Shenandoah Valley*, Confederate success,   .   May and June.
Advance on *Petersburg*, Confederate victory,   .   .   .   May and June.
Battle of *Monocacy*, Confederate victory,   .   .   .   July 9.
The great *Mine Explosion* before Petersburg, Confederate victory,   July 30.
Valley Campaign and battle of *Winchester*, Union victory,   .   .   September 19.
Battle of *Cedar Creek*, first Confederate, and then Union success,   .   . October 19.

In the West.

Sherman's Campaign from Chattanooga, begun   May 6.
Engagement at *Atlanta*, Union success, end of   .   .   . July.
Battle of *Franklin*, Union victory, ...   November 30.
Battle of *Nashville*, Union victory.   .   .   .   December 15.
Sherman's March to the Sea, ...   November.
Capture of *Fort McAllister*,   .   .   .   December 13.
Capture of *Savannah*, ...   December 21.

CAMPAIGNS OF 1865.

In the South.

Sherman's *March North* from Savannah, begun   .   .   .   February 1.
Columbia taken, ...   February 17.
Charleston taken, ...   February 17.
Actions at *Averasboro* and *Bentonville*, Union successes,   .   .   February.
Arrival at *Goldsboro*, ...   March 23.

In the East.

United forces of Sherman and Grant in *Shenandoah Valley*,   .   .   March 26.
Lee's attack on *Fort Steadman*, Union victory,   .   .   .   March 25.
Battle of *Five Forks*, Union victory,   .   .   .   April 1.
Attack on *Petersburg*, Union victory,   .   .   April 2.
Capture of *Petersburg* and *Richmond*, Union victory,   .   April 3.
Surrender of Lee's Army,   .   .   .   April 9.
Surrender of Johnston's Army,   .   .   April 26.

CALLS FOR TROOPS.

April,   1861, ...   75,000
May,   1861, ...   82,745
July,   1861, ...   500,000
July,   1862, ...   300,000
August,   1862, ...   300,000
June,   1863   100,000
October,   1863, ...   300,000
February,   1864, ...   200,000
March,   1864, ...   200,000
April,   1864, ...   85,000
July,   1864, ...   500,000
December,   1864, ...   300,000

CHAPTER V.

RECONSTRUCTION AND PEACE.

JOHNSON'S ADMINISTRATION — 1865 TO 1869.

WHEN the President was assassinated, many feared that the affairs of the government might be thrown into hopeless confusion. Such fears, however, were soon dispelled, for within a few hours of Lincoln's death the Vice-President, Andrew Johnson, took the oath of office, and was inaugurated as President, April 15, 1865.

Mr. Johnson was born in Raleigh, North Carolina, December 29, 1808. When ten years old, he was apprenticed to a tailor, with whom he served seven years, receiving no schooling. Becoming interested in hearing the reading of the speeches of some of the British orators, by a visitor to the shop, he resolved to learn for himself, which he did by improving the hours between work and sleep. Moving to Tennessee, he worked for a time as a journeyman tailor, and by the aid of his wife learned to write and cipher. Taking an active part in politics, he was repeatedly chosen to public office, and in 1843 was elected to Congress, serving four terms in the House of Representatives. In 1853, he was chosen governor of the State, and in 1857 was elected to the United States Senate. During the war, he was military governor of Tennessee, and in 1864 was made Vice-President.

RESIDENCE OF ANDREW JOHNSON.

One of the first questions being that of the reconstruction of the seceded States, Mr. Johnson, in May, 1865, issued a proclamation of amnesty to all who had been engaged in the War of Secession, except certain classes which were specified. For the

Confederate States he appointed governors, and ordered conventions of the Southern States which were required to rescind the ordinances of secession, to declare void the debts contracted for the suppression of the War of Secession, and to vote for an amendment to the Constitution which had been proposed by Congress, abolishing slavery. These requirements were complied with by the Southern States, and the thirteenth amendment to the Constitution, which had been passed by Congress in the early part of the year, having been ratified by twenty-seven States, was, on the 18th of December, announced by Secretary Seward as a part of the

ANDREW JOHNSON.

Constitution, so that slavery was forever forbidden in any part of the United States.

Serious disagreements and difficulties soon arose between the President and Congress. The President, holding that all acts of secession had been null and void, and that the Southern States had never been out of the Union, proposed a civil policy of treating them accordingly; while Congress, maintaining that such States had for the time been out of the Union, advocated a military control over them, and insisted that if they were re-admitted to the Union it must be on such conditions as Congress might impose as necessary. The President, following out his plan, in May announced the restoration of Virginia to the Union; in June, removed certain restrictions on trade with the South, and in September issued a proclamation of more extended amnesty than before.

When Congress met in December, it passed the "Civil Rights Bill," giving citizenship to all persons, both white and colored. In March, 1866, the President vetoed the bill, but it was promptly passed over his veto by a two-thirds vote. Johnson, in public speeches, strongly opposed the course of Congress, and was exceedingly bitter in his denunciations of its course, declaring that its position "was a new rebellion."

Congress going forward in its proposed course had submitted to the States, for ratification, the fourteenth amendment to the Constitution, giving equal rights to all citizens, white or black; and Tennessee, having assented to this measure, was readmitted to the Union in July, 1866. In December, Congress went on in its work, providing by bills that no State should be readmitted except on ratifying the fourteenth amendment;

RUINS OF RICHMOND AFTER THE WAR.

that the Territory of Nebraska should be admitted as a State on this condition and on giving the right of suffrage to all citizens, that the same right of suffrage should be granted in the District of Columbia, and that the South, should be divided into five districts under military governors to be appointed by the President. Johnson vetoed all these bills, but they were all passed over his veto. In March, 1867, Nebraska became the thirty-seventh State of the Union; and in June and July of the next year, North and South Carolina, Georgia, Alabama, Florida, Louisiana, and Arkansas, on the same conditions, were readmitted to the Union.

In accordance with the act of Congress which has been mentioned, Johnson appointed military governors for the five districts of the South, but afterward, on the ground that the act of Congress was unconstitutional, he gave such orders to these governors as practically to nullify the act of Congress. That body, however, passed an act declaring and re-affirming the meaning of the previous one, and despite the President's obstructions, the plans of Congress were carried out.

In March, 1867, Congress passed what was called the "Tenure of Office Bill," declaring that no officer whose appointment by the President required the assent of the Senate, should be removed from office without the Senate's permission. It was designed to prevent the President from removing officers who were not favorable to his policy, and putting in their place those who would carry out his views.

Such had been the course of the President, that as far back as 1867 there had been in the House of Representatives a movement for his impeachment. In the latter part of that year the feeling against him was greatly increased by his removal of Edwin M. Stanton, the Secretary of War, and the appointment of General Grant in his place. The Senate refused its assent to the change, and Stanton resumed the office, but was again removed in 1868, and General Thomas, who was adjutant-general, was appointed to the place. Stanton refused to vacate the office, and the House of Representatives, believing that Johnson was violating the law, the next day resolved that he should be "impeached of high crimes and misdemeanors;" and on the 3d of March they decided that the charges should be brought against him, that he had unlawfully removed Stanton, that he had declared that the thirty-ninth Congress was not a legally constituted body, and that he had failed to properly execute its acts, as he was bound to do. The articles of impeachment, eleven in number, were at once presented to the Senate, and in that body, presided over by Chief Justice Chase, the trial began on the 23d day of March. The trial continued for two months, the vote in the end being thirty-five for conviction and nineteen for acquittal, which amounted to an acquittal, as it required a two-thirds vote to convict. In July, Johnson issued another proclamation of amnesty, and in December he pardoned all who had taken part in the war against the Union. In July, 1868, the fourteenth amendment had been ratified by the requisite number of States, and so had become a part of the United States Constitution.

During Mr. Johnson's administration an important question arose as to the relation between the United States and France as to Mexico. During the war, Napoleon had sent an army which had defeated the Mexican republicans in 1863, and had made Maximilian emperor of Mexico. Occupied as the United States was with the War of Secession, nothing at the time was done; but at the close of the war Secretary Seward, carrying out the Monroe Doctrine, demanded of Napoleon the withdrawal of the French troops, which was done. The Mexicans then rose against the forces of Maximilian, and conquered them, and Maximilian, being taken prisoner, was shot in 1867.

In 1866, Cyrus W. Field succeeded in laying the second Atlantic cable in place of the one laid in 1858, a defect in which had soon prevented its successful use. The new cable was laid by the immense steamship, the Great Eastern. In 1867, a bankrupt Act was passed by Congress, and in the same year Alaska was purchased from Russia for $7,200,000, thus adding to the territory of the United States 580,000 square miles, which was more than the area of the thirteen original States of the Union. The region is of great value for its fisheries, forests and furs, and is said to have mineral deposits of immense value, though as yet they are undeveloped. The seal business of Alaska and of its islands has been a source of immense profits, as the seals have been numbered by millions, and have been taken annually by the tens of thousands for their valuable

PICKING UP THE ATLANTIC CABLE.

skins. But the slaughter of them has been so great that it was feared they would be extinct unless their destruction was for a time prohibited; and this has now been done by the united action of the United States and Great Britain, until the question of the control of Behring Sea shall be decided by arbitrators to be appointed, by whom all the questions in dispute shall be amicably settled.

In the presidential campaign of 1868, the Democrats nominated Horatio Seymour, of New York, and the Republicans nominated General Ulysses S. Grant. The Republican party, in its platform, upheld the action of Congress. And Grant was elected with Schuyler Colfax as Vice-President.

ULYSSES S. GRANT.

GRANT'S ADMINISTRATION—1869 TO 1877.

The eighteenth President of the United States, Ulysses S. Grant, was inaugurated March 4, 1869, with Schuyler Colfax, of Indiana, as Vice-President.

Mr. Grant was born at Point Pleasant, Ohio, April 27, 1822. He was graduated at West Point in 1843, and served with honor in the Mexican war, but afterward resigned from the army, and at the outbreak of the Civil War was engaged in the leather business at Galena, Illinois. Taking part in the conflict he rose rapidly in rank till he was made lieutenant-general in 1864. His course during the war, and the leading position he occupied during its continuance, and in bringing it to a close, appear fully in the account already given of the progress and results of the war.

During the first year of this administration the last of the seceded States had been restored to the Union, and three-fourths of all the States had approved the fifteenth amendment, which thus became a part of the Constitution, March 30th, 1870. In February, 1871, the Joint Commission of American and British statesmen met at Washington, to adjust the claims for injuries to our commerce from Confederate cruisers which had been built in English ship yards. By the treaty of Washington, arranged by this commission, the question in dispute was referred to a Board of Arbitration, which afterward met at Geneva, in Switzerland, and awarded to the United States as damages from England, the sum of fifteen million, five hundred thousand dollars, which was paid within the year. Between England and the United States there was also an unsettled question as to the line in the channel which separates Vancouver Island from the main land. The dispute was referred to William I., Emperor of Germany, as arbitrator, and his decision was in favor of the United States.

In 1869, the great work of connecting the Atlantic and Pacific coasts by railroad was completed, the last tie being laid and the last spike driven on the 10th of May. In the fall of the same year a disastrous panic occurred in business circles, in which many failures occurred and many fortunes were lost. In the autumn of 1871, a fearful fire took place in Chicago, sweeping over some two thousand acres in the city, destroying property to the value of two hundred millions of dollars, and causing the loss of some two hundred lives. And a year later, in November, 1872, Boston suffered from a great conflagration which swept over sixty-five acres of the city and destroyed property to the value of eighty millions. The loss of property by the fire, as well as by the long interruption of business, in each case was immense, but as the result, both cities were greatly improved in the arrangement of streets and the structure of the buildings erected.

In 1871, Mr. Lowe, the American envoy in China, and Admiral John Rodgers opened negotiations with the Corean authorities for a treaty to protect shipwrecked sailors of foreign nations, who had been cruelly treated by the natives of that country, and an expedition was allowed to make a survey of the neighboring coast and waters. The Coreans, however, were treacherous and unfaithful to their agreements, and, on the 1st of June, while two steamers and four launchers, accompanied by a French vessel, were busy with the survey, a number of masked batteries, manned by several thousand Coreans, opened upon them. Great as were the numbers of the assailants, they were no match for the civilized forces, who returned such an effective fire that the Coreans were driven shrieking from their works. The Corean government was notified that

BIRTHPLACE OF U. S. GRANT.

THE JOINT HIGH COMMISSION.

ten days would be given in which to make a suitable apology. The time passed and no apology came. Thereupon, the same vessels, together with a landing party of five hundred and fifty men, stormed the Corean forts, destroyed the guns and blew up the magazines, besides killing two hundred and forty and wounding many more of the Coreans. Of course there was no more talk about not protecting shipwrecked sailors.

The presidential election of 1872 was one of great excitement, Horace Greeley being nominated by the "liberal Republicans" and Democrats, and Grant by the Republican party. Grant was re-elected, with Henry Wilson, of Massachusetts, as Vice-President. In the spring and winter of 1873, a war arose with the Modoc Indians, caused by their removal from the lands in Oregon to a new reservation. After a long resistance, a conference was held between them and a government commission, during the progress of which, the savages treacherously murdered General Canby and another member of the commission.

STORMING OF THE COREAN FORTS.

The Modocs were then besieged, and finally they surrendered, when their chief, Captain Jack and other leaders of their tribe, were tried by a court-martial and executed.

During Grant's second term the "Credit Mobilier" scandal occurred, a law suit bringing to light the fact that several members of Congress and a late Vice-President, who were owners of its profitable stock, had probably been influenced in their vote favoring the company, by gifts

from its leaders. An investigation, ordered by Congress, left no doubt that there
had been several cases of corruption. During this second term of President Grant,
large subsidies had been granted by Congress for the construction of the
Northern Pacific Railroad, and the prospect of further help being destroyed by
the "Credit Mobilier" scandal, the credit of the road fell to a low point and brought
on the failure of the great banking house which had been engaged in the enterprise;
and other failures following, another severe and widespread panic took place, causing
stagnation in business and great injury to manufacturing and commercial interests.

THE BURNING OF CHICAGO.

In 1876, the great International Exposition, intended to celebrate the first hundred
years of our independence, was opened in Philadelphia on the 10th of May, continuing
until the 10th of November following. The matter was taken up by Congress and
large sums were appropriated by that body, and also by various State and city
governments. Fairmount Park in Philadelphia, was selected as the site of the
exhibition, and immense buildings were there erected for it. The main exhibition
building, the art gallery, the machinery, horticultural and agricultural halls, etc., all
were crowded with productions from every part of the world. Thirty-three nations
were represented by the exhibition of their productions. Nearly 10,000,000 persons,
averaging some sixty-two thousand a day, were admitted as visitors, and over $3,700,000
was received for admissions.

"I DECLARE THE CENTENNIAL EXHIBITION OPEN."

In the same year there was trouble with the Sioux Indians in the Black Hills, on the borders of Montana and Wyoming, caused by gold hunters invading their reservations, thus leading the Indians to depredations and violence. Generals Terry, Crook, Custer and Reno were sent against them, and in an attack on the 25th of June General Custer and two hundred men were killed. Reinforcements being sent, the Indians were defeated in several engagements, and finally, in the beginning of 1877, their chief, Sitting Bull, and some of his followers escaped into Canada.

In the presidential election in the fall of 1876, three candidates were brought forward, Peter Cooper, of New York, by the Greenback party, Samuel J. Tilden, of New York, by the Democrats, and Rutherford B. Hayes, of Ohio, by the Republicans. It was charged that there were serious frauds in several of the States, particularly in Florida,

ATTACK BY MODOCS ON THE PEACE COMMISSIONERS.

Louisiana and South Carolina. Great excitement existed, and threats of another civil war were more than once heard, but the difficulty was finally settled by the appointment of a commission consisting of five members each from the Supreme

CUSTER'S LAST FIGHT.

Court, the Senate, and the House of Representatives. To this body the returns of the disputed States were referred and the Republican candidates were declared elected by the close vote of 185 to 184 of the electoral college; and so a perilous crisis was passed without violence or disturbance.

The ninth census of the United States was completed in 1870, showing a population of 38,587,000. In 1876, Colorado was admitted as the thirty-eighth State to the Union.

HAYES' ADMINISTRATION — 1877 TO 1881.

The nineteenth President of the United States, Rutherford B. Hayes, was inaugurated March 5, 1877, the 4th of the month being Sunday, with William A. Wheeler, of New York, as Vice-President.

Mr. Hayes was born in Delaware, Ohio, in October, 1822. He was graduated from Kenyon College in 1842, and studied law at Harvard College three years later. At the outbreak of the war he entered the army and served with distinction in several battles, reaching the rank, first of brigadier-general, and then of brevet major-general. In 1864, he was elected to Congress, and afterward was re-elected for a second term. He was also governor of Ohio for two terms in succession.

In his inaugural address, Mr. Hayes favored a conciliatory policy toward the Southern States, which he afterward carried out by appointing as Postmaster-General, David M. Key, of Tennessee, who had been a leader in the Confederate army. He also withdrew the United States troops from Louisiana and South Carolina, where they had been sent to uphold the Republican State governments. He took strong ground in favor of Civil Service reform.

Trouble with the Nez Perces Indians of Idaho, which had begun during Grant's administration, now assumed a formidable character, and General Howard was sent against them. They were finally hemmed in by our forces and completely subdued in October, 1877. The same year a difficulty with Great Britain was settled as to the Newfoundland fisheries, by the same commission which, in 1871, had decided as to the method of settling the Alabama claims. This body met in Halifax and decided that $5,500,000 should be paid by the United States for the privilege of the fisheries for twenty years. With China our negotiations had reference to commerce and to Chinese immigration to the United States, resulting in two treaties which were satisfactory to both nations.

Financial questions were prominent during this administration. In 1875, after seventeen years of suspension, Congress passed an act for the resumption of specie payments, to begin on the first of January, 1879, after which date the legal tender notes were to be redeemed in coin. In 1878, the Bland Bill was passed, restoring the silver dollar to the currency, and providing for its compulsory coinage to a given amount, each year, by the mints. The Bankrupt Act was repealed in 1878. During this administration the national debt was diminished over $200,000,000.

In 1877, there were widespread railroad strikes, caused by a reduction of wages, which was violently resisted. In West Virginia, trains were blockaded by the strikers, who held their ground against the State militia, and were only dispersed by troops from the regular army, sent to the spot by the President. A riot occurred in Baltimore, and another in Pittsburg, where the mob, thousands in number, held the city for two days. The buildings of the railroad company, with many locomotives and hundreds of cars and valuable freight were burned, and property to the amount of $3,000,000 was

RUTHERFORD B. HAYES.

destroyed before the disturbance was suppressed by troops. Riots also occurred in New York and Kentucky, and also at Reading and Chicago, and for two weeks or more the business of the country was greatly interrupted, and the losses were very great.

In 1878, the yellow fever, beginning at New Orleans, spread through the towns and cities as far as Louisville, twenty thousand people suffering, and seven thousand dying from the plague. Liberal contributions were everywhere made at the North in aid of the suffering districts. In 1878, the admirable life-saving service, stationed on the dangerous parts of our coasts to aid endangered or shipwrecked vessels or sailors, was established.

In 1880, M. de Lesseps, who had carried through the great work of the Suez Canal, visited this country in connection with his plan for cutting a canal through the Isthmus of Panama. Great interest was felt in the matter as of immense importance to the interests of commerce if it could be successfully carried through, and the President, in a message to Congress, while approving the project, declares that if it should be constructed the United States should so far have control as to protect our National interests. The census of 1880 showed the population of the United States to be 50,152,866, with its center now as far west as Cincinnati.

During the summer of 1880, four candidates for the presidency were nominated. By the Republicans, James A. Garfield, of Ohio; by the Democrats, Winfield S. Hancock, of Pennsylvania; by the Greenback party, James B. Weaver, of Iowa; and by the Prohibition party, Neal Dow, of Maine. Garfield was elected President, with Chester A. Arthur, of New York, as Vice-President.

VIEW ON THE PANAMA RAILROAD.

ADMINISTRATIONS OF GARFIELD AND ARTHUR— 1881 TO 1885.

The twentieth President of the United States, James A. Garfield, was inaugurated March 4, 1881, with Chester A. Arthur as Vice-President. Mr. Garfield was born in Ohio, November 19, 1831. His father dying when he was an infant his mother was left

in poverty with a family to be cared for, and from an early age he began doing what he could for her help, working as a carpenter and farmer, and later as a driver and pilot of a canal boat, giving what time he could to study that he might prepare himself for future life. In 1851, he went to Hiram College, where he was both student and teacher, and in 1854, entered Williams College, from which he was graduated with distinguished honor in 1856. Afterward he was a professor in Hiram College, and finally its President. Entering, after study in Cleveland, on the practice of law, he was elected in 1859, to the Ohio State Senate. At the opening of the war he entered on active service as an officer of volunteers; soon was made brigadier-general; was chief-of-staff to General Rosecrans; was engaged in several important battles, and was afterward made major-general for distinguished services. While in the army he was elected to Congress, where for sixteen years he occupied a leading position in the Republican party. In 1880, he was elected to the United States Senate, but being elected to the presidency he never took his seat in that body.

JAMES A. GARFIELD.

The inaugural address, and the wise and prudent course of the President, gave promise of a successful and popular administration, but almost from its commencement the party which elected him became divided into two factions, each urgent for office for its adherents. One party was known as the "Half Breeds," led by Mr. Blaine, and the other called the "Stalwarts," led by Roscoe Conkling, Senator from New York. The President nominated for the Collectorship of New York a man who was disliked by the "Stalwarts," and whose confirmation by the Senate Mr. Conkling strongly opposed. But being unable to control the action of the Senate he took the strange and unheard of step of resigning his place, and persuading his associate, Mr. Platt, to do the same, hoping and expecting to have influence enough to have both reappointed, and so to be endorsed by his State, and thus to be able to rebuke and triumph over the administration. Greatly to their disappointment they utterly failed in their plan, and other senators were appointed.

PUT-IN-BAY HARBOR, OHIO.

In the midst of this excitement the country was startled and filled with alarm and sorrow by the death of the President, who was shot in the railroad depot in Washington, July 2, 1881, by Charles T. Giteau, a disappointed and angry office seeker, who thus sought to avenge the supposed neglect. The assassin was at once arrested, and afterward tried, convicted and hung. The President was taken to the White House, suffering terrible agony, and after several weeks, in which life was fast wasting away, was removed to Long Branch, where tender nursing and kindest care and medical skill were all in vain, and he died on the 19th of September, his remains being taken to their last resting place in Ohio.

When Lincoln was assassinated, Mr. Garfield had said: "God reigns and the government at Washington still lives," and the words were recalled when he himself, another chief magistrate, was stricken down by assassination and the executive power

of the nation passed quietly into the hands of the one, who, by the Constitution, succeeded to the office of President. Mr. Arthur at once took the oath of office, and in his inaugural address declared his purpose to act in the spirit and carry out the policy of his lamented predecessor.

Mr. Arthur was born in Vermont in October, 1830. He was graduated from Union College in 1848, and studying law, entered on a successful practice in New York. When the war broke out he was entrusted with arming and subsisting the New York troops, and afterward was quartermaster, general, engineer-in-chief, and inspector-general. Under his supervision sixty-eight regiments of infantry, six battalions, and ten batteries were sent into the field

CHESTER A. ARTHUR.

in four months in 1861. In 1871. he was appointed collector of the port of New York, and four years afterward was reappointed, with universal approbation. He resigned after six years of service. In 1880, he was nominated as the Republican candidate for Vice-President.

His administration was not marked by any great measures of policy, whether foreign or domestic, but the country was at peace with all the world and was steadily growing in population and prosperity. Some public acts of importance were passed by Congress. One was a bill in 1882, prohibiting Chinese immigration to the United States for a period of ten years. Another, known as the "Edmunds Law," disfranchised the Polygamists of Utah, and passed other restrictions designed to cripple the Mormon power. In January, 1883. an act was passed for reform in the civil service, and a commission, with Dorman A. Eaton, of New York, at its head, was appointed to carry the law into effect. The intent of the bill was to see that those appointed to office

23

under the government should be intelligent and every way qualified for the proper discharge of the duties that might devolve upon them. On the 3d of March of the same year a new tariff bill was passed reducing considerably duties on various imported articles. And on the 4th of March, 1885, a bill was passed authorizing the President to

GENERAL VIEW OF THE BROOKLYN BRIDGE.

place on the retired list of the army one person, with full pay, as general for life. General Grant was nominated for the position, and the Senate at once confirmed the nomination.

Other events of interest occurred during Mr. Arthur's administration. In 1883, the great suspension bridge over the East river, connecting New York and Brooklyn, was opened for travel. Its central span was 1,595 feet long, its roadway 135 feet above the

ARRIVAL OF THE FRENCH TRANSPORT ISERE.

water, the entire length of the bridge, including its approaches, 5,985 feet, and its cost about $10,000,000. This is one of the most remarkable structures in the world. In the same year the Northern Pacific Railroad was completed. In 1884, the corner stone was laid on Bedloe's Island, in New York harbor, for a pedestal to support Bartholdi's

STATUE OF LIBERTY.

colossal statue of "Liberty Enlightening the World," which was presented to this country by the people of France. The statue and pedestal are together three hundred and six feet in height above low water mark. The head of the statue is so large that forty persons can sit within it at a time. A powerful electric light at its top sends its rays for miles out to sea as a guide to vessels approaching the harbor. In 1885, the

THE FARTHEST POINT NORTH REACHED BY LIEUTENANT LOCKWOOD ON THE GREELEY EXPEDITION.

Washington Monument, in the capital of the country, was dedicated with appropriate services. It is in honor of our first President, and is in the form of an obelisk 555 feet in height, which is twelve feet higher than the great pyramid in Egypt. In its walls are some two hundred marble slabs contributed by foreign countries, States of the Union, municipal corporations and private individuals.

During this administration two expeditions which had been sent to explore Northern latitudes were heard from. The Jeanette had been dispatched by the government, in co-operation with Mr. Bennett, of the *New York Herald*, and its commander De Long and many of his party lost their lives in the Arctic regions. And in 1884, the Thetis, the Bear and the Alert, which had been sent to obtain tidings of the expedition which had gone out under Lieutenant Greeley, came back with the few survivors of that ill-fated expedition, who, with their commander, were rescued from impending starvation, after having reached the latitude of 83°, 24', the highest point ever attained. In 1882, disastrous floods in the Ohio and Mississippi Valleys caused much loss of life, destroyed large amounts of property, and rendered thousands of people homeless. And in 1884, in a public riot in Cincinnati, public buildings were destroyed, and forty-five people were killed and over a hundred wounded before order was restored. The riot was caused by dissatisfaction with the result of a trial for murder, where the populace felt that justice had not been done.

In the presidential contest in the fall of 1884, four candidates were in the field. The Republicans nominated James G. Blaine, of Maine; the Democrats, Grover Cleveland, of New York; the Prohibitionists, John P. St. John, of Kansas; and the Greenback, or "People's party," Benjamin F. Butler, of Massachusetts. The campaign was exciting, and was waged greatly on personal issues, and resulted in the election of Mr. Cleveland as President, and Thomas A. Hendricks, of Indiana, as Vice-President. For the first time in twenty-four years the Republicans failed to elect their candidate.

CALDWELL, THE BIRTHPLACE OF CLEVELAND.

CLEVELAND'S ADMINISTRATION — 1885 TO 1889.

The twenty-second President of the United States, Grover Cleveland, was inaugurated March 4, 1885, with Thomas A. Hendricks, of Indiana, as Vice-President. Mr. Cleveland was born at Caldwell, New Jersey, March 18, 1837. His early years were

passed in helping to support his widowed mother, but he acquired a good education, studied law, and entered on the practice of his profession in Buffalo, New York, where he soon became prominent as a member of the bar. In 1863, he was made assistant district attorney, and in 1870, was elected sheriff of the county. In 1881, he was chosen mayor of the city, which was strongly Republican, though he was a Democrat, because he was brought forward as the reform candidate. As mayor, his administration was able and independent, and so added to his popularity that when nominated for the office of governor of the State in 1882, he was elected by

GROVER CLEVELAND.

the very great majority of 192,854 votes, large numbers of Republicans voting for him because they were dissatisfied with the methods of their own party. While still holding this important office, he was nominated by the Democratic National Convention, and was elected to the office of President.

Entering on office he refused to make the wholesale changes demanded by the crowds of office seekers, honestly believing in the principles of the Civil Service Bill. In his message to the forty-ninth Congress which assembled in December, 1885, he advocated the reduction of duties on certain importations in ordinary use, and also suggested the suspension of the compulsory coinage of silver; advised important additions to the navy; the suppression of polygamy in Utah; the faithful enforcement of the civil service rules; and also urged that the question of presidential succession be definitely settled

DECORATION DAY.

by law. This last suggestion was acted on by Congress, and a law was passed January 19, 1886, that in case of the death of both President and Vice-President, the duties of the former shall devolve on the Secretary of State, and in case of his death or disability, on the next cabinet officer, and so in order through the list of such officers. One of the most important measures of the administration was the passage of the Inter-state Commerce Bill, the object of which was to rightly regulate railroad and other transportations between the different States of the Union.

In the spring of 1886, there were great labor agitations, and a strike that began in March extended to all the southwestern railroads so that transportation and travel were

for weeks greatly embarrassed, and at some points blood was shed. There were strikes also on the street car roads of New York; and on the Pacific coast the employment of Chinese laborers excited bitter opposition and riots, and some lives were lost. In May the demand was made in various places for the limit of labor to eight hours in the day, and there was much agitation and trouble, especially in Chicago and Milwaukee; and in Chicago a bomb was

EARTHQUAKE AT CHARLESTON, S. C.

exploded among a body of police and several persons were killed by it and by the firing on both sides. It was some time before these various troubles were quieted so that business could resume its accustomed course.

In May of this year, the old question of the Canadian fisheries came up, and an American schooner was seized on the charge of having purchased bait within the forbidden limits, but the matter after a short time was settled. In July, there was a difficulty with Mexico, our government demanding the release of an American citizen who had been held by the Mexican authorities, but this matter, too, was satisfactorily settled.

In June, the President was married in Washington to Miss Frances Folsom, of Buffalo. In the summer of 1885, General Grant died at Mount McGregor, New York, after months of great suffering, and on the 8th of August his remains, followed by an escort of thousands, were laid at rest in a vault at Riverside Park, where a monument is to be erected to his memory. The South as well as the North unitedly mourned over his death, and as a mark of the cessation of all sectional animosities, as well as of the high respect and regard of the former for the distinguished leader, two of the pall bearers were Generals Johnston and Buckner, who had been generals of the Confederate armies, while Generals Sherman and Sheridan, and Admirals Porter and Rowan, with others who were distinguished in civil life, took part with them in the sad services. In October, 1885, General George B. McClellan died; in November, Mr. Thomas A. Hendricks, the Vice-President; and in 1886, General Winfield S. Hancock, who had been one of the leaders at the battle of Gettysburg; in 1887, Rev. Henry Ward Beecher, the eloquent preacher of Brooklyn; and in 1888, Morrison R. Waite, chief justice of the United States Supreme Court.

During this administration the great exposition in New Orleans took place, to celebrate the hundredth anniversary of the first export of cotton for foreign consumption. The largest of its buildings covered thirty-three acres, and forty-five States and territories, and twenty-one foreign countries contributed articles and aid to it. During this administration, in 1886, an alarming earthquake at Charleston, South Carolina, shook the whole city and vicinity, hardly a building escaping injury, and much property being lost. Four new States during this administration were admitted to the Union, North and South Dakota, Montana and Washington. And the new department of agriculture was organized by Congress, making eight instead of seven departments of the government, each represented in the cabinet by a secretary.

HARRISON'S ADMINISTRATION — 1889 TO 1893.

The twenty-ninth President of the United States was Benjamin Harrison, of Indiana. He was inaugurated March 4, 1889, with Levi P. Morton, of New York, as Vice-President.

Mr. Harrison was a grandson of William H. Harrison, the ninth President of the United States, and was born in North Bend, Ohio, August 20, 1833. He was graduated at Miami University, and studying law, entered on its practice in Indiana. When the War of Secession broke out, he raised a regiment, in which he rose to be a colonel and then general, and was with General Sherman in his famous march through the South. In 1880, he was chosen a member of the United States Senate, where he took an active part in forwarding some of the important measures of its sessions. In 1888, he was nominated for the presidency by the Republican convention, and was elected.

During the administration of Mr. Harrison, delegates from several of the Central and South American States met in Washington to consult as to the interests of commerce between those countries and the United States, and reciprocity arrangements were made of great advantage to the different countries represented, allowing the entrance of the products of each to the others without the payment of certain duties which had previously been required. In carrying out these arrangements the "Bureau of American Republics" was organized and plans were adopted, giving promise of mutual and great advantage in the way of trade to the different States associated in the arrangements.

THE FUNERAL TRAIN OF GENERAL GRANT PASSING WEST POINT.

Another matter of importance was the Behring Sea question, having reference to the true boundaries of that sea, the lines of separation between it and the ocean, how far it was an open or a closed sea, and who had the right of taking the seals in or near it.

BENJAMIN HARRISON.

For a time the conflicting claims of the United States and Great Britain seemed to threaten the friendly relations of the two countries. But until the questions at issue could be amicably settled by common agreement between the two countries the taking of seals was forbidden by both nations, lest from the great numbers taken the seals should be exterminated. But a treaty arrangement was made between the two governments in the year 1891, to refer the questions in debate to arbitration, which, when ratified by the United States Senate, will finally settle the respective rights of the two countries as to the boundaries of that sea, and how far it is to be regarded as closed, or open, like the ocean, to all.

Another important matter during this administration, was the arrangement made for the great Columbian Exhibition to celebrate the *four hundredth anniversary of the discovery of America by Columbus.* The city of Chicago, to secure the location of the Exhibition, or Worlds Fair, subscribed millions of dollars, and other millions were appropriated by Congress to carry out the plans which were adopted, and most of the countries of Europe, as well as the different States of this country, engaged with warmest interest in efforts to make the Exhibition the greatest and most successful ever undertaken. Appropriations for immense and magnificent structures were made, and in every part of the land preparations were begun for exhibiting everything in the form of production, manufacture, invention, the treasures of art, or the applications of science, that might show the progress and prosperity of our own and other lands. Aside from the cost of the great buildings, which will be nearly $8,000,000, the cost of bridges, waterworks, railways, steam plant, sewerage, statuary, electric lighting, grading and ornamenting the grounds, etc., is estimated at about $6,000,000 more, and the expense of organization and management at nearly $5,000,000. This includes no account of what may be spent by the National or State governments or by foreign nations. All the arrangements for the exhibition were placed under the direction of an able and efficient board of managers, the presidency of which was given to Hon. Thomas W. Palmer, of Michigan, late

HON. THOMAS W. PALMER, PRESIDENT WORLD'S FAIR COMMISSION.

United States minister to Spain, and ex-member of the United States Senate, under whom and his associate managers the exhibition could not well be otherwise than a great success.

  *   *   *   *

 In concluding this review of the Federal administrations it may be well to call attention to several interesting facts concerning the public careers of some of the distinguished statesmen who have faithfully served the republic.

 The longest, and probably the greatest official career this nation has ever witnessed was that of John Quincy Adams. It is interesting in this connection to recall the well known facts. His public career began in 1794, when he was sent as minister to the Netherlands. Afterward he was minister to Prussia, member of the State Senate, United States Senator, twice minister to Russia, declined a seat on the supreme bench, was a member of the commission which negotiated the treaty of Ghent, was Secretary of State,

President of the United States, and for more than sixteen years a member of the House of Representatives, where he nobly defended the right of petition, dying at last in the Capitol.

During this unique career of fifty-four years he was fifteen years in the diplomatic service, five years senator, eight years Secretary of State, four years President, and sixteen years a representative.

The second great career was that of Henry Clay. His public life began in 1803 and ended in 1852. During these forty-nine years he was a member of the Kentucky legislature, was five times elected United States senator, six times representative, and six times speaker of the House, was a member of the commission to negotiate the treaty of peace with Great Britain, was Secretary of State, and was twice the unsuccessful candidate of his party for the presidency. He twice resigned from the Senate and twice from the House, declined the mission to Russia and a place in the cabinet offered him by President Madison, as he did a place in the cabinet offered him by President Monroe. He was United States senator at twenty-nine, speaker of the House at thirty-four, and candidate for the presidency at forty-two.

The career of James G. Blaine has often been compared to that of Clay, but it has been neither so long nor so varied. Mr. Blaine's public life began in 1859, when he was elected to the Maine legislature, continuing there four years, two years as speaker. He was seven times elected to the House of Representatives, three times speaker thereof, was once appointed and once elected Senator, and has been twice Secretary of State. He has been three times a candidate for the presidential nomination of his party, with whom he has always been popular.

Many other great careers challenge our admiration. Daniel Webster was a public man for forty years. He was twice elected congressman from New Hampshire and three times from Massachusetts. He was four times elected to the Senate, serving in that body nineteen years. He was Secretary of State under Harrison in 1841, and was continued under Tyler. He was afterward Secretary of State under Fillmore. Webster and Blaine are the only men who served twice as Secretary of State under administrations which were not successive. He was the chief instrument of negotiating some important treaties, and no man has more clearly expounded, or more nobly defended the great principles of the United States Constitution.

Mention of Clay and Webster at once brings Calhoun to mind. He was in public life forty-two years. He began in the legislature of his State, as nearly all our great publicists begin. He then served five years in the House of Representative, was Secretary of War nearly eight years, sat in the Senate fifteen years, and was Secretary of State under Tyler one year.

Thomas H. Benton's remarkable career of thirty years in the Senate still stands as the longest record of continuous service in that body. Benton was defeated for re-election, but came to the next Congress as a member of the House, and was defeated for re-election to his seat there, and was also beaten for governor of Missouri—which was the ending of his public career.

The longest congressional career in our history was that of General Samuel Smith, of Baltimore. He was a representative from 1793 to 1803, and again from 1816 to 1822, and a Senator from 1803 to 1815, and from 1822 to 1833—forty years of continuous service in Congress. Besides this remarkable career as a legislator he was once mayor of

KENTUCKY SCENE—SOUTH BANK OF THE OHIO.

Baltimore, and in the Revolutionary War rose from the rank of captain to that of brigadier-general.

Next in point of long service was Nathaniel Macon, who was twenty-four years in the House, where he served four years as speaker, and was thirteen years in the Senate, where he was for some time the presiding officer.

A noteworthy career was that of Alexander Hamilton. Brilliant in the martial field while barely out of his teens, at twenty-five in the Continental Congress, at thirty a power in the convention which formed the Constitution, Secretary of the Treasury and the father of a financial system at thirty-two; falling in a duel at forty-seven.

Robert C. Winthrop at forty-two had been five years in the Massachusetts Legislature, ten years in the National House, where he was elected speaker, and was one year in the Senate. Then his promising public career came to an end, though he is (1891) still living.

John S. Crittenden fought in the battle of the Thames, in 1812, and from that date to his death, in 1863, was almost constantly in public life. After serving a number of years in the State Legislature, he represented Kentucky in the Senate from 1817 to 1819, again from 1835 to 1848, and finally from 1855 to 1861. Meanwhile he was once governor of Kentucky and twice attorney-general of the United States. Between his first appearance in the Senate and his final exit therefrom, forty-four years passed, and then he rounded out his career by serving two years in the House.

James Buchanan's long public career has been forgotten by many people. In the forty years between 1821 and 1861, he was ten years in the House, eleven years in the Senate, minister to Russia, minister to France, Secretary of State and President.

At twenty-five Lewis Cass was a member of the Ohio Legislature. He distinguished himself in the war of 1812, was eighteen years governor of Michigan, five years Secretary of War, four years minister to France, twelve years a Senator and three years Secretary of State.

No sketch of great careers would be complete without mention of the fifty years of public service rendered by Thomas Jefferson — member of the Legislature, delegate in Congress, author of the Declaration of Independence, governor of Virginia, minister to France, and also serving in other diplomatic posts, Secretary of State, Vice-President, and President. Some of the most important of our public measures were suggested by him, and the Louisiana purchase, which added to our country a territory larger than all the thirteen original States, was a measure of his administration.

Turning to the Judicial branch of our government, it is interesting to note the length of the public careers of some of the justices of our supreme court. John Marshall's career on the supreme bench has never been equalled, either in length of service or in the distinguished character of the jurist. He was chief justice from 1801 to 1835, sitting thirty-four years and five months. He is the only man who ever held the offices of chief justice of the supreme court and Secretary of State at the same time. In January, 1801, he was Secretary of State under President John Adams. On the 20th of that month he was nominated to the Senate for chief justice, confirmed on the 27th, commissioned on the 31st, and presided on the bench from the 4th to the 9th of February. He continued to act as Secretary of State until March 3, when the Adams administration came to an end.

Justice Story sat thirty-four years. Justices McLean and Wayne thirty-two years each, Bushrod Washington thirty-one years, Justice Johnson thirty years, Chief Justice

Taney and Justices Miller and Catron each twenty-eight years, and Justices Nelson and Woodbury each twenty-seven years. Justice Field has been longer on the bench than any who are now members of the supreme court.

It is a noteworthy fact that no judge of the supreme court and no cabinet officer, other than Secretary of State, ever became President. General Grant was for a time acting Secretary of War, though not commissioned as such, and James Monroe was acting Secretary of War under Madison. Six Secretaries of State have been Presidents, viz.: Jefferson, Madison, Monroe, John Quincy Adams, Van Buren, and Buchanan.

A HARVEST SCENE IN MICHIGAN.

24

CHAPTER VI

OUR COUNTRY'S GROWTH AND IMPROVEMENT.

I.— TERRITORY.

THE earliest claim to territory in the various parts of what is now the United States, was on the ground of discovery, small settlements being made in Virginia and at several places in New England, and later in New York, and at other points of what afterward became the thirteen original States. Before 1781, only six of the thirteen States, viz.: New Hampshire, Rhode Island, New Jersey, Pennsylvania, Maryland and Delaware, had exactly defined boundaries. Of the remaining seven States some claimed to extend westward to the Pacific ocean and others to the Mississippi river, though the knowledge of the regions thus claimed was in most cases quite indefinite. But little more than fifty years ago, Daniel Webster, speaking of the region then known as Oregon, said that it was so far off that it could never be governed by the United States, and that a delegate to Congress, even if one was appointed, could not reach Washington until a year after the expiration of the term for which he was elected. And a common impression as to a large part of the great Western region beyond the Mississippi was, that it was a waste, unproductive region, large portions of which were but alkali deserts.

The States within exact boundaries ceded to the United States their claims to most if not all of their lands west of their present limits, as follows: New York, in 1781; Virginia (except 6,570 square miles of her military bounty lands), in 1784; Massachusetts, in 1785; Connecticut, in 1786; South Carolina, in 1787; North Carolina, in 1790; and Georgia, in 1802. These colonies surrendered to the general government all the territory which was ceded by Great Britain after the revolution, which was not included in the thirteen original States, as in the main they are now bounded.

In 1783, the whole area of the United States was only 820,680 square miles. Both England and France had been intending, if possible, to confine the limits of the United States to the Atlantic on the East, and the Alleghany Mountains on the West, but as an able English reviewer says, speaking of the treaty of 1783: "Three of the ablest men of the United States, Franklin, John Adams, and John Jay, succeeded by their astuteness and persistency in extending its limits to the east bank of the Mississippi, despite the insidious efforts of Vergennes, on the part of France, to hem in the new nation between the Atlantic and the Appalachian range." Similar concessions, he says, they also gained from Oswald, the English commissioner, and also valuable fishing rights on English waters, and so arranged the boundaries between Canada and the United States, "as in later times to make Canada weep tears of humiliation." By the purchase of Louisiana from France in 1803, the United States acquired 930,928 square miles, which was more in extent than all the then existing States. By the acquisition of Florida from Spain in 1819, it added 59,270 square miles; by the annexation of Texas in 1845, 247,000; by the Oregon treaty with Great Britain in 1846, 280,425; by treaties

A WESTERN PRAIRIE.

with, and purchase from Mexico, after the war with that nation, 677,260, and by the purchase of Alaska from Russia in 1867, 577,390 square miles, making in all 3,603,844 square miles, or 2,306,460,160 acres. This vast territory, which is more than sixty times as large as England, is divided, as we have seen, into forty-four States and seven Territories, including the District of Columbia, and Alaska which is not yet fully organized.

Though the United States occupies the central part of the continent, more than two-thirds of its frontiers are the shores of large lakes and oceans, with numerous bays, sounds and navigable rivers. Its rivers, some of which are the largest in the world, are those entering into the Atlantic or into its bays and sounds; those entering into the Gulf of Mexico, and those entering into the Pacific; besides which there are many smaller rivers entering into the great lakes and finding their way to the ocean through the St. Lawrence, and also the rivers which empty into the salt lakes of the great interior basin of Utah.

The chief mountains are the great eastern chain of the Alleghanies and the Rocky Mountains. The soil and climate have every variety, and the productions, which of

IMPROVING LEADVILLE, 1877.

course vary with the different regions, are those that may be found in the different zones. In the accounts given of the various States may be found more particular notice of the population, of the occupations and resources of the people, and of the sources of prosperity to the different parts of the country.

II.—POPULATION.

No country has been peopled by such a variety of races as the United States. The New England colonies were originally settled chiefly by English Puritans, with some Scotch and Welch; New York by the Dutch; Pennsylvania by Quakers and Germans; Maryland by English Roman Catholics; Delaware and New Jersey by Dutch and Swedes; Virginia by English cavaliers and large numbers of adventurers and indented servants; the Carolinas and Georgia by English and the French Huguenots; Louisiana by the French; Florida, Texas and California by the Spaniards; and Utah by Mormons chiefly from England, Wales and the northern parts of Europe. And from an early date immigration has been going on from England, Scotland, Ireland, Germany, France, Sweden, Switzerland, China, and more or less from every part of the world.

No official record was made of the influx of foreigners to this country before 1820, but from the close of the Revolutionary War to that date it is estimated that some 225,000 immigrants had come to our shores. From 1821 to 1890 the number of immigrants was 15,641,688. The arrivals from 1821 to 1830 were 143,439; from 1831 to 1840, 599,125; from 1841 to 1850, 1,713,251; from 1851 to 1860, 2,598,214; from 1861 to 1870, 2,466,752; from 1871 to 1880, 2,944,295; from 1881 to 1890, 5,176,212.

Of these numbers 4,551,719 were from Germany; 3,501,683 from Ireland; 2,460,034 from England; 1,029,083 from the British North American possessions; 943,330 from Norway and Sweden; 464,425 from Austria-Hungary; 414,513 from Italy; 370,162 from France; 356,353 from Russia and Poland; 329,192 from Scotland; 292,578 from China; 174,333 from Switzerland; 146,237 from Denmark; and from all the other countries, 606,606. Of those coming in in the last ten years, 26,257 males were of the professional classes; 514,552 were skilled laborers; 1,833,325 were of miscellaneous occupations; 73,327 made no statement as to their occupations; and 759,450 were without occupation. Of 2,040,702 females, 1,724,454 were without special occupation, though large numbers of them engaged in domestic service.

Of such various and different nationalities and their descendants, the population of the United States is made up. If their children come into our schools, learn our language, enter into our spirit, and fall into our views of liberty and into our ways of thinking, believing and acting; in a word, if they drop or outgrow the race spirit and feeling and become truly Americans, they may be a blessing alike to themselves and to the country. "One country for all, one Constitution for all, one standard of loyalty for all, one class of free, public, state, non-sectarian schools for all, one sacred ballot box for all, one type of citizenship for all, one Declaration of Independence for all, one national language for all, one flag with its stars-and-stripes for all, one sovereign for all, and that, the sovereign will of the people," educated and taught the great principles of truth and duty — in all this is the safety, the welfare, the glory of *Our Country*.

LEADVILLE IN 1897.

III.— GOVERNMENT.

In the early history of the country, the colonies, from the time of their settlements down to the Declaration of Independence in 1776, were under the dominion of Great Britain, but were governed in different ways, and most of them from time to time had changes in their mode of government. The kinds of government were :—

I. By a *Commercial Corporation*, such as the "London Company," which at first organized and ruled Virginia under a charter from the king, though afterward this company was dissolved, and Virginia became first a royal, and then a proprietary, and then again a royal province, though in 1619 it was allowed to have a colonial legislature.

II. *Proprietary* government, the control being by the authority of some proprietor or proprietors to whom the king had granted the province. Such was Pennsylvania under William Penn, and Maryland under Lord Baltimore, and at first New Hampshire and also New York, both afterward made royal provinces.

III. *Royal* government, by the king through some royal governor of his appointment. Under such government most of the colonies were at some time in the course of their history.

IV. *Charter* government, that is, under a charter or written instrument, given by the king, and granting certain political rights and privileges to the colonists.

V. *Voluntary* or *Popular* government, founded by the people themselves without the authority of king, proprietor or company, as was the case at first with the Plymouth, Rhode Island, Connecticut, and New Haven Colonies, though Plymouth, Rhode Island, and Connecticut afterward had charters, and in 1686 Plymouth was made a royal province, and then in 1692 had a new charter. Some of the colonies were allowed to have their own legislatures, and in most if not all the small towns and settlements, local matters were managed by the colonists through the leading magistrates and by deputies from the people.

Before the Revolution, the Colonial Assemblies had gained prominence, and were taking an active part in public affairs; and corresponding and consulting with each other as they did, the various colonies were becoming more assimilated as one people, planning and acting in concert in view of the oppressions of the mother country.

The first Colonial Congress met in New York, October 7, 1765, and in it nine colonies were represented by twenty-eight delegates. The first Continental Congress met in Philadelphia, September 5, 1774, and in it all the colonies were represented except Georgia, a delegation from which was prevented by the governor. In November, 1777, Congress adopted the "Articles of Confederation" which were to be the basis of a Constitution or general government for the United States when approved by all the States; and all the States did approve, but not the last of them till 1781.

The government under this plan was a *Confederation* or league of the States, but its powers were so limited and inefficient that in 1787 a convention was called to form a Constitution. After four months' deliberation the Constitution was formed, and was signed on the 17th of September, 1787; and by the middle of 1788 it was ratified and adopted by eleven of the thirteen States, and by 1790 also by the remaining two. It went into operation March 4, 1789. It is the Constitution as now existing except as it has been modified by several important amendments.

By this Constitution the government was divided into three departments, the Legislative, to make the laws; the Executive, to enforce them; and the Judicial, to interpret them. The Legislative, or law-making power, was to be in Congress; the Executive, or law-enforcing power, in the President; and the Judicial, or law-interpreting power, in certain courts, the judges of which were to be appointed by the President with the approval of the Senate.

THE LEGISLATURE.

The Legislative, or law-making department, or Congress, was to consist of the House of Representatives, chosen by the people of the States in proportion to their population, and the Senate, in which each State was to be equally represented, the representatives to hold office for two, and the senators for six years. Some were in favor of only one legislative body, while others preferred two that each might be a check on the other, and the decision in favor of the present mode of two houses is to be traced back, it is said, to a trifling personal dispute in the early history of Massachusetts. In that colony, in the days of Governor Winthrop, the custom had been for the magistrates and the delegates from the people to meet as one body for legislation and for the decision of all public questions. A poor widow had lost a pig which she claimed had been taken and killed by a prominent, and for the times, a rich man, and as she repeatedly brought the case before the public authorities, and before a jury, the decisions in each case were against her. Not a little feeling on the matter was excited in the little community, and the cry was raised that it was "the rich against the poor," and that the delegates from the people, meeting as one body with the magistrates, were influenced and overborne by the latter. Winthrop, whose remarkable and practical wisdom had more than once carried the infant colony safely through previous troubles, seeing the rising feeling, and the gravity of the possible issue, suggested the division of the council into two bodies, the magistrates and deputies of the people each to meet by themselves, each to have a chamber of its own, and to have a negative on the action of the other; and this, it is said, was the origin of the two bodies for legislation, which soon became the rule in all the colonies. "It was the first experiment of dual legislation on this continent."

More than a century later, in the great debates as to the Constitution, John Adams, taking the lesson from the early experience of Massachusetts, advocated two Houses of Congress, and in this he was seconded by Washington, while Franklin, Jefferson and others were in favor of but one House, as in France. And the anecdote is told that Washington and Jefferson taking tea together, and familiarly debating the question, Jefferson finding his tea too hot for the month, poured it out into the saucer. "There," said Washington, "is my argument — when the debates in one House become too hot and exciting, pour them out into the other and they will have time to cool, and so the wisest counsels will prevail." And Jefferson, it is said, smilingly admitted the force of the suggestion, and assented to the views of Adams, in accordance with which, the dual principal of legislation became the organic law of the United States. Strange it may seem that the quarrel about a stray pig should so excite for months the reverend divines and grave and earnest magistrates and deputies of a colony as to endanger its unity and peace. But through the guidance of Providence that trifling and ludicrous incident was made to lay a firm foundation for the wise and safe government and the

sure liberties of a nation. The loss of a screw driver decided the battle of New Orleans in 1814, and the change of the wind, from one direction to another, wrecked the mighty Armada of Spain, and sent seventy thousand tons of her hostile fleet to the bottom of the sea, and so saved England from the Spanish Inquisition!

THE EXECUTIVE.

As the Legislature was to make the laws which became valid and binding when approved by the President, the Executive department was to see that they were carried out and enforced. This Executive power was to be vested in the President who was to be chosen by electors appointed by the people. He was also to be commander-in-chief of the military and naval forces of the Nation, and by, and with, the advice and consent of the Senate to appoint embassadors and other public officers, and also consuls, and judges of the supreme and other United States courts. At first, the President had four secretaries, each having charge of a department of executive work, but this number has since been increased to eight; so that now there is a Secretary of State, of the Treasury, of War, of the Navy, of the Interior, of Agriculture, and the Attorney-General, and the Postmaster-General.

THE JUDICIARY.

The Judicial power of the government was to be vested in a supreme court and such other inferior courts as Congress might from time to time establish, the different courts to have jurisdiction in certain classes of cases which were specified by law. The judges of these courts were to be appointed by the President with the approval of the Senate. It hardly need be added that the duties of these three departments of the National government are confined to matters that pertain to the Nation as a whole, and that each of the States has its own Legislature and its Executive and Judiciary departments which take cognizance of matters that pertain especially to the State and its interests.

IV.— EDUCATION.

In every civilized or even partially civilized country, the idea seems to have been prevalent that education ought to be co-extensive with sovereignty. Despotism and aristocracy would have education, but would have it restricted to those who are to administer the government. Even Plato thought that "control should be intelligent," and Charlemagne required "that the children of all persons participating in the government should be educated, in order that intelligence might rule the empire," though the thought of educating the great masses of the common people probably never entered his mind.

But from the time of the reformation, if not earlier, the importance of general education began to be felt and acknowledged. Luther protested that every child was worthy of the best education, saying that " if there were no soul, no heaven, no future after this life, and if temporal affairs were to be administered solely with a view to the present, it would be a sufficient reason for establishing, in every place, the best schools both for boys and girls; that the world, merely to maintain its outward prosperity, has

GULF COAST NEAR GALVESTON.

need of shrewd and accomplished men and
women." And Calvin, so far as he could,
made education obligatory on all, so that
Bancroft, tracing the influence of the example
seen in the customs of Switzerland, says,
"The common school system was derived
from Geneva — the work of Calvin was introduced by Luther into Germany, and by
John Knox into Scotland, and so became the
property of the English speaking nation."
John of Nassau, Mr. Motley says, so early as
the sixteenth century "urged the States
General to establish schools where children of
quality as well as of poor families could, for
a very small sum, be well and christianly
educated and brought up;" which, he said,

would be the "greatest and most useful work they could ever accomplish for God, Christianity and the Netherlands." And Charles X, and Gustavus Adolphus "made education so common in Sweden that in 1637 not a single peasant child was unable to read and write." Holland in the previous century had not only Latin or "great schools," but lower or "small schools" for elementary training, and Motley tells us that in 1635 the Latin school at Dordrecht had been in existence for some centuries, and was one of the most famous institutions of Northwestern Europe. And he thinks the New England colonists gained their educational impulse more from the Netherlands than from England.

Whether the origin of the idea can, or cannot be traced, it is plain that all the early colonists of the United States saw and felt the importance of education, though they differed not a little in their views of its nature and extent. For the Dutch settlements in New York it was ordered in 1630 that a clergyman and a schoolmaster should be maintained, and that each householder and inhabitant should be taxed for their support. And for Boston it has been claimed, as it has been for Dorchester, Hartford, and Brooklyn, that it had the earliest existing school in the United States.

But before any of these places had schools, provision had been made for education in the older colony of Virginia, a grant of fifteen thousand acres of land having been made by Parliament in 1619, for a college and preparatory schools, for which several subscriptions of money were also made in the next two years. The terrible Indian war of 1622 prevented these plans from being carried out, but the matter was not forgotten, for in 1645 we find Richard Norwood writing "that he had been teaching school in Bermuda (Somers) islands for thirty years." In 1635 the people of Boston in town meeting voted land for school masters, and there were schools at New Haven in 1638, at Newport in 1640, and at Hartford in 1641. In all these and in other cases in the colonies, schools were endowed with lands, bequests, rents, and donations, and these were supplemented by general taxation. None of these schools, however, were free; tuition in whole or in part was paid for in all.

New England early adopted and, with a single exception, has always maintained that the public should provide for the education of all the people. What elsewhere was left to local provision, as in New York, or to charity, as in Pennsylvania, or chiefly to parental interest, as in Virginia and some of the Southern colonies, was in most of the New England colonies early secured by law. "For the purpose of public instruction," said Daniel Webster, "we have held and do hold every man subject to taxation in proportion to his property, and we look not to the question whether he, himself, have or have not children to be benefited by the education for which he pays." The Massachusetts Act of 1642 was excellent as a beginning, but in 1647 a great advance was made, every township of fifty householders being obliged to have a school for all; and every one of a hundred families to have also a grammar school in which youth could be fitted for college. Three years afterward Connecticut passed a similar law, and other New England colonies followed the good example thus set.

There was no school system in any colony south of Connecticut before the Revolution, though in all there were isolated and transient schools which did much both to express and form public sentiment. Elementary instruction was largely left to the family, and in Virginia and South Carolina the sons of those who could afford it, were sent abroad to be educated or were put under special tutors at home. But as to free schools, when Governor Berkeley of Virginia was asked by the English Commissioners what was being done in that colony for instructing the people, he replied "the same that is taken in out-of-towns in England, every man, according to his ability, instructing his children." And he also added what has become historic, "I thank God there are no free schools or printing presses in Virginia, and I hope we shall not have them these hundred years, for learning has brought disobedience and heresy and sects into the world, and printing has divulged them and libels against the best of governments. God keep us from both." And his hope was fulfilled, for he spoke in 1671, and no system of public schools was attempted in Virginia till, in the time, and mainly by the influence of Jefferson. It was not schools, but free schools for all that Berkeley disliked. More than once he was a liberal subscriber for private academies, and though his views of common schools were for a long time more or less shared not only in the Southern colonies but also in parts of New England, yet both South Carolina and Maryland had academies of high rank; and the higher class of schools or academies, and so also colleges were early established in the New England colonies.

Alongside of the first colleges of the colonies, and often connected with them, were grammar schools or academies of a high order. Before 1800, New York had nineteen of these seminaries, and Massachusetts about the same number, and some of them were to be found in almost every State both North and South. Though they were called "free," they were not so in the modern sense of the term, for fees larger or smaller were required for admission to their privileges, but they were free in contrast to similar schools in England where admission was granted only to certain members of some church or organization. Beside the eight earliest colonial colleges, sixteen others were founded before 1800; four during the Revolutionary War, and twelve soon after its close, so that the country then had as many if not more colleges in proportion to its population than it has to-day.

After the Revolution and especially after the war of 1812, the country was making rapid and substantial progress not only in population and national prosperity, but in intelligence and educational interests. Plans for various kinds of schools were discussed, and permanent school funds which had been begun by Connecticut in 1733, and by New York in 1786, were commenced in New Jersey in 1820, in New Hampshire in 1821, and in Maine about the same time. Rhode Island, Vermont, and Pennsylvania made large annual appropriations for schools. The "Literary fund" of Virginia in 1813 was about two million dollars. And other Southern States made large appropriations of lands for the benefit of common schools.

Lotteries were chartered for the benefit of schools and academies in most of the States. Congressional land grants were made for educational purposes, amounting in 1876 to some eighty million acres or one hundred and twenty-five thousand square miles, a territory greater than all of Great Britain and Ireland. Of some thirty million dollars distributed from the United States Treasury in 1836 to the different States, sixteen of the States set apart their quota, in whole or in part, for the benefit of common schools. Ten of the States in 1886 had $63,000,000 of invested school funds, giving an annual revenue of nearly three million dollars for school purposes, while the actual expenditure of these States, for the year, for the same purpose, was fifty-nine million, seven hundred and fifty-two thousand dollars.

The "District" system took its rise in the colonial period when generally the district was co-extensive with the settlement or with the parish. State supervision had a gradual growth. Massachusetts created a State Board of Education in 1837; and twenty-three of the States now have such boards, while several other States have arrangements looking to the oversight of schools. County and city supervision is also very general, and the careful education of teachers, that they may be properly qualified for their work, is everywhere provided for by Normal schools, and by lectures, institutes, associations, journals, etc. According to some of the latest accessible statistics, from which most of the following figures are quoted, there are eighty-seven Normal schools in forty of the States, having over nineteen thousand pupils, while in eighty-one private and city schools, which have the same object in view, there are over thirteen thousand pupils preparing themselves for the work of teaching. Several of the larger colleges have professorships for the instruction and training of those who expect to be teachers; and a large number of ably conducted periodicals, having the same object in view, have a wide circulation.

Of the three hundred and sixty-five colleges reported in 1887-8 thirty-three are State institutions, and ten, which were founded by wealthy individuals, have a productive endowment, exclusive of buildings and other properties, of twenty-five million dollars. The amount donated to colleges from 1872 to 1888 inclusive, was nearly fifty-three million dollars, of which about three million was for colleges for women. Two hundred and sixty-eight of the colleges are denominational, and four-fifths of those founded since 1850 are more or less under the control of church organizations. Of the total attendance of nearly seventy thousand students in these colleges, over eleven thousand are in the State institutions, so that about eight per cent. of the colleges instruct nearly twenty per cent. of the students. Ten Ecclesiastical institutions have a property of about seventeen millions; eleven State institutions have about eighteen millions; and ten privately endowed institutions have about twenty-two millions. There is also a large number of colleges for women in different parts of the country, some of them richly endowed and thoroughly furnished for all that is needed for the education of the sex, and many of the leading colleges have annexed courses of study providing for the same important end.

There are a hundred and fifty-two theological seminaries, representing twenty-seven different denominations, in twenty-eight States and Territories, having 5,775 students;

forty-nine law schools, with 2,744 students; a hundred and fifty-two medical schools, including dentistry and pharmacy, with 13,921 students; a hundred and five schools of science, with 17,086 students; two hundred and thirty-three commercial colleges, with 43,706 students; sixteen hundred and seventeen secondary schools, with 160,137 students; five hundred and forty-four kindergartens, with 25,952 pupils; 216,000 public or common schools, with an enrollment of 12,592,721 children, and an average daily attendance of 7,852,607 pupils, taught by 378,000 instructors; and also great numbers of private schools and academies in all the different States. The annual expenditures for the common schools is the enormous sum of $171,000,000, and $11,000,000 more are expended annually for the colleges and universities of the land, which are more than four hundred in number.

Besides these, there are normal schools and schools of various grades as well as colleges and seminaries for colored people; schools for the deaf and dumb, the blind, the feeble-minded; and training schools of art, technology, stenography, telegraphy, wood and metallic engraving, for smithing, jewelry, carpentry, printing press manufacture, carriage building, and for training of nurses, and in cooking, sewing, and household duties; in fact, for instructing in almost every kind of work or employment known or in use in civilized society.

In addition to all these, under land grants of more than nine million acres from the national government, aided in several States by State governments, forty-eight educational institutions have been established in the different States, having over six thousand students. The United States Military Academy at West Point, established in 1802, and since having greatly extended its course of study, gives gratuitous and thorough instruction to nearly fourteen hundred students in civil and military engineering and in all that pertains to the science or art of war. There are also under State, or local, or private control, some fifteen or more schools for military training, and in many of the colleges or academies military instruction is given by officers detailed for the purpose, from the national army.

It was nearly fifty-six years after our independence before any formal instruction was given by the United States to those who were to be active in her navy. Chaplains on ships of war were required to act as school masters, and instruction was given at the different navy yards. But in 1845, under George Bancroft who was then Secretary of the Navy, the United States Naval Academy was opened at Annapolis, where thorough instruction is given to several hundred young men in all that prepares for the navy. There is also a national school on a government vessel at Brooklyn, seventy per cent. of whose five hundred graduates have become seamen, and another on the California training-ship, the Jamestown. The Naval War School at Newport, Rhode Island, is a school of graduate instruction for officers of the navy, and its specialized and very comprehensive course of instruction is not only of military and naval science, but such as to give intelligent and broad views in all that may make cultured officers and men.

All through the country there are also houses of correction, orphans' homes, houses of detention, and industrial schools, which give certain kinds of education and training. Of reform schools proper there are sixty-six in twenty-five of the States, having some fifteen thousand inmates, and supported at an annual cost to the public of some two million dollars. Besides these, there are some four or five hundred houses and asylums for orphans and for dependent and vagrant children, in which, since 1790, it is estimated that half a million have been cared for and educated. In the various Indian schools sustained by the government, there is a school enrollment of sixteen thousand, with an actual daily attendance of about forty per cent. And of the school population of Alaska, numbering some six thousand, over twelve hundred are enrolled in thirteen schools.

In addition to all these means of general instruction, there are great numbers of evening schools, museums of art and science, literary clubs, reading circles, scientific, philosophical and historical societies; libraries, public and mercantile, endowed school district, free-town, professional, college, state and national, almost without number. The numberless newspapers and periodicals which are everywhere read, discussing all public measures and bringing news from every part of the earth, are another most important means of popular education, making the people of the United States more generally intelligent than those of any other nation on the Globe. While the

population of the United States, in the last ten years, has increased twenty-four per cent, the school gain has been twenty-six per cent, thus showing that the interests of popular education are gaining more rapidly than even the population of the country. If it is true, as Buckle has said, that America is a country in which there are comparatively few men of great learning, it is true, as he adds, "that in no other country are there so few men of great ignorance." By increasing and continually improving systems of education, "under the divine blessing, may our country," in the language of Webster, "become a vast and splendid monument, not of oppression and terror, but of intelligence, of wisdom, of peace, and of liberty, upon which the whole world may gaze with admiration forever!"

The statements and statistics thus far given were taken from the latest official reports then before the public. The census of 1890, however, has given still later returns as to the public, private, and parochial schools of the country, which are embodied in the following table :—

Statistics of Public, Private and Parochial Schools in 1890.

STATES.	TEACHERS.	WHITE PUPILS.	COLORED PUPILS.	PRIVATE PUPILS.	PAROCHIAL PUPILS.
Alabama	6,291	186,794	116,155	22,953	1,150
Alaska	18	903	741		
Arizona	233	7,828		462	418
Arkansas	5,016	163,603	59,468	11,070	1,118
California	5,434	221,756		17,720	7,123
Colorado	2,376	65,499		4,631	2,421
Connecticut	3,226	125,073	1,432	8,355	13,459
Delaware	701	26,778	4,656	1,126	1,712
District of Columbia	745	23,574	13,332	5,509	2,402
Florida	2,577	54,811	36,377	5,059	756
Georgia	7,503	209,330	133,232	48,187	287
Idaho	389	14,311		1,104	
Illinois	23,296	773,265	5,054	28,164	75,958
Indiana	13,285	507,264		17,968	25,537
Iowa	26,567	492,620	647	15,633	20,395
Kansas	12,260	389,703	9,616	11,382	9,018
Kentucky	8,722	352,955	54,612	26,969	12,328
Louisiana	2,673	74,988	49,282	17,627	7,148
Maine	6,080	130,592	87	7,330	4,015
Maryland	3,826	148,224	36,027	11,153	8,943
Massachusetts	10,324	370,893	599	28,629	38,143
Michigan	15,970	425,601	1,341	10,216	34,779
Minnesota	8,947	281,678	181	7,575	29,332
Mississippi	7,386	157,188	193,431	20,072	1,311
Missouri	13,795	587,510	32,804	27,937	31,400
Montana	549	16,718	89	1,038	384
Nebraska	10,555	239,556	744	5,278	9,426
Nevada	251	7,387		78	325
New Hampshire	3,104	59,813		2,603	4,940
New Jersey	4,465	221,634	12,438	15,250	27,827
New Mexico	472	18,215		4,093	571
New York	31,703	1,035,542	6,618	56,787	103,093
North Carolina	6,865	208,844	117,017	25,651	1,320
North Dakota	1,894	30,821		578	1,608
Ohio	25,156	797,439		35,864	57,905
Oklahoma	14	537			
Oregon	2,566	63,354		4,143	616
Pennsylvania	24,493	965,444		47,761	60,923
Rhode Island	1,378	54,170		3,814	5,940
South Carolina	4,321	90,051	113,410	13,623	634
South Dakota	4,356	66,150		2,042	1,537
Tennessee	8,376	354,130	101,602	41,827	2,391
Texas	11,097	312,802	98,107	22,310	4,573
Utah	680	36,372		10,258	536
Vermont	4,400	65,500	108	4,284	2,461
Virginia	7,523	220,210	122,059	12,831	2,005
Washington	1,610	55,432		3,328	954
West Virginia	5,491	186,735	6,558	3,498	1,109
Wisconsin	12,037	350,342		5,176	52,200
Wyoming	209	7,052		140	190
Total	361,273	11,236,072	1,327,822	686,106	673,601

Not counting colleges for women, the percentage of students in the colleges of the United States as compared with the population was one to 1,655 in 1880, and in 1890, one to 1,355, an increase of over 22 per cent. And if the average age of students is from 16 to 24, then of the college age of the total population, there was in 1880 one to 302, and in 1890, one to 252, an increase in ten years of over 19 per cent. The increase of college attendance has fully kept up with the increase of population.

V.— RELIGION.

By the early colonists of what is now the United States, the true principle of toleration was imperfectly understood, and from many of the colonies persons were driven out because they differed from the prevailing or established form of church government and opinion. Ecclesiastical and civil policies were in most of the colonies so connected that non-conformity to the prevailing views led to the persecution and the

banishment of dissenters. But as time went on, more just and liberal views gradually prevailed, until now, throughout the entire land, religion is free from any interference by either the Federal or State government, provided its doctrines or practices do not, as in case of the Mormons, teach immorality that violates the laws of the land. All denominations have entire freedom in their opinions and forms of worship, each church directing its own affairs according to its views of truth and duty as believed to be made known by the word of God.

In the historical sketches of the individual States no statistics were given as to the religious denominations, because the denominations are so numerous in most of the States

that to give accounts of them would lead to great repetition, and also because
the relative numbers of the various denominations are better made known by speaking
of them as existing not in individual States, but in the country as a whole.
The following tables, gathered mostly from the official reports of the different
denominations, show the number of the churches, ministers and communicants in each
of the various denominations in the United States as they were in 1889 and 1890, so
that the gain of each for the year may also be seen. In the Roman Catholic church the
numbers given in the tables of communicants for the year 1880, are the numbers of the
persons connected with that denomination, but in 1890, the number given is the number
of communicants. In all the other denominations the figures give the numbers of
the *communicants* in their churches.

	1800	1880
Local churches	3,030	97,090
Ministers	2,651	69,870
Communicants	364,872	10,065,963

	1889			1890		
	CHURCHES	MINISTERS	COMMUNI-CANTS.	CHURCHES	MINISTERS	COMMUNI-CANTS.
Adventists	1,575	840	100,712	1,773	765	58,742
Baptists	46,624	32,017	4,073,589	48,371	32,343	4,292,291
Christian Union	1,500	500	120,000	1,500	500	120,000
Congregationalists	4,509	4,408	475,608	4,689	4,640	491,985
Friends	763	1,017	106,930	763	1,017	106,930
German Evangelist Church	675	560	125,000	850	665	160,000
Lutherans	6,971	4,151	988,008	7,911	4,612	1,086,048
Mennonites	420	605	100,000	563	665	102,671
Methodists	50,680	29,770	4,723,851	54,711	31,765	4,980,240
Moravians	98	111	11,219	101	114	11,358
New Jerusalem	100	113	6,000	100	113	6,000
Presbyterians	13,349	9,786	1,180,113	13,619	9,974	1,229,012
Episcopalians	5,150	4,012	459,642	5,227	4,100	480,176
Reformed	2,058	1,378	277,542	2,081	1,370	282,856
Roman Catholics	7,424	7,996	7,855,294	8,765	8,332	6,250,045
Salvation Army				360	1,024	8,771
Unitarians	381	491	20,000	407	510	20,000
Universalists	721	691	38,780	732	685	42,952
Grand Total	142,767	98,436	20,667,318	151,261	103,303	21,757,171

These tables show that in 1890 there were in the United States 151,261 churches,
103,303 ministers, and 18,180,923 communicants of the churches, or if we count all who
are Roman Catholics as communicants, then there were 21,757,171 members of all the
various churches.

In addition to the statistics of the numbers connected with the various churches in
the United States, many other facts might be stated showing the progress of religion.
Over $75,000,000 are annually contributed to the support of the various churches, and
$31,000,000 more are given for the general advancement of Christianity. Within the

century now drawing to a close, 150,000,000 copies of the Bible have been printed in 226 different languages, and by the American Bible Society, a copy of the Bible or of the New Testament is printed and ready for use, every minute of the year. Fifty

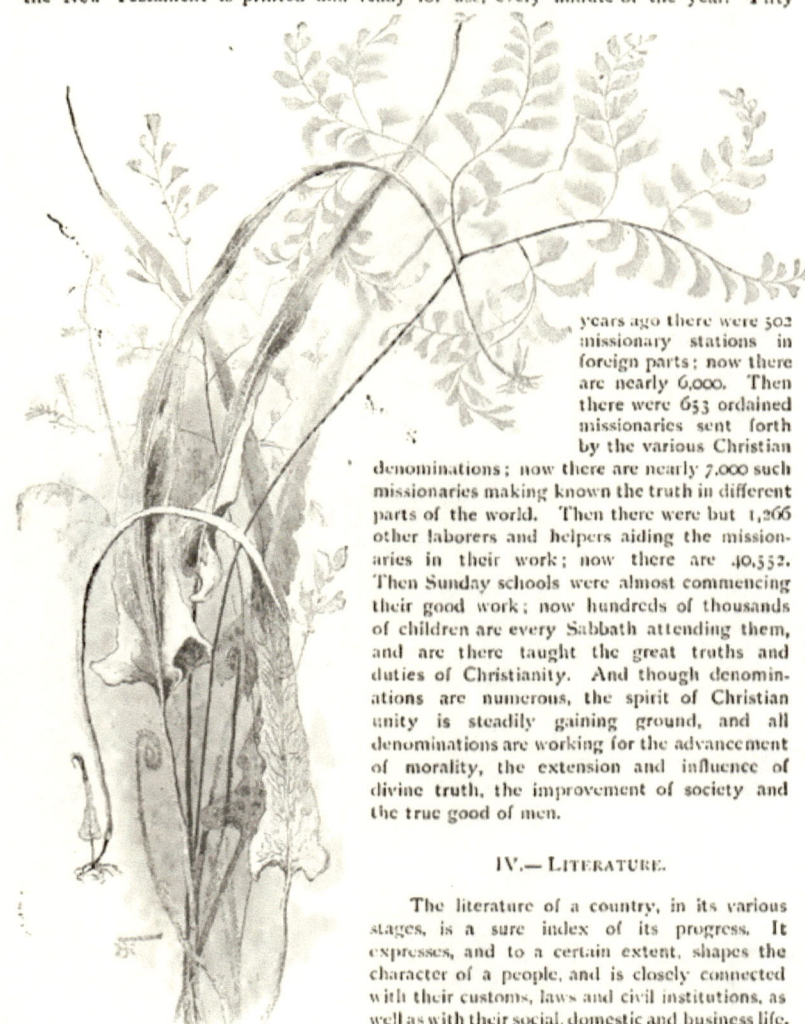

years ago there were 502 missionary stations in foreign parts; now there are nearly 6,000. Then there were 653 ordained missionaries sent forth by the various Christian denominations; now there are nearly 7,000 such missionaries making known the truth in different parts of the world. Then there were but 1,266 other laborers and helpers aiding the missionaries in their work; now there are 40,552. Then Sunday schools were almost commencing their good work; now hundreds of thousands of children are every Sabbath attending them, and are there taught the great truths and duties of Christianity. And though denominations are numerous, the spirit of Christian unity is steadily gaining ground, and all denominations are working for the advancement of morality, the extension and influence of divine truth, the improvement of society and the true good of men.

IV.— LITERATURE.

The literature of a country, in its various stages, is a sure index of its progress. It expresses, and to a certain extent, shapes the character of a people, and is closely connected with their customs, laws and civil institutions, as well as with their social, domestic and business life.

Beginning with the earliest colonies, those of Virginia and New England, the literature was limited in extent, and confined almost entirely to accounts of voyages to the new world and the experience of the earliest settlers, giving us the passing history of the times and notices of the progress and daily life of the colonies, by some of the more educated of the settlers.

The earliest writers, with perhaps two exceptions, had no thought of "Literature." They simply described to their friends in the old country their voyages over the ocean, the attractions and advantages of the new world, the appearance and character of the natives, and their own life in the new settlements. Their narratives were, of necessity, printed in England, as there was no book printing press in this country till 1640.

American literature may be considered under three distinct periods: 1. The colonial period, extending from 1607 to about 1775, or the time of the revolutionary movement. 2. From that date to about 1820. 3. From the last mentioned date to the present time.

The earliest American author was the noted Captain John Smith. Of his four American books, two, those of 1608 and 1612, give full accounts of Virginia and of his explorations and adventures with the Indians, including the romance of Pocahontas; the third and fourth, published in 1616 and 1620, are on New England and its trials. He writes with clearness and force, and his descriptions are vivid and often dramatic, though at times overdrawn. He was full of enterprise and energy, a born leader of men, and in the first twenty years of the colony, did more than any other man for its success and prosperity.

In this early period we have accounts of the country by George Percy, William Strachey, Alexander Whitaker, and John Pory, all full of interest, and also by George Sandys, a professed man of letters, who translated fifteen books of Ovid's Metamorphoses, and who was said by Dryden to be the best versifier of the age. To this early period belong Alsop's description of Maryland, and also the history of what is known as Bacon's Rebellion in Virginia.

In New England, which was eminently a thinking community, education was more general than in the other colonies. Between 1630 and 1690, there were in its settlements as many graduates of Oxford and Cambridge as would be found in any population of similar size in England itself. Among the clergy were some men of distinguished scholarship, even as judged by the high standard of the seventeenth century. No other society of pioneers ever so honored study and learning, or so promptly and liberally provided for the universal education of the people, so that, as might be expected, New England, in literature, was in advance of other parts of the country.

William Bradford, of the Mayflower and Plymouth Rock, afterward governor, has well been called "the father of American history." His "History of Plymouth Plantation," both as to time and authority, takes precedence of any other document on New England. He gives us, for twenty years, the annual record of the bright and also of the sombre aspects of colonial life, bringing the narrative down to 1646. John Winthrop, afterward governor, who was foremost among the colonists in weight of character and intellectual power, sketched the history of the colony for about the same length of time, from 1630 to 1649, giving clear views of the tone and spirit of New England society, and incidentally of his own wisdom and excellence. His definition of liberty has been said by a distinguished publicist to be the best in the English language.

Johnson's "Wonder Working Providence in New England," carries on its history from 1628 to 1651, and tells of the founding of towns and churches in the extensions of the colony, and sketches the leading men of the time.

In this period, too, come the narratives of the two great wars with the Indians, the Pequot War in 1637, and King Phillip's War in 1675, the former written, as well as fought, by Captain John Mason, and the latter narrated by Benjamin Church, and also by that noble hearted man, Daniel Gookin, who earnestly defended the Christian Indians from the charges of being unfaithful to the whites. Then we have Winslow's "Journal" and his "Good News from New England;" Higginson's "New England Plantations;" Wood's "New England Prospect;" Josscylyn's "Voyages" and his "Rarities of New England Discovered," all furnishing most interesting reading, and giving us accounts of the Indians, of the scenery, climate and productions of the new world, and of its birds, beasts, fishes, serpents, plants, etc.

In the New England colonies, where it was said "they first planted a church and then set up civil government," and that the "gospel was the making of the towns," the literature, as might be expected, was largely theological. Of the distinguished preachers of England who first came to Massachusetts, Thomas Hooker, Thomas Shepherd, and John Cotton were the most eminent. Hooker was a man of pre-eminent talents and piety, and of wonderful influence with men. His published writings number twenty-three titles, and of them a distinguished English writer has said, that "to praise them would be to lay paint on polished marble, or to add light to the sun." Shepherd was eminently practical in his writings, and his diary of meditations and experiences is rich in counsels for the Christian life. Cotton was a speaker of remarkable eloquence and great pulpit power, but his published writings do not sustain the reputation of his day, or account for his leading influence in the colony. Other ministers and writers of note were Peter Bulkley, John Norton, William Hooke, Charles Chauncey, who became president of Harvard College; Nathaniel Ward, who wrote "The Simple Cobbler of Agawan," " full of fire, wit, whim, eloquence, sarcasm, invective, patriotism and bigotry;" Samuel Stone, John Davenport, the fearless preacher of New Haven; Roger Clap, president of Yale College; John Eliot, the noted apostle of the Indians, who translated the Bible into their language, and Roger Williams, the founder of Rhode Island, and the apostle of freedom of conscience and religious toleration.

The writings of these men were mostly on theological and religious subjects, though from many of them, as was the fashion of the day, we have specimens of the crude poetry of the times in the shape of elegies, eulogies, epitaphs, and theology in verse. The "Bay Psalm Book" was published in Cambridge in 1640, and soon became quite popular both in Great Britain and America, so that in less than a century some seventy editions were published in the two countries. In the same year the first book of original poetry, a volume by Anne Bradstreet, issued in New England, for a time had a wide circulation. Eliot also published his Indian Bible, which was the first edition of the Scriptures published in America. It was three years in printing, and it is said only three copies are known to be in the United States, and only one man is known who can read it. Next came a concordance of the Bible, by John Newman, the earliest work of the kind known.

Some poetical writers of the period were John Norton, Uriah Oakes, Peter Folger, the maternal grandfather of Franklin, and Michael Wigglesworth, theologian and author of quaint religious verse, and several others who were eminent in their day.

In the latter part of the colonial period, theology was the chief department of literature. Here we have the Mathers, father, son, and grandson, Richard, Increase and Cotton, all noted for their numerous writing; the last mentioned being the author of the "Magnolia," that stupendous repository of piety, superstition and credulity, the author of fourteen books in a single year, and of no less than three hundred and eighty-three in his life-time. Samuel Sewall, John Wise and Jeremiah Dummer were noted writers of this period, as were several others of the clergy. In 1639, the first "Almanac for New England" was published. One for Boston was issued in 1676; one for Philadelphia in 1688; one for New York in 1697; one for Rhode Island in 1728; and one for Virginia in 1731. In 1733, Franklin began his famous "Poor Richard's Almanac," so noted for its "scraps of wisdom, crumbs of history, sketches of verse, proverbs, jests, etc." From several writers of this period we have historical works of value, and from Thomas Prince "The Chronological History of New England," in the form of annals, the best historical work published in America up to that date.

In this period, too, Samuel Willard published his "Complete Body of Divinity," and Solomon Stoddard issued numerous able publications on theological and other subjects. But the great author of the age and of the country was Jonathan Edwards, of whom Sir James Mackintosh declares that in profound thought and subtle and powerful argument "he was perhaps unmatched, certainly unsurpassed among men;" and of whom Chalmers says that "he was the first, not only in America, but in any country, or in any age;" and of whom a prominent historian said, that "it is perhaps impossible to name any department of intellectual exertion, in which, with suitable outward facilities, he might not have achieved superior distinction." His work on the "Will" has been pronounced a work of unequalled power; and of his "History of Redemption," Bancroft has said: "It is the only purely philosophic universal history ever written."

Other prominent theologians in this period were Jonathan Dickinson, John Witherspoon and Samuel Davies, all presidents of Princeton College; James Blair, president of William and Mary College; Samuel Johnson, president of Columbia College, and father of American episcopacy; Mather Byles, a faithful minister, but noted chiefly for his wit and humor; Ezra Stiles, president of Yale College; John Woolman, a Quaker writer and preacher, and one of the first of this country to write against slavery; Benjamin Franklin, whose essays and maxims, as well as his eminence in philosophic, scientific and political matters, have given him a world wide reputation. The historians and annalists of this period are numerous and their writings are of value. William Hubbard wrote the history of New England; William Stitt, on the discovery and settlement of Virginia; Thomas Hutchison, on the settlement of Massachusetts; Cadwallader Colden, on the five Indian nations; and David Brainerd, on the Indians to whom he was a missionary. The poetry of this period, with but few exceptions, has no great literary merit, and was of limited extent.

Passing on to the revolutionary period, we come first to the many pamphlets, letters, reports of speeches, and public documents called forth by the times, the high ability and practical wisdom of which were acknowledged by Lord Chatham, who said that "many of these productions rivalled the master pieces of antiquity." Distinguished among these early pamphleteers and writers, were James Otis, Josiah Quincy, Richard Henry Lee, John Adams, Thomas Jefferson, James Madison, John Marshall, Timothy

Pickering, Patrick Henry, Samuel Adams, Benjamin Franklin, Charles Cotesworth Pinckney, John Jay, and others whose writings or impassioned eloquence roused the entire land to resist the oppressions of the mother country and to carry out the plans of national independence. The "Common Sense" of Thomas Paine was sensible and

influential, but of his "Age of Reason," Franklin, refusing to recommend it, said to the author: "If men are so wicked with the restraints of religion, what would they be without it?" adding, "it is no mark of one's manliness or wisdom to spit in his mother's face."

The great State paper of the period was the Declaration of Independence by Jefferson, which, for dignity and eloquence, and its strong and clear statement of the oppressions of Great Britain, and for the powerful influence it has exerted, stands unrivalled among works of its class in any age or nation of the world. Jefferson also published "A Summary of the Rights of British America," and interesting "Notes of Virginia," and he left a mass of correspondence of great value to our civil and political history. The writings of Washington hold a distinguished place in this period for

WILD FLOWERS OF THE PACIFIC COAST.

their lofty patriotism and strong common sense, and his "Farewell Address," for thought, expression and wise counsel, is well nigh a model. Alexander Hamilton, who, by turns was soldier, lawyer, statesman and writer, took an important part in the formation of our national Constitution, and according to Guizot, "there is not one element of order, strength or durability in it that he did not powerfully contribute to introduce." The valuable papers of the Federalist were written chiefly by him, though in preparing them he had the important aid of James Madison and John Jay.

Among the local histories of this period were those of New Hampshire by Belknap, Connecticut by Trumbull, Massachusetts by Minot, Vermont by Williams, Pennsylvania by Prowd, and of more general interest, the histories of New England by Hannah Adams; of South Carolina by Ramsay, who also wrote the Life of Washington; the Annals of America by Holmes; the Life of Washington by Marshall; that of Patrick Henry by Wirt; the travels of Carver, one of the first to penetrate west of the Mississippi; the Journals of Ledyard, the intrepid explorer of Africa; and the Journals of Lewis and Clark, who first crossed the Rocky Mountains to the mouth of the Columbia river and led the way to what was like a new world.

The theologians of this period were ably represented by the younger Jonathan Edwards, a son of the great metaphysician, and author of several profound and able works; by Samuel Hopkins, a writer of distinguished ability; by Timothy Dwight, whose system of divinity is both eloquent and able; by William White, one of the first bishops of the Episcopal Church in this country; by Joseph Bellamy, a man of wonderful eloquence and power; by the celebrated John M. Mason, Joseph Buckminster and several others who might be mentioned.

In the department of science in this period were men like the two John Winthrops, John Ray, John Bartram, David Rittenhouse, an able astronomer and mathematician; Benjamin Rush, distinguished also as a medical writer; Alexander Wilson, whose work on the birds of America is still in high repute; and Benjamin Thompson (Count Rumford), eminent for his scientific works. Lindley Murray is well known for his work on Grammar.

Of poets, Philip Freneau was for a time highly popular; and John Trumbull, who wrote "McFingal;" Joel Barlow, author of the "Columbiad;" Timothy Dwight, who wrote "The Conquest of Canaan;" Joseph Hopkinson, who wrote "Hail Columbia;" and Robert Treat Paine, whose "Adams and Liberty," was the rallying song of the Federalist party, all in their day were highly regarded. About the only novelist of this period was Charles Brockden Brown, who wrote several tales, now but little known even by name. Among the miscellaneous writers whose productions appeared chiefly in newspapers and magazines, were Francis Hopkinson, a humorous writer, and author of "The Battle of the Kegs;" Henry Breckenridge, who wrote the vigorous satire, "Modern Chivalry;" Joseph Dennie, one of the earliest of our magazine writers and editors, and others well known or even prominent in their day, but comparatively unknown now.

The last period in American literature, from about 1820 to the present time, is in marked contrast to the period before it, both in the variety and extent as well as the finish of its productions. In 1820 Sydney Smith, in the Edinburgh *Review*, sneered at the poverty of American literature, and it must be confessed with some reason. But since that time there is no department of human knowledge which has not been explored and ably set forth by American authors. In history, jurisprudence, poetry, natural science, theology, medicine, fiction, essays, and in magazine and newspaper literature, the advance has been wonderful, and to give even a list of authors and notices of their works might fill volumes. As statesmen, we have men like Webster, Clay,

Calhoun, Benton, and John Quincy Adams; in jurisprudence, Marshall, Kent, Story, Greenleaf and Parsons; as poets, Sprague, Bryant, Halleck, Drake, Hillhouse, Percival, Poe, Willis, Brainard, Stoddard, Aldrich, Holmes, Pierpont, Longfellow, Lowell, Stedman, and Whittier; in history, Bancroft, Ticknor, Prescott, Parkman, Motley, Hildreth, Higginson, and Palfrey, to say nothing of local historians and industrious analysts; in literature, Irving, Verplanck, Paulding, Kennedy, Cooper, Sparks, Everett, Channing, Hawthorne, Ticknor, Thoreau, Phillips, Whipple, Sands, Holland, Fisher, Draper, Starr King, Emerson, Warner, Howells, James, Mitchell, Alcott, Stockton, and Mrs. Stowe, whose " Uncle Tom's Cabin " has had a wider reading than any work ever written by a woman; as lawyers and advocates, Hamilton, Parsons, Wirt, Pinckney, Binney, and Choate; in political economy, Wayland, Lieber, and Carey; in constitutional history and principles, Wheaton, Livingston, Sedgwick, Parsons, and Woolsey; in theology and religion, Stuart, Channing, the Alexanders, H. B. Smith, Crosby, and Charles Hodge, whose theology is now a text book to most of the evangelical denominations in the land; in philology, Webster, Worcester, Whitney; in language, Duponceau, Marsh, Pickering, Gallatin, and Schoolcraft; in works of travel, Ledyard, Hillard, Silliman, Stephens, Taylor, Robinson, Thompson, and Stanley; in natural history, Audubon, Wilson, and Agassiz; in botany, Gray, Eaton, and Dewey; in mineralogy, and geology, Hitchcock, Shepherd, Silliman, and Dana; in mathematics, Bowditch, Davis, Day, Pierce, and Loomis; in medicine, Dewees, Beck, Rush, Hosack, Parker, Wood, and Agnew; in education, Mann, Barnard, and Hopkins; in applied science, Henry, Morse, and Edison; in astronomy, Mitchell, and Peters; in the science of war, Scott, Hardee, Upton, Mahan, Dahlgreen, and Barnard; in the fine arts, Smibert, Copley, Trumbull, Jarvis, Allston, Greenough, Story, and Church; in school books of a high character, a host of able writers; and in architecture, agriculture, statistics, mechanics, memoirs, antiquities, biography, essays, reviews, magazines, and newspapers, names without number, and of decided ability.

In all these departments, style has improved, originality, research and industry have been manifest, and the literary standard has been steadily rising, until now American books on almost every subject are published abroad as well as at home, and acknowledged to be of standard excellence. The activity and enterprise which, as a people, we carry into business and public improvement, extend also to thought and mental progress. The extent of our country, the variety of its climate and scenery, its lofty mountains and fertile valleys, our broad and noble rivers and inland lakes; the vast stretch of our ocean border, where now the storms sweep in their power, and now the music of the rippling waves lulls the senses as twilight comes on; and our immense works of public improvement — all these things influence and shape the literature of our people, and mould it to the likeness of the land in which it originates. Everything in the country tends to make us original in thought, bold in expression, vivid in imagination, and impressive in language, so that we may well expect, in the progress of our national life, to see our oratory and eloquence, our poetry and prose, our works alike of science and art, our published volumes and daily papers, take on a national type and excellence far beyond what are now known.

Already our publications in the various departments of which we have spoken are libraries in themselves. Appleton's Cyclopedia of American Biography, out of its 14,243 names, gives us 2,051 names of American writers devoted to literature, and if to

these we add the 2,164 of the clergy, the 462 under the title of Art, the 564 under
Science, and the 586 under Education, we have no less than 5,827 persons in the history
of our country more or less contributing to its literature. And of poets alone, Griswold
in his collection of American poets, published some fifty years ago, gives the names of
no less than ninety-six persons whom he considers worthy of being counted as
American poets, and seventy more who, he says, if they had written more might justly
be ranked with the former. And since he wrote the number has been nearly doubled.
New names are constantly coming forward to fill the places of those who are passing
away, and to add to the bright galaxy of our country's authorship. As every age of
the past has brought forth its distinguished orators, statesmen, jurists, historians,
essayists, and poets, so the future will do the same. The sons and daughters of genius
may have their various types of thought and expression, different as their faces, but
each may be instinct with life and strength and intelligence, with thought to instruct,
imagination to quicken, and beauty to attract us, and so, as we would hope and
believe, the improvement will go on till the millennium of intellect and taste shall by
and by come in the fullness of its glory, to continue till time shall be no more.

American literature, especially in its later periods, owes much to its female writers.
Several of these, Anne Bradstreet, Hannah Adams, Mrs. Sigourney, Mrs. Sedgwick, and
some others have already been mentioned. In addition to these may well be mentioned
Abigail Adams, Mrs. Child, Mrs. Whitman, Mrs. Stephens, Mrs. Kirkland and Margaret
Fuller (Countess Ossoli), a thorough scholar and a critic of ability in art, literature, and
social science. Of later days are Mrs. Stowe, Mrs. Ellis, Mrs. Southworth, Miss
Warren, Mrs. Judson (Fanny Forester), Mrs. Welby, Mrs. Howe, author of the "Battle
Hymn of the Republic," Mrs. Neal, Mrs. Lippincott (Grace Greenwood), the Carey
sisters, Mrs. Hunt (H. H.), Mrs. Terhune (Marion Harland), Mrs. Parton, and more
recently, such writers as Mrs. Jewett, Miss Murfree, and others.

In considering American literature, our magazine and newspaper writers are not to
be overlooked; for in no country do the monthly, weekly, and daily journals have so
wide a circulation or so great an influence as in this; and for terse, condensed, and well
put thought some of them are models.

The first newspaper in America was published in Boston, in 1690, under the name
of *Public Occurrences*, but it was at once suppressed by the authorities for speaking too
freely of public matters, so that a second number was never issued. It was not till 1704
that the *News-Letter* of Boston, the first newspaper that lived, was issued in that city.
But the fashion soon spread, so that by 1765 forty-three newspapers had been
established in the various colonies, of which eleven were in Massachusetts. Most of
them were diminutive sheets, mostly filled with items of news and advertisements. It
was not till the time of the Revolution that journalism began to be an important
literary force, and that public questions and interests were discussed in the papers with
both freedom and talent. And from that day to this the periodical press has been
steadily extending its circulation and gaining in influence, until now there are probably
as many newspapers published in the United States as in all the world beside. In 1840
the daily and weekly and other periodicals of the country were 1,404; in 1850, 2,032;
in 1860, 3,542; in 1870, 4,896; in 1880, 7,954; in 1890, 19,011, sending out for the year
some 3,000,000,000 numbers, enough to give to every person some fifty copies of some
publication every year. Of these periodicals 955 were religious publications, having a

circulation of 3,972,650 copies each issue. And as the reading of newspapers and periodicals is well nigh universal, their influence on the literature as well as the intelligence of the people is very great, for they contain not only news, but essays, tales, poems, discussions, and information of every kind. Some of our ablest and most popular writers, in every age of the country, have been editors, and scores of men might be mentioned, among them some of the most famous of our authors, who have been connected with the periodical press. The character of newspaper and magazine writing has for years been steadily improving,

till now some of the best talent of the land is engaged in its work, and it is an important part of the literature of the country.

VII.—INVENTIONS, DISCOVERIES, IMPROVEMENTS.

The progress of a people, as well as its genius and enterprise, is seen in its inventions, in its application of old principles to new uses, and in all its improvements in mechanical art which abridge distance, annihilate time, extend commerce, aid agriculture, economize labor, transmit speech, give to night the brilliancy of day, prevent or alleviate pain, give prosperity to business, and comfort and enjoyment to every day life. And in all such inventions and improvements no country has been more prominent or successful than the United States.

A leading London paper gives a list of fifteen American inventions and discoveries which it says "have

MOUNTAIN FLOWERS.

been adopted all over the world." These it enumerates as "the cotton gin, planing machine, grass mower and grain reaper, rotary printing press, navigation by steam, hot air or caloric engine, sewing machine, India rubber industry, manufacture of horse shoes and nails by machinery, sand blast for carving and cutting, gauge-lathe, grain elevator, artificial ice making, electro magnet, and the composing or type-setting machine for printers."

Beside these, for which credit is given to the inventive genius of Americans, there are many other inventions and improvements everywhere in use in the country and so connected with every day life as to be worthy of notice. Some of these are of American origin, and some American improvements on the inventions of other countries, but all showing as well as aiding in the progress of our country. Among these are the type-writer, sewing machine, steel pen, sulphur and phosphorus match, electric light, revolving pistol, repeating rifle and shot gun, gatling gun, telegraph, telephone, spectroscope, screw propellor, monitors, natural gas, petroleum or kerosene, ocean steam ships, street and elevated railways, ocean cables, steam fire engines, chemical fire extinguishers, anæsthetics and painless surgery, nitro-glycerine, giant powder, dynamite, electro-plating, pneumatic tubes, electric bells, cheap postage, vestibule cars, cantilever bridges, several new metals, etc., etc. Some of these are of foreign, and some of home invention, and all are so extensively used in this country that a brief notice of several of them may be interesting and instructive as connected with our progress as a people.

The Cotton Gin.—One of the earliest and most valuable inventions of the country, which has given immense value to our Southern States, was that of the cotton gin by Eli Whitney, in 1793. As early as 1621 cotton seeds had been planted in Virginia as an experiment, and at a later date the plant was introduced into Carolina. Small quantities of cotton had now and then been exported, but when, in 1784, eight bags of it were sent to Liverpool it was seized at the custom house on the ground that so much cotton could never have been grown in America. But as the production of the crop increased the great drawback to its value was the difficulty of separating the fibre from the seeds. It was a full day's work for a man to clean a single pound of cotton, a rate so slow as to make the extensive production of the crop unprofitable.

To meet the difficulty Mr. Eli Whitney, then a school teacher in Georgia, invented the cotton gin, in which by passing the cotton through fine wire teeth the seed is separated from the fibre, and by which a thousand pounds of cotton are as thoroughly cleaned by one man's daily work as a single pound could be by hand. In 1791, only 2,000,000 pounds had been raised in the South; in 1793, the amount was 5,000,000 pounds; in 1820, 160,000,000; in 1880, 3,200,000,000; and in 1890, 3,461,031,600 pounds, or 8,652,579 bales of 400 pounds each, of which about 2,000,000 bales were exported to England. And a cotton-picking machine has been invented which it is claimed will save 80 per cent. in the cost of picking the crop, and if so, will almost, if not quite equal the value of the cotton gin. In addition to the value of the cotton itself, the cotton seed of the eight million bales of cotton, which is over four million tons, is worth some seventy million dollars for oil, oil-cake and feed. And there are in the cotton-growing regions 194 cotton-seed oil mills, with a capital of $20,000,000; and forty of these mills have fertilizer factories in connection with their oil business, using the cotton-seed meal, after the oil has been extracted, as a basis for manufacturing fertilizers. It shows the progress of the cotton-growing region, that in 1880 there were but forty of such cotton-seed mills with a capital of only $3,500,000.

Though Whitney's invention made the prosperity of the cotton growing States, agriculturally, commercially, and financially, and in one important department changed the commerce of the world, all his rights in the patent were shamefully disregarded, and he was deprived of the profits he should have received from his invention.

The Rotary Printing Press.—The art of printing is of comparatively modern origin, some four hundred and fifty years having elapsed since the first book was issued from the press. The great discovery of forming each of the letters on a separate type so that they could be taken one by one and combined in printing was made between 1420 and 1438, and is said to have been made about the same time by Laurens Coster and also by Johann Gutenberg. The types at first used were made of wood, but metal soon came into use. Between 1450 and 1455 Gutenberg succeeded in printing the Bible; and in 1471 Caxton introduced printing into England, and in 1474 put through the press the first book ever printed in the English tongue. Of the ninety-nine productions of his press, thirty-eight survive in single copies or in fragments only.

The first kind of printing press was a simple and crude affair. It was worked slowly by hand, producing a single small sheet at a time, which had to be pressed four times to complete the impression on both sides of the paper. Then came the Stanhope press; then the Columbian; then the cylinder press which was propelled by steam and by which the impressions were made, not from flat surfaces, but from revolving cylinders to which types were attached; then the Hoe press in which stereotype plates took the place of movable types, a machine which from each of its cylinders could print two thousand papers an hour; then the Walter press, which printed both sides of the paper at the same time, and some seventeen thousand copies in an hour; then others, each of which, like those first mentioned, claimed some improvement on those that had been before them; then the Hoe perfecting and folding press, which not only printed but folded the sheets; and these followed by others, each claiming improvements, till now we have the great sextuple press, weighing fifty-eight tons, and printing ninety thousand four-page papers in an hour, or twenty-five copies every second, and using up twenty-six miles of paper in an hour. Franklin's press printed only a hundred sheets in an hour, and Eliot's Indian Bible, of which but one sheet was printed in a day, was three years in the process of being printed. Now the American Bible Society prints, binds, and every way completes a copy of the Bible or Testament every minute for the three hundred and twelve working days of the year. Some of the most important improvements of the printing press are of American invention.

Type Setting Machines.—Type setting by hand is comparatively a slow process, each letter having to be taken by itself and put in its proper place for printing. To facilitate the work, several inventions have been patented for setting and distributing type by machinery. In 1820 Mr. William Church of Connecticut, patented a composing machine, but it did not become popular. One was afterward invented by Copenhagen, which met with better success, and was exhibited in the Paris exposition in 1855, setting up and distributing type at the same time. Its capacity was considered equal to that of three compositors. In 1856 Mr. Robert Hattersley, of England, invented a machine which set from four thousand to six thousand types per hour, and which also distributed the type after it had been used.

PENNSYLVANIA SCENERY.

In 1871, Mr. A. Mackie, an Englishman, invented a machine which worked by steam, and in the same year a machine, also worked by steam, was invented in Warrington, England, of which it was claimed that it would do the work of eight men. Several other machines have been invented each of which seems to have worked well, but none have come into general use, owing to the cost of construction and repair, the amount of type-breaking which they cause, and their liability to get out of order. The machines show great ingenuity, and in perfected forms may by-and-by come into general use, and if so, may prove an important addition to the industries of the country. It is hoped they will be so perfected that the operator of the telegraph, from the sounds of the instrument, may at once set type by machinery without first writing the message.

Type-writers.—Another important and comparatively recent invention is that of the type-writer, a machine for printing with movable types, and so to take the place of writing with the pen. The first patent for a practical machine of this kind was taken out in 1868. The types were arranged in parallel rows, and the impression or printing was done by a striker or plunger which was moved by keys, as in the piano, the operator pressing the key corresponding to the letter which he wished to use, and thus rapidly printing words. In other type-writers the letters are placed on the periphery of a wheel, and are brought to the printing point by its revolution. In most type-writers the types are at the end of levers, which are so arranged as to strike at a common printing point, and the paper is made to pass that point by machinery, and so receives the impression of the types. For a long time type-writers were used by but few persons, but now they are in use almost everywhere, in office work, for correspondence, etc. There is quite a variety in their construction, there being numerous patents for them issued to different inventors. Their use is steadily increasing.

Metallic Pens.—In ancient times a kind of reed was used for writing, though sometimes letters were printed with fine hair pencils or brushes, as among the Chinese of the present day. Quill pens are said to have come into use soon after the introduction of paper; the name pen coming from *penna*, the Latin word for feather, as pens were made from the quills of birds. Early in the century, Mr. Joseph Gillot, a working jeweler of Birmingham, England, accidentally split one of his fine steel tools, and being suddenly called on to sign a receipt, and not finding his quill pen at hand, he used the split tool as a ready substitute, and this incident is said to have suggested to him the idea of making pens of metal.

Carrying out the idea with secrecy and promptitude, he began making pens of steel, in which he was so successful that he invented machinery for making them. As at first made by hand, a single pen was retailed for half a crown, a price which was gradually reduced to sixpence. By the machinery which he invented, he was able in 1821 to sell his improved pens at $35.00 per gross, which was then thought quite cheap. Better pens are now sold from the same manufactory for twopence a gross, that is, over eight hundred pens are now sold for what in 1821 was the price of a single one. And one hundred and fifty million pens are made in that factory annually.

In 1870 there were three factories of steel pens in the United States, and in 1880 there were several others. In 1870 there were in the United States twenty-one manufactories of gold pens and pencils, employing two hundred and fifty hands in the work. And fountain pens, giving a constant supply of ink, are also extensively made and used. The art of making metallic pens has been so perfected that ten millions of the tiny bits of steel can be cut into shape and prepared for completion by one man in a single day. The manufacture of steel and other metallic pens has been as important an invention as any connected with business and education since that of printing.

Sewing Machines.— Sewing machines are one of the most important inventions of the century, and like the stocking-frame, which in principle they resemble, they are the invention of a poor mechanic, striving to lessen the labor of his wife and other poor women. Elias Howe, a native of Massachusetts, was the inventor. After many experiments and long and patient labor, he completed the first working machine, the patent for which was granted to him in May, 1841. For a long time he met with discouragement in this country, and going to England, sold his patent for that country to a stay-maker for $1,000 and a royalty of $15.00 on each machine made and used. When he came back he found his American patent had been pirated by a wealthy company, but asserting his rights in the courts and finally establishing them, his machine soon came into use and he became a wealthy man.

His machine made what is called the lock-stitch, but since his invention many improvements and modifications have been introduced by other inventors. The principal ones of these are: 1. Machines that work with one thread and with a needle pointed at each end which is pushed through by pincers on one side and caught by pincers on the other, and so pulled backward and forward for its work. 2. A single thread machine which makes a running stitch, which was patented in 1844. 3. A single thread machine which makes the chain or tambour stitch, in which the thread is looped upon itself by a curved shuttle after it has passed through the cloth. This was patented in 1848. 4. The Wheeler and Wilson, which is a double thread machine, and is used extensively both in this country and in Great Britain. Special sewing machines are also made for sewing leather in binding books, or for shoes, for sewing harness, gloves, embroidery, and for various other purposes. One for sewing the soles upon boots and shoes is said to have sewed a hundred and fifty pairs of soles on army boots in a single day. Sewing machines are now made and sold by the tens of thousands. The Singer Company is said to have made a hundred and forty-one thousand of their machines in a single year.

Mowing and Reaping Machines.— From time immemorial, grass and grain have been cut with the scythe or the sickle. The sickles in use among the ancient Jews, Egyptians, and Chinese, seem to have differed but little from those in use at the present day. The process of reaping and mowing, however, by the sickle and scythe, were so tedious and expensive that during the present century many attempts have been made to do the work by machinery, and in the last fifty years these attempts have been crowned with complete success.

Reaping by machinery, however, is not a modern invention, though the great improvements in the machines have given them about all their value. Pliny, the elder, who lived in the first century, describes a reaping machine which he saw in Gaul. It was a large van with projecting teeth on the side, driven on two wheels through the standing grain by oxen pushing it from behind. And four hundred years later, Palladius saw the same kind of machine working in Gaul.

In modern times Mr. Capel Loft, in 1785, suggested a machine somewhat like the ancient one first spoken of. Between that time and 1851 the patents taken out for reaping and mowing machines were numerous. In 1826, Mr. Patrick Bell, of Scotland, constructed an efficient and simple machine which long continued in use, and several features of which are still used in later machines. Before 1832 there were eight patents taken out for machines.

In 1833, Obed Hussey, and in 1834, C. H. McCormick, each invented such machines, and other machines have also been patented. Most of these carry mechanical binders, binding the grain as it is cut, with wires or twine, thus saving the labor of many men, and enabling them to do other work. Reapers and mowers are now used everywhere, and the work they do is an hundredfold what was accomplished by the old-fashioned method of hand work.

In connection with reapers and mowers, mention may well be made of threshing and winnowing machines which are of modern invention. In former times the ripened grain when reaped was spread upon the ground, and then trampled on by oxen, or beaten out by the flail till the kernel was separated from the straw, and then what had been beaten out was tossed in the air till the wind had blown away the chaff from the kernel which was thus secured for use. Now both these processes are superseded by machines which at the same time thresh out the grain and by rapidly moving fans blow away the chaff, a single machine doing the work of a score of men and thus largely saving both time and expense.

Planing Machines.— The ordinary hand plane is known to almost everyone. It did its work well but slowly, giving to wood, for its various uses, a smooth and even surface. The planing machine, which is an important modern invention, accomplishes the same kind of work by the power of machinery, either by pushed, or more commonly, by rapidly revolving knives, one machine doing in the same time the work of sixty men.

Planing machinery is also applied to metal of all kinds. In this case, however, the chisel-edged steel cutter is pressed down upon the metal and the latter is moved forward against it by powerful machinery. And when a groove of a given width has been cut, the metal is returned to its first place, and then is again pressed forward till another groove is cut in the same manner, and so on till the work is completed. By this process, slow as it may seem, metals are smoothed or worked in various ways with a facility and rapidity before unknown. The value of the planing machine, as applied to every kind of dressed wood work, as for doors, boards, the wood work for buildings and for furniture of all kinds, can hardly be over-estimated.

Bessemer Steel.—The old method of making steel from iron was a slow and expensive process, and made the cost of steel so great that its use was comparatively limited. But the discovery of Sir Henry Bessemer, made some twenty-five years ago, has changed all this, and made steel so cheap that it is everywhere taking the place of iron except for minor purposes. It is a process for changing molten iron into molten steel cheaply and almost instantly, and so substituting steel for iron in some of the most important industries of the world.

Before this invention, steel had but a limited and comparatively insignificant use; now its production is more than a third of the total consumption of iron in the world. With the exception of printing, the mariner's compass, the discovery of America, the

26

introduction of the steam engine, and the application of electricity to the telegraph, telephone, and lighting of streets and dwellings, but few, if any, discoveries more mark the world's progress, or are of greater usefulness than this. It reduces immensely the cost of railroads and their repairs, so that they can be extended to new regions; diminishes the cost of transportation so as to bring to the markets of the world products that otherwise would not pay for removal, and so cheapens transportation; increases production; multiplies the resources of the people, and thus benefits the country.

Since the introduction of this great invention, and it is said largely owing to it, the cost of railroad transportation has been reduced two-thirds, and the difference to the country in a single year has been reckoned as $1,000,000,000, a large part of which saving is due to the fact that steel rails give greater strength and stability, and so the capacity of increased loads in transportation, thus bringing the distant areas of a vast country nearer to each other, and giving ready and profitable market to products that otherwise would be of little or no value to the producers.

The Screw Propellor.— The screw propellor which has so extensively taken the place of the paddle wheel, both in vessels of war and in commercial vessels, is comparatively a late invention. The screw, as applied to vessels, was first used to produce motion in 1802, by Mr. Shorter, an Englishman, but the discovery was at that time comparatively valueless, as the steam engine had not then been applied to navigation. But in 1832, by Mr. B. Woodcroft; in 1836, by Mr. F. P. Smith; and in 1837, by Mr. Ericson, improvements were made in its form and application, till now it is in almost universal use. Sometimes it has two, sometimes four, and sometimes six blades or arms, and these arms vary in length, some, as in the Great Eastern, being twenty-four feet in diameter. Many vessels are built with two screws, one under each quarter, which not only adds to the power for motion, but is a great advantage in rapidly turning a vessel. The screw is generally preferred to the wheel for navigation, and its invention and use mark, as well as aid, the progress of commerce.

Electric Lighting.— All known methods of generating electricity can produce light, and a century ago we find Cavallo speaking of a light which he thought was different from the electric spark, produced by friction. But light from battery electricity was first discovered by Sir Humphrey Davy in 1810, when on breaking the continuity of the electric current a brilliant light was produced. In 1820, Oersted proved, as he thought, the identity of electricity and magnetism, and in 1831, Faraday, by his great discovery of induced currents, was the first to make practical the application of electricity to the production of artificial light.

It was not, however, till 1853, that the magnetic electro machine was actually applied for this purpose, and in 1857, the first practical trial which was successful took place. Since then inventions and improvements have been made by various persons, and lately wonderful improvements by Edison, who has made electric lighting for streets and buildings simple and everywhere common. Though thus far more expensive than gas, the wonderful brilliancy of its light is likely to make its use everywhere general, and the facts that it does not consume the oxygen of the air, and causes so little heat, are likely to make its use everywhere general both for stores and dwellings, as well as for public streets.

The Telegraph.—The idea that signs for words might be sent from one point to another by means of electricity was early entertained. Galileo, in 1632, suggested a way in which, by the aid of the magnetic needle, persons might converse with each other when two or three thousand miles apart. And in 1753 a Scotch writer proposed a crude and clumsy apparatus by which electric currents passing through wires should make letters and stamp messages on paper.

But it was not till 1832–5 that the telegraph, as now so successfully and extensively used, was made practical by Mr. S. B. F. Morse. The Morse line was first laid between Washington and Baltimore in 1842, and the printing telegraphic instrument was invented by Mr. Alfred Vail, of New Jersey, in 1837. At first Morse made use of the fountain pen to dot down his characters, but in the end steel points were found best. Various improvements have been patented for the transmission of messages, but most of them have been bought by the Western Union Company, which now controls most of the telegraph operations of this country.

Telegraphing, which was first used on land, has since been extended to the ocean, and thousands of miles of telegraphic cable now connect the ends of the earth with each other. The postal telegraph system has been adopted by the government of Great Britain, telegraphic messages being sent by the post office department, and the adoption of the same system has been urged by the Postmaster-General of this country. According to the latest statistics, there are in various countries about 500,000 miles of telegraph lines, using about 1,200,000 miles of wire. Of this extent the United States has more than any other country. Messages, at the rate of 800 a day, are now sent from New York to London, and the answer returned in four minutes, the whole 800 messages being sent between ten o'clock A. M. and two o'clock P. M.

The Telephone.—This instrument is designed to convey articulate sounds to a distance by means of electricity. The principle of the telephone was first recognized in 1860 by Reis, of Frankfort, but in his instrument the quality of the sound was entirely lost. The discovery of the principle of the articulating telephone seems to have been made about the same time by Gray, of Chicago, and by Bell, of Edinburgh, who is now living in the United States. The articulating telephone of Bell was first shown at the centennial exhibition at Philadelphia, and is of very simple construction. By it words spoken into the telephone are faithfully reproduced at great distances, and by the use of what is called the microphone the sounds have even been magnified. For domestic and business purposes the telephone is everywhere used in the United States, especially in cities and large towns.

Matches.—Matches are, as all know, pieces of inflammable material prepared for the purpose of kindling fire readily. Before their invention fire was preserved by burying sticks of wood under the ashes over night, so that in the morning it would be burning coal; or if the fire went out a common resource was to go with an iron or tin pan to a nearest neighbor and borrow a few coals with which to kindle the wood afresh. And among savages fire was kindled by the rapid friction of dry sticks upon each other.

One of the first forms of what we now know as matches, was made by dipping one end of little strips or pieces of wood in melted sulphur. Thus prepared, the sulphur points at once took fire when applied to a spark obtained by striking fire from a flint and steel into tinder made from burnt cloth and usually kept in a small tin box. This was in almost universal use up to the first quarter of the present century. After this, several ingenious inventions rapidly followed each other and so displaced the old brimstone matches that now they are almost unknown.

The first of these inventions was the instantaneous light box, which consisted of a small tin box containing a bottle in which was some sulphuric acid soaking in asbestus, and a supply of properly prepared matches coated with a mixture of chlorate of potash, powdered loaf sugar and gum arabic, and these being dipped in the bottle at once took fire. Next came the "lucifer match," which dispensed with the sulphuric acid and was tipped with an inflammable mixture of chlorate of potash and sulphuret of antimony, and also with brimstone. These matches were ignited by friction, being drawn rapidly over sand-paper. Then came the "Congreve" match, which is much used by some, and which is still often called "the lucifer." They are tipped with phosphorus and nitre, or phosphorus, sulphur and chlorate of potash, and require but a slight friction to ignite them, for which purpose one side of the paper box in which they come is generally sanded. One of the latest forms of this match is the "safety match," which was invented in Sweden, which leaves out the phosphorus, and can be lighted only by rubbing on a composition which is put on the side of the box containing the matches, thus preventing the danger of their taking fire by ordinary friction like the other kinds of matches.

The wooden splints for matches, which are either square or round, are made rapidly by machinery. The business of match making, and the trade in matches, has attained enormous proportions both in this country and in Europe. One firm in Bohemia employs 2,700 persons in their manufacture, and more than one firm in England produces 10,000,000 of them every day. A Birmingham firm manufactures daily eight miles of thin wax taper to convert into Congreve matches. And several establishments in the United States manufacture matches by the millions daily. The machinery for cutting the tiny sticks which are made into matches, has been so perfected that one machine can cut 10,000,000 of these little sticks, ready for dipping, in a single day.

Gas Light.—Lighting by gas is one of the best and most economical modes of obtaining artificial light which has thus far been brought into use. As compared with the old-fashioned tallow candles and oil lamps, it is a wonderful improvement, and though likely to be largely superseded by electric lighting, will still be everywhere extensively used. For the same amount of light, it is said to cost but one-fifth as much as common whale oil, and but one-ninth as much as sperm oil. Though electric lights are far more brilliant, gas light is thus far found to be the cheapest, and improvements are from time to time made reducing the cost of making it. It can be made from wood, rosin, oil, or kerosene, but that made from coal is thus far found to be the best.

From 1658 to 1739, the attention of men of science in England had repeatedly been called to streams of inflammable air issuing from crevices and mines in the coal districts, and before 1800, some experiments were made toward lighting houses or factories with gas, but they seem to have been unsuccessful or little known. When in 1810, a company was formed in London for lighting with gas, it is said that Sir Humphrey Davy ridiculed the idea, saying "one might as well talk of lighting houses or streets by slices of moonlight," and when, after strong opposition, the pipes for gas were introduced into the houses of parliament, a member, looking at the iron burners, said it was "absurd to talk of light from those tips, for they had no wicks" as in oil lamps.

And when it was first proposed to introduce gas into Philadelphia, it was strongly objected to by a large number of leading citizens on the ground that it would cause explosions in the streets and endanger the lives of the people.

The use of gas, however, rapidly increased, till most of the cities of Great Britain and Europe were lighted with it, and it was extensively used in this country. Gas is also used for cooking and heating purposes, and for facility of regulation, ease of application, and perfect cleanliness, it is greatly approved. Since the discovery of gas wells, "natural gas," as it is called, is coming into extensive use for heating purposes in manufactories of various kinds, as well as for heating and cooking in private dwellings. It is piped for great distances from the wells, and its use in cities is increasing.

Petroleum or Kerosene.— Petroleum or kerosene was known for a long time before any one thought it of much value. For many years it was known to the Indians and early settlers in the State of New York as Seneca oil, and was used for medical purposes, chiefly as a liniment. But that it was so extensively a natural product and good for lighting and other practical purposes was a discovery of the present century. It had indeed been made in small quantities by distillation from shale and bituminous coal, but its wonderful discovery in the bowels of the earth put a stop to its manufacture and opened new sources of commerce and domestic use and comfort.

The first systematic boring for it began about 1857-59, and in a few years the product increased enormously. Wells sunk in Pennsylvania, Ohio, and West Virginia vary in depth from less than two hundred up to two thousand feet, and from them the kereosene or petroleum flows, often spouting with force, and is gathered into enormous tanks and transported to the refineries where it is purified for use.

Pipe lines also are constructed from the oil regions to the refineries, and huge tanks on railroad cars carry great quantities of it for the same purpose and for use to various parts of the country. At present the yearly output is variously estimated from 30,000,000 to over 40,000,000 barrels, and though many of the old wells are exhausted, new fields are constantly being opened. For home purposes kerosene is everywhere used in the United States, and its export to foreign countries is great and constantly increasing. The total value of its exports for the year ending June 30, 1891, was $51,313,454. Its use for lighting purposes has largely taken the place of candles and of whale oil, especially in the smaller places which electric or gas lighting has not reached. The largest oil well ever known was opened in 1891, and yields 14,000 barrels of oil a day.

India Rubber.— India rubber or caoutchouc is the dried milky juice of plants or trees growing in tropical or semi-tropical climates. In Herreros' account of the second voyage of Columbus, he mentions elastic balls made of the gum of a tree which he says is found in Hayti, and in 1615 it is mentioned by Torquemada as yielded by trees in Mexico, from the gum of which he says shoes were made and "cloaks were so waxed" as to make them water-proof. It was first known in this country as *elastic gum*, and afterward received the name of *India rubber* from its use in rubbing out the marks of lead pencils, for which purpose it was imported into Great Britain, and was sold at high prices. It was also used for flexible tubes for the use of surgeons and chemists.

It was not till about 1820 that it began to be used in the United States in the manufacture of water-proof cloths and for making overshoes and various other articles.

In that year the first pair of India rubber shoes was seen in this country. They were thick and clumsy, covered in part with gilding, and in shape like the heavy shoes of the Chinese. They were made of solid rubber, not as now made thin and flexible by vulcanizing. They were made by first forming a last of clay of the size and shape of the foot which the shoe might fit, and on this last the fluid from the tree, almost the color of milk, was allowed to flow and harden, to aid which it was held over a smoking fire which at the same time dried and blackened it. When the rubber was thoroughly dried and hardened, the clay last was broken up and the pieces taken out. The rubber shoe thus made was often a quarter of an inch thick in the thickest parts and thinner at the edges. In its vulcanized form, the mode of making India rubber articles as now known was discovered by accident by Mr. Charles Goodyear in 1843, and its applications are very numerous and important. The patents for its use in different forms are said to be between two and three thousand in number. Belting, buffers, wheel tires, washers, valves, pipes, fire-hose, bands, and articles for water-proof clothing are made of this material, as are many articles for medical and surgical purposes. One English firm manufactures three thousand pounds of India rubber thread a day; in another factory three thousand tobacco pouches are made daily. In Great Britain, in France, and in the United States thousands of operatives are constantly engaged in the manufacture of India rubber in its various forms, and the sale of such goods is immense and steadily increasing.

The Sand Blast.—The sand blast is a method of engraving figures on glass or metal, or any hard substance, by the percussive force of a rapid stream of sand driven against either of them by artificial means. It was invented by Benjamin Tilghman, of Philadelphia, who took out a patent in 1870. The hard surface to be cut is covered with a plate of metal or wax, with openings for the parts to be cut, and against these openings the stream of sand is forcibly driven by steam or compressed air, thus cutting letters or engravings in a very short time. At one of the great marble quarries of Vermont, the sand blast has been used to cut the names and dates on tombstones. Metal plates, with openings for the letters or figures, are fastened on the stone with shellac, and the sand blast cuts the word, or in this case the name of the soldier, with the company, regiment, rank, and dates in the stone in less than five minutes. Two hundred and fifty-four thousand headstones for soldiers have been cut for national cemeteries at this one quarry, at a cost of $864,000. Beautiful engravings can be cut on glass or metal in the same manner. Its practical uses are almost unlimited, and the cost of work done by it is far cheaper than by other methods.

Monitors.—The monitor or turret-ship is a recent invention in naval warfare, and consists of an iron or steel-plated vessel, rising but slightly above the water, and having one or more turrets encased in massive iron or steel plates, each holding guns of heavy caliber.

These guns can be pointed by machinery in any direction. Turret-ships were first proposed in England, and about the same time "monitors" were constructed in the United States, differing somewhat from those of the former country. One advantage of the monitors is that heavier guns can be carried at the middle of the ship than at broadside; another is the fact that they are made of iron or steel; and still another, that so small a part of the vessel is exposed to the guns of an enemy. In our late war the monitors were of great and efficient service, being proof against shots that might sink a wooden vessel.

The first monitor in the United States navy was constructed by Mr. John Ericsson, the distinguished inventor and engineer. It was built in three months in 1862, and in that year defeated and sunk the Confederate iron-clad Merrimac. It is to be hoped that such terrible instruments of slaughter as the monitor and repeating guns and cannon may make warfare so fearfully destructive that nations will be led to settle their difficulties by arbitration rather than by the wholesale carnage of men.

Revolvers and Gatling Guns.—Gunpowder, or something very like it, seems to have been known to the Chinese long before the Christian era, and to have been used in Europe with artillery as early as the 12th century. Its connection with fire-arms of various kinds is obvious, and cannon (from *canna*, a reed), having small bores not larger than those of modern muskets, were used in the 14th century. As time passed on, fire-arms of various kinds and sizes were made, the arquebuse, the clumsy matchlock, the firelock, the flint musket, then the percussion musket and rifle, and then the beautiful

AN EARLY STEAMBOAT.

shot-guns of the present day, and the rifles culminating in the breech loaders, repeating guns, and revolvers of various kinds with their multiplied shooting power.

The revolver, in fire-arms, is a weapon which, by means of revolving barrels, can be made to fire several times without reloading. In a very crude form, it was known two hundred years ago, and in the time of George IV a pistol with from four to twenty barrels bored in a solid mass of metal, was so made as to revolve when the trigger was drawn back, but its great weight and cumbrous mechanism made it comparatively useless.

In 1835, Col. Samuel Colt, who, it is said, had seen this pistol in England, after long experiments, patented his world-renowned "Colt's revolvers," which are now so largely manufactured in this country and in Europe. The revolver consists of one strong rifled barrel and a chamber perforated with six or seven barrels, each of which, in turn, is brought to the main barrel by the action of the trigger, so that all can be fired in quick succession. These revolvers are now extensively used in naval and military service, as well as by individuals in every part of the world.

The revolver principle has also been applied successfully to artillery. The Gatling gun, a revolver of this kind, was extensively used in the late war of secession. It was invented in 1861 by the man whose name it bears, and has five or ten barrels, each one having a corresponding lock, the barrels and locks revolving together. The gun is fed

A MODERN STEAMER — MIDNIGHT ON LAKE ERIE.

by feed cases which fit into a hopper connected with the chamber, so that continuous firing can be carried on at the rate of a thousand shots a minute, each case being replaced by another as fast as the firing goes on. It is one of the most destructive weapons of modern warfare. The principle of rapid feeding, so as to keep up rapid and continuous firing, is applied to fire-arms of every kind.

Steam Navigation.—When once steam had been thought of as a moving power, its application to navigation was obvious, and as early as 1543, Blasco de Garay endeavored so to apply it in the harbor of Barcelona. He exhibited a steamboat of his own invention, but apparently without success, as nothing further is known about it. It was not till 1777 that, in the hands of Watt, steam became an efficient power, and from that time on many efforts were made in Europe to apply successfully the power of steam to navigation.

Before the close of 1787, Fitch at Philadelphia, and Rumsey at Shepherdstown, Virginia, had each moved vessels by steam. A vessel built by Fitch, and propelled by steam, was on the Delaware river in 1790; and by 1800, Samuel Morey had gone up the

Connecticut river in a steamer of his own construction, and Elijah Ormsbee, a Rhode Island mechanic, had, on the Seekonk river, a boat, the paddles of which were driven by steam. Early in this century, Stevens on the Hudson, and Oliver Evans on the Delaware and Schuylkill, exhibited small vessels moved by steam. And in 1807, Robert Fulton made the first really successful voyage by steam, from New York to Albany in the Clermont, which went one hundred and ten miles in twenty-four hours against both wind and tide, thus having been the first to prove the practical utility of steam navigation.

But even then the idea of steam navigation was opposed as both useless and dangerous, and "no man in his senses," it was said, "would risk his life in such a fire boat as the Clermont, when the river was full of good sailing packets." Soon after this time a small vessel, not much larger than a large row boat, went up the Connecticut river propelled by steam. The cylinders of the engine played horizontally, pushing out on each side of the boat four oars, which turned as in sculling, and then were drawn back towards the sides of the boat, the motion of which was about four miles an hour, but which, for some reason, did not make a second trip.

From this time on improvements were rapidly made and the application of steam to navigation steadily increased. Before 1820 the first steamboat had passed down the Mississippi river to New Orleans; the first steamboat had appeared on the lakes; and the Atlantic had been crossed by the little steamship Savannah. Now magnificent steamboats are found on all our lakes and navigable rivers, and war steamers have taken the place of old ships of the line; and where formerly sailing vessels often were for weeks and even months in coming from Havre to New York, bringing but few passengers, now our huge steamers crossing the Atlantic in less than six days, bring more human beings in a single passage than a hundred years ago crossed the ocean both ways in a year. In 1793 a gentleman who had been abroad was a curiosity, and as he walked the streets of America he was pointed out with the remark, "There goes a man who has been in Europe!" Now in a single year hundreds of thousands of emigrants from Europe land at the port of New York alone.

Railroads.—Railroads, those wonderful instrumentalities of travel and transportation, owe their origin, not to men of education or high scientific attainments, but to the laborers or mechanics of the coal mines in the north of England who thus sought to simplify the transit of coal from the mines to the places of shipment or sale. These first railroads were made by two parallel lines of wooden beams laid and fixed on the ground, with flanges to prevent the wheels of the crude box cars from slipping off the track. Where seventeen hundred pounds made a one-horse load on the common road, forty-two hundred weight could easily be drawn by a horse on these beams or tramways as they were called.

The date of their invention and first use is uncertain, but it was between 1602 and 1649. It was not, however, till about 1700 that any improvements were made in their construction. Thin strips of iron were laid on the wood, and in 1740 cast iron rails took the place of the iron strips. Soon a connected series of small wagons took the place of one large wagon, and flanges on the wheels took the place of flanges on the rails. In 1802 a patent was taken out for a steam carriage which drew the wagons about five miles an hour. This crude form of locomotion was improved by Stephenson, and about 1821 passengers were carried, for the first time, in railroad coaches.

SCENE IN THE ROCKIES.—EMERGING FROM A SNOW SHED.

The first railroad in the United States was at Quincy, Massachusetts. It was run by horse power and was used to transport granite from the quarries. It was not till 1829 that the first locomotive was introduced into America, and that was built in England. The Baltimore and Ohio railroad was begun in 1828, and the road from Albany to Schenectady in 1831. The cars and locomotives, as compared with those of the present day, were of crude and simple construction. (*See cut on page 72.*) For some time it seemed a question whether railroads or canals were to be the great modes of travel and transportation for the country. As late as 1827 a leading professor of Yale college, in a lecture to his classes, took the ground that railroads were so expensive, and if built, would be so unreliable, and if attempting any great speed, would be so dangerous, that the great reliance of the country for transportation and travel would probably be by canals. And Chancellor Livingston is reported as having said that for building railroads a solid foundation of stone would have to be laid, strong stone walls built on each side of the track, and that to say nothing of the expense of building the roads, they probably could not go more than four or five miles an hour, and that canals would be our chief reliance for traveling and for the transportation of goods and produce.

The improvements in railroads, cars, and locomotives steadily went on, till now the United States has more well appointed railroads than any other country, their mileage being more than half of that of the world. The railroads already built have cost over $10,000,000,000, and employ more than 1,000,000 men; and trains have run from New York to Chicago at the rate of about a mile a minute.

The railroads of the country carried the last year 520,439,082 passengers and 701,344,437 tons of freight. The elevated railway of New York carries some 525,000 passengers a day, or 191,625,000 a year. The Hoosac tunnel, between four and five miles long, and the tunnel between Canada and Michigan, at the outlet of Lake Huron, are among the wonders of modern engineering. The railroad bridge at Poughkeepsie has a single span of 548 feet, and the highest railroad viaduct in the United States is on the Erie railroad and is 305 feet high. The fatal accidents in railway travel are said to average but one in ten million passengers. And a train has gone from New York to San Francisco in less than four days.

Patents.—The first statute organizing the Patent office was passed by Congress in 1790, and the first patent issued by the United States was granted to Samuel Hopkins, for making pot and pearl ashes, about a hundred years ago. Up to 1830 the business of the office was so limited that it was conducted by a single clerk. In that year four clerks, one to act as examiner, and one as draughtsman, one as machinist, and one as messenger were appointed, and a library was commenced. From this small beginning has grown the present immense establishment occupying a building 453 feet long, 331 feet wide and 75 feet high. The model halls in the upper story are 1350 feet in length and contain over 350,000 models. In the ten years ending in 1850, 5,941 patents were issued; from 1850 to 1860, 21,428; from 1860 to 1870, 77,315; from 1870 to 1880, 140,375; in 1889, 23,360; and up to 1890, in all, 433,432 have been granted. The ratio of the increase of patents is far greater than that of the population, and the receipts of the office for fees, etc., are nearly $1,500,000 a year. The average weekly issue of patents at the present time is about 450.

Pins.— Pins are small things, but used as they are by millions, the wonderful improvement in their manufacture, and their cheapness as now made, may well be mentioned as marking the progress of mechanical invention in modern times. As a requisite of the toilet, pins were first used in England in the latter part of the 15th century, and in 1540 brass pins were imported from France for the use of the queen of Henry VIII. For a long time they were made by hand and were very expensive, as there were fourteen processes gone through in making a pin, requiring one man for each process. The expression "pin money" came from the fact that an old English tax was assessed on the people to meet the great expense of supplying the queen with pins, and when at a later date pins became cheaper, so much of the money given by the husband to his wife for personal expenses was required to pay for pins that for a long time the sum continued to be called "pin money." It was not till 1824 that a machine for making pins was invented by Mr. Wright, an American, and since improvements have been made on his invention, the fourteen old hand processes are now all performed by machines which though simple in principle, are wonderful in their details and in the work they accomplish. The entire process of cutting and straightening the wire, making the head and point, polishing and whitening the pin, creasing the paper and making in it holes for the pins, and then putting each pin in the hole in the paper prepared for it, all this is now done by machinery, and pins, which once were so few and so expensive, are now made and sent to market by car loads, and at the most moderate prices.

Watches and Clocks.— The earliest measure of time seems to have been by the shadow of an upright pole, which of course varied in its length and position; then by crude sun dials; then by the dropping of water from one vessel to another; then by the hour glass, in which sand took the place of water, or, as with King Alfred, by the gradual shortening of lighted candles; and the earliest notice of anything like a clock was in 1379: one of a very crude kind was made by a German for the palace of Charles V, king of France. The portable timekeeper or watch, was first made with a pendulum, and was about the size of a dessert plate, sometimes round like the plate, and sometimes oblong in shape. It was first called the "pocket clock," but in 1552 was named a "watch." One made for Edward VI. was of iron gilded, and had plummets of lead working like the weights of a clock. A plain watch then cost over $1500, and it took a year to make one. Now we have clocks of every kind and price. One factory in New England makes over eighty thousand in a year; while a single watch factory at Waltham, Massachusetts, employs some two thousand five hundred workmen, and makes about fifteen thousand watches a year. An ordinary watch has about a hundred and fifty pieces or parts in its construction, and a stem-winder has about one hundred and eighty-five parts. It is estimated that the number of watches made in the United States and imported here from foreign countries, is at least one hundred and fifty thousand every year. So great, for a long time, was the cost of a clock or watch that only persons of great wealth could afford either. Now, for a dollar, any family may have a clock, and any laborer with the wages of a few days may purchase a watch.

The Gauge Lathe.— The art of shaping wood, metal, ivory or other hard substances into various forms by the turning lathe, has long been known, and in modern times has been applied to the most delicate articles of luxury and ornament, as well as to the most ponderous machinery; from the beautiful and fine tracing on the watch case to

THE HUNTER'S RETREAT.

the huge cylinder for the steam engine. Formerly the wooden stock of the musket or shot-gun was slowly carved by hand, but by the gauge lathe, one end of which moves on an iron model and the other on the block of wood, the latter is rapidly and perfectly turned to the desired shape, to the great saving of time and expense. This use of the gauge lathe, which is said to have been first made by Whitney, the inventor of the cotton gin, is but one of the many important applications of the turning lathe for the saving of labor and rapidly and accurately completing work. By late improvements in the application of the principle, spools for the winding of thread are now said to be perfectly made at the rate of one every second of time for each set of the knives used.

Wearing Apparel.-- In the last, and in the early part of the present century, such things as ready-made hats, shoes and clothing, were comparatively unknown. The head was measured for the size of the hat, the foot for the size and shape of the shoe; and for clothing, as a common thing, the flax was raised, spun, and woven, or the sheep were purchased, and at the proper time sheared, and the wool cleansed, spun and woven into clothing for the family.

For shoemaking, for example, nothing that could be called machinery was in use, and ready-made shoes as an article of trade, were almost unknown. Every village had its shoemaker who measured the foot, prepared a wooden last of the proper size and shape, furnished the leather, made his own wax and paste, sawed and split blocks of wood for shoe pegs, which he sharpened with his knife before using, made his own blacking, and did everything for the completion of the shoe except the binding, which was commonly done by women at home. Where the population was scattered and the dwellings isolated the shoes for the family were usually made in the house, the shoemaker going with his lap board, awls, hammer, thread, etc., from house to house, and staying with each family till his work was done. Now, as is well known, shoemaking is largely done by machinery, and one factory in one of our large cities, employing about six hundred men, turns out three thousand pairs of shoes a day. As showing how rapidly such machines work, at a late public exhibition the foot of a lady was measured and a pair of shoes made for her in thirty-two minutes, while she waited for them.

Tailors, or clothes-makers, in the same way, often went from house to house in villages, or in the country took the measure of each person, and remained with the family till the work was done. And the fact has been published that about 1740 a minister in Rhode Island sent the measure of his head to a hat maker in Massachusetts, by whom, in the course of a few weeks, the hat was duly made and sent on to the one who had ordered it. The well-known and immense establishments for ready-made clothing, for the sale of hats and shoes of every kind, shape and price, show most remarkably the changes that in this respect have taken place, and the progress of the country.

There are many other inventions and improvements, in addition to those above mentioned, which show the progress of the country, and are well worthy of

notice. Among them are the air brake and vestibule cars for railroads; the street cars; the grain elevator; elevators for stores and dwellings; the electro-magnet; the pointed screw; steel nails; the steam fire engine; paper from wood pulp; the manufacture of artificial ice; the construction of tunnels through miles of earth and rock, as under the Hoosac mountains, or under broad rivers, as at Port Huron; natural gas, brought by pipes from great distances, for manufacturing purposes or heating of dwellings; and the increase and extension of postal facilities, till now we have in the country some 63,000 post offices receiving on an average 8,000 pieces of mail matter every minute, distributing some 8,000,000,000 pieces by postal cars every year, and in cities delivering letters and papers daily, and in some cases several times in the day. All such advances in invention and improvement mark the progress of the country, and largely contribute to the prosperity and comfort of the people.

FORT SCENES, MACKINAC.

The general history of our country is, of course, the history of its growth, and the account of its various inventions and improvements which economize labor, increase production and add to the comforts of life and the increase of wealth, makes plain the nature and extent of our prosperity and progress. Tables of statistics on almost every subject might be added to what has already been presented, and such tables would show the steady progress of the country from the earliest dates to the present time. The census returns for 1890 have not as yet been fully published. But the contrasts of 1870 and 1880 may show the advance of the country in some important particulars, and give some idea of what the advance, in all probability, has been from 1880 to 1890. The agriculture of a country and its products are so closely connected with its prosperity in other departments of growth, that most of the statistics which follow have reference to them,—and they are, to a great extent, an index of prosperity in other things.

	1870.	1880.
Number of farms in the United States....	2,659,985	4,002,907
Acres in farms.........	407,735,041	536,081,835
Value of farms.	$8,202,803,861	$10,197,096,776
Value of farming implements............................	$336,878,429	$406,520,055
Barley, bushels.....	29,761,305	43,997,495
Buckwheat, "	9,821,721	11,817,327
Indian corn, "	760,944,549	1,754,591,676
Oats, "	282,107,157	407,858,999
Rye, "	16,918,795	19,831,595
Wheat, "	287,745,626	459,483,137
Potatoes, "	143,337,473	169,458,539
Cotton, bales	3,071,966	5,755,359
Hay, tons	27,316,048	35,205,712
Wool, lbs....	100,102,387	153,681,751
Hops, "	25,456,660	26,546,378
Rice, "	73,635,021	110,131,373
Tobacco, "	262,735,341	472,661,157
Horses, ...	7,145,370	10,357,488
Milch cows, ...	8,935,332	12,443,120
Other cattle, ...	13,566,005	22,488,550
Sheep, ...	28,477,951	35,102,074
Swine, ...	25,134,559	47,681,700
Number of manufactories................................	252,148	263,852
Capital invested in them................................	$2,118,306,769	$2,790,272,606
Value of products......................................	$4,282,325,412	$5,369,579,191

	1870.	1880.	1890.
Iron mined, tons........................	4,500,000	9,500,000	13,400,000
Coal mined, tons........................	33,000,000	55,000,000	81,000,000

MONEY IN CIRCULATION.

1860..	$ 435,408,252
1870..	675,212,794
1880..	973,382,228
1890..	1,429,251,270

The whole cereal crop of the United States for 1891, is placed by the government crop report at 3,465,000,000 bushels, as against 2,515,000,000 for 1890.

CHAPTER VII.

NATIONAL AND OTHER PARKS.

THERE are other matters connected with the story of our country, some of which have been briefly mentioned in connection with the different States, but which have so much of national interest as to call for a somewhat fuller notice.

We have, for example, sixty-seven national or public cemeteries, in which are the remains of thousands of soldiers who perished in the late Civil War, giving their lives for the preservation of the Union. These cemeteries are located in twenty-two different States, and are under the care of superintendents appointed by the government. In that at Arlington, which is two hundred acres in extent and occupies part of the estate once owned by General Robert E. Lee, lie the bodies of more than eighteen thousand of these soldiers, the names of some twelve thousand of whom are on their monuments, while between six and seven thousand more, gathered from various battlefields after the

ROBINSON'S FOLLY, MACKINAC ISLAND.

war was over, but not identified, are also buried there. And in various parts of the South are similar burial places, where rest the remains of thousands of brave soldiers of the Confederacy, who, under leaders like Jackson and Lee, were so often successful in conflict, and whose valor was fully acknowledged by those against whom they fought.

Visitors at places like Andersonville, Gettysburg, Mackinac, Alexandria, Yorktown,

and other public cemeteries, both North and South, are often seen among these silent dwellings of the honored dead, looking for the monuments and names of those once so near as well as dear, but now no more to be seen on earth.

One of the most interesting of the cemeteries alluded to, especially in its associations, is that of Mackinac, for though comparatively small, it is on the beautiful island which is famous for its history, for its Indian traditions and conflicts, as the stronghold of Pontiac, for its connection with the early fur traders of the great Northwest, and for its pure atmosphere and splendid scenery, which make it one of the most delightful and attractive pleasure resorts in the country.

Another interesting feature of our country is seen in the large and elegant parks of many of our chief cities, prepared at great expense as resorts for the people, where they may find not only health but recreation and pleasure. New York has its grand Central Park of eight hundred and forty-three acres, with its walks, drives, lakes, statues, and trees and shrubbery gathered from different regions. Baltimore has its Druid Hill, of six hundred and eighty acres of varied surface, magnificent oaks, the growth of many years and walks and drives of exceeding beauty. Philadelphia has its widely extended Fairmount, the largest city park in the world, covering over three thousand acres, and giving in its drives and walks every variety of scenery. And Chicago has its six splendid parks, connected by a broad boulevard, in four of which are over sixteen hundred acres, and in all more than thirty-three miles of drives, with broad avenues of trees, and opening views of the lake.

But the natural parks, as they are called, of the great West, in their extent and the variety of their wonders, surpass the mightiest and proudest works of man, and speak in visible accents of almighty power. For the most part they are extended ranges of comparatively level lands, surrounded by mountains or towering cliffs, with wonderful

SUGAR LOAF ROCK, MACKINAC ISLAND.

scenery—cataracts, waterfalls, mammoth trees and vast geysers sending up huge jets or columns of water to a height of fifty, and in one case, two hundred and fifty feet. Some of these are: the North Park, of Colorado, having an altitude of eight thousand feet above sea level, and containing an area of twenty-five thousand square miles; the

ARCH ROCK, MACKINAC ISLAND.

Middle Park, lying south of the one just mentioned, containing some three thousand square miles, and encircled by majestic mountains, some of whose peaks are from thirteen thousand to fourteen thousand feet high; South Park, still further south, two thousand square miles in extent, and nine thousand feet above the level of the sea, surrounded by lofty mountain ranges; San Luis Park, south of that last mentioned, and also in Colorado, having an area of eighteen thousand square miles, a beautiful lake, and numerous hot or warm springs; Monument Park, eight miles from Colorado Springs, with its lofty sandstone columns, some of them fifty feet high; and the Garden of the Gods, four miles from the Springs, some fifty acres in extent, surrounded, like the others, by mountains, ravines and cliffs, with large upright rocks, some of which are three hundred and fifty feet high.

YOSEMITE VALLEY.

Of these vast natural parks, two, the Yosemite Valley and the Yellowstone region, have been reserved from sale or settlement under the laws of the United States, and made *National Parks* by acts of Congress, the former in 1864, and the latter in 1872. They are forever set apart as places of public resort and recreation, and great improvements have been made, and still greater are in progress to make them attractive to tourists and to all who would see some of the wildest, grandest and most beautiful

GRAND CAÑON, COLORADO RIVER.

scenes which can anywhere be found. The Yosemite Valley was granted, conditionally, to the State of California. It is in Mariposa county, about one hundred and fifty-five miles from San Francisco, and not far from the center of the State. It is nearly level, and what is included in the park is about six miles long, and from half a mile to a mile in width, and though about four thousand feet above the level of the sea, its perpendicular depth below the surrounding level is about a mile. Its walls are nearly vertical, and the Merced river flows through it at almost right angles to the mountain ranges. It is accessible in summer by stage and saddle-horse, but in winter only by snow-shoes. One of its objects of interest is the Bridal Veil Fall, where the water of the creek makes a precipitous descent of six hundred and thirty feet to a slope below, and then descends by a series of cascades to the valley, the entire fall being over nine hundred feet. Another is Cathedral Rock, a massive granite formation, two thousand six hundred and sixty feet high; and near it the Spire, a single column of granite five hundred feet high and tapering toward the top; and then Sentinel Rock, towering three thousand and forty-three feet in the air, and terminating in a slender obelisk one thousand feet high. Sentinel Dome, and the Virgin's Tears Falls, are the next striking features, the latter a cataract descending one

thousand feet. El Capitan and the Three Brothers are monster masses of rock, and above the latter is the great Yosemite Fall, having first a vertical descent of fifteen hundred feet, and then cascades of six hundred, and fifty, and a final fall of four hundred feet. These, with other and smaller falls, form a combination of the sublime and beautiful nowhere else to be found.

About sixteen miles south of the valley are the Mariposa and other groves of the mammoth trees, the *Sequoia Gigantea*, found only in California, and also the *Sequoia Semper Virens*, or red wood. Three of these groves are in Mariposa county, and have one hundred and thirty-four trees, each of which is more than fifteen feet in diameter, and some three hundred of smaller size. In the different groups are trees from two hundred and seventy-five to three hundred and seventy-five feet in height, and from twenty-five to thirty-five feet in diameter; and some have been cut down, which, judging from the rings in the wood, are thought to have been growing for from two thousand to two thousand five hundred years.

STEEPLE ROCKS, YELLOWSTONE.

THE GROTTO.

But the great National Park is the Yellowstone, the wonders of which were first discovered in 1871 by the United States engineers. It is in Montana and Wyoming, and its area is three thousand five hundred and seventy-eight square miles. Its general elevation above the sea is about six thousand feet, with mountain ranges about it rising to the height of from ten to twelve thousand feet. And the region approaching, as well as within and about it, is probably the most sublime and impressive in the world. The region is volcanic in character, and picturesque masses of rock, tall columns of basalt, the warm and hot springs, the wonderful geysers, and the mud volcanoes are all objects of ceaseless wonder and interest. The entrance to the great cañon is so gloomy and

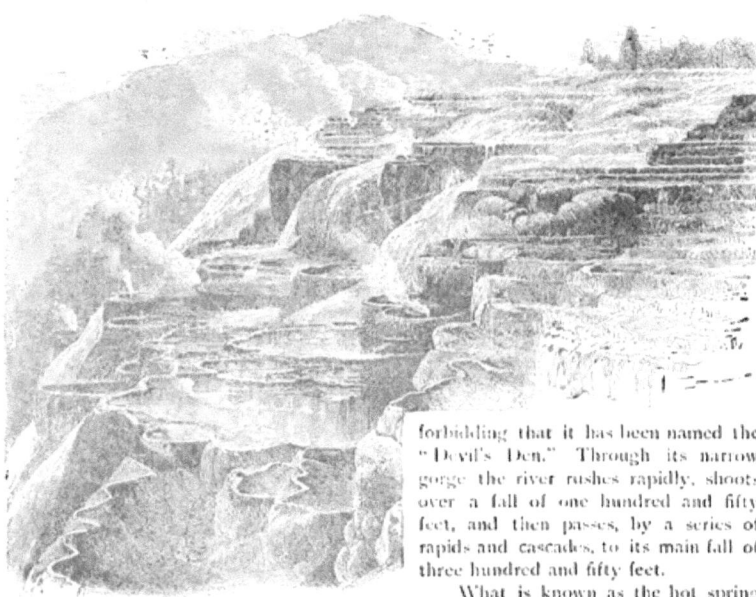

BOILING SPRINGS, YELLOWSTONE PARK.

forbidding that it has been named the "Devil's Den." Through its narrow gorge the river rushes rapidly, shoots over a fall of one hundred and fifty feet, and then passes, by a series of rapids and cascades, to its main fall of three hundred and fifty feet.

What is known as the hot spring region is remarkable for its mud geysers, and particularly for a "mud volcano," the crater of which is twenty-five feet wide and thirty feet deep, and which is constantly sending up its bubbling stream. One of the geysers of the region has a basin sixty feet in diameter and spouts at intervals of six hours. About eight miles from here is the beautiful Yellowstone lake, twenty-two miles long, from ten to fifteen miles wide, and three hundred feet deep. Further on, in the Fire-hole basin, is a system of hot springs having the appearance of vast lime-kilns in active operation and movement. But the chief wonder is the great geyser basin, which is entered from the north, following the course of the Madison river, on the sides of which are two geysers in active operation, known as the Sentinels. Beyond these are the Well geyser, which has a crater like a well, and spouts eighty or ninety feet, and the Castle geyser, on a platform of its own deposit, one hundred feet by seventy. At the head of the valley is Old Faithful, playing regularly every three-quarters of an hour, and throwing a stream of from one hundred to one hundred and fifty feet high. Then there are the Giant, the Giantess, the Beehive, the Grand, the Fan, the Saw Mill, the Turban, the Riverside, and several others, each wonderful in its way, and all showing volcanic power at work beneath. No other locality contains so many attractions both of climate and scenery, and no other, probably, has so many singular and wonderful formations and sights. The number of springs, large and small and of various kinds, is from 5,000 to 10,000, of which at least fifty are geysers. Perhaps we can give a better description of this wonderful region by quoting from the report of Dr. Hayden, who explored it as government surveyor:

"These springs cover an area of four square miles, but those in active operation are to be found within an area of about one square mile. The margins of the basins are beautifully

BOILING SULPHUR SPRINGS, YELLOWSTONE PARK.

scalloped, and formations of exquisite beauty are encrusted on them. The wonderful variety of these deposits excites the admiration of all visitors. But it is to the wonderful variety of exquisitely delicate colors that this picture owes the main part of its attractiveness. The little orifices from which the hot water issues are beautifully enameled with a porcelain-like lining, and around the edges a layer of sulphur is precipitated. As the water flows along the valley, it lays down in its course a pavement more beautiful and elaborate in its adornment than art has ever yet conceived. The sulphur and the iron, with the green microscopic vegetation, tint the whole with an illumination of which no decoration-painter has ever dreamed. From the sides of the oblong mound, which is here from thirty to fifty feet high, the water has oozed out at different points, forming small groups of the semicircular, step-like basins.

"If we look at the principal group of springs from the high mound above the middle terrace, we can see the same variety of brilliant coloring. The wonderful transparency of the water surpasses anything of the kind to be seen in any other

GREAT FALLS OF THE YELLOWSTONE RIVER.

portion of the world. The sky, with the smallest cloud that flits across it, is reflected in its clear depths, and, the ultramarine colors, more vivid than the sea, are greatly heightened by the constant gentle vibrations. One can look down into the clear depths and see, with perfect distinctness, the minutest ornament on the inner sides of the basin; and the exquisite beauty of the coloring, while the variety of forms baffles any attempt to portray them, either with pen or pencil. And then, too, around the borders of these springs, especially those of rather low temperature, and on the sides and bottoms of the numerous little channels of the streams that flow from these springs, there is a striking variety of the most vivid colors. One can only compare them to the most brilliant aniline dyes—various shades of red, from the brightest scarlet to a bright rose tint; also yellow, from deep-bright sulphur, through all the shades, to light cream-color. There are also various shades of green, from the peculiar vegetation. These springs are also filled with minute vegetable forms. There are also in the little streams that flow from the boiling springs great quantities of a fibrous, silky substance, apparently vegetable, which vibrates at the slightest movement of the water, and has the appearance of the finest quality of

OLD FAITHFUL GEYSER.

cashmere wool. When the waters are still these silken masses become incrusted with lime, the delicate vegetable threads disappear, and a fibrous, spongy mass remains, like delicate snow-white coral.

"Between Mount Washburn and the Upper Falls there are some seven or eight boiling springs of great size, which emit large quantities of sulphurous vapor. They look like nothing earthly one has ever seen, and the pungent fumes which fill the atmosphere are not unaccompanied by a disagreeable sense of possible suffocation. Entering the basin cautiously, one finds the entire surface of the earth covered with the incrusted sinter thrown from the springs. Jets of hot vapor are expelled through a hundred natural orifices with which it is pierced, and through every fracture made by passing over it. The springs themselves seem as diabolical in appearance as the witches' caldron in Macbeth, and need but the presence of Hecate and her weird band to realize that horrible creation of poetic fancy. They were all in a state of violent ebullition, throwing their liquid contents to the height of three or four feet. The largest has a basin twenty by forty feet in diameter. Its greenish-yellow water is covered with bubbles, which are constantly rising, bursting, and emitting sulphurous gas from various parts of its surface. The central spring seethes and bubbles like a boiling caldron. Fearful volumes of vapor are constantly escaping it. Near it is another, not so large, but more infernal in appearance. Its contents, of the consistency of paint, are in constant, noisy ebullition. A stick thrust into it, on being withdrawn, is coated with a lead-colored slime a quarter of an inch in thickness. Nothing flows from this spring. Seemingly, it is boiling down. A fourth spring, which exhibits the same physical features, is partly covered by an overhanging ledge of rock. We tried to fathom it, but the bottom was beyond the reach of the longest pole we could find. Rocks cast into it increase the agitation of its waters. There are several other springs in the group, smaller in size, but presenting the same characteristics.

"Between the Upper and Lower Falls and Yellowstone lake, which is the central gem of that wonderful collection of long-hidden treasures, lies a marvelous region, filled with boiling springs and craters, with two hills, three hundred feet high, formed wholly of the sinter thrown from the adjacent springs; and at the base of one of them is a cavern whose mouth is seven feet in diameter, from which a dense jet of sulphurous vapor explodes with a regular report like a high-pressure engine. A few yards off is a boiling spring, seventy feet long by forty wide, the water of which is in unceasing agitation; and in another direction is a boiling alum spring, surrounded by beautiful crystals. No wonder that the first beholders of these things called the various points by names of infernal significance. There are now no true geysers in this group, but in ancient times there were very powerful ones. The steam-vents on the side, and at the foot of these hills, represent the dying stages of this once most active group.

"But the real geyser region is just over the margin of the Yellowstone Basin, on the Firehole river. The valley in which these wonderful phenomena are located is about twelve miles in length with an average width of three miles. It is said that there are more of these natural wonders in this small area than can be found in the rest of the world.

"The Firehole river flows from Madison lake, one of the most beautiful of the many lovely sheets of water in the mountains, and the volume of its waters is increased by the accession of mountain torrents, until just before reaching the geyser-basin, it falls over two cliffs, one twenty, and the other fifty feet in height. These pretty falls, if located in an Eastern stream, would be

LIME TOWER NEAR HOT SPRINGS.

celebrated in history and song; here amid objects so grand as to stagger belief, they were passed without a halt."

The boiling springs, all in active eruption, with craters from three to forty feet high, are scattered along the banks of the Firehole river. A description of one of the geysers will answer for all, though they differ in dimensions. "The great beauty of the prismatic colors," writes Dr. Hayden, "depends much on the sunlight; about the middle of the day, when the bright rays descend nearly vertically, and a slight breeze just makes a ripple on the surface, the colors exceed comparison; when the surface is calm there is one vast chaos of colors, dancing, as it were, like the colors of a kaleidoscope. As seen through this marvelous play of colors, the decorations on the sides of the basin are lighted up with a wild, weird beauty, which wafts one at once into

THE YELLOWSTONE.

the land of enchantment, all the brilliant feats of fairies and genii in the Arabian Nights' Entertainment are forgotten in the actual presence of such marvellous beauty; life becomes a privilege and a blessing after one has seen and thoroughly felt its cunning skill."

"Castle Geyser" is the most imposing formation in the valley, and receives its name from its resemblance to the ruins of an old fortress. The deposited silica has crystallized in immense globular masses, like cauliflowers, or spongiform corals, apparently formed about a nucleus at right angles to the centre. The mound is forty, and the chimney twenty feet high, and the lower portion rises in steps formed of thin laminæ of silica, an inch or two thick. The base of the crater is three hundred

THE GROTTO GEYSER.

and twenty-five feet in circumference, and that of the turret one hundred and twenty-five. At the base of the turret lies a large petrified pine-log, covered with a brilliant incrustation several inches thick."

"The Giant Geyser," writes Lieutenant Doane, "played several times while we were in the valley, on one occasion throwing constantly for over three hours, a stream of water seven feet in diameter, from ninety to two hundred feet perpendicularly, while it doubled the size of the Firehole river."

Near the Giant is the Grotto, so called from its curious formation, which plays a volume of water six feet in diameter to a height of sixty feet. Both these National Parks are constantly and more and more visited by tourists from our own and foreign countries, offering as they do, attractions of various kinds that are unsurpassed in any part of the world.

It was a wise foresight in our government when Congress passed an act, forever preserving these parks in their natural grandeur, that those of coming generations as well as the present may have the opportunity of personally viewing what it is impossible fully to describe.

LOWER FALLS, YELLOWSTONE PARK.

AREA OF THE UNITED STATES IN 1783, AND TERRITORY
SINCE ACQUIRED.

	SQ. MILES
Area of the United States in 1783,	827,844
Louisiana Purchase, 1803, with the portion of Oregon Territory retained in 1846,	1,171,931
Florida Purchase, 1819,	59,268
Texan Annexation, 1845,	375,239
Mexican Cessions, 1848–53,	591,318
Alaska, 1868,	577,390
United States since 1867,	3,602,990

GREAT HISTORICAL PAPERS.

TO KNOW thoroughly the history of a country is to be familiar, not merely with the ordinary events of its annals, but to be also acquainted with its great political changes and their causes. Those that mark the great eras of our country are, of course, mentioned in the preceding pages which speak of them at the times of their occurrence. They cannot, however, be fully understood, but by the important State papers which explain their origin and causes, and mark the steps of their progress to final results. The importance of such papers as an essential part of our history is too often overlooked. Instead of being prominently presented as they ought to be, they are too often printed in small type and labeled " Appendix," as though of comparatively little consequence, and so are too often unknown. How few, even of the intelligent readers of our history, are familiar with " Franklin's plan" for the union of the colonies, with the old " Articles of Confederation," with the " Declaration of Independence," and with the present " Constitution of the United States" and its various amendments! All these important papers should be familiar to our people that they may know the progress of our republican institutions and the fundamental principles of our National life. In a Republic like ours every citizen is a law-maker, and as such he should know not only the laws, but the great fundamental principles on which they rest. And that they may be known they are here given, in full, together with Washington's " Farewell Address," and Lincoln's " Emancipation Proclamation," all of which are essential parts of our history.

FRANKLIN'S PLAN OF UNION.

The compact of the Mayflower, made before the pilgrim fathers left their little vessel, may be seen on page 41. While the settlements were small, such brief agreements well expressed the union and aim of those who, as to their plans and government, were substantially of one mind. But as colonies were multiplied, in different parts of the country, and as their populations increased, different and conflicting views arose and each colony looked chiefly to its own local interests. The New England merchant had little sympathy with the Southern planter, and the adjacent colonies too often disputed about boundaries, and were filled with commercial jealousies. So numerous and decided were these opposing interests that Jeremiah Dummer, in his noted "Defense of the New Charters," said it was impossible for the different colonies ever to unite; and another prominent writer thought that if the oppressive "hand of Great Britain were once taken off, there would be chronic civil war all the way from Maine to Georgia."

This state of things was the cause of no little anxiety to the most thoughtful leaders of the colonies. And in 1754, in the prospect of war with the French, a Congress of the colonies was called to meet at Albany to prepare for the expected conflict, and also to form some plan of confederation which all the colonies might adopt. Franklin, who had broad views and a clear foresight of the future growth and greatness of the country, was earnestly anxious to bring about a permanent union of the colonies, and at the head of his paper, the *Pennsylvania Gazette*, he placed a union device, with the motto, "Unite or Die." And a plan was prepared, chiefly by him, known afterward as the "Albany Plan," though it might better have been entitled "Franklin's Plan," which was much more complete than the Confederate scheme of 1777, and in some of its main features greatly resembled the Federal Constitution of 1787, under which, with its amendments, our government is now administered.

His plan was that the Legislature of each colony should, once in three years, choose representatives to a Grand Federal Council which should make treaties and regulate trade with the Indians, legislate on all matters concerning the colonies as a whole, levy taxes, enlist soldiers, build forts, and nominate civil officers, all laws passed by it to be subject to approval or veto by the king within three years. No colony was to send more than seven or less than two representatives, and except matters which were to be controlled by the Federal Council, each colony was to retain all other powers. The supreme executive power was to be vested in a president or governor-general, to be appointed and paid by the crown, who was to nominate all military officers subject to the approval of the Grand Council, and to have a veto on its acts, and no money was to be issued but by the joint order of the Executive and the Council.

This plan, it will be seen, was that of a Federal Government, and not a mere compact or league. It was designed to confer on the representatives of the people the power of making laws acting directly on individuals, and appointing officers to execute them, and yet not to interfere with the execution of the laws operating on the same individual by the laws of States. It contemplated the two great and important ideas, on the one hand, of a central Federal Government, and on the other, of colonial or State rights, each supreme in its own sphere. "It was," says Fiske, "in its main features, a noble scheme, and the great statesman who devised it was already looking forward to the immense growth of the American Union, though he had not yet foreseen the separation of the colonies from the mother country." "In less than a century," he said, "the great country beyond the Alleghanies must become a populous and powerful dominion," and he recommended that two new colonies should at once be founded in the West, one on Lake Erie, and the other in the valley of the Ohio, with free chartered governments, like those of Rhode Island and Connecticut.

THE DECLARATION OF INDEPENDENCE.

Two years before the adoption of the plan of the Confederation by the last of the States, the *Declaration of Independence*, prepared mainly by Jefferson, had been adopted by the "Representatives of the United States in Congress assembled, July 4, 1776." It declared the separation of the colonies from the mother country, and gave in clear and vivid language the reasons of the separation. It is a document of which many speak, but with the details of which, it is feared, comparatively few are familiar. But as showing the great principles and noble courage of the founders of our Union, and the reasons why we are no longer dependent colonies, but an independent *nation*, it ought to be known in every family and by every one who is a citizen of the land where, in the language of Lincoln, "there is a new birth of freedom, and the government of the people, by the people, and for the people," it is hoped, may never "perish from the earth."

THE DECLARATION.

When in the course of human events, it becomes necessary for one people to dissolve the political bands which have connected them with another, and to assume, among the powers of the earth, the separate and equal station to which the laws of nature and of nature's God entitle them, a decent respect to the opinions of mankind requires that they should declare the causes which impel them to a separation.

We hold these truths to be self-evident, that all men are created equal; that they are endowed by their Creator with certain unalienable rights; that among these are life, liberty, and the pursuit of happiness; that, to secure these rights, governments are instituted among men, deriving their just powers from the consent of the governed; that, whenever any form of government becomes destructive to these ends, it is the right of the people to alter or to abolish it, and to institute a new government, laying its foundation on such principles, and organizing its powers in such form, as to them shall seem most likely to effect their safety and happiness. Prudence, indeed, will dictate that governments long established, should not be changed for light and transient causes; and, accordingly, all experience hath shown, that mankind are more disposed to suffer, while evils are sufferable, than to right themselves by abolishing the forms to which they are accustomed. But, when a long train of abuses and usurpations, pursuing invariably the same object, evinces a design to reduce them under absolute despotism, it is their right, it is their duty, to throw off such government, and to provide new guards for their future security. Such has been the patient sufferance of these colonies, and such is now the necessity which constrains them to alter their former systems of government. The history of the present king of Great Britain is a history of repeated injuries and usurpations, all having, in direct object, the establishment of an absolute tyranny over these States. To prove this, let facts be submitted to a candid world:

He has refused to assent to laws the most wholesome and necessary for the public good.

He has forbidden his governors to pass laws of immediate and pressing importance, unless suspended in their operation till his assent should be obtained; and, when so suspended, he has utterly neglected to attend to them.

He has refused to pass other laws for the accommodation of large districts of people, unless those people would relinquish the right of representation in the Legislature; a right inestimable to them, and formidable to tyrants only.

He has called together legislative bodies at places unusual, uncomfortable, and distant from the depository of their public records, for the sole purpose of fatiguing them into compliance with his measures.

He has dissolved representative houses repeatedly, for opposing, with manly firmness, his invasions on the rights of the people.

He has refused, for a long time after such dissolutions, to cause others to be elected; whereby the legislative powers, incapable of annihilation, have returned to the people at large for their exercise; the State remaining, in the meantime, exposed to all the danger of invasion from without, and convulsions within.

He has endeavored to prevent the population of these States; for that purpose, obstructing the laws for naturalization of foreigners; refusing to pass others to encourage their migration hither, and raising the conditions of new appropriations of lands.

He has obstructed the administration of justice, by refusing his assent to laws for establishing judiciary powers.

He has made judges depend on his will alone for the tenure of their offices, and the amount and payment of their salaries.

He has erected a multitude of new offices, and sent hither swarms of officers to harass our people, and eat out their substance.

He has kept among us, in times of peace, standing armies, without the consent of our legislatures.

He has affected to render the military independent of, and superior to, the civil power.

He has combined, with others, to subject us to a jurisdiction foreign to our Constitution, and unacknowledged by our laws; giving his assent to their acts of pretended legislation.

For quartering large bodies of armed troops among us.

For protecting them by a mock trial, from punishment, for any murders which they should commit on the inhabitants of these States.

For cutting off our trade with all parts of the world.

For imposing taxes on us without our consent.

For depriving us, in many cases, of the benefits of trial by jury.

For transporting us beyond the seas to be tried for pretended offenses.

For abolishing the free system of English laws in a neighboring province, establishing therein an arbitrary government, and enlarging its boundaries, so as to render it at once an example and fit instrument for introducing the same absolute rule into these colonies.

For taking away our charters, abolishing our most valuable laws, and altering, fundamentally, the powers of our governments.

For suspending our own legislatures, and declaring themselves invested with power to legislate for us in all cases whatsoever.

He has abdicated government here, by declaring us out of his protection, and waging war against us.

He has plundered our seas, ravaged our coasts, burnt our towns, and destroyed the lives of our people.

He is, at this time, transporting large armies of foreign mercenaries to complete the works of death, desolation, and tyranny already begun, with circumstances of cruelty and perfidy scarcely paralleled in the most barbarous ages, and totally unworthy the head of a civilized nation.

He has constrained our fellow-citizens, taken captive on the high seas, to bear arms against their country, to become the executioners of their friends and brethren, or to fall themselves by their hands.

He has excited domestic insurrections among us, and has endeavored to bring on the inhabitants of our frontiers the merciless Indian savages, whose known rule of warfare is an undistinguished destruction of all ages, sexes, and conditions.

In every stage of these oppressions we have petitioned for redress in the most humble terms; our repeated petitions have been answered only by repeated injury. A prince, whose character is thus marked by every act which may define a tyrant, is unfit to be the ruler of a free people.

Nor have we been wanting in attention to our British brethren. We have warned them, from time to time, of attempts made by their legislature to extend an unwarrantable jurisdiction over us. We have reminded them of the circumstances of our emigration and settlement here. We have appealed to their native justice and magnanimity, and we have conjured them, by the ties of our common kindred, to disavow these usurpations, which would inevitably interrupt our connections and correspondence. They, too, have been deaf to the voice of justice and consanguinity. We must, therefore, acquiesce in the necessity which denounces our separation, and hold them, as we hold the rest of mankind — enemies in war, in peace, friends.

We, therefore, the representatives of the United States of America, in general Congress assembled, appealing to the Supreme Judge of the world for the rectitude of our intentions, do, in the name, and by the authority of the good people of these colonies, solemnly publish and declare, that these United Colonies are, and of right ought to be, free and independent States; that they are absolved from all allegiance to the British crown, and that all political connection between them and the state of Great Britain is, and ought to be, totally dissolved; and that, as free and independent States, they have full power to levy war, conclude peace, contract alliances, establish commerce, and to do all other acts and things which independent States may of right do. And, for the support of this declaration, with a firm reliance on the protection of Divine Providence, we mutually pledge to each other our lives, our fortunes, and our sacred honor.　　　　　　　　*Signed by*

Massachusetts Bay.

JOHN HANCOCK.
SAMUEL ADAMS.
JOHN ADAMS.
ROBERT TREAT PAINE.
ELBRIDGE GERRY.

Rhode Island.

STEPHEN HOPKINS.
WILLIAM ELLERY.

New Hampshire.

JOSIAH BARTLETT.
WILLIAM WHIPPLE.
MATTHEW THORNTON.

Delaware.

CÆSAR RODNEY.
GEORGE READ.
THOMAS M'KEAN.

OUR COUNTRY.

Connecticut.

ROGER SHERMAN.
SAMUEL HUNTINGTON.
WILLIAM WILLIAMS.
OLIVER WOLCOTT.

New York.

WILLIAM FLOYD.
PHILIP LIVINGSTON.
FRANCIS LEWIS.
LEWIS MORRIS.

New Jersey.

RICHARD STOCKTON.
JOHN WITHERSPOON.
FRANCIS HOPKINSON.
JOHN HART.
ABRAHAM CLARK.

Pennsylvania.

ROBERT MORRIS.
BENJAMIN RUSH.
BENJAMIN FRANKLIN.
JOHN MORTON.
GEORGE CLYMER.
JAMES SMITH.
GEORGE TAYLOR.
JAMES WILSON.
GEORGE ROSS.

Maryland.

SAMUEL CHASE.
WILLIAM PACA.
THOMAS STONE.
CHARLES CARROLL, of Carrollton.

Virginia.

GEORGE WYTHE.
RICHARD HENRY LEE.
THOMAS JEFFERSON.
BENJAMIN HARRISON.
THOMAS NELSON, Jr.
FRANCIS LIGHTFOOT LEE.
CARTER BRAXTON.

North Carolina.

WILLIAM HOOPER.
JOSEPH HUGHES.
JOHN PENN.

South Carolina.

EDWARD RUTLEDGE.
THOMAS HEYWARD, Jun.
THOMAS LYNCH, Jun.
ARTHUR MIDDLETON.

Georgia.

BUTTON GWINNET.
LYMAN HALL.
GEORGE WALTON.

THE CONFEDERATION OF 1778.

Comprehensive and excellent as the plan of Franklin now seems to us, it did not meet with favor either on the part of the royal governors or with the people, and though adopted by the Albany assembly, it was nowhere approved by the colonies or in the mother country.

The importance of union, however, was more and more felt, especially after the Declaration of Independence, and in July, 1778, the representatives of eight of the colonies which afterward formed the " United States of America," agreed to the " Articles of confederation and perpetual union between the States of New Hampshire, Massachusetts Bay, Rhode Island and Providence Plantations, New York, New Jersey, Pennsylvania, Delaware, Maryland, Virginia, North Carolina, South Carolina and Georgia."

But it was March, 1781, before Maryland, the last to adopt it, ratified the instrument, and it went into full operation in the thirteen States. In these articles were set forth the great principles of government, which a few years later were embodied in the Constitution of the United States, but the plan was rather that of a compact or agreement than a government — a system of good provisions, but with no authority to enforce or carry them out in practice. It was, in fact, but little more than a name.

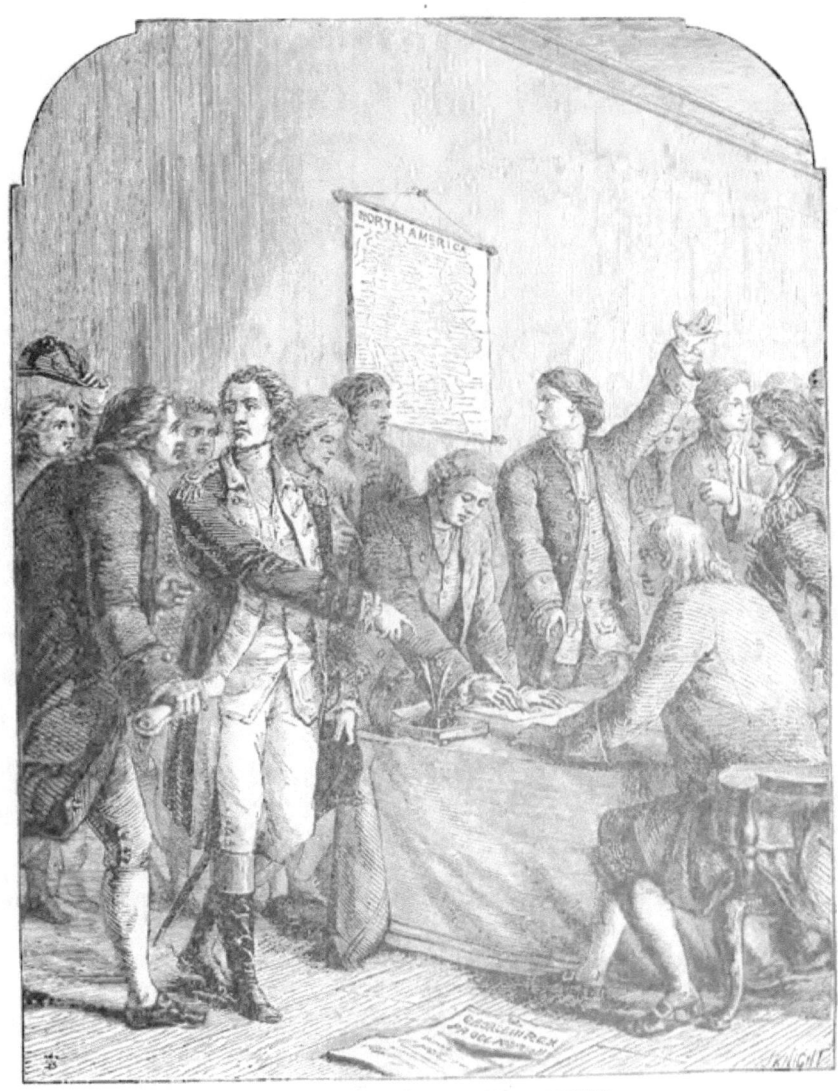

SIGNING THE DECLARATION OF INDEPENDENCE.

Jay, one of the wisest of our public men, said of Congress, which was the seat of its power: "They might declare war, but had no power to raise men or money to carry it on; might make peace, but had no power to see its terms observed; might form alliances, but without the ability to comply with their own stipulations; might enter into treaties of commerce, but without power to enforce them; might borrow money, but without means to repay it; might regulate commerce, but without authority to enforce their ordinances; might appoint ministers and other officers of trust, but without power to try or punish them for misdemeanors; might resolve, but could not execute either with dispatch or secrecy." In a word, he says, "they may consult and deliberate, recommend and make requisitions, and only those who please may regard them." (See page 161.)

This estimate of so wise and thoughtful a man was more and more seen to be correct, and the feeling became general that a new Constitution should be formed which should give to the United States the oneness of a great nation, and instead of leaving everything to Congress, should separate the three great departments of sovereignty — the Legislative, Judicial and Executive, and give to each its appropriate sphere and power. And the result was the formation of the present Federal Constitution, adopted by eleven States in 1788, and going into operation March 4, 1789.

THE CONSTITUTION OF THE UNITED STATES AND ITS AMENDMENTS.

What was said of the Declaration of Independence may justly be said, and in even stronger terms, of the Constitution of our country. How few, even of our intelligent men, whether in business or professional life, are familiar with the details of its provisions and the guarantees it gives for the rights and privileges of the people. Ought it not to be a study in our colleges and higher seminaries of learning, and its principles to be taught in the schools and families of the people if they would be intelligently free? And instead of being overlooked and unknown, ought it not to be regarded as a most important part of the history of our country in connection with which it is here printed, that it may be studied and understood in every family, and by every reader? It is as follows:

THE CONSTITUTION.

PREAMBLE.

We, the people of the United States, in order to form a more perfect union, establish justice, insure domestic tranquility, provide for the common defense, promote the general welfare, and secure the blessings of liberty to ourselves and our posterity, do ordain and establish this Constitution for the United States of North America.

ARTICLE I.

SECTION I.

All legislative powers herein granted shall be vested in a Congress of the United States, which shall consist of a Senate and a House of Representatives.

Legislation vested in Congress.

SECTION II.

1. The House of Representatives shall be composed of members chosen every second year by the people of the several States, and the electors in each State shall have the qualifications requisite for electors of the most numerous branch of the State legislature.

Representatives for two years from States.

2. No person shall be a representative who shall not have attained to the age of twenty-five years and been seven years a citizen of the United States, and who shall not, when elected, be an inhabitant of that State in which he shall be chosen.

Must be citizens not under twenty-five years of age.

3. Representatives and direct taxes shall be apportioned among the several States which may be included within this Union, according to their respective numbers, which shall be determined by adding to the whole number of free persons, including those bound to service for a term of years, and excluding Indians not taxed, three-fifths of all other persons.* The actual enumeration shall be made within three years after the first meeting of the Congress of the United States, and within every subsequent term of ten years, in such manner as they shall by law direct. The number of representatives shall not exceed one for every thirty thousand, but each State shall have at least one representative; and until such enumeration shall be made, the State of New Hampshire shall be entitled to choose three, Massachusetts eight, Rhode Island and Providence Plantations one, Connecticut five, New York six, New Jersey four, Pennsylvania eight, Delaware one, Maryland six, Virginia ten, North Carolina five, South Carolina five, and Georgia three.

Proportioned to population.

4. When vacancies happen in the representation from any State, the executive authority thereof shall issue writs of election to fill such vacancies.

Vacancies, how filled.

5. The House of Representatives shall choose their speaker and other officers; and shall have the sole power of impeachment.

House to choose its officers — and has sole power of impeachment.

SECTION III.

1. The Senate of the United States shall be composed of two senators from each State, chosen by the legislature thereof, for six years; and each senator shall have one vote.

Senate, how organized.

*Altered by Fourteenth Amendment, Section II.

Classes of members, and vacancies.

2. Immediately after they shall be assembled in consequence of the first election, they shall be divided as equally as may be into three classes. The seats of the senators of the first class shall be vacated at the expiration of the second year, of the second class at the expiration of the fourth year, and of the third class at the expiration of the sixth year, so that one-third may be chosen every second year; and if vacancies happen by resignation, or otherwise, during the recess of the legislature of any State, the executive thereof may make temporary appointments until the next meeting of the legislature, which shall then fill such vacancies.

Who senators.

3. No person shall be a senator who shall not have attainted to the age of thirty years and been nine years a citizen of the United States, and who shall not, when elected, be an inhabitant of that State for which he shall be chosen.

Presiding officer of Senate.

4. The vice-president of the United States shall be president of the Senate, but shall have no vote, unless they be equally divided.

Chooses its officers.

5. The Senate shall choose their other officers, and also a president pro tempore, in the absence of the vice-president, or when he shall exercise the office as President of the United States.

Tries all impeachments.

6. The Senate shall have the sole power to try all impeachments. When sitting for that purpose, they shall all be on oath or affirmation. When the president of the United States is tried, the chief-justice shall preside; and no person shall be convicted without the concurrence of two-thirds of the members present.

Effect of conviction.

7. Judgment in cases of impeachment shall not extend further than to removal from office and disqualification to hold and enjoy any office of honor, trust, or profit under the United States; but the party convicted shall nevertheless be liable and subject to indictment, trial, judgment, and punishment, according to law.

SECTION IV.

Elections.

1. The times, places, and manner of holding elections for senators and representatives, shall be perscribed in each State by the legislature thereof; but the Congress may at any time by law make or alter such regulations, except as to the places of choosing senators.

When Congress meets.

2. The Congress shall assemble at least once in every year, and such meeting shall be on the first Monday in December, unless they shall by law appoint a different day.

SECTION V.

Who its members.

1. Each house shall be the judge of the elections, returns, and qualifications of its own members, and a majority of each shall constitute a quorum to do business; but a smaller number may adjourn

from day to day, and may be authorized to compel the attendance of absent members, in such manner and under such penalties as each house may provide.

2. Each house may determine the rules of its proceedings, punish its members for disorderly behavior, and, with the concurrence of two-thirds, expel a member.

Rules of proceeding and behavior.

3. Each house shall keep a journal of its proceedings, and from time to time publish the same, excepting such parts as may in their judgment require secrecy; and the yeas and nays of the members of either house, on any question, shall, at the desire of one-fifth of those present, be entered on the journal.

A journal to be kept.

4. Neither house, during the session of Congress shall, without the consent of the other, adjourn for more than three days, nor to any other place than that in which the two houses shall be sitting.

As to adjournments.

SECTION VI.

1. The senators and representatives shall receive a compensation for their services, to be ascertained by law, and paid out of the treasury of the United States. They shall, in all cases, except treason, felony, and breach of the peace, be privileged from arrest during their attendance at the session of their respective houses, and in going to and returning from the same; and for any speech or debate in either house, they shall not be questioned in any other place.

Compensation and privilege.

2. No senator or representative shall, during the time for which he was elected, be appointed to any civil office under the authority of the United States, which shall have been created, or the emoluments whereof shall have been increased during such time; and no person holding any office under the United States, shall be a member of either house during his continuance in office.

Hold no other office

SECTION VII.

1. All bills for raising revenue shall originate in the House of Representatives; but the Senate may propose or concur with amendments as on other bills.

Revenue bills to originate in House of Representatives.

2. Every bill which shall have passed the House of Representatives and the Senate, shall, before it becomes a law, be presented to the president of the United States: if he approve he shall sign it, but if not he shall return it, with his objections, to that house in which it shall have originated, who shall enter the objections at large on their journal, and proceed to reconsider it. If after such reconsideration two-thirds of that house shall agree to pass the bill, it shall be sent, together with the objections, to the other house, by which it shall likewise be reconsidered, and if approved by two-thirds of that house, it shall become a law. But

Bills to be approved by the president, but may be passed by two-thirds vote.

in all such cases the votes of both houses shall be determined by yeas and nays, and the names of the persons voting for and against the bill shall be entered on the journal of each house respectively. If any bill shall not be returned by the president within ten days (Sundays excepted) after it shall have been presented to him, the same shall be a law, in like manner as if he had signed it, unless the Congress by their adjournment prevent its return, in which case it shall not be a law.

Adjournment. 3. Every order, resolution, or vote to which the concurrence of the Senate and House of Representatives may be necessary (except on a question of adjournment) shall be presented to the president of the United States; and before the same shall take effect, shall be approved by him, or being disapproved by him, shall be re-passed by two-thirds of the Senate and House of Representatives, according to the rules and limitations prescribed in the case of a bill.

SECTION VIII.

Powers of Congress. The Congress shall have power to:

1. To lay and collect taxes, duties, imposts, and excises, to pay the debts and provide for the common defense and general welfare of the United States; but all duties, imposts, and excises shall be uniform throughout the United States;

2. To borrow money on the credit of the United States;

3. To regulate commerce with foreign nations, and among the several States, and with the Indian tribes;

4. To establish a uniform rule of naturalization, and uniform laws on the subject of bankruptcies throughout the United States;

5. To coin money, regulate the value thereof, and of foreign coin, and fix the standard of weights and measures;

6. To provide for the punishment of counterfeiting the securities and current coin of the United States;

7. To establish post-offices and post-roads;

8. To promote the progress of science and useful arts, by securing for limited times to authors and inventors the exclusive right to their respective writings and discoveries;

9. To constitute tribunals inferior to the supreme court;

10. To define and punish piracies and felonies committed on the high seas, and offenses against the law of nations;

11. To declare war, grant letters of marque and reprisal, and make rules concerning captures on land and water;

12. To raise and support armies; but no appropriation of money to that use shall be for a longer term than two years;

13. To provide and maintain a navy;

14. To make rules for the government and regulation of the land and naval forces;

15. To provide for calling forth the militia to execute the laws of the Union, suppress insurrections, and repel invasions;

16. To provide for organizing, arming, and disciplining the militia, and for governing such part of them as may be employed in the service of the United States, reserving to the States respectively the appointment of the officers, and the authority of training the militia according to the discipline prescribed by Congress;

17. To exercise exclusive legislation in all cases whatsoever, over such district (not exceeding ten miles square) as may, by cession of particular States, and the acceptance of Congress, become the seat of the government of the United States; and to exercise like authority over all places purchased by the consent of the Legislature of the State in which the same shall be, for the erection of forts, magazines, arsenals, dock-yards, and other needful buildings;—and

18. To make all laws which shall be necessary and proper for carrying into execution the foregoing powers, and all other powers vested by this Constitution in the government of the United States, or in any department or officer thereof.

SECTION IX.

1. The migration or importation of such persons as any of the States now existing shall think proper to admit, shall not be prohibited by the Congress prior to the year one thousand eight hundred and eight, but a tax or duty may be imposed on such importation, not exceeding ten dollars for each person.

Immigration.

2. The privilege of the writ of habeas corpus shall not be suspended, unless when in cases of rebellion or invasion the public safety may require it.

Habeas corpus.

3. No bill of attainder or ex post facto law shall be passed.

4. No capitation, or other direct tax shall be laid, unless in proportion to the census or enumeration hereinbefore directed to be taken.

Attainder and ex post facto laws. Taxes proportioned to population.

5. No tax or duty shall be laid on articles exported from any State.

6. No preference shall be given by any regulation of commerce or revenue to the ports of one State over those of another; nor shall vessels bound to, or from, one State, be obliged to enter, clear, or pay duties in another.

Ports of all States on the same footing.

7. No money shall be drawn from the treasury, but in consequence of appropriations made by law; and a regular statement and account of

No moneys to be drawn from treasury but by law.

the receipts and expenditures of all public money shall be published from time to time.

Titles and gifts forbidden.

8. No title of nobility shall be granted by the United States; and no person holding any office of profit or trust under them shall, without the consent of the Congress, accept of any present, emolument, office, or title, of any kind whatever, from any king, prince, or foreign State.

SECTION X.

Limitations of States in various matters.

1. No State shall enter into any treaty, alliance, or confederation; grant letters of marque and reprisal; coin money; emit bills of credit; make anything but gold and silver coin a tender in payment of debts; pass any bill of attainder, ex post facto law, or law impairing the obligation of contracts, or grant any title of nobility.

2. No State shall, without the consent of the Congress, lay any imposts or duties on imports or exports, except what may be absolutely necessary for executing its inspection laws; and the net produce of all duties and imposts, laid by any State on imports or exports shall be for the use of the treasury of the United States; and all such laws shall be subject to the revision and control of the Congress.

3. No State shall, without the consent of Congress, lay any duty of tonnage, keep troops, or ships of war in time of peace, enter into any agreement or compact with another State, or with a foreign power, or engage in war, unless actually invaded, or in such imminent danger as will not admit of delay.

ARTICLE II.

SECTION I.

The president.

1. The executive power shall be vested in a president of the United States of America. He shall hold his office during the term of four years, and, together with the vice-president, chosen for the same term, be elected as follows:

Presidential elections.

2. Each State shall appoint, in such manner as the legislature thereof may direct, a number of electors, equal to the whole number of senators and representatives to which the State may be entitled in the Congress; but no senator or representative, or person holding an office of trust or profit under the United States, shall be appointed an elector.

Duties of electors.

3. The electors shall meet in their respective States, and vote by ballot for two persons, one of whom, at least, shall not be an inhabitant of the same State with themselves. And they shall make a list of all the persons voted for, and of the number of votes for each; which list they shall sign and certify, and transmit sealed to the seat of the government of the United States, directed to the president of the Senate. The president of the Senate shall, in the presence of the Senate and House

of Representatives, open all the certificates; and the votes shall then be counted. The person having the greatest number of votes shall be the president, if such number be a majority of the whole number of electors appointed; and if there be more than one who have such majority, and have an equal number of votes, then the House of Representatives shall immediately choose, by ballot, one of them for president; and if no person have a majority, then, from the five highest on the list, the said house shall, in like manner, choose the president. But, in choosing the president, the votes shall be taken by States; the representation from each State having one vote; a quorum for this purpose shall consist of a member or members from two-thirds of the States; and a majority of all the States shall be necessary to a choice. In every case, after the choice of president, the person having the greatest number of votes of the electors shall be vice-president. But, if there should remain two or more who have equal votes, the Senate shall choose from them, by ballot, the vice-president.

4. The Congress may determine the time of choosing the electors, and the day on which they shall give their votes; which day shall be the same throughout the United States. *To vote on same day.*

5. No person except a natural-born citizen, or a citizen of the United States at the time of the adoption of this Constitution, shall be eligible to the office of president; neither shall any person be eligible to that office who shall not have attained to the age of thirty-five years, and been fourteen years a resident within the United States. *Who may be president.*

6. In case of the removal of the president from office, or of his death, resignation, or inability to discharge the powers and duties of the said office, the same shall devolve on the vice-president; and the Congress may by law provide for the case of removal, death, resignation, or inability, both of the president and vice-president, declaring what officer shall then act as president, and such officer shall act accordingly, until the disability be removed, or a president shall be elected. *If office vacant.*

7. The president shall, at stated times, receive for his services a compensation, which shall neither be increased nor diminished during the period for which he shall have been elected, and he shall not receive within that period any other emolument from the United States, or any of them. *His compensation*

8. Before he enter on the execution of his office, he shall take the following oath or affirmation: *His oath of office.*

"I do solemnly swear (or affirm) that I will faithfully execute the office of president of the United States, and will, to the best of my ability, preserve, protect, and defend the Constitution of the United States.

SECTION II.

Commander-in-chief.

1. The president shall be commander-in-chief of the army and navy of the United States, and of the militia of the several States, when called into the actual service of the United States; he may require the opinion, in writing, of the principal officer in each of the executive departments, upon any subject relating to the duties of their respective offices, and he shall have power to grant reprieves and pardons for offences committed against the United States, except in cases of impeachment.

Power of appointment and treaties.

2. He shall have power, by and with the advice and consent of the Senate, to make treaties, provided two-thirds of the senators present concur; and he shall nominate, and by and with the advice and consent of the Senate, shall appoint ambassadors, other public ministers and consuls, judges of the supreme court, and all other officers of the United States, whose appointments are not herein otherwise provided for, and which shall be established by law; but the Congress may by law vest the appointment of such inferior officers, as they think proper, in the President alone, in the courts of law, or in the heads of departments.

Vacancies in office.

3. The President shall have power to fill up all vacancies that may happen during the recess of the Senate, by granting commissions, which shall expire at the end of their next session.

SECTION III.

President and Congress.

He shall from time to time give to the Congress information of the state of the Union, and recommend to their consideration such measures as he shall judge necessary and expedient; he may, on extraordinary occasions, convene both Houses, or either of them, and in case of disagreement between them, with respect to the time of adjournment, he may adjourn them to such time as he shall think proper; he shall receive ambassadors and other public ministers; he shall take care that the laws be faithfully executed, and shall commission all the officers of the United States.

SECTION IV.

Impeachments

The President, Vice-President, and all civil officers of the United States, shall be removed from office on impeachment for, and conviction of, treason, bribery, or other high crimes and misdemeanors.

ARTICLE III.

SECTION I.

The judiciary.

The judicial power of the United States shall be vested in a supreme court, and in such inferior courts as the Congress may from time to time ordain and establish. The judges, both of the supreme and inferior courts, shall hold their·offices during good behavior, and shall, at stated times, receive for their services a compensation which shall not be diminished during their continuance in office.

SECTION II.

1. The judicial power shall extend to all cases, in law and equity, arising under this Constitution, to the laws of the United States, and treaties made, or which shall be made, under their authority; to all cases affecting ambassadors, other public ministers and consuls; to all cases of admiralty and maritime jurisdiction; to controversies to which the United States shall be a party; to controversies between two or more States; between a State and citizens of another State; between citizens of different States; between citizens of the same State claiming lands under grants of different States, and between a State, or the citizens thereof, and foreign States, citizens, or subjects. *Extent of jurisdiction.*

2. In all cases affecting ambassadors, other public ministers and consuls, and those in which a State shall be a party, the supreme court shall have original jurisdiction. In all the other cases before mentioned, the supreme court shall have appellate jurisdiction, both as to law and fact, with such exceptions, and under such regulations as the Congress shall make. *What to judge.*

3. The trial of all crimes, except in cases of impeachment, shall be by jury; and such trial shall be held in the State where the said crimes shall have been committed; but when not committed within any State, the trial shall be at such place or places as the Congress may by law have directed. *Trial by jury.*

SECTION III.

1. Treason against the United States shall consist only in levying war against them, or in adhering to their enemies, giving them aid and comfort. No person shall be convicted of treason unless on the testimony of two witnesses to the same overt act, or on confession in open court. *Treason.*

2. The Congress shall have power to declare the punishmet of treason, but no attainder of treason shall work corruption of blood, or forfeiture except during the life of the person attainted. *Its punishment.*

ARTICLE IV.

SECTION I.

Full faith and credit shall be given in each State to the public acts, records, and judicial proceedings of every other State. And the Congress may by general laws prescribe the manner in which such acts, records, and proceedings shall be proved, and the effect thereof. *Decisions valid in every State.*

29

SECTION II.

Citizens in different States.

1. The citizens of each State shall be entitled to all privileges and immunities of citizens in the several States.

Offences — where tried.

2. A person charged in any State with treason, felony, or other crime, who shall flee from justice, and be found in another State, shall on demand of the executive authority of the State from which he fled, be delivered up, to be removed to the State having jurisdiction of the crime.

Obligation to labor.

3. No person held to service or labor in one State, under the laws thereof, escaping into another, shall, in consequence of any law or regulation therein, be discharged from such service or labor, but shall be delivered up on claim of the party to whom such service or labor may be due.

SECTION III.

New States.

1. New States may be admitted by the Congress into this Union; but no new State shall be formed or erected within the jurisdiction of any other State; nor any State be formed by the junction of two or more States, or parts of States, without the consent of the legislatures of the States concerned as well as of the Congress.

Territories.

2. The Congress shall have power to dispose of and make all needful rules and regulations respecting the territory or other property belonging to the United States; and nothing in this Constitution shall be so construed as to prejudice any claims of the United States, or of any particular State.

SECTION IV.

Republicanism guaranteed.

The United States shall guarantee to every State in this Union a Republican form of government, and shall protect each of them against invasion; and on application of the legislature, or of the executive (when the legislature cannot be convened), against domestic violence.

ARTICLE V.

Amendments to the Constitution.

The Congress, whenever two-thirds of both Houses shall deem it necessary, shall propose amendments to this Constitution, or, on the application of the legislatures of two-thirds of the several States, shall call a convention for proposing amendments, which, in either case, shall be valid, to all intents and purposes, as part of this Constitution, when ratified by the legislatures of three-fourths of the several States, or by conventions in three-fourths thereof, as the one or the other mode of ratification may be proposed by the Congress: provided that no amendment which may be made prior to the year one thousand eight hundred and eight shall in any manner affect the first and fourth clauses in the ninth section of the first article; and that no State, without its consent, shall be deprived of its equal suffrage in the Senate.

Article VI.

1. All debts contracted and engagements entered into, before the adoption of this Constitution, shall be as valid against the United States under this Constitution, as under the Confederation.

Former debts valid.

2. This Constitution, and the laws of the United States which shall be made in pursuance thereof, and all treaties made, or which shall be made, under the authority of the United States, shall be the supreme law of the land; and the judges in every State shall be bound thereby, any thing in the Constitution or laws of any State to the contrary notwithstanding.

National laws supreme.

3. The senators and representatives before mentioned, and the members of the several State legislatures, and all executive and judicial officers, both of the United States and of the several States, shall be bound by oath or affirmation to support this Constitution; but no religious test shall ever be required as a qualification to any office or public trust under the United States.

Oaths of office.

Article VII.

The ratification of the conventions of nine States shall be sufficient for the establishment of this Constitution between the States so ratifying the same.

Validity of the Constitution.

Done in convention by the unanimous consent of the States present, the seventeenth day of September, in the year of our Lord one thousand seven hundred and eighty-seven, and of the Independence of the United States of America the twelfth. In witness whereof we have hereunto subscribed our names.

When signed.

GEORGE WASHINGTON,
President and Deputy from Virginia.

New Hampshire.
JOHN LANGDON.
NICHOLAS GILMAN.

Delaware.
GEORGE READ.
GUNNING BEDFORD, Jr.
JOHN DICKINSON.
RICHARD BASSETT.
JACOB BROOM.

Massachusetts.
NATHANIEL GORHAM.
RUFUS KING.

Maryland.
JAMES McHENRY.
DANIEL OF ST. THOMAS JENIFER
DANIEL CARROLL.

Connecticut.

    WILLIAM SAMUEL JOHNSON.
    ROGER SHERMAN.

New York.

    ALEXANDER HAMILTON.

New Jersey.

    WILLIAM LIVINGSTON.
    DAVID BEARLY.
    WILLIAM PATTERSON.
    JONATHAN DAYTON.

Pennsylvania.

    BENJAMIN FRANKLIN.
    THOMAS MIFFLIN.
    ROBERT MORRIS.
    GEORGE CLYMER.
    THOMAS FITZSIMONS.
    JARED INGERSOLL.
    JAMES WILSON.
    GOUVERNEUR MORRIS.

Virginia.

    JOHN BLAIR.
    JAMES MADISON, Jr.

North Carolina.

    WILLIAM BLOUNT.
    RICHARD DOBBS SPAIGHT.
    HUGH WILLIAMSON.

South Carolina.

    JOHN RUTLEDGE.
    CHARLES COTESWORTH PINCKNEY.
    CHARLES PINCKNEY.
    PIERCE BUTLER.

Georgia.

    WILLIAM FEW.
    ABRAHAM BALDWIN.

Attest:

WILLIAM JACKSON,

Secretary.

AMENDMENTS TO THE CONSTITUTION.

PROPOSED BY CONGRESS AND RATIFIED BY THE LEGISLATURES OF THE SEVERAL STATES.

ARTICLE I.

Freedom in religion, in speech, in the press and in petition.

Congress shall make no law respecting an establishment of religion, or prohibiting the free exercise thereof; or abridging the freedom of speech, or of the press; or the right of the people peaceably to assemble, and to petition the government for a redress of grievances.

ARTICLE II.

Keeping and bearing arms.

A well-regulated militia being necessary to the security of a free State, the right of the people to keep and bear arms shall not be infringed.

ARTICLE III.

No soldier shall, in time of peace, be quartered in any house without the consent of the owner, nor in time of war but in a manner to be prescribed by law.

ARTICLE IV.

The right of the people to be secure in their persons, houses, papers, and effects, against unreasonable searches and seizures, shall not be violated, and no warrants shall issue but upon probable cause, supported by oath or affirmation, and particularly describing the place to be searched, and the persons or things to be seized.

ARTICLE V.

No person shall be held to answer for a capital, or otherwise infamous crime, unless on a presentment or indictment of a grand jury, except in cases arising in the land or naval forces, or in the militia, when in actual service in time of war or public danger; nor shall any person be subject for the same offense to be twice put in jeopardy of life or limb; nor shall be compelled in any criminal case to be a witness against himself, nor be deprived of life, liberty, or property without due process of law; nor shall private property be taken for public use without just compensation.

ARTICLE VI.

In all criminal prosecutions, the accused shall enjoy the right to a speedy and public trial by an impartial jury of the State and district wherein the crime shall have been committed, which district shall have been previously ascertained by law, and to be informed of the nature and cause of the accusation; to be confronted with the witnesses against him; to have compulsory process for obtaining witnesses in his favor, and to have the assistance of counsel for his defense.

ARTICLE VII.

In suits at common law, where the value in controversy shall exceed twenty dollars, the right of trial by jury shall be preserved, and no fact tried by a jury shall be otherwise re-examined in any court of the United States than according to the rules of the common law.

ARTICLE VIII.

Excessive bail shall not be required, nor excessive fines imposed, nor cruel and unusual punishments inflicted.

ARTICLE IX.

Limitation of rights.

The enumeration in the Constitution of certain rights shall not be construed to deny or disparage others retained by the people.

ARTICLE X.

Reserved to the States

The powers not delegated to the United States by the Constitution, nor prohibited by it to the States, are reserved to the States respectively, or to the people.

ARTICLE XI.

Cases to be tried.

The judicial power of the United States shall not be construed to extend to any suit, in law or equity, commenced or prosecuted against one of the United States by citizens of another State, or by citizens or subjects of any foreign State.

ARTICLE XII.

Choice of president.

The electors shall meet in their respective States, and vote by ballot for President and Vice-President, one of whom, at least, shall not be an inhabitant of the same State with themselves; they shall name in their ballots the person voted for as President, and in distinct ballots the person voted for as Vice-President, and they shall make distinct lists of all persons voted for as President, and of all persons voted for as Vice-President, and of the number of votes for each, which lists they shall sign and certify, and transmit sealed to the seat of the government of the United States, directed to the president of the Senate. The President of the Senate shall, in presence of the Senate and House of Representatives, open all the certificates, and the votes shall then be counted; the person having the greatest number of votes for President, shall be the President, if such number be the majority of the whole number of electors appointed; and if no person have such majority, then from the persons having the highest numbers, not exceeding three on the list of those voted for as President, the House of Representatives shall choose immediately, by ballot, the President. But in choosing the President, the votes shall be taken by States, the representation from each State having one vote; a quorum for this purpose shall consist of a member or members from two-thirds of the States, and a majority of all the States shall be necessary to a choice. And if the House of Representatives shall not choose a President whenever the right of choice shall devolve upon them, before the fourth day of March next following, then the Vice-President shall act as President, as in the case of the death or other constitutional disability of the President. The person having the greatest number of votes as Vice-President, shall be the Vice-President, if such number be a majority of the whole number of electors appointed; and if no person have a majority, then from the two highest numbers on the list, the Senate shall choose the Vice-President: a quorum for the purpose shall consist of two-thirds of the whole number of senators, and a majority of the whole number shall be necessary to a choice. But no person constitutionally ineligible to the office of President shall be eligible to that of Vice-President of the United States.

ARTICLE XIII.

SECTION I.

Neither slavery nor involuntary servitude, except as a punishment for crime, whereof the party shall have been duly convicted, shall exist within the United States, or any place subject to their jurisdiction.

Slavery forbidden

SECTION II.

Congress shall have power to enforce this article by appropriate legislation.

ARTICLE XIV.

SECTION I.

All persons born or naturalized in the United States, and subject to the jurisdiction thereof, are citizens of the United States and of the State wherein they reside. No State shall make or enforce any law which shall abridge the privileges or immunities of citizens of the United States; nor shall any State deprive any person of life, liberty, or property, without due process of law, nor deny any person within its jurisdiction the equal protection of the laws.

Who citizens,

SECTION II.

Representatives shall be apportioned among the several States according to their respective numbers, counting the whole number of persons in each State, excluding Indians not taxed. But when the right to vote at any election for the choice of electors for President and Vice-President of the United States, representatives in Congress, the executive and judicial officers of a State, or the members of the legislature thereof, is denied to any of the male inhabitants of such State, being twenty-one years of age, and citizens of the United States, or in any way abridged, except for participation in rebellion or other crime, the basis of representation therein shall be reduced in the proportion which the number of such male citizens shall bear to the whole number of male citizens twenty-one years of age in such State.

Representatives proportioned to population.

SECTION III.

Who may not hold office.

No person shall be a senator or representative in Congress, or elector of president or vice-president, or hold any office, civil or military, under the United States, or under any State, who, having previously taken an oath, as a member of Congress, or as an officer of the United States, or as a member of any State legislature, or as an executive or judicial officer of any State, to support the Constitution of the United States, shall have engaged in insurrection or rebellion against the same, or given aid or comfort to the enemies thereof. But Congress may, by a vote of two-thirds of each house, remove such disability.

SECTION IV.

Public debts.

The validity of the public debt of the United States, authorized by law, including debts incurred for payment of pensions and bounties for services in suppressing insurrection or rebellion shall not be questioned. But neither the United States nor any State shall assume or pay any debt or obligation incurred in aid of insurrection or rebellion against the United States, or any claim for the loss or emancipation of any slave; but all such debts, obligations, and claims shall be held illegal and void.

SECTION V.

Power to enforce legislation.

The Congress shall have power to enforce, by appropriate legislation, the provisions of this article.

ARTICLE XV.

SECTION I.

Who may vote.

The right of citizens of the United States to vote shall not be denied or abridged by the United States, or by any State, on account of race, color, or previous condition of servitude.

SECTION II.

The Congess shall have power to enforce this article by appropriate legislation.

The history of our country would be incomplete without Washington's "Farewell Address," and Lincoln's "Emancipation Proclamation," the former abounding in wise suggestions as to the true welfare of our country, and the latter giving freedom to our millions of slaves and freedom to our land forever.

THE FAREWELL ADDRESS OF GEORGE WASHINGTON,

FIRST PRESIDENT OF THE UNITED STATES, ON HIS DECLINING A RE-ELECTION.

Friends and Fellow-Citizens:—

The period for a new election of a citizen to administer the executive government of the United States being not far distant, and the time actually arrived when your thoughts must be employed in designating the person who is to be clothed with that important trust, it appears to me proper, especially as it may conduce to a more distinct expression of the public voice, that I should now apprise you of the resolution I have formed, to decline being considered among the number of those out of whom a choice is to be made.

I beg you at the same time to do me the justice to be assured that this resolution has not been taken without a strict regard to all the considerations appertaining to the relation which binds a dutiful citizen to his country ; and that in withdrawing the tender of service which silence in my situation might imply, I am influenced by no diminution of zeal for your future interest ; no deficiency of grateful respect for your past kindness ; but am supported by a full conviction that the step is compatible with both.

The acceptance of, and continuance hitherto in the office to which your suffrages have twice called me, have been a uniform sacrifice of inclination to the opinion of duty, and to a deference for what appeared to be your desire. I constantly hoped that it would have been much earlier in my power, consistently with motives which I was not at liberty to disregard, to return to that retirement from which I had been reluctantly drawn. The strength of my inclination to do this previous to the last election, had even led to the preparation of an address to declare it to you ; but mature reflection on the then perplexed and critical posture of our affairs with foreign nations, and the unanimous advice of persons entitled to my confidence, impelled me to abandon the idea.

I rejoice that the state of your concerns, external as well as internal, no longer renders the pursuit of inclination incompatible with the sentiment of duty or propriety, and am persuaded, whatever partiality may be retained for my services, that in the present circumstances of our country, you will not disapprove of my determination to retire.

The impressions with which I first undertook the arduous trust were explained on the proper occasion. In the discharge of this trust, I will only say, that I have with good intentions contributed toward the organization and administration of the government the best exertions of which a very fallible judgment was capable. Not unconscious, in the outset, of the inferiority of any qualifications, experience in my own eyes, perhaps still more in the eyes of others, has strengthened the motives to diffidence of myself ; and every day the increasing weight of years admonishes me more and more, that the shade of retirement is as necessary to me as it will be welcome. Satisfied that if any circumstances have given peculiar value to my services, they were temporary, I have the consolation to believe, that while choice and prudence invite me to quit the political scene, patriotism does not forbid it.

In looking forward to the moment which is intended to terminate the career of my public life, my feelings do not permit me to suspend the deep acknowledgment of that debt of gratitude which I owe to my beloved country, for the many honors it has conferred upon me; still more for the steadfast confidence with which it has supported me, and for the opportunities I have thence enjoyed of manifesting my inviolable attachment, by services faithful and persevering, though in usefulness unequal to my zeal. If benefits have resulted to our country from these services, let it always be remembered to your praise, and as an instructive example in our annals, that under circumstances in which the passions, agitated in every direction, were liable to mislead, amidst appearances sometimes dubious—vicissitudes of fortune often discouraging—in situations in which not unfrequently want of success has countenanced the spirit of criticism—the constancy of your support was the essential prop of the efforts, and a guarantee of the plans by which they were effected. Profoundly penetrated with this idea, I shall carry it with me to my grave, as a strong incitement to unceasing wishes that Heaven may continue to you the choicest tokens of its beneficence—that your union and brotherly affection may be perpetual—that the free constitution which is the work of your hands may be sacredly maintained—that its administration in every department may be stamped with wisdom and virtue—that, in fine, the happiness of the people of these States, under the auspices of liberty, may be made complete, by so careful a preservation, and so prudent a use of this blessing, as will acquire to them the glory of recommending it to the applause, the affection, and adoption of every nation which is yet a stranger to it.

Here, perhaps, I ought to stop. But a solicitude for your welfare, which cannot end but with my life, and the apprehension of danger natural to that solicitude, urge me, on an occasion like the present, to offer to your solemn contemplation, and to recommend to your frequent review, some sentiments, which are the result of much reflection, of no inconsiderable observation, and which appear to me all-important to the permanency of your felicity as a people. These will be offered to you with the more freedom, as you can only see in them the disinterested warnings of a parting friend, who can possibly have no personal motive to bias his counsel. Nor can I forget, as an encouragement to it, your indulgent reception of my sentiments on a former and not dissimilar occasion.

Interwoven as is the love of liberty with every ligament of your hearts, no recommendation of mine is necessary to fortify or confirm the attachment.

The unity of government which constitutes you one people, is also now dear to you. It is justly so; for it is a main pillar in the edifice of your real independence, the support of your tranquility at home and your peace abroad; of your safety; of your prosperity; of that very liberty which you so highly prize. But as it is easy to foresee that from different causes and from different quarters, much pains will be taken, many artifices employed, to weaken in your minds the conviction of this truth; as this is the point in your political fortress against which the batteries of internal and external enemies will be most constantly and actively (though often covertly and insidiously) directed, it is of infinite moment that you should properly estimate the immense value of your national Union to your collective and individual happiness; that you should cherish a cordial, habitual, and immovable attachment to it; accustoming yourselves to think and speak of it as of the palladium of your political safety and prosperity; watching for its preservation with jealous anxiety; discountenancing whatever may suggest even a suspicion that it can in any event be abandoned; and indignantly frowning upon the first dawning of every attempt to alienate any portion of our country from the rest, or to enfeeble the sacred ties which now link together the various parts.

For this you have every inducement of sympathy and interest. Citizens by birth or choice, of a common country, that country has a right to concentrate your affections. The name of American, which belongs to you, in your national capacity, must always exalt the just pride of patriotism, more than any appellation derived from local discriminations. With slight shades of difference, you have the same religion, manners, habits, and political principles. You have in a common cause fought and triumphed together; the independence and liberty you possess are the work of joint councils and joint efforts, of common dangers, sufferings, and successes.

But these considerations, however powerfully they address themselves to your sensibility, are greatly outweighed by those which apply more immediately to your interest. Here every portion of our country finds the most commanding motives for carefully guarding and preserving the union of the whole.

The North, in an unrestrained intercourse with the South, protected by the equal laws of a common government, finds in the productions of the latter great additional resources of maritime and commercial enterprise and precious materials of manufacturing industry. The South, in the same intercourse, benefiting by the agency of the North, sees its agriculture grow and its commerce expand. Turning partly into its own channels the seamen of the North, it finds its particular navigation invigorated; and while it contributes, in different ways, to nourish and increase the general mass of the national navigation, it looks forward to the protection of a maritime strength, to which itself is unequally adapted. The East, in a like intercourse with the West, already finds, and in the progressive improvement of interior communications, by land and water, will more and more find a valuable vent for the commodities which it brings from abroad or manufactures at home. The West derives from the East supplies requisite to its growth and comfort —and what is perhaps of still greater consequence, it must of necessity owe the secure enjoyment of indispensable outlets for its own productions to the weight, influence, and the future maritime strength of the Atlantic side of the Union, directed by an indissoluble community of interest as one nation. Any other tenure by which the West can hold this essential advantage, whether derived from its own separate strength, or from an apostate and unnatural connection with any foreign power, must be intrinsically precarious.

While then every part of our country thus feels the immediate and particular interest in union, all the parts combined cannot fail to find in the united mass of means and efforts, greater strength, greater resource, proportionably greater security from external danger, a less frequent interruption of their peace by foreign nations; and what is of inestimable value, they must derive from union an exemption from those broils and wars between themselves, which so frequently afflict neighboring countries, not tied together by the same government; which their own rivalship alone would be sufficient to produce, but which opposite foreign alliances, attachments, and intrigues would stimulate and embitter. Hence likewise they will avoid the necessity of those overgrown military establishments, which under any form of government are inauspicious to liberty, and which are to be regarded as particularly hostile to Republican liberty. In this sense it is, that your Union ought to be considered as the main prop of your liberty, and that the love of the one ought to endear to you the preservation of the other.

These considerations speak a persuasive language to every reflecting and virtuous mind, and exhibit the continuance of the Union as a primary object of patriotic desire. Is there a doubt whether a common government can embrace so large a sphere? Let experience solve it. To listen to mere speculation in such a case were criminal. We are authorized to hope that a proper organization of the whole, with the auxiliary agency of governments for the respective subdivisions, will afford a happy issue to the experiment. It is well worth a fair and full experiment. With such powerful and obvious motives to union, affecting all parts of our country, while experience shall not have demonstrated its impracticability, there will always be reason to distrust the patriotism of those, who in any quarter may endeavor to weaken its bands.

In contemplating the causes which may disturb our union, it occurs as matter of serious concern that any ground should have been furnished for characterizing parties by geographical discriminations — Northern and Southern — Atlantic and Western; whence designing men may endeavor to excite a belief that there is a real difference of local interests and views. One of the expedients of party to acquire influence, within particular districts, is to misrepresent the opinions and aims of other districts. You cannot shield yourselves too much against the jealousies and heart-burnings which spring from these misrepresentations; they tend to render alien to each other those who ought to be bound together by fraternal affection. The inhabitants of our Western country have lately had a useful lesson on this head; they have seen, in the negotiation by the executive, and in the unanimous ratification by the Senate, of the treaty with Spain, and in the universal satisfaction at the event throughout the United States, a decisive proof how unfounded were the suspicions propagated among them of a policy in the general government, and in the Atlantic States, unfriendly to their interests in regard to the Mississippi; they have been witnesses to the formation of two treaties, that with Great Britain and that with Spain which secure to them everything they could desire, in respect to our foreign relations, toward confirming their prosperity. Will it not be their wisdom to rely for the preservation of these advantages on the Union by which they were procured? Will they not henceforth be deaf to those advisers, if such there are, who would sever them from their brethren, and connect them with aliens?

To the efficacy and permanency of your Union, a government for the whole is indispensable. No alliances, however strict, between the parts can be an adequate substitute; they must inevitably experience the infractions and interruptions which all alliances in all times have experienced. Sensible of this momentous truth, you have improved upon your first essay, by the adoption of a Constitution of Government better calculated than your former for an intimate Union, and for the efficacious management of your common concerns. This government, the offspring of your own choice, uninfluenced and unawed, adopted upon full investigation and mature deliberation, completely free in its principles, in the distribution of its powers, uniting security with energy and containing within itself a provision for its own amendment, has a just claim to your confidence and your support. Respect for its authority, compliance with its laws, acquiescence in its measures, are duties enjoined by the fundamental maxims of true liberty. The basis of our political systems is the right of the people to make and to alter their Constitutions of Government. But the Constitution which at any time exists, until changed by an explicit and authentic act of the whole people, is sacredly obligatory upon all. The very idea of the power and the right of the people to establish government, presupposes the duty of every individual to obey the established government.

All obstructions to the execution of the laws, all combinations and associations, under whatever plausible character, with the real design to direct, control, counteract or awe the regular deliberation and action of the constituted authorities, are destructive of this fundamental principle, and of fatal tendency. They serve to organize faction, to give it an artificial and extraordinary force — to put in the place of the delegated will of the nation, the will of a party, often a small but artful and enterprising minority of the community; and, according to the alternate triumphs of different parties, to make the public administration the mirror of the ill-concerted and incongruous projects of faction, rather than the organ of consistent and wholesome plans digested by common councils and modified by mutual interests.

However combinations or associations of the above description may now and then answer popular ends, they are likely, in the course of time and things, to become potent engines, by which cunning, ambitious, and unprincipled men will be enabled to subvert the power of the people, and to usurp for themselves the reins of government; destroying afterward the very engines which have lifted them to unjust dominion.

Toward the preservation of your government, and the permanency of your present happy state, it is requisite, not only that you steadily discountenance irregular oppositions to its acknowledged authority, but also that you resist with care the spirit of innovation upon its principles, however specious the pretexts. One method of, assault may be to effect in the form of the Constitution alterations which will impair the energy of the system, and thus to undermine what cannot be directly overthrown. In all the changes to which you may be invited, remember that time and habit are at least as necessary to fix the true character of governments as of other human institutions; that experience is the surest standard by which to test the real tendency of the existing constitution of a country — that facility in changes upon the credit of mere hypothesis and opinion, exposes to perpetual change from the endless variety of hypothesis and opinion; and remember, especially, that for the efficient management of your common interests, in a country so extensive as ours, a government of as much vigor as is consistent with the perfect security of liberty, is indispensable. Liberty itself will find in such a government, with powers properly distributed and adjusted, its surest guardian. It is, indeed, little else than a name, where the government is too feeble to withstand the enterprises of faction, to confine each member of the society within the limits prescribed by the laws, and to maintain all in the secure and tranquil enjoyment of the rights of person and property.

I have already intimated to you the danger of parties in the State, with particular reference to the founding of them on geographical discriminations. Let me now take a more comprehensive view, and warn you in the most solemn manner against the baneful effects of the spirit of party, generally.

This spirit, unfortunately, is inseparable from our nature, having its root in the strongest passions of the human mind. It exists under different shapes in all governments more or less stifled, controlled, or repressed; but in those of the popular form, it is seen in greatest rankness, and it is truly their worst enemy.

The alternate domination of one faction over another, sharpened by the spirit of revenge, natural to party dissension, which in different ages and countries has perpetrated the most horrid enormities, is itself a frightful despotism. But this leads at length to a more formal and permanent despotism. The disorders and miseries which result, gradually incline the minds of men to seek security and repose in the absolute power of an individual, and sooner or later the chief of some prevailing faction, more able or more fortunate than his competitors, turns this disposition to the purposes of his own elevation, on the ruins of public liberty.

Without looking forward to an extremity of this kind (which nevertheless ought not to be entirely out of sight), the common and continual mischiefs of the spirit of party are sufficient to make it the interest and duty of a wise people to discourage and restrain it.

It serves always to distract the public councils, and enfeeble the public administration. It agitates the community with ill-founded jealousies and false alarms; kindles the animosity of one part against another, foments occasionally riot and insurrection. It opens the door to foreign influence and corruption, which find a facilitated access to the government itself through the channels of party passions. Thus the policy and the will of one country are subjected to the policy and will of another. There is an opinion that parties in free countries are useful checks upon the administration of government, and serve to keep alive the spirit of liberty. This within certain limits is probably true; and in governments of a monarchical cast, patriotism may look with indulgence, if not with favor, upon the spirit of party. But in those of the popular character, in governments purely elective, it is a spirit not to be encouraged. From their natural tendency it is certain there will always be enough of that spirit for every salutary purpose. And there being constant danger of excess, the effort ought to be, by force of public opinion, to mitigate and assuage it. A fire not to be quenched it demands uniform vigilance to prevent its bursting into a flame, lest, instead of warming, it should consume.

It is important, likewise, that the habits of thinking, in a free country, should inspire caution in those entrusted with its administration, to confine themselves within their respective constitutional spheres, avoiding in the exercise of the powers of one department to encroach upon another. The spirit of encroachment tends to consolidate the powers of all departments in one, and thus to create, whatever the form of government, a real despotism. A just estimate of that love of power, and proneness to abuse it, which predominates in the human heart, is sufficient to satisfy us of the truth of this position. The necessity of reciprocal checks in the exercise of political power, by dividing and distributing it into different depositories, and constituting each the guardian of the public weal against invasions by the others, has been evinced by experiments ancient and modern; some of them in our country and under our own eyes. To preserve them must be as necessary as to institute them. If, in the opinion of the people, the distribution or modification of the constitutional powers be in any particular wrong, let it be corrected by an amendment in the way which the Constitution designates. But let there be no change by usurpation; for though this, in one instance, may be the instrument of good, it is the customary weapon by which free governments are destroyed. The precedent must always greatly overbalance in permanent evil any partial or transient benefit which the use can at any time yield.

Of all the dispositions and habits which lead to political prosperity, religion and morality are indispensable supports. In vain would that man claim the tributes of patriotism, who should labor to subvert these great pillars of human happiness, these firmest props of the duties of men and citizens. The mere politician, equally with the pious man, ought to respect and to cherish them. A volume could not trace all their connections with private and public felicity. Let it simply be asked, where is the security for property, for reputation, for life, if the sense of religious obligation desert the oaths which are the instruments of investigation in courts of justice? And let us with caution indulge the supposition that morality can be maintained without religion. Whatever may be conceded to the influence of refined education on minds of peculiar structure, reason and experience both forbid us to expect that national morality can prevail in exclusion of religious principle.

It is substantially true that virtue or morality is a necessary spring of popular government. The rule, indeed, extends with more or less force to every species of free government. Who that is a sincere friend to it, can look with indifference upon attempts to shake the foundation of the fabric?

Promote then, as an object of primary importance, institutions for the general diffusion of knowledge. In proportion as the structure of a government gives force to public opinion, it is essential that public opinion should be enlightened.

As a very important source of strength and security, cherish public credit. One method of preserving it, is to use it as sparingly as possible—avoiding occasions of expense by cultivating peace; but remember also that timely disbursements to prepare for danger, frequently prevent much greater disbursements to repel it; avoiding likewise the accumulation of debt, not only by shunning occasions of expense, but by vigorous exertions in time of peace to discharge the debts which unavoidable wars may have occasioned, not ungenerously throwing upon posterity the burden which we ourselves ought to bear. The execution of these maxims belongs to your representatives, but it is necessary that public opinion should co-operate. To facilitate to them the performance of their duty, it is essential that you should practically bear in mind, that toward the payment of debts there must be revenue; that to have revenue there must be taxes; that no taxes can be devised which are not more or less inconvenient and unpleasant; that the intrinsic embarrassment inseparable from the selection of the proper objects (which is always a choice of difficulties) ought to be a decisive motive for a candid construction of the conduct of the government in making it, and for a spirit of acquiescence in the measures for obtaining revenue which the public exigencies may at any time dictate.

Observe good faith and justice toward all nations, cultivate peace and harmony with all: religion and morality enjoin this conduct; and can it be that good policy does not equally enjoin it? It will be worthy of a free, enlightened, and, at no distant period, a great nation, to give to mankind the magnanimous and too novel example of a people always guided by an exalted justice and benevolence. Who can doubt but that in the course of time and things, the fruits of such a plan would richly repay any temporary advantage which might be lost by a steady adherence to it? Can it be, that Providence has not connected the permanent felicity of a nation with its virtue? The experiment, at least, is recommended by every sentiment which ennobles human nature. Alas! is it rendered impossible by its vices?

In the execution of such a plan, nothing is more essential than that permanent, inveterate antipathies against particular nations, and passionate attachments for others, should be excluded; and that in place of them just and amicable feelings toward all should be cultivated. The nation which indulges toward another an habitual hatred or an habitual fondness, is in some degree a slave. It is a slave to its animosity or to its affection, either of which is sufficient to lead it astray from its duty and its interest. Antipathy in one nation against another, disposes each more readily to offer insult and injury, to lay hold of slight causes of umbrage, and to be haughty and intractable, when accidental or trifling occasions of dispute occur. Hence frequent collisions, obstinate, envenomed, and bloody contests. The nation, prompted by ill-will and resentment, sometimes impels to war the government, contrary to the best calculations of policy. The government sometimes participates in the national propensity, and adopts through passion what reason would reject; at other times, it makes the animosity of the nation subservient to projects of hostility instigated by pride, ambition, and other sinister and pernicious motives. The peace often, sometimes perhaps the liberty, of nations has been the victim.

So, likewise, a passionate attachment of one nation for another produces a variety of evils. Sympathy for the favorite nation, facilitating the illusion of an imaginary common interest in cases where no real common interest exists, and infusing into one the enmities of the other, betrays the former into a participation in the quarrels and wars of the latter, without adequate inducement or justification. It leads also to concessions to the favorite nation of privileges denied to others, which is apt doubly to injure the nation making the concessions, by unnecessarily parting with what ought to have been retained; and by exciting jealousy, ill-will, and a disposition to retaliate, in the parties from whom equal privileges are withheld. And it gives to ambitious, corrupted, or deluded citizens (who devote themselves to the favorite nation) facility to betray or sacrifice the interests of their own country, without odium, sometimes even with popularity; gilding with the appearance of a virtuous sense of obligation, a commendable deference for public opinion, or a laudable zeal for public good, the base or foolish compliances of ambition, corruption, or infatuation.

As avenues to foreign influence in innumerable ways, such attachments are particularly alarming to the truly enlightened and independent patriot. How many opportunities do they afford to tamper with domestic factions; to practice the arts of sedition, to mislead public opinion, to influence or awe the public councils! Such an attachment of a small and weak, toward a great and powerful nation, dooms the former to be the satellite of the latter. Against the insidious wiles of foreign influence (I conjure you to believe me, fellow-citizens) the jealousy of a free people ought to be constantly awake; since history and experience prove that foreign influence is one of the most baneful foes of Republican government. But that jealousy to be useful must be impartial; else it becomes the instrument of the very influence to be avoided, instead of a defense against it. Excessive partiality for one foreign nation, and excessive dislike of another, cause those whom they actuate to see danger only on one side, and serve to veil and even second the arts of influence on the other. Real patriots, who may resist the intrigues of the favorite, are liable to become suspected and odious; while its tools and dupes usurp the applause and confidence of the people, to surrender their interest.

The great rule of conduct for us, in regard to foreign nations, is, in extending our commercial relations, to have with them as little political connection as possible. So far as we have already formed engagements, let them be fulfilled with perfect good faith. Here let us stop.

Europe has a set of primary interests, which to us have none, or a very remote relation. Hence she must be engaged in frequent controversies, the causes of which are essentially foreign to our concerns. Hence, therefore, it must be unwise in us to implicate ourselves, by artificial ties, in the ordinary vicissitudes of her politics, or the ordinary combinations and collisions of her friendships or enmities.

Our detached and distant situation invites and enables us to pursue a different course. If we remain one people, under an efficient government, the period is not far off when we may defy material injury from external annoyance; when we may take such an attitude as will cause the neutrality we may at any time resolve upon to be scrupulously respected; when belligerent nations, under the impossibility of making acquisitions from us, will not lightly hazard the giving us provocation; when we may choose peace or war, as our interest, guided by justice, shall counsel.

Why forego the advantages of so peculiar a situation? Why quit our own to stand upon foreign ground? Why, by interweaving our destiny with that of any part of Europe, entangle our peace and prosperity in the toils of European ambition, rivalship, interest, humor, or caprice?

It is our true policy to steer clear of permanent alliances with any portion of the foreign world, so far, I mean, as we are now at liberty to do it; for let me not be understood as capable of patronizing infidelity to existing engagements. I hold the maxim no less applicable to public than to private affairs, that honesty is always the best policy. I repeat it, therefore, let those engagements be observed in their genuine sense. But, in my opinion, it is unnecessary, and would be unwise to extend them.

Taking care always to keep ourselves, by suitable establishments, on a respectable defensive posture, we may safely trust to temporary alliances for extraordinary emergencies.

Harmony, and a liberal intercourse with all nations, are recommended by policy, humanity, and interest. But even our commercial policy should hold an equal and impartial hand; neither seeking nor granting exclusive favors or preferences; consulting the natural course of things; diffusing and diversifying by gentle means the streams of commerce, but forcing nothing; establishing, with powers so disposed, in order to give trade a stable course, to define the rights of our merchants, and to enable the government to support them, conventional rules of intercourse, the best that present circumstances and mutual opinion will permit, but temporary, and liable to be from time to time abandoned or varied, as experience and circumstances shall dictate; constantly keeping in view that it is folly in one nation to look for disinterested favors from another; that it must pay with a portion of its independence for whatever it may accept under that character; that by such acceptance it may place itself in the condition of having given equivalents for nominal favors, and yet of being reproached with ingratitude for not giving more. There can be no greater error than to expect, or calculate upon real favors from nation to nation. It is an illusion which experience must cure, which a just pride ought to discard.

30

In offering to you, my countrymen, these counsels of an old and affectionate friend, I dare not hope they will make the strong and lasting impression I could wish — that they will control the usual current of the passions, or prevent our nation from running the course which has hitherto marked the destiny of nations. But if I may even flatter myself that they may be productive of some partial benefit, some occasional good, that they may now and then recur to moderate the fury of party spirit, to warn against the mischiefs of foreign intrigue, to guard against the impostures of pretended patriotism, this hope will be a full recompense for the solicitude for your welfare by which they have been dictated

How far in the discharge of my official duties I have been guided by the principles which have been delineated, the public records and other evidences of my conduct must witness to you and to the world. To myself, the assurance of my own conscience is, that I have at least believed myself to be guided by them.

In relation to the still subsisting war in Europe, my proclamation of the 22d of April, 1793, is the index to my plan. Sanctioned by your approving voice and by that of your representatives in both Houses of Congress, the spirit of that measure has continually governed me, uninfluenced by any attempts to deter or divert me from it.

After deliberate examination, with the aid of the best lights I could obtain, I was well satisfied that our country, under all the circumstances of the case, had a right to take, and was bound in duty and interest to take, a neutral position. Having taken it, I determined, as far as should depend upon me, to maintain it with moderation, perseverance, and firmness.

The considerations which respect the right to hold this conduct, it is not necessary on this occasion to detail. I will only observe, that according to my understanding of the matter, that right, so far from being denied by any of the belligerent powers, has been virtually admitted by all

The duty of holding a neutral conduct may be inferred, without any thing more, from the obligation which justice and humanity impose on every nation, in cases in which it is free to act, to maintain inviolate the relations of peace and amity toward other nations.

The inducements of interest for observing that conduct will best be referred to your own reflections and experience. With me, a predominant motive has been to endeavor to gain time to our country to settle and mature its yet recent institutions, and to progress, without interruption to that degree of strength and consistency which is necessary to give it, humanly speaking, the command of its own fortunes.

Though, in reviewing the incidents of my administration I am unconscious of intentional error, I am, nevertheless, too sensible of my own defects, not to think it probable that I may have committed many errors. Whatever they may be, I fervently beseech the Almighty to avert or mitigate the evils to which they may tend. I shall also carry with me the hope that my country will never cease to view them with indulgence, and that after forty-five years of my life dedicated to its service with an upright zeal, the faults of incompetent abilities will be consigned to oblivion, as myself must soon be to the mansions of rest.

Relying on its kindness in this as in other things, and actuated by that fervent love toward it, which is so natural to a man who views in it the native soil of himself and his progenitors for several generations I anticipate with pleasing expectation that retreat, in

which I promise myself to realize, without alloy, the sweet enjoyment of partaking, in the midst of my fellow-citizens, the benign influence of good laws under a free government—the ever favorite object of my heart, and the happy reward, as I trust, of our mutual cares, labors and dangers.

G. WASHINGTON.

UNITED STATES,
17th September, 1796.

PROCLAMATION OF EMANCIPATION.

BY ABRAHAM LINCOLN, PRESIDENT OF THE UNITED STATES.

WHEREAS, On the 22d day of September, in the year of our Lord one thousand eight hundred and sixty-two, a proclamation was issued by the President of the United States, containing, among other things, the following, to wit:

"That on the 1st day of January, in the year of our Lord one thousand eight hundred and sixty-three, all persons held as slaves within any State or designated part of a State, the people whereof shall then be in rebellion against the United States, shall be then, thenceforward, and forever free; and the Executive Government of the United States, including the military and naval authority thereof, will recognize and maintain the freedom of such persons, and will do no act or acts to repress such persons, or any of them, in any efforts they may make for their actual freedom.

"That the Executive will, on the first day of January, aforesaid, by proclamation, designate the States and parts of States, if any, in which the people thereof, respectively, shall then be in rebellion against the United States; and the fact that any State, or the people thereof, shall on that day be in good faith represented in the Congress of the United States, by members chosen thereto at elections wherein a majority of the qualified voters of such State shall have participated, shall, in the absence of strong countervailing testimony, be deemed conclusive evidence that such State, and the people thereof, are not then in rebellion against the United States."

Now, therefore, I, Abraham Lincoln, President of the United States, by virtue of the power in me vested as commander-in-chief of the army and navy of the United States in time of actual armed rebellion against the authority and government of the United States, and as a fit and necessary war measure for suppressing said rebellion, do, on this first day of January, in the year of our Lord one thousand eight hundred and sixty-three, and in accordance with my purpose so to do, publicly proclaimed for the full period of one hundred days from the day first above mentioned, order and designate, as the States and parts of States wherein the people thereof, respectively, are this day in rebellion against the United States, the following, to wit:

Arkansas, Texas, Louisiana (except the parishes of St. Bernard, Plaquemines, Jefferson, St. John, St. Charles, St. James, Ascension, Assumption, Terre Bonne, Lafourche, St. Mary's, St. Martin, and Orleans, including the city of New Orleans), Mississippi, Alabama, Florida, Georgia, South Carolina, North Carolina, and Virginia (except the forty-eight counties designated as West Virginia, and also the counties of Berkeley, Accomac, Northampton, Elizabeth City, York, Princess Anne, and Norfolk, including the cities of Norfolk and Portsmouth), and which excepted parts are, for the present, left precisely as if this proclamation were not issued.

And by virtue of the power and for the purpose aforesaid, I do order and declare that all persons held as slaves within said designated States and parts of States are, and henceforward shall be free; and that the executive government of the United States, including the naval and military authorities thereof, will recognize and maintain the freedom of said persons.

And I hereby enjoin upon the people so declared to be free to abstain from all violence, unless in necessary self-defense; and I recommend to them that, in all cases when allowed, they labor faithfully for reasonable wages.

And I further declare and make known that such persons, of suitable condition, will be received into the armed service of the United States, to garrison forts, positions, stations, and other places, and to man vessels of all sorts in said service.

And upon this act, sincerely believed to be an act of justice, warranted by the Constitution, upon military necessity, I invoke the considerate judgment of mankind, and the gracious favor of Almighty God.

In testimony whereof I have hereunto set my name, and caused the seal of the United States to be affixed.

Done at the city of Washington, this first day of January, in the year of our Lord one thousand eight hundred and sixty-three, and of the Independence of the United States the eighty-seventh.

ABRAHAM LINCOLN.

By the President:
WILLIAM H. SEWARD,
Secretary of State.

THE GOLDEN GATE.

INHABITANTS BEFORE OUR HISTORICAL PERIOD.

THE MOUND BUILDERS AND THEIR WORKS.

THE preceding pages contain only the written history of "Our Country," which practically begins with the year 1492, the date of the first voyage of Columbus to a new world before unknown. Yet there pertains to the preceding period quite a variety of very interesting material of a semi-historical character — in part traditional and legendary, and in part based upon researches in the languages, customs and antiquities of the Mound Builders and Indians. There is no longer doubt that this country was many years ago, inhabited by a hardy, energetic, and partly civilized race; and a fuller notice of the facts and of the abundant and deeply interesting literature relating to this earlier epoch, seems desirable as a closing chapter of this work.

Who were the Mound Builders? What was their origin? When and how did they live? And when as a people did they pass away, and disappear from the land? These are questions that no one can satisfactorily answer, though their works remain to testify of their past existence and numbers, of which written history gives us no account.

These works—the mounds which they built--are found in the region lying between the Great Lakes on the north and the Gulf of Mexico on the south, and between the Mississippi river on the west, and on the east by a line drawn through about the middle of New York, Pennsylvania and Virginia, and extending south so as to include South Carolina and the whole of Georgia and Florida. Similar works are here and there found outside of these limits, but by far the greater part of them are within this region, and especially in Ohio. Those which, from their shape, have been called the "Animal Mounds," are found in Wisconsin, as the "Enclosures" are in Ohio, and the "Truncated Mounds" in the States further south, though all kinds are found in the Ohio Valley where they are more numerous, of larger size, and of more varied forms than elsewhere in the United States.

Taken as a whole these works have been described under two great divisions— embankments and mounds — and these again have been divided into several different groups. The Embankments or enclosures are generally of earth, rarely of stone, and are situated on the level terraces of rivers, on the tops of hills, and on other elevated and strong positions, and according to their location are supposed to have been works of defense, or, as they have been called, "hill-forts" and "fortified villages." The former follow the outline of the hill, sometimes enclosing but part, and sometimes the whole hill-top with a wall, while the latter are stretched on the level bank or terrace of the river. They are of various shapes and sizes, the square and circle predominating, though the two are often united and run into each other, and are generally surrounded by walls which are from a few to thirty feet in height from the bottom of the ditch below.

In point of size these works differ greatly, some being not more than fifty feet in diameter, while the groups in which several works are united often cover hundreds of acres, or, as in case of the works at Newark, Ohio, are scattered over an area of two miles square. Some of these works were formerly surmounted by stockades, showing they were for defense. The ditch was sometimes on the outside, sometimes within the wall, and sometimes on both sides. The material from which these embankments were built was taken from the surrounding soil, no hewn or prepared stone or mortar being used, and embankments, in part of rough stone, were found only in localities where that material is abundant.

Turning now from the embankments to the second great division — the Mounds— they are composed of earth and stone, and vary in location, size, shape and contents. Divided according to their forms, they have been classed :

1. As the *temple* or *truncated* mounds, which are conical in shape, commonly having graded ways to the top, and often truncated sides. Their bases are of different

forms, round, square, oval or oblong, and all are alike in having flat or level tops which are supposed to have been sites of rude temples for worship, or for the cabins of their chiefs. In height they vary from five to ninety feet, and at the base are from forty feet in diameter to, in one case, twelve acres. Like the embankments, they are simply heaps of earth, some of them

OBSERVATORY MOUND, NEWARK WORKS.

of immense size, but all thrown up from the earth or material on the spot, with apparently no choice or care as to the material, or the order of its deposit.

2. The next class, known as "Animal Mounds," from their supposed resemblance in form to animals, birds, and even human beings, are more or less irregular, varying in height from one to six feet, while their dimensions on the ground are often very large

Some in human form are over a hundred feet in length; quadrupeds have bodies and tails each from fifty to two hundred feet long; birds have wings of a hundred feet; lizard mounds are two and even four hundred feet in length; straight and curved lines of embankments extend over a thousand feet, and the forms of serpents are equally extensive. Mounds of this class are common in Wisconsin, and are also found in Ohio and Georgia. They are usually constructed of earth, stones being rarely used, except perhaps in Georgia, where some bird-shaped mounds are constructed entirely of that material.

3. The third class of mounds consists of conical truncates that are scattered over the whole area which has been mentioned, and are far more numerous than all the others combined. They are generally round or oval, and vary in height from a few inches to several feet, and in diameter from three or four to three hundred feet. A height of from three to thirty feet, and a diameter at the base of from fifteen to fifty feet, would include a large proportion of them. Though alike in form, they differ widely in location, being found on the highest hills, and in the lowest valleys, alone and in groups, and in connection with the hill-forts or fortified villages, of which they seem to have been parts. Most of them are of earth, though stone mounds or cairns are not uncommon, and in Florida they are often made almost entirely of shells.

This is believed to be a fair statement of all that is known of mounds, as mounds, without regard to their contents, or what is known of them historically. It is taken from Force and Carr, the latter of whom takes his account almost literally from Bancroft whose "Summary of the results of the Explorations of Squier, Lapham, and others," he says, "is just and comprehensive." The various groups of these structures, showing but little difference among themselves, consist of numberless mounds and circumvallations, fifteen hundred of the latter and ten thousand of the former being found in Ohio alone, to say nothing of those in other parts of the country.

Their uses and the objects for which they were built vary according to the kind of the structures. Some seem to have been for defense against enemies, as the stockades and trenches, the extent and elevation of which and the fact that they were provided with wells or cisterns for water, show that they were for protection against the possible attack of foes. Some seem to have been for the purpose of worship, whatever the form of that worship might have been. And some evidently were burial places, and when of great extent were cemeteries, where for generations the dead were laid at rest, with the utensils, personal ornaments, and weapons of warfare which among savage tribes are generally buried with those to whom in life they belonged, and thought in some sense to go with them to the spirit land.

The *stone heaps* or *cairns* were apparently to commemorate some notable event, some treaty of peace, some victory over foes, the settlement of some village, or were thrown up as landmarks or memorials over the dead. The *bone mounds* were burial places on a larger scale, in which, after battle, the numbers that were slain were laid in tiers, one above another, and a high mound raised over them. In such mounds large numbers of skeletons have been found, and in many cases there were bones scattered on the surface, and even projecting from the sides.

The *truncated* or *temple* mounds were apparently arranged for the cabins of the chiefs and the dwellings of their attendants, or as the beginnings of their villages, and also as places of worship. These larger mounds were elevated in location and had at one point a graded way easy of approach to the top, while at every other point the sides were so steep as to be difficult of ascent, and so, easily defended from enemies.

Whether these various mounds were built by the ancestors of the modern Indians, or by some prehistoric people that have passed away leaving no descendants on the continent and no evidence of their existence but the monuments they have left, is still an unsettled question. But whoever may have built them, they must have been erected many ages ago. The growth of trees upon these mounds gives one indication of the times when they must have been built. Squier and Davis mention a tree six hundred years old on the great mound at Point Creek; Barrandt tells of another at least six hundred years old on one of the mounds of the upper Missouri; and Dr. Hildreth speaks of another eight hundred years old on a mound at Marietta, Ohio. Some of the works then, it would seem, must have been abandoned at least six or eight hundred, and some think a thousand years ago, but whether by a people that were conquered or exterminated, or by ancestors of the modern Indians, is still a question not fully settled.

Whoever the Mound Builders may have been, it is evident they were a numerous people, for their mounds and enclosures are found by thousands scattered through the various States, from the great lakes to the Gulf of Mexico, and from central New York, Pennsylvania, the Carolinas and Georgia on the east, to the Mississippi on the west. They were probably divided into clans or tribes, for their cemeteries extended and in layers, as some of them are, seem to indicate the burial of large numbers at a time, as if of those slain in great conflicts, and some of their connected mounds or defensive works are in communication with each other by signal stations at conspicuous points, forming lines of notification and defense for great distances. As one of many instances of this, a mound at Norwood, back of Cincinnati, commands a view through a depression of the hills eastwardly to a mound in the valley of the little Miami river, and northwardly through a valley and low lands to similar works at Hamilton, and then by a series of mounds westward to the fort at the mouth of the great Miami river. There is also a series of these signal mounds extending a distance of over one hundred miles along the Scioto, from the northern boundary of Franklin County to the Ohio river; thus alarm signals could easily have been transmitted by the Mound Builders through the entire length of the valley to their works at Portsmouth. Such arrangements show preparations for danger and for giving alarm, if need be, to friends or confederates at a distance, that they might be put on their guard against foes, or called promptly in aid of those who were in danger.

The Mound Builders were also an enterprising, and more or less a trading people, far in advance of the Indian tribes who succeeded them, and who, it is believed by some, are their descendants. Modern investigations show that the mining of native copper was carried on by these ancient people to an extraordinary extent. In a single district of eighteen miles square on Isle Royal, near the northern shore of Lake Superior, more ore was taken out by them by their crude processes than has been taken out in the last twenty years from the largest single mine on the lake, with all the aid of modern machinery. There is no trace of dwellings of any kind near the ancient excavations or mines. But fragments of native copper from which pieces have been chipped off, have been found in the mounds in Ohio. The miners evidently visited the mines in summer, and left when winter closed the lake, and then came back again when spring had melted the ice and re-opened navigation. In the frail boats which they used, they must have coasted hundreds of miles along the shores of the lake with their heavy loads, or without compass must have crossed its wide and often boisterous surface, in either case, showing their enterprise and persevering courage.

They could not in the modern sense be called a commercial people, though they manifestly exchanged their various products from different parts of the country. Copper implements from the North found their way to the South, and sea shells were taken from the coast to the interior. Mica was carried from the Alleghany Mountains to the valley of the Ohio. Flint chips and implements were taken from Ohio to Illinois, and fragments of obsidian found their way to Ohio from the Rocky Mountains and New Mexico. Stone-pipes found in the Scioto valley so faithfully represented the sea-cow that the makers must have been acquainted with that animal which now is nowhere

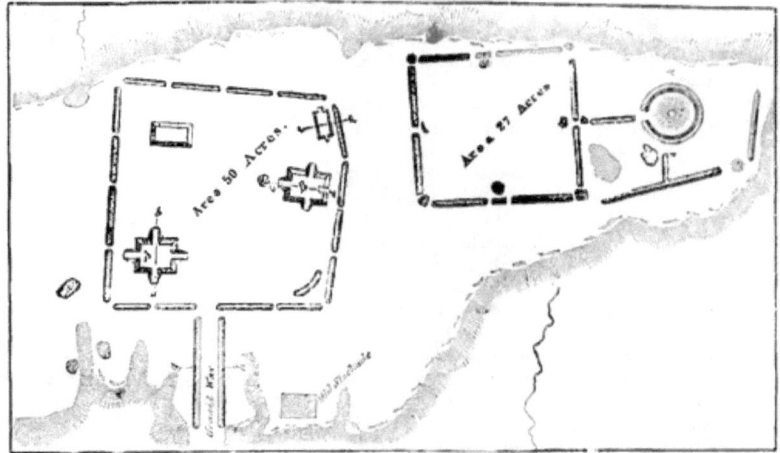

WORKS AT MARIETTA, OHIO.

found in the United States except on the coast of Florida. One pipe represents a bird which is an inhabitant of the West Indies and South America. Such facts show communication between different parts of the country, and the interchange of commodities of different kinds and from different regions.

The carving of the Mound Builders, as seen in their pipes and ornaments, exhibits greater skill and artistic taste than are found in the works of modern Indians. Native copper has been found with its outer surface plated with silver, not hammered on, but apparently united by fusion. In a large collection of copper instruments belonging to the Wisconsin Historical Society, one or more specimens were thought to have been cast, not hammered, though the casting is doubted. Skill of a different kind is seen in the embankments of the Mound Builders, especially in the Scioto valley, where the squares, circles, octagons, and ellipses are found to be mathematically accurate, showing

a knowledge of mathematics and engineering. Circles of more than a thousand feet
and one of them seventeen hundred feet in diameter, show that their builders had some
means of accurately measuring angles, and the fact that so many of these circles are
precisely a thousand and eighty feet on the side is proof that they had some fixed
standard of measurement. All these facts show a condition of life, and a kind and
degree of knowledge and taste unlike those which we associate with our Indians, and so
far go to show that they were a people different from and superior to them, or that if
they were ancestors of the modern Indians, then the latter must have been gradually
sinking in the scale of civilization.